WITCH HIGH

edited by Denise Little

DAW BOOKS, INC.
DONALD A. WOLLHEIM, FOUNDER
375 Hudson Street, New York, NY 10014

ELIZABETH R. WOLLHEIM
SHEILA E. GILBERT
PUBLISHERS

www.dawbooks.com

DAW Book Collectors No. 1453.

DAW Books is distributed by Penguin Group (USA) Inc.

First Printing, October 2008

1 2 3 4 5 6 7 8 9

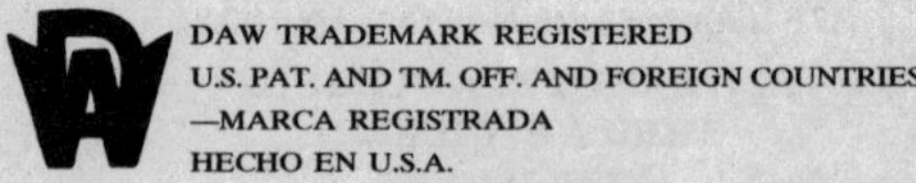

PRINTED IN THE U.S.A.

ACKNOWLEDGMENTS

Contents

Introduction

Denise Little

I spent a good percentage of my youth wanting to be a witch. I watched way too much television, and it seemed to me that being able to wiggle my nose and make things happen, like on *Bewitched*, would solve any number of my problems. Most notably, my weekly parentally mandated effort to put my room to rights would be a lot easier. And magic use would have helped a lot with the wretched burden of memorizing mathematical facts that haunted my second and third grade years. I mentioned my fantasies of gaining mystical power to my mom, and she doused them immediately with a giant dose of common sense. She said, "It's probably a lot harder to learn to be a witch than it is to clean your room and remember the times tables. So do your chores and count your blessings that you're not trying to study witchcraft."

Put that way, the reasons I personally didn't know any magic users (even though books and movies and the TV were full of them) suddenly made sense to me. Learning magic was hard work. Of course witches were rare.

Of course, I later discovered that magic—at least the way I envisioned it—didn't exist. Along with other such delightful childhood illusions as the Easter Bunny and the Tooth Fairy, I gave up on the idea that I could make things happen by spell casting. Learning that the world doesn't have powerful witches in it wasn't all bad—my nightmares were a lot less complicated once I internalized that concept. If I couldn't zap people, then it stood to reason that other people couldn't zap me.

But I never fully let go of the sense that somewhere out there, magic lived. Some of the things I learned in school seemed an awful lot like magic. Subatomic nuclear particle physics comes powerfully to mind here. Also calculus and differential equations. But magic itself, wielded by a trained practitioner . . . I finally decided that there was no such thing.

I thought that was a pity, of course. And I always wondered what kind of training it would take to turn out a proper witch. If school was tough for a bunch of ordinary kids, what must it be like for powerful magic users? Were the bullies unbearable? How did the teachers keep the strongest kids from blowing the weaker ones into sizzling wet spots?

My musings on the nature of a magical education found their way to the written page in the end. I wondered where the modern witch went to polish her skills, learn her history (both magical and mundane), and try out for the wildest pom-pom squad in the history of higher learning. I decided she went to Witch High, of course. Naturally, Witch High doesn't go by that name officially. Salem Township Public High School #4 is the name on the redbrick front gate. But everybody knows what the school is really about. Between high school angst, gym class, and witchcraft, it's a wild ride for students and teachers both at Witch High!

The result of that fantasy voyage into training modern witches is the book you hold in your hand. The stories range from the frothiest humor to the deepest pathos. Among all the other things that were clear from an adult perspective that I didn't consider as a child wiggling my nose, it was obvious to all the writers that magic couldn't solve every problem. At best, it just exchanged one set of troubles for another, something they utilized a lot in these stories. But gathering a lively bunch of kids together to teach them the tricks of the trade would certainly make for a lively school day, and the writers used that to the fullest.

All the writers in this book took my simple musings and ran with them, producing some amazing tales.

I hope you enjoy them as much as I did.

Domestic Magic

Kristine Kathryn Rusch

Kristine Kathryn Rusch is a multiple award-winning author and editor whose latest book is *The Recovery Man*. She also writes as Kristine Grayson and Kris Nelscott and a whole bunch of other names too numerous to mention.

THE dream is like the scenes on television, only with magic. J. Rutherford Wisenhauer the Third comes into the cafeteria wearing his father's black robes, points a finger at June Bauer, and immediately she's burning. Alive. A couple of other kids use water spells to put her out, but when they do, he shoots flames at them, and they go down.

Water spells are beyond the expertise of almost everyone in the room—one of the higher levels that a lot of us will learn in college (at least that's what Mrs. Parnham says. She also says don't worry about it; you won't ever need them, which is bad advice considering the dream).

I'm in line to pay for the slice of pizza I'm not supposed to be eating—Mom says you can't use magic to get rid of fat (it's not fair, and it won't hold, which turned out to be true in the case of my older sister)—when J. Rutherford starts his rampage. I scurry behind the steam tables, taking my tray with me—God knows why I think pizza will be helpful—and I watch him burn down half a dozen other students before Principal Haas, who is still in his office, douses the entire cafeteria in an ocean of water.

We—everyone in the caf—get swept outside, but not before six die. They'll stay dead too. Resurrection spells are black magic, and, worse than that, they're flawed. You create zombies or ghosts unless you're really, really good at it. So as drenched kids run across the lawn—slow motion, just like on TV—everyone knows that what happened in there was awful, permanent, and terrible.

And then I wake up.

In tears.

I'm not a precog. I don't have a lot of magic skills, and the ones I do have are disgustingly domestic—I can turn McDonald's french fries into the best garlic mashed potatoes you've ever tasted; I can clean your house with an eyeblink; I can iron your clothes just by rubbing my forefinger and thumb together. It's so damn sexist. Boys almost never get the domestic magic gene. Some of our geneticists (yes, we have geneticists and other scientists as well) think that the domestic magic gene is carried on the X chromosome and becomes stronger in girls than it'll ever be in boys.

So I've accepted that I have girl magic—the most stereotypical type. I've also accepted what I can't do.

Among the many things I can't do is see the future. Not in flashes, not in visions, and certainly not in dreams.

So no one is going to believe that what I dreamed might come true.

Maybe not even me.

But I'm scared, too. Because if I did see the future, then I'm duty-bound to stop this thing.

Except I'm not the right person for the job. J. Rutherford and I have history.

Bad history.

The kind that makes anything I say about him sound suspiciously like I'm out for revenge.

Which I'm not.

At least, not anymore.

* * *

J. Rutherford and I grew up on the same block. He lived three houses down from me in this single-story suburban ranch thing that everyone thinks is trendy now, but they thought it down-market then.

His dad had just started the Magic Revival Hour on local cable access, but the show hadn't yet been picked up by the Sci-Fi Channel, which led to repeat airings on USA, which made J. Rutherford Wisenhauer the Second (known around here as Number Two) the most famous real magic proponent in the country.

That's when the Wisenhauers bought the mansion on Pendergast Hill, although you'd more properly call that white elephant a castle, and after the rumors about Number Two dabbling in the black arts started.

There's lots of jealousy in the magic community. My mom always attributed the comments to sour grapes—it was pretty clear from the beginning that Number Two's TV show was going to take off, especially when the Conservative Right sent its minions from all over the country to picket outside his cable access studios.

But I wasn't so sure jealousy was the source of the talk. I'd seen J. Rutherford around the neighborhood, and he knew how to do stuff long before it got taught in Salem Township Elementary. Mean stuff, too, like hanging someone by his feet from an invisible rope or morphing a litter of puppies into a single entity attached at the tips of the tails.

That stuff may not be black magic, but it is precursor black magic, and something most parents would never, ever allow their kids to read about, let alone try.

Some kids knew how to undo—which made me wonder about them too—and more than a few parents got involved, privately talking to Number Two or his wife. They always promised to do something—and they did, but only about the problem at hand. The puppies got separated, or someone cut the invisible rope and floated the poor victim to the ground so he wouldn't break anything.

But the Wisenhauers never really did anything about J. Rutherford, and we all breathed a sigh of relief when he moved to that hilltop.

We figured he wouldn't be our problem anymore.

But, of course, he was.

As for me and J. Rutherford, here's the text message version. But first, you need a little background.

What most people don't know about small domestic magic is that it's practical magic. I can do all kinds of small useful things that no one else even thinks of. I can stop your casserole from burning or add golf spikes to your shoes so you won't slip down an icy hill.

I'm like the white vinegar of magic; no one even thinks of me until they spill red wine on their shirt.

The thing I learned from my mother is that practical magic is subtle. I can't resuscitate a blackened banana into nutritious food, but I can prevent a perfect yellow banana from going stale for an entire week. And that's valuable, especially when you only have so much food, and it'll all spoil before you get to it.

Sometimes, by thinking small, you can make great changes.

Mom told me all this by way of a lecture one night after a long crying jag—mine, of course. I was upset because I couldn't make rats jump over the walls of their maze like show ponies. Everyone else could do it, but not me.

I could, however, clean their cages with a wave of a hand.

Mom said that cage cleaning is a lot more important to real life than rat wall jumping, which of course I didn't believe. But she talked about the practical magic, subtle magic, small equals great thing, and I finally believed her.

Then I decided to test it on J. Rutherford.

Okay. I didn't decide right then and there, but the next day, I'm outside and I see J. Rutherford picking on the new kid from down the block.

The new kid looks pickable, the kind who just by his clothes is asking for trouble. He's wearing obvious hand-me-downs—the worn knees on his jeans actually puddle around his ankles—and he's way too skinny. He has a bruise along one side of his chin and fragile glasses that someone has attached to his head with one of those rubber things that goes around the back of the skull.

To make things worse, he doesn't approach the world with confidence. He cringes as he walks, which is a neon red KICK ME sign to someone like J. Rutherford.

J. Rutherford has the new kid in his sights. He's calling to the kid, putting on the personal charm that he learned from Number Two, and making the kid feel welcome. I've seen J. Rutherford do this a dozen times, and it always ends badly.

Actually, it always ends with the invisible rope and a kid hanging by his feet from some obscure spot in the neighborhood until someone sees him and gets him down.

Only I think this kid isn't going to survive the upside down trick. It's going to break what little spine he has left.

I'm about to find a grown-up when I remember what Mom says about small things. I know magic theory. I know that the invisible items created—heck, any item created—has to be made of the same kind of materials it would have in the real world. Which is why, to go back to the banana example, I can't create a new banana from a spoiled one (my magic isn't big enough) but I can preserve a good one for a limited period of time.

J. Rutherford's invisible ropes are made of hemp. He's never been any good at tying those plastic ropes or those slick ropes you buy at the hardware store. He can only tie—and we're talking by hand here—the ropes made from coarse natural materials.

Now, if I were better at magic, I'd change the natural ropes to plastic ropes, but I'm not. I have to think domestically.

I have to think small.

And as J. Rutherford conjures his invisible hemp rope, I stand on the curb, just outside his line of sight, and fray the weave. I fray it so badly the rope has no tensile strength at all. J. Rutherford doesn't notice because rough unfrayed hemp feels pretty much the same as rough frayed hemp, especially when you can't see what you're doing.

So he commands this thing, with its hangman's noose, to wrap itself around the new kid's feet. It does, but the minute J. Rutherford pulls the thing tight—that moment in which so many of us fell flat on our backs and screamed with surprise—the thing just kinda slips away from the kid's ankles, leaving rope burns and little else.

The kid still screams like the hounds of hell are after him and runs home.

I slide along the curb until I find a good tree and wait there, but J. Rutherford never sees me. Instead, he picks up the rope and tries to figure out what went wrong.

He did that every single time I thwarted him—and I thwarted him a lot that spring. Then he finally gets the bright idea to make the rope visible, something the rest of us would have done right away (I never said J. Rutherford was the sharpest knife in the drawer), and sees the fraying.

Even then he doesn't figure out it's me. He blames a bunch of other kids. None of them know how to fray a magical rope like that—the magic is too small, and most people never learn the small stuff because it seems too unimportant.

So it takes him another month to find me.

But when he does . . .

Oh, when he does . . .

I don't like to remember that. It involved hanging—by the neck, actually—and real torture and six weeks in the hospital for me. By the time my throat had healed enough so that I could talk and my hands had healed enough so that I could write, Number Two had moved his family to their little castle and had given lots of money to local charities.

So when I blamed J. Rutherford, no adult believed me.

The kids did, of course. They knew how mean he could be.

But the adults wondered why I was lying about such a nice kid (he knew to turn on the charm with them too) and urged me to tell them what really happened.

The local police (magical branch) figured some drifter had done this. There'd been a lot of torture murders of little girls in nearby communities, and they figured this was just a different version of the same old song.

Only they caught the torture murderer guy, and he confessed to killing dozens of kids all over the country, but he wouldn't admit to attacking me.

Even after that no adult believed me, and the more I pointed at J. Rutherford, the more people forgot my six weeks in the hospital (and the very real fear that I wasn't going to survive), and the more they started thinking of J. Rutherford as the victim of some poor little girl's delusion.

Once I asked my mom if Number Two had cast a spell on the whole town, making them believe that J. Rutherford was a good kid.

But she just shook her head. "If he cast that kind of spell, you would never say anything about J. Rutherford, and I would think he's a saint too."

Still, I wondered if such a spell would work on people who'd suffered at J. Rutherford's hands. Maybe the spell only worked on people who hadn't paid much attention to J. Rutherford.

Only I didn't say that theory to Mom because she'd tell me to let it all go and to stay away from the Wisenhauers. It was just safer that way.

And I couldn't look up black magic spells without setting off alarms all over town. I was already seen as the kid who went crazy when that drifter tortured her. If I got viewed as the crazy kid who dabbled in black magic, I'd get sent away somewhere.

So I successfully avoided J. Rutherford for four years—from elementary school to our first year of high school—and I never talked about him.

But that didn't stop everybody else from wondering if I ever got over the "trauma." I have to see counselors every other week, and no matter how much I claim I'm over it, they don't believe me.

In fact, sometimes they act as if I'm the one who's going to blow up the school—even though girls never do those things, not even at the magical schools.

Mom thinks I'm just paranoid, and she says that I'm not over it either and won't be until we move somewhere far away from the Wisenhauer family (although I wonder how that's possible to do, with Number Two being internationally famous and all).

So I'm just hanging on until I get out of high school. I'm hoping for college somewhere that'll appreciate my domestic talents or maybe even a trade school, like that magic chef school in Paris that I've been reading about.

At least, I was hanging on until the night I had that stupid dream.

The first time the dream comes, it's at 3 A.M., and scares me so deep that I don't want to go back to sleep. So I go downstairs and make Mom the best breakfast ever—without magic (or much of it anyway). It's just the two of us now, with my older sisters married and making babies and my dad long gone—as in he ran off, not as in he's dead.

I kinda like it being me and Mom, but I've never cooked anything just for her before, so when she gets up at her normal 5:30, she's stunned.

Over bacon, eggs, toast, and this amazing pastry that

I got from my latest French cookbook, I tell her about the dream, and she says, "What an awful nightmare," which sounds like she's dismissing it.

So I say, "What if it's a premonition?"

And she stifles a laugh with a mouthful of scrambled eggs, probably thinking I don't notice.

"Honey, no one in our family has ever had precognitive abilities. Visions don't come to us. It's just not possible."

I set down my fork. The food is good, but not good enough to eat when I'm this upset. "What if you're wrong?"

She freezes for a minute, then sighs. "Has he said anything to you?"

"J. Rutherford? Are you *kidding?*"

"No," she says, but she's talking like she's not really paying attention to me. "So have the other kids said something, something you might have overheard?"

"You mean like J. Rutherford confessing his plans to his friends?" I can't keep my voice from rising. "Mom, that would mean he has friends."

She frowns at me. "You can't tell anyone about this, hon. Everyone knows that we don't have that kind of magic, and then there's your reputation."

She makes it sound like I did something wrong.

"I don't have a reputation," I snap.

"You know what I mean."

The thing is that I do know what she means. But that doesn't make it right. "*He* hurt *me*. How come everyone around here thinks I did something to him?"

"I didn't mean it that way, hon."

"But you said it that way."

"Just like the school officials will when you bring this to them." Mom leans over her plate of eggs. She hasn't touched the pastry yet, and it's the best part. "Hon, listen. It makes sense that you'd have a nightmare about J. Rutherford. I'm amazed you don't have more of them."

"I do." I get up, grab my pastry and my coat and

leave the house. Mom can handle the mess I made. And I don't need my books.

I just need to get out of there.

The one person who usually believes me, the one who understands me, and she tells me to blow this off. I'd love to, but I meant what I asked her.

What if this is a true premonition? What if I have developed some kind of Sight?

What if J. Rutherford walks into the cafeteria with a fire-loaded finger and kills six of my classmates?

What if I could have prevented it just by telling the right person?

I don't want to live through that. I don't want to be the cause of six deaths.

I just don't.

So when I get to school, I go straight to the counselor's office. I have a private therapist, Mr. Marx, on Tuesdays outside of school, but my every-two-weeks meetings are with Ms. Emerson who works in the guidance office. She doesn't have a psychology degree. Her degree is in magical brain phenomenon, which is more like neurology and psychiatry as it pertains to magic.

Or that's how she explained it to me once.

Mrs. Emerson is younger than my mom and skinnier too. She wears designer rip-offs, which automatically makes her suspect to me because I think anyone who wears designer rip-offs has to have low self-esteem.

But still, she's the only person with some authority I can think of telling. Or, to clarify, the only person with some authority who has even the slightest chance of believing me.

Her office has windows that overlook the parking lot. She has covered those windows in plants, many of which are hanging medicinal herbs. She makes me sit in that fake leather chair across from her desk and she listens attentively as I tell her about the dream and my fears. I don't tell her what Mom said, although

Ms. Emerson repeats Mom's sentiments almost word for word.

(Except she doesn't say our family; she says your family. But still.)

So I lie. I tell Mrs. Emerson she's one of the people burned to death.

That at least makes her stop offering petty reassurances. For a half a second she even looks a little scared.

Then she says, "You know, with all the recent mundane television coverage of school shootings, it's not surprising you'd dream about something like that here. And as focused as you are on J. Rutherford Wisenhauer, it makes sense that he'd be the villain in your dream."

I stand up. I'm so mad that I can hardly see. I knew no one would take me seriously, and here they are, not taking me seriously.

"It's not a dream," I say. "At best, it's a nightmare. At worst, it's true."

That scared look comes back on her face and stays there longer this time. Then she gets up and goes to the filing cabinets behind her desk. She pulls open one in the middle, waves a hand over it so that I can't even see the folders, and peers inside.

She heaves a small sigh of relief, closes the drawer, and comes back to her desk.

"He doesn't have the ability to create fire like that," she says. "None of the students do."

"What about the teachers?" I ask.

She shakes her head. "That's a black magic."

"No, it's not," I say. "It's been around longer than almost all magic. The ability to make a flame so that you can light a room or ignite kindling to keep the family warm. It's a survival skill."

Which makes it a domestic magic. A small magic. I hope she doesn't figure that out. Because then that would turn the suspicion back on me.

Her jaw hardens, and she says, "Is there anything else you'd like to tell me?"

Meaning, am I planning this thing? As if my ability

to create a tiny flame could turn into those jets of fire that I saw in my dream.

I decide to misunderstand her, even though I want to scream at her. There's a lot I want to tell her, much of which might get me expelled.

I walk to the door, put my hand on the knob, and then stop. "I just want to tell you this. If he does spray up the school and kill a bunch of people, it's not my fault. I've tried to warn you. If you die at lunchtime, it'll be your own damn fault."

Then I let myself out, only to find myself grabbed by two of the school's four security guards.

They pull me into the principal's office. Seems half of what I said in Ms. Emerson's office sounded like a threat, so she pressed some button, notifying them. Now they're detaining me.

The good part is I'm not going to the cafeteria today.

The bad part is that I've only managed to make my crazy victim reputation worse.

Which means no one will believe me now. And the longer this day goes on, the more I think they should.

Of course no one talks to J. Rutherford to see what he's planning. So when they finally let me out of Principal Haas's office with a warning not to threaten counselors again and a reminder that they'll be watching all of my interactions with authority figures, I realize that only one person can prevent this whole thing.

Me.

By the time they let me out of Principal Prison, it's long past lunch. No one's in the caf and no one will be again until tomorrow morning at 10:40 when the first lunch begins.

And nothing happened, which means everyone'll say that my dream was a nightmare and nothing more.

But there wasn't a timeline on the dream. It could've happened today, or it might happen tomorrow.

Or, if I'm being charitable, it might never happen.

And that would be the best.

But it is a function of what I think about J. Rutherford that makes me believe he will attack the school and that he'll do it sooner rather than later.

So as soon as they let me out of Principal Prison, I scout the hallways. I'm looking for J. Rutherford, and I find him in the library, actually cracking a book.

He's a lot bigger than he was when he put me in the hospital. He's six foot five and built like a football player, even though he's not that athletic. He dresses in black, but that doesn't mean much since half the school does.

What he doesn't have are tats or piercings or other things that would scare the grown-ups. All he has are those sharp blue eyes that, if anything, have gotten meaner.

I stop at the door. My heart is pounding. I haven't voluntarily gotten near J. Rutherford in four years. But I'm going to do it now.

I square my shoulders and walk across the thick pile carpet until I reach his table. He's looking at old spell books—studying them in fact—and I can't tell if it's for a class or because he wants to.

He doesn't look up when I sit down. So I lean forward and put my hand over the page he's studying. Dust rises from the parchment.

He raises his head slowly, and when his gaze meets mine, I nearly run from my seat.

It takes all of my strength to stay there.

"I know what you're planning," I say. "Don't do it."

He frowns.

"It'll hurt you more than anyone else." Which isn't technically true—the kids that burn alive and survive will always remember it even though healing magic'll ensure that their skin won't scar, and the kids that die, well, their families'll be hurt the worst.

But my lie sounds good.

For a moment, tears line his eyes, then they disappear as quickly as they appeared.

"What are you talking about?" he snaps.

"Is this spell book about the black arts?" I ask. "Is that how you learn the fire-jet spell?"

His cheeks flush. For a moment—just a moment—he looks as terrified as Mrs. Emerson did.

Then he slams the book closed, right on top of my hand, and says in a really loud voice, "How come you always accuse me of stuff? I haven't done anything to you. I've *never* done anything to you."

Everyone turns and stares at us. I can see them out of the corner of my eye. But I don't look away from J. Rutherford, and I say softly, "We both know that's not true."

He starts to say something, but that's when my personal security guards—the same creeps that took me to Principal Prison—grab my arms again and drag me back there.

I get a lecture on harassing other students, and when I'm not repentant (I'm angry; no one is believing me), that's when I get suspended.

For three days.

Like I'm the bad guy.

Which I most decidedly am not.

Three days away from school—Wednesday, Thursday, Friday—and then the weekend. I figure nothing's going to happen this week because I'm not there, and I'm absolutely there in the dream, right down to rescuing my own personal slice of pizza because I somehow deem it important.

Mom is "disappointed" in me and she actually makes me go see Mr. Marx, like I'm the one who's crazy, not J. Rutherford.

Mr. Marx is, at least, sympathetic. But I have a hunch that's because the insurance company pays him more than $100 an hour to be as nice to me as he can.

Still, he says all the right things and makes me choke up when he says, "That took a lot of courage to face J. Rutherford by yourself."

He's right. It did take a lot of courage. More courage than I thought I had. But I really believe lives are at stake.

He also says, "You've done everything you can. You've warned the principal and the administration, you've even challenged J. Rutherford himself. There's not much more you can do."

And he's right about that too. Because I can't spell away J. Rutherford's powers, nor can I dunk him in water every five seconds. I can't get those stupid school security guards to follow him, and I don't have enough magic to fight him.

I've warned everyone, and no one's listening.

"So now what am I supposed to do?" I ask Mr. Marx.

He shrugs. "It's a tough situation. Let's just hope everything you've done changes the tide."

It sounds as though he believes me. In fact, when he said that, I *thought* he believed me. But as I'm leaving, I realize he never actually said that. In fact, he was careful not to say he believed me.

I've got to say, Mr. Marx is pretty good at making me feel like I've had a sympathetic ear. But a sympathetic ear isn't what I want. I want someone to stop J. Rutherford. Or I want someone to prove to me that J. Rutherford isn't about to finger-burn kids in my school.

I'm depressed again by the time I get home. Depressed and angry and frightened.

So I do what any good old domestic magician does when she loses control of her world.

I cook and cook and cook. I use real recipes, and I cheat on a few others. I make pastries and cakes and pies and two different dinners and a salad that has both fruit and vegetables and a dressing I invent myself.

I cook until I can't anymore. (And Mom eats until she can't eat anymore.)

Then I stagger to bed, so exhausted I know that nothing will ever wake me up.

* * *

Except that stupid dream.

I have it again. Only this time, when J. Rutherford comes into the cafeteria, he looks right at me, and his eyes are filled with tears.

But he doesn't point at me or at Jane Bauer. He starts with a different kid, a boy I don't recognize, and then when the same kids try to help, J. Rutherford goes after them.

I still manage to hide behind the steam tables, only this time I don't rescue my piece of pizza. And it takes the same amount of time for Principal Haas to get his act together and drown the entire cafeteria in water.

I wake up even more terrified, and this time, I wake up Mom. She's starting to worry now too, and she promises, in the morning, we'll hire a true precog and see exactly what is going on.

The true precog is Willard Pruitt, the great-great-grandfather of last year's prom queen, Willa Pruitt. No one knows how old Willard is, but everyone knows he's the best precog in a family full of them.

He shows up at our house fifteen minutes early (Mom later jokes that precogs never do anything on time), banging on the door before I finish making Mom's breakfast. So I have to use a bit of magic to double everything, just so I can offer him some.

When he comes into the kitchen, I'm glad I made the effort. He has that weird look some old guys get when it's pretty clear they were really big once and aren't anymore. It's not that his clothes don't fit—they do—it's just that they look like the kind of clothes a six foot six guy would wear instead of a guy who's a little under five foot seven.

His bones are big, too—his hands are twice the size of mine, but they look frailer somehow—and so is his nose. Hairs grow out of it and out of his ears, and when he sits at the table, he says, "I've been looking forward to this meal all week."

Which, I was about to say, was impossible, until I realize that he probably knows everything that's going to happen at this meeting. That creeps me out and makes me not want to talk to him.

Instead, I give him a serving of waffles sprinkled with powdered sugar and covered with strawberries so fresh they look like they've been airbrushed. He asks for and gets coffee, then he loads the waffles with butter and eats as though he hasn't seen food in a week.

Mom and I wait until he's finished before telling him why we've called.

He listens but with that distracted air people get when you're telling them something they already know.

Finally, I say, "You know how this is going to come out. Why don't you just tell us?"

He smiles, grabs the full glass of orange juice in front of his empty plate, and leans back in his chair.

"Precognition isn't quite like that," he says. "Some events are certain—like this spectacular breakfast—and others are in flux. I have no idea what is going to happen in your school cafeteria, if anything. I am not privy to the future of the Wisenhauer family. It's blocked. It's always been blocked, which leads me to believe Number Two cast some kind of shield spell over the whole family about the time he decided to do his cable-access show."

For some reason that news makes me shudder.

"So," Willard Pruitt says, "I'm here partly to see if I can help you, partly to see if there's any truth to your dream, and partly for that breakfast. You should open a restaurant, honey. You're the best chef I've ever encountered."

I flush in spite of myself.

Mom nods.

"Yes," she says. "My daughter is an amazingly talented domestic."

I look at her in shock, thinking maybe she's talking

about one of my sisters. Only my sisters aren't domestics. So Mom has to be talking about me. Except she's never talked about me like that before.

"What she isn't," Mom is saying, "is a visionary or a precog. This dream of hers, while scary, can't be true. Our family doesn't have the magic for it."

Willard Pruitt clears his throat. Then he drinks some orange juice. Then he clears his throat again.

He's obviously thinking about something, and he's battling with himself about whether or not to say it.

Finally, he says, "There're precogs and people who have a bit of the visionary magic, and then there's everyone else."

Mom nods. She knows this. *I* know this.

"But then there are break-through moments. Do you know what those are?"

Mom frowns. I frown. I've never heard of this.

"Breakthrough moments are future moments so powerful that even the nonmagical get a sense of them. That's why the nonmagical talk about having déjà vu. They've had a wisp of a vision about that moment and haven't even acknowledged it on a conscious level. Usually they can't acknowledge it—they don't have the tools to access it."

I'm beginning to feel like I'm in magical theory class. All this talk about stuff most of us just do irritates me and gives me a headache at the same time.

But I'm trying to pay attention to Willard Pruitt because he is, after all, trying to help me.

"The magical," he's saying, "no matter what their talents, can have these break-through moments and can remember them. Usually they come in a vision, not a dream and usually—forgive me, hon . . ."

And he looks at me for that.

". . . usually, they're about the visionary's impending death."

I let out a small breath. That revelation doesn't really surprise me. I had a hunch this might be about my death. Although that doesn't explain why I can see how the whole thing resolves—from the ocean of water the principal unleashes to the drenched kids running across the schoolyard in slow motion.

Mom picks up her coffee mug, spills some coffee, and sets it down again.

Willard Pruitt looks at her shaking hands, then reaches over and pats them. "I do not think your daughter is having a breakthrough moment."

Mom purses her lips, and I can tell she's thinking he's patronizing her.

"This could be a sending, a warning, that's coming directly to her, something that could happen. Or it could be, as her counselor says, a manifestation of your daughter's fear of this young man, which is—"

And he looks at me again.

"—entirely justified. The Wisenhauers are terrifying people, and they get away with a lot."

I let out a small sigh. He's the only person, except maybe Mom, who has ever really believed me.

"I happen to think, however, that it's a metaphor."

I blink. We're not in English class. Metaphor is not a word I expected this nice old guy to say.

"A metaphor?" Mom asks.

"Your daughter sees a potential in young Mr. Wisenhauer. She understands how destructive he is. Her subconscious is sending messages to her conscious via dreams, using the imagery of modern life. This doesn't mean that young Mr. Wisenhauer is going to destroy her school, but he is going to damage something important. Something important to your daughter. It's not by accident that she has this dream about the cafeteria, which is the only place in the high school where her talents are relevant. He's messing inside her magic, and the fact that in the first dream she saves her food is important. How important I do not know. I think you should hire a dream interpreter. Then you'll get to the bottom of this."

A dream interpreter. I can see dollar signs in the sadness on Mom's face. Willard Pruitt is already costing us a small fortune. We can't afford any other help.

"What's a sending?" I ask. He had mentioned that first, before all the other possibilities.

He sighs, as if he had hoped I hadn't heard that part.

"A sending," he says, "comes from someone else. Like a message or a warning. It too can be a metaphor."

"How do I know if it's my subconscious or someone trying to contact me?" I ask.

"Well, you can hire someone to trace the dream to its source. It's a highly specialized form of magic. No one here has that ability, but I can give you some names—"

"What about you? Why can't you do it?" Mom asks.

"If it's not a vision or a true prophecy or a breakthrough moment, my magic can't help you either."

Her cheeks are flushed. Mom is getting mad. Next thing you know, she's going to deny him his fee, which she can't do since he already told us some valuable things.

And, I think, he's probably the only person who really, truly believes me. That's worth the fee too.

"Can I do anything to see if it's a sending?" I ask. "I mean, there's got to be a way to tell if it's just a dream or a sending, right, without going to the source?"

He looks at me for a long time. Then he says, "You might try dedicated dreaming."

He doesn't have to explain that to me. We all learn dedicated dreaming in Head Start. Naptime is supposed to be about dedicated dreaming, although you learn later in the biology of magic that four-year-olds really can't control their dreams. That ability doesn't come until puberty. But it's a good way to get little kids to close their eyes for a half an hour.

Dedicated dreaming, not that I've tried it since I

came of age, is the ability to control your dreams. If it's a true dream, you can turn it, make it into what you want. You can even ask the dream questions and it'll answer you.

Essentially, dedicated dreaming is about talking to your own subconscious and having it answer.

So I can see the logic of his suggestion. If I can control the dream, then my subconscious is trying to tell me something. If I can't, then there's a good chance something else is going on.

Mom sighs. "Now I'm finally beginning to understand how all the mundanes feel."

By mundanes, she means the nonmagical. I don't ask her what she means—I know Mom, and I know she makes comments like this as a setup for some angry comment.

But Willard Pruitt doesn't know Mom at all, so he asks her what she means.

She glares at him. "This all sounds like mumbo jumbo. It's a colossal waste of time and—"

"Mom," I say.

He's leaning back, startled at the vehemence in her tone.

"—a waste of money, and if we hadn't already paid you—"

"Mom!"

"—we wouldn't be."

"Which is why," he says as he stands up, "I always ask for up front payment. It doesn't take a precog to know that sometimes customers don't want to hear what you have to say."

He nods at me, and I see warmth in his eyes.

"Good luck," he says softly. "The future is dark on this topic. I hope your dream is wrong, but if it's right, I know you will do the best you possibly can."

Note he doesn't say I would do the right thing. Or even that I would do the heroic thing. Only that I would do my best.

Which I'm already trying to do.

Mom's still yelling at him as he heads for the door. I stay and clean the kitchen, feeling unsettled by the encounter. Not because Mom is angry—she always gets angry when she thinks we spent money we don't have—but because, really, Willard Pruitt has no idea if my dreams predict the future or not.

He only has what we have—an idea that they don't and a fear that they might.

I'd be back to square one if it weren't for two things: He actually believes (like I do) that J. Rutherford is a threat; and I can try dedicated dreaming.

When I finish cleaning my mess, I go upstairs and log onto our household computer. I read all I can find on dedicated dreaming, and there's not a lot, at least from the magical perspective.

What there is is all about ritual, the kinda stuff I usually scoff at.

But I need to know, so I go through all the goofy rituals from the scented oil bath to the vanilla candles to the overturned mirrors and the quiet bedroom. I'm prepared to have the dreams of my life.

And, of course, I don't dream at all.

Until Sunday night, the night before my suspension ends. I was right about one thing—nothing happened while I was away. School lunch is normal, and nothing, not even threats, make the news. I monitor the My-Space pages of everyone I can think of and don't even see rumors.

Which both relieves me and terrifies me. It leads me to believe I'm onto something when in fact, I might just be delusional.

Certainly the fact that I can't even dedicated dream makes me wonder if I have much magic at all. According to the Web sites, dedicated dreaming is one of those basic spells everyone can perform after a certain age.

Everyone but me, apparently.

So I don't go through the stupid dedicated dreaming

rituals at all on Sunday, and I actually fall asleep on the couch, watching some Monster Truck Rally thing.

One minute I'm watching giant trucks drive over other giant trucks, and the next I'm back in the cafeteria, holding onto my silver tray with its lonely little slice of pizza. Kids are sitting at various tables, talking, and Mrs. McGuillicuty—the cafeteria supervisor—is telling me about this luscious lemon pie she makes, and I'm pretty convinced none of that happened before, but I'm not sure I'm making the changes.

So I consciously choose to set down my tray (and its delectable slice of pizza), and I turn around long before J. Rutherford comes into the cafeteria.

In fact, I'm beginning to think he's not going to when he does, his father's black robes flapping around him. J. Rutherford raises that deadly finger, and then he stops. He stares at me.

I stare at him and realize how stupid he looks, all in black like a TV magician, with one finger pointed and this frown of concentration on his face. He's conjuring up how to do the spell, that's what he's doing.

And no one can stop him.

Except . . .

I wave a finger at Ms. McGuillicuty's asbestos gloves, the ones she keeps behind the counter for removing things like pizza from the double-hot ovens. I command those gloves to cover J. Rutherford's hands and not to come off until he leaves the cafeteria and gives up his dream of killing people.

The gloves soar across the caf just as he turns toward Jane Bauer, the kid he burned alive in the first dream. And as the fire jets out of his finger, the gloves slide on, interrupting the flow. Jane's clothes light on fire, the boys around her put it out, and those evil security guards—the ones that took me to Principal Prison—cart J. Rutherford away.

Then I wake up.

The TV's playing some Japanese game show, the point of which seems to be to make everyone fall so that their back bends into an unnatural position. Mom's covered me with a blanket, but she hasn't sent me to bed.

And my heart is pounding.

Okay. That had to be dedicated dreaming since I set down my tray and actually stopped J. Rutherford with domestic magic. That couldn't happen in real life.

I push off the blanket and go into the kitchen, my domain. There I drink some water, wipe off my sweaty face, and lean against the counter for a while.

It's done. The whole dream thing is over.

At least, I hope it is.

Especially as I head for school that morning.

And walk into the cafeteria at lunch.

Of course, stupid me, I decide to have pizza to celebrate. I've been dreaming of pizza for a week now, and I deserve some. I mention that to Mrs. McGuillicuty as I'm getting my slice. She pulls off her asbestos gloves to serve it to me, fresh and bubbly, looking better than I even dreamed it would.

Then she tells me about this lemon pie she's making, and the hair rises on the back of my neck.

I turn just as J. Rutherford comes into the caf. Only he's not wearing his dad's robes, and he's being trailed by those evil security guards. They're not quite touching the backs of his arms.

He comes directly at me. I snap my fingers, and instantly I'm holding those asbestos gloves instead of my cafeteria tray.

He sees that move, and he smiles. Then he blinks hard. Against tears.

Tears again from J. Rutherford Wisenhauer the Third. What the heck is this all about?

He crowds so close to me that I wedge my back against the railing around the steam tables.

"I just had to tell you," he says, "I've turned myself in."

He says it real soft, so no one else can hear, except maybe those guards.

My mouth is dry.

"The gloves got me," he says. "Good move. Made me realize that not all magic is about power. And someday, we're going to tell that to my dad."

Before I can even say, "Huh?" he heads out of the cafeteria again. Next thing I know, it's all over the school that J. Rutherford Wisenhauer the Third has voluntarily committed himself to some treatment facility for suicidal kids. Suicidal magical kids.

Seems he'd been dreaming about dying for a week or more because (rumor has it) he can't stand living with Number Two and Number Two's expectations.

Only I know different. Maybe he's been dreaming of suicide, but only after he takes out part of the school.

Because he was sending me the dreams.

Me, the person he beat up so bad she went to the hospital.

Me, the person with such small magic that no one pays attention to it.

Me, the person who used that small magic to stop him once before.

The whole thing is a big scandal, the kind the tabloids love: J. Rutherford the Second's namesake is so miserable he's thinking of suicide. What's really happening in that mansion on the hill? Rumors of black magic, Satanism—and all that stuff the mundanes are afraid of.

When really, Mom thinks it was just the same stuff that mundanes deal with. A depressed kid, a distant and demanding father, an alcoholic mother (yep, that came out too). The kid decides he's going to go out, but in a way that'll destroy his father forever.

It's not enough to kill Number Two, after all. J. Rutherford has to demolish everything Number Two stands for.

Only some spark in J. Rutherford's subconscious, some little teeny part of himself, maybe the part that started all that self-loathing in the first place, knows it's wrong. So it sends out feelers to the one person who actually knows J. Rutherford for who he really is.

Lucky me.

J. Rutherford'll be in his mental health facility for the next five years or so. His father's not on TV anymore, and the mansion's up for sale.

I've been accepted to the magical version of Le Cordon Bleu in Paris, and Mom, she vacillates between being really proud of me and wondering what she'll do when she no longer has a resident chief cook and bottlewasher.

And I try not to do much dreaming. Sleep dreaming, that is. I'm up a little later than I used to be, and I drink a lot more caffeine.

Mr. Marx says it's a natural reaction to all I've been through. Mom thinks I should get past it because dreaming's a normal part of life.

But I just don't want the responsibility. Or the angst over the life-and-death philosophical questions.

I'd rather just spend my life cooking—and not mopping up someone else's spilled red wine.

Temporal Management

Laura Resnick

Laura Resnick is the award-winning author of such fantasy novels as *Disappearing Nightly, In Legend Born, The Destroyer Goddess,* and *The White Dragon,* which made the "Year's Best" lists of *Publishers Weekly* and *Voya*. She has also published more than sixty short stories. You can find her on the Web at www.LauraResnick.com.

THE problem was, I didn't have time to prepare for my midterm in Moans and Groans, more formally known as Historical Persecutions of Occult Practitioners. It's a required course here at Salem High, and it's taught by good old Gray and Grizzled himself, a.k.a. Mr. Flavius Junius. He's so ancient, it's rumored he was actually *around* during most of the historical persecutions he lectures about in his class. (The alternate but not incompatible theory is that he's trying to get into future history books by persecuting his students *now*.)

Junius is also so old that he has no memory of what it was like to have an actual life, with stuff to *do*—you know, besides studying all the time. So he assigns a boatload of homework as well as a major project each term, and his exams are a nightmare. (Last year, Yasmine Perkins actually had a nervous breakdown in the second hour of her final exam for this class. Okay, Yasmine's a little high-strung, but *still*. And when she recovered and came back to school this past fall, Junius made her complete the test! Honestly, I think someone in admin needs to investigate whether old Gray and Grizzled is possessed by a particularly vicious kind of demon.)

Anyhow, since Junius the Persecutor is the one who teaches Moans and Groans, we're talking about *weeks* of reading and *reams* of note taking—just to get through the midterm!

And, well, I hadn't had time for that.

For one thing, my project team in my third year Practical Skills class (a.k.a. Toil and Trouble) was working overtime on our levitation project, which wasn't going so well. (We should have picked a less ambitious target than the entire gymnasium for the twenty minute free float we needed to achieve to get a good grade. But we were stuck with it now.) I also had a huge midterm paper due on the uses and limitations of talismans for my Alchemy II class. And I was worried about my grades in Chiromancy, so I was reading Robert Fludd's *Utriusque Cosmi Historia* for extra credit (and let me tell you, boy, is *that* a slow-moving book).

Plus, I was this year's chairperson of the Winter Solstice Dance committee, and we were planning a particularly cool total eclipse of the moon effect to fall on the stroke of midnight while the DJ would be playing a CD by the Moody Blues, which is a band from olden days. And you can't get an effect like that j-u-s-t right without a lot of planning and practice, after all.

So I was a little too busy to get fully prepped for a famously unfair midterm in a required course that's focused entirely on horrible stuff that happened years ago, okay?

I'm not excusing what happened. I'm just explaining that I had my reasons for needing to find an effective solution to a scheduling problem that wasn't my fault. (Why do they give all the midterm tests and make all the midterm papers due the exact same week, after all? Why don't they stagger them? Wouldn't that make more sense?)

I wasn't trying to cheat. I was just trying to buy some time. I was *applying* myself to the problem, exactly the way the teachers here encourage us to do.

How was I to know that it would cause so much trouble?

I got the idea in Metaphysics (a.k.a. Airy Fairy class), the only course I was taking that didn't have a midterm test, paper, or project. (There's no final exam, either. It's a pass-or-fail class, based entirely on whether the psychics who probe your mind on the first day and then again on the last day of class think you've achieved a higher level of consciousness over the course of the year.) This term, we were studying the Threefold Law of Return, esoteric thought, theosophy, divine consciousness, the nature of good and evil, yada yada yada, and it was all pretty much a big yawn. Frankly, I think I deserve a passing grade just for not running screaming from the classroom.

But then one day the teacher, Ms. Celeste Divine (like *anyone* believes that's her real name), started talking about temporal magic. And, by coincidence, it was the same day I was really freaking about not having even *started* the mountains of reading I needed to do to survive Gray and Grizzled's midterm exam in two days.

Temporal magic! Playing with time. Folding seams of time backward and forward on themselves. According to Ms. Divine, a deft practitioner of temporal magic whose client realized on Sunday that she had lost her wallet could turn the clock back to Saturday, to the exact moment the client last remembered seeing the wallet, so the missing object could be reclaimed. Or, if a tragic accident occurred, the practitioner could fold time back in order to relive that moment and make sure the accident was averted.

"Before being licensed as temporal practitioner,

however," Ms. Divine said, "the artiste must swear in blood—or in some other cherished bodily fluid—that he or she will never use this power for personal gain or evil intent."

(Cherished bodily fluids. Yeah, *that* one drew a few snickers from Robbie Marciano, who sat right behind me.)

Well, this got me to thinking. And, come on, they're always saying around here that they *encourage* us to think, right?

So I went to the library, which is something *else* the teachers are always encouraging us to do, and used my lunchtime that day to do a little cramming on the practical aspects of temporal magic. It's complicated stuff, in general, involving paradox, multiple dimensional threads, and a boatload of morality clauses. But what I specifically wanted to do seemed pretty straightforward—just turn the clock back a few days to give me enough time to prepare for my Historical Persecutions midterm. So that my parents wouldn't persecute *me* when report cards were issued.

Anyhow, it *seemed* straightforward.

Time is circular, according to my reading. And we had studied circular magic spells in Practical Skills the previous year.

Clockwise circular movement is used in witchcraft for casting positive spells and for creating the Magic Circle, a sacred, protected space for conducting rituals. In practical magic, the clockwise direction of circular magic is associated with positive blessings and good fortune. Its opposite direction is widdershins, a counterclockwise movement used to cast binding and banishing spells. In some traditions, widdershins circular magic is considered negative and unnatural, and it's even associated with black magic. But this depends strictly on the intentions of the practitioner, and, in fact, it can be very effective in counteracting negative spells and bad juju. So there.

And in temporal magic, I learned during my lunchtime cramming, clockwise or deosil (turning to the right) magic is associated with the movement of the sun across the heavens and the forward movement of time.

The bell rang before I was done reading, and I had to get to Chiromancy class to do my extra-credit presentation on Fludd's deadly-dull *Utriusque Cosmi Historia.* But in final period that day, while sitting through one of Junius the Persecutor's familiar diatribes on "the laziness of young people today" in Moans and Groans, I thought about temporal magic some more. And I reasoned (because they're *always* encouraging us to reason at Salem High, right?) that if deosil or clockwise circular magic represents the forward movement of time . . . then widdershins must represent a backward movement.

In which case . . . I could buy myself some time! All I needed to do was look up a temporal spell and perform it widdershins. And I could turn back the clock!

Not all the way back to the days of historical persecutions of occult practitioners, obviously, but maybe back to, say, Monday. Which was when I had spent five hours with my Practical Skills team trying to make the locker room levitate (as a warm-up to trying to float the whole gym this Friday, for our final grade). Now that I knew what it had taken us five hours to figure out then . . . I could polish off that task in ten minutes and use the rest of that day to study for my Friday midterm in Historical Persecutions.

Like I said, this wasn't about cheating, it was about effective time management.

So that night I slipped out of the house after lights-out, while my dad was sleeping in his chair and my mom was watching a cable minimarathon of *What Not to Wear.* (My life has never been the same since she discovered that program. I pray to Hecate nightly to protect me from a mother who suddenly thinks she knows everything about fashion because she watches that stupid show.) Salem's not exactly a lively and happening place after ten o'clock on a weeknight, but there was nonetheless a chance of getting hit on my bicycle after dark, so I walked to the school.

Everyone in town with a functioning cerebellum knows what goes on at Salem Township Public High School #4, so we don't exactly need tight security on campus. By the time you're a sophomore here, ordinary locks can't keep you out of any building; and ordinary people in Salem don't come around our school after dark (also not a whole lot by day, either). I'm a junior, and I'd slipped into school after dark a few times before this. So I knew exactly how to do it by now.

The teachers' offices are so securely warded that you'd need a whole team of advanced adepts to get into them covertly. And high-powered security on the computer systems databases ensures that students can't use their skills (magical *or* worldly) to change their grades when no one's looking. But so many students of the Craft work better after dark that the school has fairly flexible rules about us using the library and workshops at night, as long as nothing gets damaged or stolen.

However, I was here *very* late that night, since I wanted to do something that's not on the syllabus. But I figured I was just bending the rules, not really breaking them.

Once I was in the library, it took longer than I'd hoped to find what I wanted. Unfortunately for modern students like me, ancient tomes don't tend to have handy appendices with useful subject headers like, "Temporal spells, short-term." And forget about the internet; you'd grow old before you managed to sort out the useful stuff from the ignorant garbage and derivative, watered-down crap. No, this is the sort of research you always have to do the old-fashioned way. So I spent about three hours of really dull reading, in French, Latin, and English, before I found what I needed. It happened to be in English, which was lucky for me because sometimes I get bad results when I work spells that I've translated from other languages. (Junius says I need to study harder. Yeah, whatever.)

Codified in 1617 in Vienna (the one in Austria), then translated a century later in York (the one in England), the *Temporal Spell for the Effective Dislocation of One Solar Day* could be multiplied in its power by a factor of three (according to the text) with the use of some simple supplies I could easily find in the Practical Skills workshop. So if I did that, then performed the ritual widdershins, I figured that would get me back to Monday.

I made my way to the workshop and started gathering the materials I needed: chalk, candles, rosemary, yarrow, deadly nightshade, sea salt, toad's blood, sulfur (I *hate* sulfur, and you need it for just about everything), wolfberries, two pebbles from the Euphrates River, grated lemon peel, the jawbone of a tortoise, blah blah blah.

By the time I got everything set up according to the three-hundred-year-old instructions I was following, it was nearly dawn. And by the time I was done performing the ritual, people were starting to drift into school for another day of classes.

I realized my mom must be wondering why I wasn't home when she woke up. I also realized that, not having expected to be gone all night, I hadn't brought my cell phone with me. So I borrowed a cell phone from the first person I saw and called home.

"Sorry, Mom," I said when she answered. "I forgot to tell you that I had to leave for school super-early today."

"What are you wearing?" she asked.

"Huh? What does it matter?" I was wearing gray sweatpants and a blue flannel shirt. Not my best look, no; but I hadn't expected anyone to see me. The research and ritual took longer than expected. These things always do, I guess.

"I just want to make sure you're not wearing those black hip-huggers," my mother said. "The episode of my show that I watched this weekend made me realize those pants aren't a good look for a girl of your height."

"Oh, good grief! We already talked about this on Monday, Mom, and I told you then—"

"Today *is* Monday, dear."

"—I like those pants, I think they look fine, and I *wish* you would stop watching . . . watching . . . " I frowned and my jaw dropped as I realized what she had just said. "*Today* is Monday?"

"All day," she said, with exaggerated patience.

"Oh, my God! It's *Monday?*" I shrieked. "It worked! It's Monday! Monday, Monday, Monday, *yipppeeeeee!*"

"Er, are you feeling all right, dear?"

"Mom! It's Monday!"

"Yes. And this is the first time since kindergarten that you've been happy about that."

"I've gotta go," I said. "Busy day. I'll see you tonight."

"Wait! Are you still planning to stay late to work on your levitation project?"

"Yes, I'm still staying late," I confirmed. "But I won't have to work on *that* today! Hah!"

"I'll set aside some dinner for you. It'll be in the fridge whenever you finally get home."

I remembered what she had cooked Monday night. "Oh, no, *not* that chicken casserole, Mom." Words cannot describe how bland it was.

"How did you know I was planning—"

"I'll get a burger or something on the way home. Gotta go. Bye, Mom!"

I cleaned up the mess I'd made with my temporal spell, then I whizzed through the exercises in that morning's Practical Skills class since I knew this time exactly how to solve the problems presented. Next, I took a nap during the Monday morning Metaphysics lecture, since I'd already heard it and had taken good notes. That afternoon, my levitation team thought I was a genius when I single-handedly "solved" the problem we'd jointly spent five hours working our way through the first time I'd lived through this day. Accepting their praise and thanks, I grabbed a stack of reading for my Moans and Groans midterm, and I retreated to a study carrel in the library for the rest of Monday.

After two more days of similarly effective time management and cramming, I felt I could probably get through Junius the Persecutor's midterm exam with an acceptable grade on Friday. The next day, Thursday, was the day I had dreamed up and enacted this plan. Since I already knew what would happen all day, I figured I could work in a little more Persecutions studying, then go home early for a good night's sleep.

But when I woke up the next day . . . it was dawn, and I was in the Practical Skills workshop. I was wearing gray sweatpants and a blue flannel shirt, and I was standing in the middle of the temporal circle I had made . . . at exactly this moment in time three days earlier.

"This can't be right," I said.

I borrowed a cell phone—the same one I had borrowed before—to phone my mother. She wondered if I was wearing black hip-huggers and offered to leave some chicken casserole in the refrigerator for me that night, since I'd be staying late at school to work on my levitation project.

I decided not to panic.

I had deliberately tripled the effect of the temporal dislocation spell. As planned, it had folded time backward by a factor of three days.

Now, perhaps, I was experiencing an unforeseen side effect of tripling the spell. Maybe I had inadvertently done something that ensured I'd have to live through these same three days *three* times.

Sure, that made sense. That *must* be what had gone

wrong. A lot of spells have odd side effects. And while I hadn't translated this one from a foreign language, I had translated it from early eighteenth-century English, which is a lot *like* a foreign language.

No, indeed, no need to panic. I'd just ride out this three-day temporal spell period two more times, until the cycle was fully completed and time once again flowed forward in its normal way. Meanwhile, I'd use the repetitions of these three days to prepare so well for my Moans and Groans final *and* for my levitation project that I'd be able to bring home the best report card of my life.

Now *that's* a plan for effective time management, I figured.

However . . . when I woke up a *fourth* time in gray sweatpants and a blue flannel shirt, to find myself once again standing in the temporal circle I had made in the Practical Skills workshop, on a Monday morning that I had already lived through multiple times . . .

Okay, it was clearly time to panic.

I skipped all my classes and spent the entire day—and night—in the library, trying to figure out what I had done wrong and how I could fix it. Never mind passing my midterms. If I didn't undo what I had done, I'd be in high school for the rest of my life, living these exact same three days over and over and *over.*

By the seventh time we went through this cycle, people were starting to talk.

"Am I having another nervous breakdown?" Yasmine Perkins wondered aloud in Metaphysics on that seventh Tuesday. "I feel like I've lived through this exact same day a gazillion times. Or least half a dozen. Yesterday, too. And tomorrow, I think."

"My God, I thought it was just me!" exclaimed Robbie Marciano. "We talked about this at home last week, and my mom confessed that she smoked pot a few times when she was pregnant with me, so we thought maybe this was a family hallucination. Like, you know, the shit you do comes back on you—and also on your kids."

"It's not a nervous breakdown or a marijuana dream," Ms. Divine said crisply. "We're caught in a broken temporal cycle. *Someone* . . ." She looked around the classroom with a dark expression. ". . . has been messing with the Wheel of Time. Someone here in Salem. Someone . . . *among* us."

"How do you know that?" Yasmine asked, wide eyed.

"Because in the rest of the country, it's Christmas Day and everyone's off work and out of school. Call your relatives in other towns and ask them. Only here in Salem is it Tuesday, December tenth. *Again.*"

I decided to confess. As bad as things get when you confess what you've done, experience has taught me that it's not as bad as what happens if you get caught and then have to explain why you *didn't* confess.

So I stood up and said, "I cannot tell a lie, Ms. Divine. It was me. I've broken the Wheel of Time. But I swear it was an honest accident. I was just trying to, um . . . make time a little bit flexible, that's all."

"Were you doing this for your own personal gain?" Ms. Divine asked sternly.

"Huh? Who me? What? No, no, no, of course not," I said, perhaps not as convincingly as I might have done.

"Because that would certainly explain why the wheel is broken and the cycle is stuck," she said.

"It would?"

"Teenagers!" She threw up her hands in exasperation. "Hecate's breath! Weren't you paying any attention the day we discussed this in class?"

"Um . . . I remember something about bodily fluids," I said.

Robbie Marciano snickered.

"Temporal spells are very delicate!" Ms. Divine

snapped. "They disintegrate into chaos if you use them for evil intent or—how much clearer do I have to make this to you, young lady?—*personal gain.*"

"Oh," I said. Then, *"Ohhhhhh."*

Divine sighed and rubbed her forehead. "I take it you fucked with time for a less than perfectly altruistic reason?"

Yasmine gasped at hearing a teacher use the "F" word.

I said, "Um, well, er, uh . . ."

"The principal's office!" Divine said to me, opening the classroom door and leading the way. "*Now!*"

It turned out that it had taken a mere five identical Mondays in a row in Salem High for the faculty to start suspecting foul play. (And they say education is going downhill in America.) But although they had started investigating, they'd been pretty lost until I confessed.

Now, once I showed them exactly what I had done and explained the intent behind the working of the spell, they were able—with the help of fee-charging specialists whom they phoned in York and Vienna (in England and Austria)—to end the cycle and restore time in Salem to the same schedule the rest of Massachusetts (and the world) was on.

So we went to bed one night on December 13 (yet again) . . . and woke up the next morning in early January of the following year. We missed the Christmas holidays entirely . . . and because of the exams and class days we had missed while repeatedly cycling through the same three days for several weeks, the administration decided we'd have to extend our school calendar the following summer to make up for lost time.

All of this, as you can imagine, has not made me the most popular girl in school. But I haven't been around Salem High lately to endure the glares and snipes of my fellow students in the Craft, because I've been suspended. Indefinitely. Pending a disciplinary hearing. A hearing that will only be scheduled once they get the clocks in Salem working correctly again. (Not *everything* went back to normal time when the faculty broke the temporal spell.)

But I learned my lesson.

Sometimes, time just doesn't pay.

Boil and Bubble

Phaedra M. Weldon

Phaedra M. Weldon has written short stories for several anthologies, as well as novellas published in shared universe fields such as *Star Trek* and *BattleTech. Wraith,* her first novel, was published by Ace Books. Its sequel, *Spectre,* was recently released in trade paperback, also from Ace.

I sometimes suspect I have a universal KICK ME sign on my back.

Then came the day I became *certain* it's there.

The day that changed my life. Which I'm not supposed to remember, technically.

It started when my dad moved us from central Georgia up to Salem a year ago, right *before* my senior year. No explanation, no warning, and suddenly I'm attending Salem Township Public High School #4, otherwise known to the locals as Witch High.

Yes, witches. Like me.

I'm a guy. And I'm a witch. And don't try telling me that a male witch is a warlock. To be warlocked has a completely different meaning—literally locked away in another dimension, only a step away from execution. Latest rumor I heard was that Salem Township's public enemy number one was up for final sentencing.

Rush Nevortes.

Never met him. Never wanted to. He was warlocked into the Mirror of Souls before I was born for a series of murders and other crimes. It's been hard to avoid hearing about him, though, since I've been told—repeatedly—that I have the same magical specialty that he did.

More on that later.

Being a witch in the south was a bit different from in the north. There, families teach their own—no special schools. But here in Salem, tradition is tradition, and tradition says that young witches go to Witch High. And speaking of tradition, at that moment, on the morning of April 29, the day of the May Dance, a week before the township's Beltane celebration—I was holding the biggest tradition in Salem history in my hand.

"So, what'd you want to show me?"

I glanced over at my best friend, Charles "Chaz" Valdez, unable to say anything.

I knew what the five-by-five gold envelope I held in my trembling hands had to be. The bloodred wax sealing the back flap and the symbol pressed deep into its center were classic telltale signs.

"Lemme see," Chaz said impatiently as he pulled at my hand, hoping to get a better look and breaking me out of my stupor.

As soon as he saw the symbol in the wax, his own eyes grew to the size of small chicken eggs. "This can't be," he said, fixing me with an accusing stare. "Where did you steal this from?"

I snatched it back from him, just a tad put out by his accusation. "I did *not* steal it. It was in my locker. Maybe somebody else stole it and used a teleportation spell." In fact, there *was* an odd tingle to it against my fingers.

"Or," Chaz gulped, "you really *are* the next candidate for the Omega Honor Society. Wow! They choose one every year before Beltane—and you're it!"

His words, echoing my own thoughts, were too far

out there for me to handle at that moment. No way was I, the newcomer with average grades, the single student picked for an honor like this.

"Hey, Kyle, what you got in the death grip?" Halie Pennington, my locker neighbor and date for the dance that night, bounced up to me at that moment and ogled my hands. Before I could put the invitation away, she too had snatched it away from me.

Don't they teach manners here?

"No. Way. Do you know what *this* is?"

I sighed before snatching it back from her—though, oddly enough, the paper didn't look manhandled. Definitely enchanted in some way. "Of course I know what this is." I lowered my shoulders. "I'm just not sure what it's doing in my locker."

"Burn it," Halie said as she snapped her fingers angrily at her locker, which clicked and opened. Halie was good with locks. I'd never seen one she couldn't zap—or at least intimidate the crap out of. "I'm not sure I trust the Omega."

"How can you say that?" Chaz moved around me and nearly grabbed Halie's shoulders in disbelief. "If Kyle here were one of the Omega Triumvirate, then his future at any magical college in the country would be a given. No tuition. No penny magic. His future would be secured, and they don't even make you pay dues. And if he makes it onto the Triumvirate . . ." He opened his mouth wide and pointed at her. "Oh, I get it! You're just put out because he got the invite and you didn't!"

"Don't be ridiculous."

I pursed my lips as I looked at the invitation. Chaz was right—being a member of Omega meant a good choice of schools and scholarships. And making the Triumvirate, the three leaders of the society, would guarantee I could get a job pretty much anywhere I wanted.

With this I could let my dad off the hook. He worried too much about money and how he was going to afford my education. He'd taken a substantial pay cut to come up here, but he'd insisted a diploma from Witch High meant more in the occult community than the less formal schooling back home.

Halie took a few books from her locker before slamming it. "That's what they want you to think, Chaz. That there's no payback." She looked at me with such a fierce expression I wanted to crawl into my locker. "The Omega Triumvirate—the ruling three—has a history, Kyle. I know it's supposed to be the ultimate in honor societies, but they're too secretive." She paused and looked around, her eyes wide. "Kyle—" her voice was a whisper. "Once you're a member, you're always a member. They never let you go."

That weirded me out—which is sort of hard to believe given the circumstances of my existence. But hey, some things can freak out anyone, whether a witch or the most normal cowen.

The bell rang for first period. She grabbed my wrist. "We'll talk at lunch. Whatever you do, do *not* open that," she nodded to the invite. "Promise me."

"I promise."

A quick kiss on my cheek and she was gone.

Chaz stood beside me as fellow students ran, skated, floated as well as surfed by. "Don't listen to Halie, Kyle. Do it. It'll brighten your future."

"Chaz," I grabbed his arm as I hoisted my backpack over my shoulder. "Don't tell anyone, okay? I get the feeling it's supposed to be secret."

"Sure. You can count on me."

I'm not sure if it was my wishful thinking or a countercommand on the envelope. Word got back to me around third period that Chaz had been sent to the apothecary with a strange case of *Administered Silence*. Arthur Jones, Chaz's lab-mate in Better Living Through Potions, was accused of putting the curse on him.

And it would serve Chaz right—he *did* talk a lot. But I had a suspicion he'd been about to blab about the invitation when the mysterious spell hit him.

Third period for me was Alchemy Today, something I was interested in. Though no one had really turned lead into gold, I was fascinated by the relationship between objects, properties, and their relativity to time and space.

It sort of went with my natural abilities.

Mr. Patrick Selenium ran the class with what he called an open-air policy. He believed that students learned best by pursuing their own studies. The style suited me, and it made me realize how much I enjoyed the subject. It also convinced me that I wanted to be a teacher, just like Mr. Selenium.

That would make Dad happy, I think—anything that kept me out of the Dark Forces would. Don't get me wrong, that's not as ominous as it sounds—Dark Forces is our version of the local police. They're the ones responsible for watching out for the cowens—making sure errant wee withes weren't tormenting them. And, if needed, it was their job to arrange a formal warlocking.

I was sitting in the back, grimoires sprawled all over the table, when Mr. Selenium approached. He looked young—maybe in his mid-thirties—but with witches that was hard to tell. *Glamour* was an easy spell and used often. So a witch's true age could only be seen when they slept.

Today he wore his usual khaki pants, blue long-sleeved shirt, and brown belt. His blond hair was cut short away from his long, thin face. He wore small, round silver-framed glasses. "Kyle, might I have a word with you? In the hall?"

I blinked up at him and nodded. It wasn't an odd request—Mr. Selenium often had small conferences with the students to see how well they were doing or to see what direction their papers were going.

Once outside his expression turned serious. "You haven't opened your invitation."

My face fell for an instant—I'd been so preoccupied with my experiment that I was honestly unsure what he was talking about until I remembered the gold envelope in my back pocket. "Oh. Yes. Sorry. I've been a little busy."

"You do realize, Mr. Daniels, that out of the entire student body, only one is chosen every year to be a member of Omega. And eventually he or she could be chosen to be a part of the Triumvirate."

I nodded. I knew the rumors. "Yes, sir. I was just—" I narrowed my eyes at him. "How did you know I had it?"

"Because I'm the one that put it in your locker, Mr. Daniels." He smiled. "I am on the Board for Omega oversight."

I knew that. Well, maybe not all of it. But I knew he had something to do with it. "Then can you tell me why I was chosen? Mr. Selenium, I'm a new student. I haven't been here as long as the students here. And I'm not the smartest—Halie Pennington is much better at schoolwork than I am. Shouldn't this honor have gone to someone else?"

"Oh, no. No. We took into consideration your grade-point average in Cowen and Witch studies, as well as your Magical rating."

"Ah," I felt my shoulders lower. "You know I'm a Correlation specialist. That's why you chose me."

With that mention a smile wide enough to crack glass crossed his face. "Of course we do, Mr. Daniels."

Most witches had inherent talents, something they're really good at naturally. My Aunt Beulla was a Tarot Specialist—her card predictions were dead on. Well, when she wasn't swigging the mead.

And my mom, before she died, was a whiz with fire spells. I'm lucky if the firesparks didn't stick their tongues out at me when I wanted to light a candle.

Dad was a Force Witch, meaning he could move objects with his mind. No spells. No potions. No incantations. Of course, it took a lot out of him—the larger the object, the harder the force needed.

Which brings us to me—

—remember how I said I had that same talent as Nevortes?

Correlation.

I found out at a very young age that I could call things to me. I would just think of something and fold space enough to bring it into my hands. Not creating something new, just moving stuff around. When I was much younger, I had to be able to see something before I could call it. Lately the ability had moved beyond that, and I was able to bring things just from my memory, but that was still a bit hit or miss.

"Kyle," Mr. Selenium was saying, "trust me. You belong in Omega. Among the elite." He smiled again, but his voice remained serious. "Perhaps even a Triumvirate member."

I wasn't sure what to say. I was a little put off that it wasn't my grade-point average, which wasn't all that ace, but it was decent, that caused my being chosen. Nor was it because I was a good person.

Just because of my magic.

I reached into my pocket and pulled out the envelope. It still looked and felt as crisp as ever.

"Open it."

His voice took on a lilting tone, and it seemed to wrap itself around my head, dulling my senses. I wanted to tell him no—I couldn't open it because I promised Halie I wouldn't—but the words couldn't find a way out of my head. I watched my hands move over the envelope, my index finger slip between the back flap and wax seal, and with a slight tug, it was broken.

"Good," Mr. Selenium said. His voice still bothered me as it tugged and pulled at my senses. "Read it carefully. And don't be late."

I'm not sure how long I stood in the hallway, my hands gripping the cream colored invitation that had been tucked neatly inside the gold envelope. When the bell sounded, Mr. Selenium was in front of me again, my book bag in his hand. He nodded once to me before I headed off to the cafeteria, still slightly dazed.

"You did what?"

I didn't duck in time, and Halie hit me over the head with a rolled copy of *Modern Witch.* We were seated at a table outside near a clump of flowering pink and white azaleas. I have a slight allergy problem and would rather have eaten my lunch inside, but Halie insisted we go somewhere more private to talk.

Rubbing the top of my head with one hand I held up the other. "Hey—I told you. Mr. Selenium told me I had to. And what's the big deal? It's just an invitation to the Honor Society for crying out loud."

"Are you so sure about that?" Halie lowered her magazine. She set it on the table and let it uncurl. A squirrel jumped up on the table, and she fed it a couple of nuts. "Why you? Why the secrecy? How come he had to jinx you to get you to open it?" She nodded to the offensive envelope and invite on the table between us. "And why can't Chaz talk?"

She had a point, but I didn't want to discuss the real reason I'd gotten the invitation. My particular talent drew enough unwanted attention. "With my grades, I should have been offered membership a long time ago."

She was right—even her mundane studies on human history and civics were exemplary. But it gave me an excuse to avoid her questions.

"So you are jealous," I said before starting in on my apple.

"I am *not,*" she insisted. "I just—well, okay, a little, but I'm still worried about you. What did the invitation say you had to do?"

I reached out for the card, but she swatted at my hand. I nearly choked on the apple as I swallowed. "What the hell? How am I supposed to tell you—"

"I want you to do it from memory. There's magic around that damned invitation. I don't like it."

"P'ssshhh," I took another bite of apple, but the words on the cream colored paper came back to me. "I'm supposed to attend a meeting tonight at Town Hall, midnight. Alone."

"Tonight? After the dance?"

"Yeah," I frowned. "Might have to cut our date a little short."

"No chance. I'm coming too."

I felt a tug at my stomach when she said that. "I don't think that's a good idea."

"Oh, not that anyone will know, silly. I just plan on being nearby."

"Hey!"

We both turned to see Chaz bounding toward us, his PDA in his hand, his bookbag slung over his shoulder. "You guys!"

When he'd taken the seat beside me, he handed me the PDA. "Read this."

"I see you got your voice back," Halie commented, almost disappointedly.

"The weirdest thing," Chaz said as he settled his bag on the floor. "Even the nurse couldn't figure out how to counteract the spell. She did finally figure it was from a different source—the manifestation of cerullian energy that she found guarding my larynx was originating from a different location. Anyhow, while I was stuck there, I started pulling in stuff to read, and check this out!"

I looked at the PDA, which was displaying a colorful picture of the town newspaper. "I didn't know the *Salem Scroll* was online."

"It's not," Chaz said as he started pulling snack foods out of his backpack.

Oh. I started scrolling through the article. Front

page news, dated this morning. Nevortes' fate had been decided, and his execution was scheduled for tomorrow at an undisclosed time and place—to avoid crowds and protestors. I handed the PDA to Halie. "Wow."

Chaz nodded as he dug into a bag of cheesy badness. "I'll say. This is the talk of the whole town. A lot of people who lost loved ones because of this creep are threatening to protest all over town, regardless of the cowen's tourist presence." He shook his head, munching. "It's all very sad. They want to *see* him die."

Nodding, Halie put the PDA back on the table. "Mister Fixit, tell me what you see when you look at that," she pointed to the invitation.

"See what?" He looked over at the invitation, his eyes wide. He pushed at my shoulder. "Dude! You got the Omega invitation."

Halie and I exchanged glances. "Chaz," I started and set my apple core down on my tray. "You already knew that. Remember? This morning before homeroom?"

Chaz frowned and shook his head slowly. "No, 'fraid not, Kyle. But," he reached out and snatched it up—and then put it back down. He shivered and dropped his bag of snacks.

"Hey, what is it?" I reached out to touch him, and Chaz was shaking, his eyes wide as he stared at the invitation.

"I gotta go." He grabbed up his bag and his PDA. "I'll see you later."

"Don't forget the dance," I said as he walked away.

I turned back to a glaring Halie. "What?"

"Now will you believe me that something's wrong?" She pointed to the invitation. "That thing just creeped Chaz out. Nothing creeps Charles out. Not even eating scorpions."

She had a point. Rumor had it that Chaz actually ate a scorpion when he was ten. Luckily his mother's a Healer and was able to counteract any poisons. "Yeah."

"Send it away."

"Scuse me?"

"Send it away," she pointed to it. "You can call it back—just see if you can send it away."

I picked it up, thought about that place I had in my house, the box of things I kept hidden in the basement, and decided to send it there.

Nothing happened.

I tried again.

"It's boil and bubble, Kyle. Something's up. And for some reason, you're in the middle of it."

I've often wondered from what universal decoration book dance committees pulled their ideas. Whatever it was called, this committee wasn't using it. There wasn't a shred of wadded up toilet paper anywhere.

What there was—well, that was spectacular. The theme was The Little Mermaid. Magic sizzled in the air, lifting and floating never-popping bubbles. Colorful tropical fish floated by and through the underwater kingdom as bits of confetti turned and moved about on invisible currents.

Even the floor resembled an ocean with its sand and moving kelp, coral and sea anemones. Several times while dancing to the live band I stepped on one or two of the coral—but there wasn't any sort of crack or crunch.

They were all bits of magic.

In fact, I was having such a good time, I'd nearly forgotten my excursion to Town Hall later on.

But Halie wasn't about to let me forget. She and Chaz met me outside of the school, and we piled into her black Honda CR-V.

"I've got a backpack in the seat with Chaz," Halie said as she pulled out of the parking lot. I checked my watch—it was 11:48. Luckily we weren't that far away. "I've packed several torches, a listening bug, and two carrier pigeons."

Chaz and I just blinked at her.

She grinned, her teeth flashing as we passed beneath a green light. "I'm just joking!"

"You got the invite?" Chaz asked me.

I nodded. What I didn't tell either of them was that I'd left the invitation at home, on purpose. And that I'd found it later in the pocket of my suit jacket.

Creepy.

The courthouse was dark, as I expected. The invitation didn't say where the meeting was to take place, but somehow I knew it would be in the basement. And any meeting in any basement couldn't be good.

Halie parked the car on the street a few feet down, and the three of us made our way to the back door, which was at the bottom of a set of steps leading a meter down into the ground. The windows on the door were painted black, and the locked handle rattled under my touch.

Halie smiled as she pushed up invisible sleeves—'cause trust me, the dress she was wearing wasn't leaving anything to the imagination. And don't think I hadn't noticed. "Allow me, boys."

I put my hand on her shoulder. "Be careful."

She put her hand on the doorknob. There was a click, and then it moved inward just a tad. Halie then stepped back and looked up at me. "Okay, let's go see."

But when she started in, I pulled her back. "I think I should go in first—in case there's danger. Okay?"

Both of them nodded like bobblehead dolls.

Great.

I pushed the door open and stepped inside. There was a lurch in the dark, and then I was standing in a huge, brightly lit lobby.

Lights blazed from the chandelier overhead as two men in suits approached. I couldn't see their faces, though—the light was too bright. I turned to see if Chaz or Halie was behind me. They weren't there.

"Ah!" one of the men said as I put my hand up to stave off the light. Was it getting brighter? "Mr. Daniels, I'm so glad you could make it." He took my arm and after a few moments of wincing I could make out Mr. Crucifix's, my dad's boss's, face.

I allowed him to lead me through the empty room, our footsteps echoing off the marble tile. We walked along the hallway past several doors and then turned a sharp right to a dark door. The door handle was in the shape of the Omega letter.

"Sir . . ." I started.

But he put a hand on my shoulder. "It's best you go on down. They're waiting on you."

"This isn't just an honor society, is it?"

But he only smiled and nodded to the door.

There was something decidedly wrong here.

I opened the door and carefully went down several flights of steps that crisscrossed one another. When I reached the bottom, there was nothing. Just a black so dark that everything disappeared. I couldn't even see my hand when I raised it to within an inch of my face.

The clock on the tower struck midnight.

On the last stroke the room before me lit up.

Of all the things I expected to see, a courtroom did not rank high on the list. Let me rephrase that—a *crowded* courtroom.

I was in the back, as if I'd just stepped in through the usual set of double doors. There were rows of benches—maybe twenty people wide—set on either side of me so that there was a path between them. That path led directly to a round podium with a cage around it, and beyond that was a three meter high desk with three people seated behind it.

"Will the candidate please come forward."

The voice echoed all through the room. All eyes turned to me. There wasn't another sound in the room, and as I slowly put one foot in front of the other, I realized that most of the faces were people I knew. Teachers, people from town. Chaz's mother narrowed her eyes at me as I passed.

Was this it? This was the Omega Society? This was the grand honor society? How could that be? They were all *adults*. Not students.

"Mr. Daniels, please step onto the podium."

I glared at the cage surrounding it. Did they think I was going to run off? With another deep breath I neared the cage. It didn't appear to have an opening. I looked around it to the three people sitting behind the desk. They all wore dark black robes and hoods with large silver Omega symbols on their chests. "It's not opening."

"You open it."

It was obviously a test, and I also suspected there wasn't a key. They wanted me to use my magic to send the cage away and then bring it back. With a wave it vanished; I stepped on the podium and then made it reappear, surrounding me. There were murmurs all around.

And I have to admit, I felt a little impressed with myself.

"I always thought it was a mistake to let him retain that ability," the man on the right said. He had a gray beard and ponytail as well as a sour expression.

"Now, now, Osiris," the center person said. This was a woman, somewhere about my grandmother's age, who wasn't wearing a glamour spell. Which I liked. "It was agreed upon. And he hasn't abused that power. Not once."

"He tried to send the invitation away!" declared the man on the left. He was bald and had several chins.

"Which we expected." The woman smiled at me. "Kyle Daniels, I am Priestess Odessa. To my left is Lord Osiris, and to my right is Lord Belinus. We are the Omega Triumvirate."

Silence swept through the room, and I felt a chill from the power contained in that single statement.

"We are the council that retains and commands the Dark Forces. We make the law, we carry out the law, and we are the law. Do you understand?"

I nodded.

Abruptly several men and women in dark robes stepped in through a side door on my right. I moved a bit within the cage to see what they were doing. They carried a single large, triangular mirror whose surface reflected back only a milky white mist. When they set it on a stand between me and the Triumvirate, I immediately recognized it, though I'd never seen it before.

The Mirror of Souls. The place the High Council of Witches sent criminals.

But—why was it here? Why was it in front of *me?*

"Mr. Kyle William Daniels, you stand before us here as a symbol of our justice system. Before you is the Mirror of Souls, where the warlocks are cast out. It is time for the execution to begin." She hit a hammer to a gong, and the mirror's surface moved.

I moved back against the cage as the face of Rush Nevortes appeared, his eyes closed, his expression blank. And suddenly it all came clear to me—why I'd been chosen, why they wanted me here.

"You—you want me to transport him out of there?" I pointed to the mirror. "You want me to get him out so you can kill him!"

"Silence!" Barked Lord Osiris. "You will not speak again until asked."

Something closed in on my throat, constricting my breathing. I grabbed at my neck with both hands and gasped for breath. I definitely couldn't speak—and forget that whole breathing thing.

"Now, now Osiris," Priestess Odessa said in a calm voice. "That is no way to address our candidate. Mr. Daniels, eighteen years ago you stood before this court to be judged. It was our decision that you be warlocked."

What—me—warlocked? Eighteen years ago . . .

The grip on my neck eased, and I took in several mouthfuls of air and coughed. I looked down at the mirror, all too aware that it wasn't just a face hanging there.

But a reflection.

"Ma'am," I coughed again. "I—I don't understand. You have me confused with someone else. I'm only seventeen. I couldn't have been here—"

"Silence!"

But this time Odessa held up her hand and blocked Osiris' spell. A slight whiff of smoke was the only sign of the battle. "Osiris, put your grievances aside for now."

"You're treating him as though he were an innocent."

"He *is* an innocent." Odessa looked back at me. "Mr. Daniels, for over a century this Triumvirate has warlocked hundreds of criminals. But some truly wish to reform, and for them we grant an option of reincarnation. Our own version of intelligent design."

Everyone paused. As did I.

"You are the incarnation of Rush Nevortes. You are his second chance."

I felt my legs giving beneath me as I went down on my knees. I—I—I was Rush Nevortes? Me? No, that's not possible. I—I was Kyle Daniels. I was born in rural Georgia—

"Kyle," Odessa's voice was soft and soothing in my ears. I looked up at her through the bars. "This is a cruel thing to reveal to you—but as set down in the agreement reached those years ago, it is time for your execution."

"My what?" I still wasn't sure I understood any of this. "What—what does that mean? I'm Kyle Daniels—not some criminal. I'm me!"

"Control yourself," Osiris said, but I could tell from his tone he wasn't as angry as before. "Every year at Samhain we reincarnate a soul, and eighteen years later, at Beltane, if he or she has truly reformed, that soul is given the right to destroy the old life and become one of the Omegas."

Omega.

The end of all things.

"You mean . . ." I put a hand on the bars.

"Exactly." Osiris nodded. "You must end your former self, those vestiges of evil that still remain warlocked in the Mirror."

As preposterous and outrageous as it all sounded, it made sense. Certain memories I'd always had. Dad's abrupt move to Salem. His insistence that I always use my magic for good. He knew what his son was. And he wanted me to succeed.

I wanted to vanish out of there at that moment, with all eyes on me.

I wanted to make all of them go away.

But most of all, I wanted to make that face in the mirror disappear.

End the reflection, end the evil. For good.

I vanished the bars and stood up, my eyes watering from the mixed emotions racing around inside my head. It felt as if everyone were watching on the edge of their seats; even the Triumvirate were eager to see what I would do.

I looked at my hands. Correlation—was it a curse or a choice? Whatever it was, it wasn't my power. It wasn't who I am.

It was the last vestige of a dead criminal.

With a yell, I thrust out my hands and imagined my talent—my understanding of Correlation—as a small glowing ball of light. I felt it leave me in a burst of pain, and with the last of my strength I pushed it into the mirror. The surface cracked, the face opened its eyes and screamed, his mouth forming a perfect O.

There was no sound. Only the slight music of a piano from somewhere above us.

"I—I do not want to remember." I sniffed and wiped at my nose. I was getting dizzy—as if I hadn't eaten in some time. To shove out my own magic, if only temporarily, was exhausting. "I don't want any of it."

"Are you sure, Kyle Daniels?" It was the voice of the man on Odessa's right, Belinus. A voice I recognized as that of Mr. Selenium.

I nodded. I was starting to pitch forward, unsure of what was happening. I heard the sound of distant applause, and felt hands reaching out to catch me as I fell. The last thing I remembered was looking up into my teacher's face and hearing him whisper, "I'm sorry."

"What do you mean you don't remember?"

Halie was beyond mad at me. And she had every right to be. She and Chaz had stepped in after me to an empty basement, complete with dirt and spiders. I had disappeared. She had not been happy. The two of them had waited outside for hours, but I never showed up.

We were sitting in the park across from the school, enjoying a lazy Saturday afternoon.

"I don't remember," I shrugged. It wasn't the truth, but it was what I wanted her and Chaz to know. I remembered far more than I wanted but less than a full story. "I do know I passed the test, and I'm officially a member of Omega."

"And set for life," Chas said from where he sat behind us, reading his PDA. "You get all the luck."

Luck? I suppose getting a second chance was lucky. But I still had that KICK ME sign on my back. Omega members got privileges, true, but only so that the rest of the order could keep an eye on them. "Oh, ho, ho," my friend finally said and turned the PDA around for us to see. "Look here—Rush Nevortes was executed at 12:21 this morning. I guess they had the hearing at midnight to avoid the press."

Halie nodded, but she was looking at me funny. "It's never straight with you, is it? Boil and bubble."

And sometimes I look at me funny too, and I wonder who really is staring out at me from the mirror. I had an odd sense of loss on my shoulders. But they were my shoulders, and come what may, I was a witch graduating from Witch High.

The future? I had my entire life to do over again.

Chemistry 101

Pamela Luzier

Pamela Luzier is a voracious reader of science fiction, fantasy, humor, and romance, and her stories usually include two or more of these elements. Five of her short stories have appeared in other collections, and she has published romance novels under the name Pam McCutcheon. A former industrial engineer for the Air Force, she now lives in the mountains of Colorado with her terrier/poodle mix, Mo.

"IT'S so unfair," I complained to my BFF, Melisande, as I slumped against my school locker the second week of school. "Why do I have to take Elemental Chemistry?"

Meli placed one hand on her hip. She usually used both hands and hips when she wanted to get my attention, but the other hand held her book bag. "Kenina Bailey, you know darned well why you have to take it—it's required for all elemental witches." Meli flipped her hair over her shoulder for emphasis.

Her long blond hair was straight, shiny, and beautiful. I ought to hate her for that, not to mention her perfect skin and model-thin body, but she was so clueless about being a knockout that I felt kind of responsible for keeping boys from drooling on her all the time. She simply didn't get how hot she was.

Now me, I'm a different story. I'm kind of short

and pudgy with a mop of wild curls I can't seem to tame, so I look more like Little Orphan Annie . . . if she had dark brown hair, that is. Everyone talks about how gorgeous Meli is. Me, I get called cute. Gag me.

"I know it's required," I grumped. "But it sucks being the only fire witch in the class." Especially a fire witch who'd really rather be doing something that didn't involve math or science. Art, now there was something to get excited about. I'd rather experiment with fire to mold ice or wax into cool shapes, or melt silica sand into glass baubles and beads, or try fusing different kinds of materials together. It was totally awesome to make something no one had ever seen before, all from little old me.

And Elemental Chemistry was so *not* fun. "We're not allowed to use our powers there at all. It's so bogus." And with five earth witches, three airy types, and a bunch of water witches in the class, I felt stifled by all that dampening water energy. I frowned at my best friend for not supporting me. "You're lucky you're not an elemental."

"Yes, I like being an animal empath." Meli smiled and flipped her hair again, not noticing or caring how it caught the attention of several seniors walking by. The guys checked her out thoroughly, nudging each other and whispering. I didn't need to earjack their conversation to know what they were saying.

I glared at them. "She's only a sophomore—*and* she has a boyfriend." Plus, the guys really needed to be small and furry to get her attention.

I think it was my scowl more than my words that scared them off. Whatever. So long as they left her alone.

Meli didn't even seem to notice. "Besides," she added with a sly smile, "it can't be too bad. Didn't you say Mr. Dennis assigned Brad Harrison as your lab partner, and you get to partner up today?"

Yeah, Brad was a total hottie despite being a water witch, but the water bitches were real protective of what they considered their territory. And Brad was definitely prime lakefront property . . . with NO FISHING signs clearly posted.

I shrugged as if I didn't care. "He's okay." Uh huh. Like who wouldn't like tall, dark, and dimpled?

Meli elbowed me in the ribs. "Yeah, sure. Tell the truth. You're crushing on him, aren't you? He's your McDreamy."

"Don't be McStupid." But my burning face gave me away, damn it. That was the only thing I hated about being a fire witch—color blazed too easily on my cheeks.

She chortled. "I knew it. So, are you going to invite him to the Sadie Hawkins dance?"

As if. I rolled my eyes. "Like he'd go with me."

"Why not? You're funny, talented, cute . . ."

There was that "c" word again. ". . . a dork, a freak, and an art geek," I finished for her.

Meli scowled. "Stop putting yourself down. I hate it when you do that."

I shrugged. Better me than someone else. "Well, it's not gonna happen, so just drop it." No way was I going to set up myself up for the humiliation of rejection, not to mention the added bonus of sneers and jeers from the water bitches when they found out. Not even for one night with Brad Harrison. One long, hot, summer night . . .

Meli jerked me out of my daydream with another dig to the ribs. She stared over my shoulder. "Hey, there he is. Grab your chance." She had no right to look so darned smug. She already had a date for the dance—her boyfriend, Ernie Potts. I'm not sure what she saw in him, though he was kind of cute, in a geeky way. Maybe it was because they were both animal empaths. Or maybe there was something else to this chemistry stuff I didn't get.

"Chill," I growled, refusing to eyeball Brad and embarrass myself more. "Or I'll give you a hot seat."

Thank the powers that be that she knew when to

quit. "Okay, but if you want to go out with him, you'll have to make the first move. You know he won't."

I winced. "Ouch." Unfortunately, she had a point.

"Come on, Kenina, you know I didn't mean it like that. But whenever he walks by, it's almost like you turn invisible or something—and I know you don't have that power. You at least need to make him aware that you exist. Let him get to know the real you and he'll love you like I do."

"I don't know . . ." It was just so darned awkward. But as I finally got up the courage to watch his retreating back, my heart pounded like a drummer on speed just from seeing his dark hair curling on the back of his neck. It was all I could do to keep from sighing like some lovesick loser. Damn, I had it bad. "He probably already has a date." The Student Council had announced the dance last week. Surely someone had asked him already.

"You won't know unless you ask."

I gave her my best "as if" look.

Meli sighed. "At least you could say a word or two today as you pass him a beaker or something," she urged.

"Okay," I said grudgingly. She was right in a way. It *was* the only time I was sure to have his attention without the other watery types hanging too close. I didn't want them going all tidal wave on my ass.

"But try to talk about something other than lab tests . . . like casually mention the dance or something."

"Not sure I can go *that* far."

Meli patted my shoulder. "You'll do fine, Kenina. But you have to promise to tell me aaaaaall about it later."

"Yeah, right." I wasn't making any promises. And, for the first time since I'd arrived at Witch High, I was really glad that the school was enchanted as a no-texting zone. Otherwise, my cell phone wouldn't stop ringing with Meli's texts every five minutes after class.

And speaking of ringing, there went the bell for class. I headed off to Chemistry. Great, now I had to find a way to say something to Brad, or I'd never hear the end of it from Meli.

I slid into my seat in the back, as far away from all that water energy as possible.

Chelsea Tipton, the most obnoxious of the water witches, said, "Gee, where's Dennis the Menace today?"

The little court surrounding her snickered as if her dumb joke were actually funny. Sooooo original.

Mr. Dennis arrived, looking more like a sad bulldog than a cartoon character. "All right class, today we are going to familiarize ourselves with the lab equipment. Leave your books here and follow me, please."

We followed him into the lab next door. The water bitches were all whispering and giggling, and most of the girls in the class were clearly jealous that Brad had been assigned as my partner, even the earth and air witches. But all I could think about was finally being close to Brad. My heart was thumping, and my stomach churned like the first time I'd flown in the flightorium. If I didn't know better, I'd think I had the flu.

Just what I needed, for my first words to Brad to be, "Excuse me while I hurl on your shoes." Not.

Mr. Dennis told us to take our assigned places and introduce ourselves to our lab partners, so I got control of my stomach and gave Brad a smile, hopefully not as sickly as it felt.

"Hi," he said as he stuck out his hand. "I'm Brad Harrison, water witch."

Like I hadn't been lusting after him from afar for over a year now. *Say something.* "Uh, Kenina Bailey, fire," I muttered, then mustered up the courage to accept his handshake.

"I know," he said and his dimples deepened. "You're the one who made that glass sculpture at the freshman art show last year."

"You . . . you saw that?"

"Yes, I was impressed. It was great—I wish I had a talent like that."

Oh, my. He actually smiled at me *and* he knew who I was? A surge of . . . something . . . surged within me like a jet of flame through my insides. As we shook hands, I felt little pops of electricity zing through my hand, travel up my arm, and spread throughout my body. Tiny sparks flew where we touched. Not the imaginary kind of electricity you read about in romance novels. I'm talking real live sparks here, the kind you see on the Fourth of July sparklers.

I don't think anyone else noticed, but I jerked my hand back.

"Holy cow," he exclaimed. "What was that?"

"I don't know. It's never happened before." Oh, no. Did I do that on purpose? What did it mean? That I had the hots for him? Heck, I already knew that, but I didn't want the whole world to know it, too. Why didn't Mom and Dad *tell* me about this? Quick, find an explanation.

"Uh, it must be static electricity," I muttered. Yeah, it was totally lame, but how else was I supposed to explain it? "Maybe because I'm a fire witch, it comes out as sparks." Whatever it was, I'd better get it under control and not touch him again until I was sure I wasn't going to set him on fire. Damn it.

"Cool." He grinned at me, and those dimples almost made me self-combust right then and there. "Hey, do you like—"

But I never did hear what he was going to ask, because Mr. Dennis chose that moment to interrupt and give us a lecture. "Before you can learn to handle your element magically, you need to understand it and how it interacts with others."

"Like water puts out fire," Chelsea called out, giving me a sly glance.

Her court giggled, but Mr. Dennis ignored them. "True, and earth can smother fire, while air feeds it.

But don't forget, fire can scorch earth and set water to boiling."

And wouldn't I like to do that to one smart-ass water witch right now?

Mr. Dennis blathered on about the basic ways the elements interacted and lab safety, but I barely heard him. I was too conscious of Brad standing next to me, smelling all clean and fresh and looking positively scrumptious. Well, at least I'd have *something* to report to Meli, even if it was only that he liked my art . . . and sparks flew, literally, when we touched. Even now, I felt the arm that was closest to him prickle, as if the fire wanted to jump to him and eat him all up.

A collective groan arose from the class, and I tuned in again. Mr. Dennis raised his arms in a shushing motion. "That's right, no magic in the lab until you've mastered the basics first—it's too dangerous otherwise." He ignored the reactions from the class and flicked a finger toward a crystal ball at the front of the lab. It turned red. "That means the spell detection enchantment is in place. If anyone uses magic, for any reason, in this class, an alarm will go off, and the witch who set it off will be severely punished. Do you understand?"

It sucked, but we all nodded solemnly.

"All right then, please familiarize yourself with the equipment."

As I fiddled with the Bunsen burner, a guy took advantage of the chatter and sidled up to Brad. "Hey, Brad."

"Yeah, Jon?" Brad said warily, keeping an eye on Mr. Dennis.

"Anyone ask you to the Sadie Hawkins dance yet?"

"Not yet." Brad gave Chelsea a wary glance. "I've been avoiding some people," he said in low voice.

Yes! Inside, I felt like shouting with joy, doing a happy dance, and bursting into flame, but somehow managed to control myself.

"Who do you want to ask you?" Jon asked.

But I didn't hear the answer to that all-important question as Mr. Dennis ordered Jon back to his lab station. "And Brad and Kenina, back to work."

Brad and Kenina . . . that had a nice ring to it.

Brad flashed his dimples at me again. "Sorry about that."

I shrugged. "No biggie." I wished I was brave enough to ask him to answer Jon's question, but that wasn't going to happen anytime this century.

But maybe I could hint a little. My heart pounding like mad, I tried to sound casual. "Well, uh, you know, if someone asks you . . . you, uh, don't have to say yes." Like a certain water bitch who shall remain nameless.

"Yeah, I guess girls know all about that—you get asked out a lot I bet."

Me? He thought I got asked out a lot? I didn't know whether to be happy that he thought I was popular or upset because he'd think I was unavailable. I fiddled with the burner, avoiding his eyes, and decided just to ignore that part. "If you don't want to hurt her feelings, you could tell her someone else already asked you. Or ask someone yourself—I'm sure no one would mind."

My bravery didn't extend to looking at him while he answered. "I guess," he said and his voice deepened. "Do you have anyone in mind?"

Me, me. Pick me! But my courage ran out then. Instead of carpe-ing the diem, I pretended it didn't matter and shrugged.

To cover my embarrassment and hide the sudden blush I felt heating my face, I reached past the Bunsen burner to grab a pair of safety goggles. But Brad did the same thing at the same time, and our arms brushed.

Baby sparks flew once more, and I jerked my arm back.

"It's okay," Brad said. "I think it's cool."

He reached out to stroke my arm again to see the tiny flickers pop, and I thought I'd die of pure pleasure. I gazed up into his eyes and, like in one of those slow motion commercials, I watched his smile spread as a cool breeze blew one of his dark curls into his eyes.

Whoosh! Suddenly, the tiny bits of fire burst into full flame, setting my shirt sleeve ablaze.

Before I could even react with anything other than horror, Brad made a quick gesture and it was as if someone had dumped a bucket of water over my head. I was drenched with water from head to foot.

Whoooooop! Whoooooop! Whoooooop!

Damn, damn, damn. Not only had I lost control of myself, but we'd set off the alarm, and I was soaking wet—a real loser. At that point, I really wished the water would melt me into a puddle of mortification like the Wicked Witch of the West.

"Are you hurt?" Brad asked me.

Only my pride. I shook my head without meeting his eyes. "More scared than hurt." Oh great, now he'd really think I was a dork. Especially since he'd had to save my life . . . or at least save me from a bad burn. "Thanks."

Mr. Dennis made a furious gesture, and the alarm turned off. "Who did that?" he demanded.

"I saw it all," Chelsea piped up. "Kenina tried to show off by lighting the Bunsen burner with her magic and lost control of it. She set herself on fire. Thank goodness Brad was there to put it out immediately or we could have all been killed." She put a hand dramatically to her meager chest. She fancied herself an actress, but I, for one, wasn't fooled.

Mr. Dennis gave me a jowly scowl. "Ms. Bailey, is that true? Did you use magic in this lab after I expressly told you not to?"

I gulped as water dripped off my nose. "No, sir. I didn't." At least, not on purpose. If I didn't do it on purpose, it didn't count, did it? But teachers were notorious for not seeing a student's side of things. Oh, hell, now I was really in deep doo-doo.

"It was probably my spell that set off the alarm," Brad said. "When Kenina's shirt caught on fire, I reacted automatically with a water spell. I'm sorry, sir."

He gestured at the state of my clothes, just in case no one had noticed that I was standing in a puddle and dripping all over the lab.

Wow, what a guy. He was even trying to take the blame for my mistake. It almost made up for the humiliation of looking like a drowned cat in front of the water bitches.

"That was quick thinking on your part, Mr. Harrison, and it probably prevented Ms. Bailey from getting badly burned. There will be no repercussions for using a spell to prevent someone else from harm." Mr. Dennis looked thoughtful then checked the crystal ball. A straight line appeared in the crystal, moving from left to right, then spiked twice, like one of those heart monitors I've seen on television.

Mr. Dennis nodded. "The enchantment registered two spells, one right after the other. If one was Mr. Harrison's, someone else must have used a spell right before his to set the fire."

A skinny little air witch named Ariana Sherman said, "I saw the same thing Chelsea did . . . and there's only one fire witch in the class."

Mr. Dennis scowled. "I'm aware of that." He glanced at me. "Would you like to change your story, Ms. Bailey?"

"No, I didn't use a spell, I swear it. I know it looks bad, but it wasn't me." I might not be totally in control of my power, but I knew the difference between an accident and a deliberate spell.

Mr. Dennis's mouth firmed up until he looked even more like a bulldog. "Then who was it?"

"I don't know."

Mr. Dennis looked at Brad. "Did you see Ms. Bailey use a spell?

Brad looked confused. "I–I'm not sure."

My heart sank.

"Who else could it be?" Chelsea asked in a shrill voice. Obviously, she was thrilled by the thought that the fire witch who was lucky enough to be partnered with Brad—the guy she considered to be the exclusive property of one Chelsea Tipton—was about to be humiliated.

"That remains to be seen," Mr. Dennis said solemnly. "Ms. Bailey, Mr. Harrison, Ms. Tipton, and Ms. Sherman, come with me. The rest of you, return to your seats and stay there quietly until the bell rings for the next class."

Mr. Dennis grabbed my arm as if I were a criminal he was afraid was going to escape and led me out the door and down the hall. I could hear Chelsea and Ariana whispering fiercely to Brad. They were trying to get his attention and diss me, I'm sure. Pathetic.

I squished and sloshed my way down the hall until Mr. Dennis apparently had enough of it. He gestured with his free hand, and I was suddenly dry. I glanced back, and even my wet footprints were gone. Wow—now that was a useful spell. I'd really like to learn how to do that, but right now didn't seem like quite the right time to ask.

It soon became clear we were headed for the principal's office. Oh, no, now I was about to be expelled. Brad would never speak to me again, my parents would be ashamed of me, and everyone would pity me . . . all for something I didn't do.

I am so screwed.

But only cowards gave up. My mind raced, searching for a way out. But how could I win when the evidence was so clearly against me? A slim hope dawned. After working with her at the art show last year, I knew that Ms. Jones, the principal, was fair. Maybe I wasn't as screwed as I thought.

Fortunately, she was free, so the whole parade marched into her office. Mr. Dennis finally let go of my arm, and I rubbed the spot, hoping I wouldn't have a bruise later.

Ms. Jones didn't look like a principal. She was about my mother's age, pretty, and had a sweet-looking face framed by soft brown hair. My hopes rose again. Maybe she'd be nice and I'd only get detention or something.

She raised a delicate eyebrow. "Please, sit down and tell me why you're all here."

We sat, Brad sandwiched between the two other girls, as Mr. Dennis explained the facts baldly without saying one way or another if he thought I was guilty. He placed the crystal ball on Ms. Jones's desk and showed her the spiked line. "The second spell is the one Mr. Harrison used to put out the fire. What's in contention is who cast the first spell." He nodded toward the girls. "Ms. Tipton and Ms. Sherman witnessed the infraction."

"Yes," Chelsea blurted out, giving me a malicious look. "Kenina was trying to show off and light the Bunsen burner with her magic."

"That doesn't sound like you, Kenina," Mrs. Jones said calmly.

"It isn't. I didn't," I said miserably.

Ms. Jones glanced back at Chelsea. "Why do you believe Kenina was trying to show off?"

Chelsea tried hard to look angelic, but maybe I was the only one who could see those horns propping up her halo. And the devil in her made her say, "Because she has a crush on Brad. A friend of mine heard her friend say so right before class."

Kill me now . . . I tried hard to sink through the chair and into the floor, but it wasn't working. Now Brad knew I liked him. Could anything be more mortifying? I gave Ms. Jones a pleading look, hoping she'd save me from this torture.

She looked apologetic and was kind enough not to ask me to confirm it. Instead, she asked Chelsea,

"What makes you think Kenina deliberately set herself on fire?"

"Oh, I don't think she did that on *purpose*. But she was throwing off little tiny sparks, like she was trying to get his attention."

I peeked out from under my bangs to see how Brad was taking this. He was frowning . . . not a good sign. If I got through this, how could I ever look him in the face again? Let alone be his lab partner or, heaven forbid, actually ask him to the dance . . .

"I saw the sparks, too," Ariana said. "And when she put out her hand to make the spell light the Bunsen burner, Brad reached out to stop her, but it was too late—she lost control of the spell, and it flared up."

"Exactly," Chelsea said smugly.

"Is that how it happened?" Ms. Jones asked Brad.

"Not exactly. I wasn't trying to stop her from doing anything—we both reached for the goggles at the same time, and sparks came off her arm. I don't know why they flared up this time. They didn't earlier. It was just static electricity."

Mr. Dennis and Ms. Jones exchanged a knowing glance. Uh-oh, what did that mean?

"Oh, he's just being nice," Chelsea said. "He hates to get anyone in trouble."

Ariana nodded vehemently. "Everyone knows that about Brad."

Brad looked surprised and a little pleased. Darn it, even he was buying into their little fabrication.

"Thank you," Ms. Jones said. "Mr. Dennis, will you please take Chelsea and Ariana and wait outside?"

They left, the girls looking smug with the realization that I was about to be history.

So it was only Brad, me, and Mrs. Jones left. The principal looked at me. "Is that true about the sparks?"

"Yes," I admitted. "But it's never happened before

today. It was an accident, I swear. I didn't do it on purpose—it wasn't a spell."

She nodded. "I'm sure the sparks were accidental, but it wasn't static electricity. During adolescence, when fire witches are attracted to someone, sparks will fly—literally—when they touch that person, until they learn to control it."

I could just die. And kill my parents for not explaining this to me along with the birds and the bees. Hell, now I wished she'd sent Brad out as well.

"I apologize for embarrassing you, Kenina, but the reason I'm telling both of you this is because it isn't something Kenina can help." She smiled at me. "But we can get you help to learn to control it. And Brad, you needed to understand why as well, which is why I asked you to stay."

Why? To make sure he never touched me again? This was the most humiliating day of my life. My cheeks had been burning so much I think they were permanently red.

"I understand," Brad said. "You need her to practice touching me so I can help her learn to control it."

Ms. Jones beamed. "Exactly."

He didn't sound disgusted by the thought. I peeked at him again and he grinned at me.

A tiny hope surfaced. He didn't mind . . . and the principal was actually encouraging the two of us to touch. Cool!

Unfortunately, my hopes plummeted at her next words. "But first, we need to get to the bottom of this fire . . . and who cast the first spell in the lab despite the school rules." She gave me a questioning glance. "You were aware of the rule against spells in the lab, weren't you?"

"Yes, ma'am," I answered honestly. "Mr. Dennis explained it to everyone. But I didn't do it."

"Then who did? Do you know?"

Brad shook his head.

I sighed. "I wish I knew. The only one who seems

to really dislike me is Chelsea—and her water witch friends." But even I could tell how brainless that sounded. It was pretty unlikely that a water witch would cast a fire spell.

"Ariana didn't seem to like you much, either," Brad said, with an apologetic look.

"Yeah, but why would an air witch—" The light dawned. "Wait a minute." I turned to Brad. "Didn't Mr. Dennis say . . ."

". . . air feeds fire," we said together.

"That's true," Mrs. Jones said slowly. "A blast of pure oxygen could fan a spark into a blaze. Do you have reason to believe that's what happened?"

"Yes," Brad said excitedly. "Right before the flare-up, I remember feeling a cool breeze on my face."

"That's right," I confirmed. I remembered it blowing that lock of hair into his eyes. "I felt it, too."

"And what reason would Ariana have to do this and blame it on you?" Ms. Jones asked.

Wasn't it obvious? My face burned again, and I wouldn't look at Brad or her. He remained silent, too.

"I see," the principal said.

The door opened and Mr. Dennis came back in with Ariana and Chelsea. Ms. Jones must have sent him some kind of signal I didn't notice.

Ms. Jones folded her hands on the desk. "Ariana, is there something you'd like to tell us about this situation?"

The skinny girl looked surprised. "No, we told you everything already."

"Did you?"

Oh, my. I would hate to be on the receiving end of that stern look.

Ariana burst into tears, covering her face. "I didn't mean to do it," she wailed.

"Do what?" Chelsea demanded. "What did you do?"

So, the water bitch wasn't in on it? That was a surprise, too.

Ms. Jones looked sympathetic. "I believe she did

see the sparks between Brad and Kenina, and cast a spell to enrich the oxygen in the area to make them flame up. Is that right?"

Ariana hiccoughed back a sob and I kind of felt sorry for her. "Ye–es. I'm sorry. Mr. Dennis said air fe–feeds fire, and I just did it. I didn't me–mean to. It just happened."

"Why?" Ms. Jones asked gently.

"Be–because." She gave Brad this kicked puppy dog look and it was obvious to everyone why she'd done it. Hell hath no fury like a scorned witch.

"I can't believe you were so dumb," Chelsea declared. But it was obvious to me, even if no one else got it, that Chelsea thought Ariana was dumb for thinking Brad could ever be attracted to her, not for setting me on fire.

"That's enough," Ms. Jones said. "Mr. Dennis, if you would take Chelsea back to class?"

After they left, Ms. Jones said, "You could have endangered everyone in the school, Ariana. Especially Kenina. If it hadn't been for Brad's quick thinking, Kenina might have been badly injured—and the fire might have spread to Brad. You owe them both an apology."

"I'm sorry," Ariana murmured, looking down at the floor. "I didn't mean to hurt either of you. It was just a dumb impulse."

Now I really did feel sorry for her. "That's okay. I know you didn't mean it." I perfectly understood the desire to have Brad all to myself. Not that *that* would ever happen now.

Ms. Jones nodded in approval as Brad echoed my words. "Ariana, please stay here so we can discuss your punishment. Kenina and Brad can return to Mr. Dennis for lessons in . . . spark control."

Damn, there went the heat in my cheeks again.

"But first, a word, Kenina?"

She beckoned me closer and leaned over to whisper so only I could hear. "Because you were so generous to Ariana just now, I thought you should know . . . the sparks only happen when the feeling is mutual."

I jerked back to look her in the eye. "Really and truly?"

She smiled. "Really and truly."

Oh, wow. Brad liked me, too? Awesome!

But for some reason, knowing that made it more difficult than ever to look him in the eye.

"So," he said, as we walked slowly down the empty hall together, "shall we continue our earlier conversation?"

"Wha–what conversation?"

"You know, the one where you were advising me on the Sadie Hawkins dance."

"Oh." Oh, yeah. Could I sound any more brilliant? *Come on, Kenina. Grow some guts. Ask him.* But how could I when I couldn't even look him in the eye?

"You mean you don't want to ask me to the dance?" He sounded disappointed.

My head flew up. "Of course I do—" But when I saw the expression on his face, I realized he was teasing me.

Brad Harrison was teasing *me*. Awesome!

"So, you will?" I ventured.

"I thought you'd never ask." He gave me a mock bow. "I'd love to."

Just the thought of it made my heart zing and fire pop through my veins. Maybe Elemental Chemistry wouldn't be so bad after all. Just wait until I told Meli!

I couldn't resist testing him, though, to make sure he really meant it. "But . . . fire and water don't mix."

"Sure they do. Don't you know your chemistry?" He wiggled his eyebrows at me. "Fire and water make steam."

A Perfect Ten

Christina F. York

Christina F. York was once a closet romantic. She is learning to embrace her "sappy side," and it shows in her work. Her stories in anthologies like this one and *Fantasy Gone Wrong,* as well as romance novels like *Dream House* (Five Star Books), display her belief in the power of love stories. But romantic doesn't mean weak, as her *Alias* novels (Simon Spotlight Books) clearly illustrate—girls can kick ass, too! Chris is living her own love story with husband and fellow writer J. Steven York, on the romantic Oregon coast, where the couple is supervised by the obligatory writers' cats, Oz and Sydney.

THE music was loud, loud enough to cover Cassie's voice as she counted the beat. She linked arms with Lynn on the third level of the human pyramid, and waited, a huge smile locked in place.

Behind her, unseen, and unheard beneath the pounding beat, Cassie knew Allison was starting her run.

Four beats, and Allison jumped into the waiting hands.

Two beats, she landed on Cassie and Lynn's shoulders.

One beat to catch her balance.

One beat to raise her arms in a giant "V" for victory.

"Go, Salem!" Cassie screamed in unison with the rest of the squad.

They had rehearsed the routine a thousand times, maybe several thousand, but each time Cassie held her breath as Allison's foot landed on her shoulder, as her toes, in their soft slipper, dug in and Allison stood atop the pyramid. Each time Cassie knew they teetered twenty feet in the air, a split second from disaster; from broken bones and career-ending injuries.

Allison's foot slid, as it had before, and Cassie felt her struggle to keep her balance. In that instant, she knew it was too late. Allison was falling.

Then, as though pushed by an invisible hand, Allison straightened and stood tall, and the squad below moved into position for the dismount.

Seconds later, Allison dived gracefully from her perch, her brush with disaster apparently forgotten.

On the gym floor, two strong boys caught her, breaking her fall and tossing her lightly onto her feet, where she slid into a split, her arms high in the air.

Lynn followed, then Cassie, as the pyramid came apart with practiced precision.

In the locker room after practice, Cassie lingered in the showers. When she emerged, wrapped in the scratchy gym towel, her hair dripping down her back, she found Allison alone in the locker bay. She was already dressed, with her letter sweater thrown carelessly over her shoulders.

"Allison."

Allison turned to look at Cassie. Her expression wasn't unfriendly, just dismissive, as though Cassie wasn't worth the effort to dislike. "What?" she asked, making no effort to disguise her impatience.

"You know what. You nearly fell. And it isn't the first time." Cassie felt her face growing hot.

She didn't want this confrontation, shouldn't have to do it. But if Coach Barkley wasn't going to call Cassie on her missed landing—which was totally his responsibility—somebody had to. She couldn't be the only one who had noticed, could she?

"I didn't 'nearly fall,' " Allison said. "I landed just fine. Maybe my foot slipped a little, but it wouldn't have, if you weren't sliding all over the place."

A hot flash of anger raced through Cassie. She had not been sliding around! She had been steady and solid, and Allison knew it.

"That is such a lie!"

"Oh, yeah? Well, who do you think Coach will believe? His top, or," she waved a dismissive hand at Cassie, "the jealous little girl who had to settle for second place?"

Allison tried to look unconcerned, but Cassie sensed a moment of hesitation. Allison knew she was right.

"This isn't about me. Or you, Allison. It's about the team, and winning, and not getting my friends hurt because you won't admit you can't cut it."

Cassie turned away in disgust, yanking clothes from her locker. She wrestled a T-shirt over her head, and tried to ignore the tightness in her throat and the stinging in her eyes.

She would not let that bitch make her cry!

"Don't kid yourself, Cassie. I can cut it. I did it today, and I'll do it tomorrow, and I'll do it at the competition next week. And all your saying otherwise won't make it so."

Allison's locker slammed shut, the clash of metal echoing through the empty building. Cassie heard her stomp away, keeping her back turned until she was sure Allison was gone.

Was she really just jealous? Sure, Allison was the top. She was the smallest, lightest girl on the squad—the easiest for the guys to toss high into the air. Her long blond ponytail fanned out just-so when she tumbled, and her dad had paid a fortune for her dazzling smile.

There was a lot to be jealous of, but that wasn't it.

Allison *had* stumbled. She had nearly fallen, and Cassie knew it. Allison knew it, too. Cassie had seen it.

So what had saved her? It couldn't be witchcraft; that was strictly forbidden in competition. Get caught using a spell, or a wand, and you were off the squad, and getting cut was like total social suicide. Even Allison couldn't get away with that one.

Still, she was right about one thing. Nobody was going to believe Cassie, not without something to back up her suspicions.

So, what was she going to do about it?

Alone in her backyard, Cassie bounced on the trampoline her parents had installed for her to train on. It was supposed to help her practice, to make her the best, but that plan hadn't quite worked.

Cassie bounced on her butt, then back onto her feet, and turned a somersault in midair. She didn't need to be jealous of Allison; she could have everything Allison had, if she wanted it badly enough. All she needed was to starve herself, use lots of bleach, and spend a fortune on dentist bills—and she didn't want it that bad.

The tramp rolled under her feet, with the weight of another body, dropping her onto her back.

Cassie looked up at Dave, the cheerleader-next-door, and her best friend since second grade. Dave grinned and held out his hand, hauling her back onto her feet.

They bounced in companionable silence for a minute, then Cassie said "Dave?"

"That's me."

"Can I ask you something?"

Dave furrowed his brow. "Of course. Isn't that what friends are for?"

"Yeah." She paused a second before the words rushed out. "Am I a jealous bitch?"

"Did I say you were?"

"No. But someone else did."

Dave put his hand on her shoulders, forcing her to stop bouncing. He gave her a little shove toward the side of the tramp and sat down, patting the rubber next to him.

"And the person was—hmmm, let me guess—Allison?"

Cassie dropped down next to him. "Well, duh! Guess that was pretty obvious, huh?"

"Yep." Dave smiled at her. "You don't have anything to be jealous about, anyway. Your spells are better, your grades are higher. If anything, she should be jealous of you."

Cassie thought for a minute before she spoke. "But Allison thinks I want her spot. Not that I wouldn't like it," she added quickly.

"Hello? I know all this already. Tell me something new."

"Well," Cassie drew the one word out, until it was nearly a whole sentence. "See, I kinda think, that is, I know, that Allison, well, it's like." Cassie shook her head, annoyed at herself for stalling.

"Allison almost fell." There, she'd said it out loud.

"When?"

"Today, on the final pyramid. I felt her slip, and I thought we were all going down, but she pulled it out. And it wasn't the first time, either. She's come close to falling a lot of times, but she never does."

Dave hopped to his feet. Now it was his turn to think, to avoid looking at Cassie. He turned several flips while Cassie bounced at his side, waiting for him to say something, anything.

"You think she's cheating." It wasn't a question.

"I don't know what I think," Cassie said. "I mean, her spells aren't that good—you're right—she'd totally give herself away. And Coach won't even allow a wand into the gym, so there's no way . . ." Her voice trailed off.

"Then how—?" Dave began.

"I don't know," Cassie cut him off, feeling foolish. "I'm just saying, if she is, and we get caught, there goes the season. And probably next year, too."

She bounced higher, turning a somersault. "You'd tell me if I was being a bitch, wouldn't you?"

Dave grinned at her. "How could I pass up the opportunity?" Then he stopped smiling, and his voice lowered. "No, you're not. Really. I saw it, too." He shook his head. "I didn't want to believe it, told myself I was imagining things, she was too far away for me to be sure. But I knew."

Cassie threw her arms around Dave's neck. "Thank you. I *knew* it wasn't just me!"

"No, not just you," Dave said. He plopped back down onto the trampoline and rested his head on one fist. "But how do we get anybody to believe us? Like you said, Allison will just say you're jealous."

Cassie sat down beside him, and stared into the growing darkness. "Whatever we do, it better be fast. The finals in Worcester are in five days. After that, we're toast."

The next afternoon, Cassie dragged herself to the gym. She didn't know what to expect from Allison, and she dreaded another confrontation.

In the locker room, Allison was holding court, going out of her way to compliment the other squad members on their outfits.

Two days earlier, Cassie had heard her making barking noises to her friends when Cindy Martin walked past. Now, she was offering her makeup tips and patting her shoulder as if they were old friends.

Cassie spun the dial on her lock, glancing in Allison's direction. Allison avoided her glance, until she though no one else was looking, then glared. The message was as clear as if she had shouted, "Don't screw with me!" and Cassie knew she had been warned.

This was war, and Allison was quickly gathering her allies.

Despite Cassie's fears, the practice seemed to go

well. Each movement was precise, the timing was flawless, and Allison landed the final pyramid solidly.

When she finally followed Lynn, diving into the waiting arms of Dave and Robert, Cassie knew they had a winning routine.

If they could do this every time. But could they?

She hurried through her shower, trying to time her exit to avoid Allison, yet still be part of the noisy crowd spilling out of the locker room.

As she stepped outside, she could see Allison a few feet away. Cassie slowed her steps, putting more distance between them. Then Allison climbed into Brad's red Miata and was gone.

Cassie considered her options. As though she had any. She could try to talk to Coach Barkley, but after their perfect practice, why would he have any reason to believe her?

Still, she had to try.

But when she poked her head in the coach's office, the only person there was the team manager, Franklin Pearson. He was writing awkwardly with his left hand on equipment forms. The long sleeves of his sweatshirt were pulled down, nearly covering his right hand.

"Uh, hi, Franklin." Nobody ever called him by anything but Franklin. "Coach's gone, huh?"

"Right after practice. Left me in charge." Franklin puffed his chest out, stressing his importance. "I was just finishing up. What can I do for you?"

"Oh, nothing. I just had a question for the coach, but it can wait."

"All right." Franklin sounded disappointed that he didn't get to be "in charge" of some problem. "You're sure?"

"Sure," Cassie said. "Well, I better get going. Lots of homework."

Franklin shrugged. "If you say so." He stared at her for a second, and she was suddenly aware that they were alone in the building. "Sure you don't want to hang around? I'll be through here in just a minute."

"Naw, I gotta run," she said, stepping back from the door. "Later!"

As she hurried toward home, Cassie wondered why she had felt so uncomfortable around Franklin. He was team manager, but she didn't know him that well, since he had transferred to Witch High—oops, Salem Township Public High School #4—last fall.

She had heard rumors, though. He was a star tumbler at his last school, until an accident ended his career. His right arm, which he kept hidden, had been damaged. Some people said he'd lost it completely, but no one had ever actually *seen* it, and nobody really knew.

The one thing Cassie was sure of was that Franklin knew just about everything there was to know about cheering and about competitions. Even though he couldn't flip, or tumble, or do a cartwheel, he was still a part of the team.

And he wanted to win.

It took Cassie two more precious days to get an opportunity to talk to Coach Barkley. She changed her mind at least half a dozen times, and she was still not sure what she was going to say when she finally walked into Coach's office and found him by himself.

"Can I talk to you, Coach?"

"Certainly, Cassie. Sit down." Coach gestured to beat-up folding chair next to his desk. "What's the problem?"

Cassie closed the door behind her before she sat down. "I, uh, I don't know. That is, I *do* know, but I don't really know if it's a problem. It's just that, well," she swallowed hard, "I think there *might* be a problem, and I don't know what to do about it."

A flash of impatience crossed Coach's face, but he sat quietly, waiting for her to go on.

"It's Allison." There she'd said it. "She's missed a couple landings. One last week and again this afternoon. She didn't fall, I know," she hurried on. "But I felt her slip. Really."

The coach's face hardened, and Cassie felt her stomach drop somewhere around her sneakers. Even before he opened his mouth, she knew he didn't believe her.

"Ms. Stevens." Oh, shit. She'd gone from "Cassie" to "Ms. Stevens." She'd be lucky if she wasn't cut from the team right here.

"That's a very serious accusation. Have you thought about what you're saying?" He held up his hand and slowly unfolded his fingers as he talked.

His voice was soft, and serious. "First, Allison did not fall, despite what you say. In fact, she looked just fine from where I was. Second, if she did slip, and that's a very big 'if,' it was not apparent. Third, no one else saw or felt this slip. Fourth, there was no fault, no foul, no fall. Nothing that would mark down points in competition."

He stared at her, daring her to argue, and she knew she was defeated. He hadn't threatened to cut her—yet—but the hard look in his eyes was enough. She knew better than to say anything more, but she couldn't help herself.

"But, Coach," she said, trying to control the quaver in her voice. "It felt like she slipped, and then something just *pushed* her back into place."

Coach's eyes were hard and angry, and his face turned red. When he finally spoke, his voice cut through Cassie, sending a chill down her back. "Are you saying Allison was cheating somehow? That there was something else involved?

"You know how I feel about witchcraft in my gym, Ms. Stevens. It is strictly forbidden. Spells and tricks are just lazy shortcuts that prevent you from actually learning our routines. None of my athletes would dare break that rule."

Cassie knew she had already gone too far, and she struggled to keep from answering. Nothing she could say would make things better, and anything she could say would make things worse.

She nodded silently and rose from her seat. Fighting for control, willing her eyes not to flood with tears of humiliation and rejection, she turned quickly and opened the door. The best thing she could do was leave, before coach threw her out of his office and off the squad.

Franklin was waiting next to the door, his face as hard and cold as the coach's. Had he been listening? Did he know what she had told Coach? Judging by his expression, the answer was yes.

She ran down the corridor, headed for the gym doors. Her chest was tight, and she needed to get outside, to get a breath of fresh air. She burst through the door and didn't stop running until she reached her trampoline.

The familiar bouncing, up and down, soothed Cassie's frazzled nerves. As she calmed down, she wondered if what she had done was really as bad as she first thought.

She had spoken to the coach, and no one else. She hadn't gossiped with the other girls or tried to confront Allison again. Coach Barkley was the only one who knew about her suspicions, and he had clearly dismissed them.

So why did she think he was wrong?

She was still trying to figure out how to get back on the coach's good side when Dave jumped up beside her.

"What's wrong?"

They had been friends a long time. Cassie knew she couldn't fool him. No sense in trying. "I talked to Coach after practice today. I told him Allison slipped and that it has happened before."

"And—let me guess—he didn't believe you, right?" Dave shook his head. "What did you expect, Cassie? You knew he wouldn't believe it."

"I know," she said miserably. "But I at least thought he'd listen. Instead, he said I was accusing Allison of cheating, and he didn't allow witchcraft on the squad, and nobody would break that rule."

She told him about nearly running into Franklin at the office door and her suspicion that he'd been listening in.

"The worst part, though," she continued, "is that he's right. Not even Allison would break that rule. Nobody would. The squad is too important, we've worked too hard, to do anything that would hurt the team."

Cassie sat down, hanging her head and once more near tears. Maybe Allison wasn't her BFF, but she still wasn't a cheat, and Cassie hadn't really meant to imply she was.

"Then why did you say anything to Coach? You knew better!"

"But something's wrong, Dave! You said so yourself. Allison isn't sticking her landings, and she almost fell the other day." Cassie looked up at Dave. "You saw her today, too! I know you did."

She could see the answer in his eyes. He had seen Allison slip. He knew she was right.

Dave sat down next to her and nodded his head. "That still doesn't solve anything, though. Just because I think I saw something from the floor doesn't make it so. And if Coach didn't see it, it doesn't matter."

"Then what can we do about it? I want to win at semis—we all do—and if Allison doesn't make her landing, or if she's doing something that gets us disqualified, then we all lose!"

Dave patted Cassie's shoulder. "If Coach says it's okay, then it's okay. No matter what we think we saw. He wouldn't let anything hurt the squad's chances. You know that."

Cassie leaned her cheek against Dave's hand. "I know." She sighed and dropped to the ground. "Guess I better go get my homework done. Thanks for being such a good listener, Dave."

Dave grinned at her and waved as he went through the high wooden gate between their backyards. Cassie waved back before the gate closed and went in the house.

If Cassie had accepted what Dave said, and she had, there was only one thing she could do. Apologize. She needed to build a bridge and just get over herself, and the sooner the better.

As soon as the bell rang for lunch, she hurried across campus to Coach Barkley's office. When she got there, Coach was sitting behind his desk, and Franklin was in the other chair.

Coach greeted her politely, without a trace of his anger from the previous day, but Franklin glared at her and didn't speak.

"Coach, can I talk to you for a minute?" Cassie asked. She didn't say "alone," but the coach got the idea anyway.

So did Franklin. He glared at Cassie, then turned to Coach Barkley as though looking for instructions. The coach nodded quickly at Franklin.

Franklin stood up and kicked the chair away, still glaring at Cassie. He brushed past her, not close enough to actually push her, but enough that she pulled back as he passed.

"Sit down, Cassie."

Well, at least she was "Cassie" again, and not "Ms. Stevens." That was a good sign, wasn't it?

Still, she preferred to stay standing. Her breakfast felt like a lump in her stomach, and she twisted her fingers together to keep her hands from shaking. If she sat down, she might never be able to stand back up.

Cassie could dive from the top of the pyramid, do a double flip from a standing start, or walk a tightrope if she had to, all without a single nervous twitch or second of anxiety. But just thinking about this conversation had her weak in the knees.

She swallowed past the lump in her throat. "I came

to apologize," she said. "I really though Allison had slipped, but I must be wrong. I shouldn't have said anything, and I apologize."

With the worst part out of the way, she took a deep breath and went on. "I didn't talk to anyone else about this. Except I tried to talk to Allison before I came to you, which didn't go so well, and I'll apologize to her as soon as I can. I just wanted to talk to you first."

Coach Barkley fiddled with a small glass paperweight from his desk. It was in the shape of a crystal ball. Cassie watched him turning the ball over in his hands, and she wondered if he had powers, like the rest of the faculty. She had never thought about it before. Witchcraft was strictly forbidden in the gym, but Coach could still practice outside the gym, right?

"Yes."

Cassie jumped, startled to have him answer her question out loud, even though she hadn't said a word.

"I don't allow anyone to use their power in here, usually not even me. It isn't fair to use our skills in competition with the mundane world, so they are banned from practice. If we rely on wands and spells, we don't gain the athletic skills we need to be competitive, and we don't learn sportsmanship and fair play."

"I never meant to say Allison was a cheat. She wants to win as much as the rest of us, but she wouldn't cheat. We may not be best friends," Cassie shrugged, "but she isn't a cheat."

"I know that," Coach answered, looking at the glass ball in his hand. "I wouldn't tolerate a cheat on my squad. And believe me," he said, gently laying the ball on his desk, "I *know* my squad."

"Understood, sir," Cassie said. Now that she had said what she needed to, she wanted to get out of there. Fast. Before her shaky knees stopped working entirely.

"I better hurry, if I want to talk to Allison before lunch is over," she said as she opened the door. "Thanks, Coach."

"Thank you, Cassie. See you at practice."

Cassie darted out the door and turned toward the cafeteria, only to find her way blocked by Franklin.

"Haven't you done enough?" he said, his voice low. "Just leave Allison alone. She doesn't need any more of your interference; she's fine just the way she is."

"What I do is none of your business, Franklin. That was a private conversation."

"I'm the team manager." He stood tall, and looked down at her. "Coach expects me to keep track of everything, so it *is* my business. I have to take care of the squad at all times."

Cassie stared into Franklin's cold eyes. "I'm not so sure Coach Barkley," she raised her voice a little, wondering if the coach could overhear the conversation outside his door, "would appreciate you eavesdropping when he's got the door closed."

"I need to know what's going on."

There was no point in arguing with Franklin, and Cassie had to go find Allison. She wanted this over with.

"Whatever!" she said, stepping around Franklin.

As she walked away, she heard him go in Coach Barkley's office and close the door.

Creepazoid, much?

She shook her head, and hurried on toward the cafeteria.

For once, Allison wasn't the center of an adoring crowd in the cafeteria, and Cassie was able to slide onto an empty bench across from her. She glanced at Allison's plate, where a squashed lemon wedge and a few droopy lettuce leaves were considered a meal. Yuck!

"What do *you* want?" Allison said, as soon as she sat down. She wasn't pleased to see Cassie, especially without her audience of adoring fans, but this time Allison's mood wouldn't control Cassie.

"I came to apologize," she said. She kept her voice low and soft, trying to feel some sympathy for the girl across the table. After all, she carried a lot of responsibility on her thin shoulders, and Cassie had added to that this week.

"I really am sorry. I did think you slipped, and I was worried about the semis. We all want to win, and I was afraid. But if you say you didn't slip, well, maybe I was nervous or something, and I was wrong."

Cassie bit her lip, and looked at Allison. There was something—fear?—deep in Allison's eyes, but it disappeared before Cassie could be sure.

Allison shrugged, and a smile curved her mouth, though it didn't change the blank look in her eyes. "Apology accepted."

Cassie blew out a deep breath. "Thanks, Allison. I just wanted to get this out of the way. I mean, we have semis in just a couple days, and I know we can win."

Allison nodded. "Yes, we can." But there was a hesitation in her voice.

Or maybe Cassie was just imagining things again. After all, Allison had done the same routine about a million times, and she was perfect almost every time. There was nothing to worry about.

The music was loud, loud enough to cover Cassie's voice as she counted the beat. She linked arms with Lynn on the third level of the human pyramid and waited, a huge smile locked in place.

Behind her, unseen, and unheard beneath the pounding beat, Cassie knew Allison was starting her run. In front of her, the audience in the Worchester Arena was a sea of faces, all run together. They clapped in time to the music, adding to the noise, and the insistent rhythm.

Beat, beat, beat, beat. Lift. Beat, beat. Land.

Allison's weight, all eighty-seven pounds of her, was steady on Cassie's shoulder, a perfect landing. She felt Allison shift slightly, as she threw her arms in the air, still solid and steady.

Beat.

"Go, Salem!"

The crowd exploded in cheers and applause, shrill whistles echoing from the left side. Cassie's dad was sitting there, and even though she couldn't see him, she knew he had his fingers in the corner of his mouth, whistling wildly.

Relief was a warm tide, flowing through Cassie's body. They were perfect! The only thing left was the dismount. The crowd loved them! And if the crowd loved, them, the judges would love them, too!

Allison tensed, shifting slightly, as she braced herself, then dove for the floor. Cassie held her head high, eyes forward, but she heard another explosion of applause, and she knew Allison had landed in a perfect split in front of the pyramid.

Beside her, Lynn launched herself, and a few beats later Cassie dove into the waiting arms of the catchers.

But Dave wasn't there.

Charlie and Wade caught her and swung her onto her feet. She tried to look around, to spot Dave, without breaking the routine, but she couldn't find him.

There was no time for distractions. Cassie made her last move, a stag leap into Charlie's arms, and held her position, as the crowd cheered and stomped.

A whistle blew from the edge of the stage, a signal for the squad to break formation and make their exit.

As Cassie moved toward the wings, her heart turned a flip, higher and wilder than any the squad had performed in the last four minutes.

Franklin was on the floor, his shirt ripped away. Dave knelt with one knee on his chest, his uniform torn and a trickle of blood on the side of his face. Franklin was twisting awkwardly on the ground, trying to get away.

A judge was standing over the two boys, his hands in fists on his hips, and a security guard was reaching for something clutched in Dave's hand.

Her stomach lurched at the sight of the blood on

Dave's face. She raced to the spot where the boys still struggled, as the security guard tried to intervene. Coach Barkley was only a step or two in front of her.

She was within a step or two when her brain finally registered what Dave was holding. She stopped dead, staring, as the realization hit her.

Franklin's right shoulder was bare, a horrifying mass of scar tissue and strap marks, where his prosthetic arm had been ripped away. And Dave had hold of an arm.

A *wooden* arm.

An arm that could double as a wand.

Dave caught her eye. His head moved slightly, a little shake that no one else noticed.

The security guard pulled Dave off Franklin and helped the manager to his feet. Dave surrendered the arm to Coach Barkley, refusing to return it to Franklin.

Coach's eyes widened as he realized what he was holding, but Dave said quietly, "It's okay, Coach."

"We'll sort this out in the office." The security guard gestured for the group to follow him down a hallway.

Cassie ran to Dave before the guard could lead them away and threw her arms around his neck.

"You said—" she whispered in Dave's ear.

"I know. But you were so sure. And you were right," Dave interrupted. "I was watching, and I stopped him before he could interfere. Allison did it by herself."

The guard pulled her away, and Cassie reached up to brush the blood away from Dave's temple.

"It'll be okay," Dave assured her, as he walked down the hall, Coach Barkley at his side. I'll tell you all about it later."

The cheers of the audience still rang in her ears. They'd earned it fairly and honestly. For today, they were perfect.

Another Learning Experience

Jody Lynn Nye

Jody Lynn Nye enjoys recreational shopping, particularly for books, cooking gadgets, art supplies (and who doesn't?), and esoterica. She lives with two black cats and one husband in the northwest suburbs of Chicago. Her latest book is *An Unexpected Apprentice.*

THYRA Sanmussen held a cloth to Elaine Bargrim's bleeding nose and surveyed the bruise on the girl's forehead. The guidance counselor shook her head.

"That's why the broomstick field is lined with sandbags," she said. Anyone might be forgiven for thinking that the tall, athletic redhead in a no-nonsense, short-sleeved white blouse and a short, yellow denim skirt was one of the gym teachers, a misconception she was used to correcting for new students and parents. "You will have to serve detention here in my office for taking a training broom out of the fieldhouse. Three days. You'll be relieved to hear you won't have to stop flying lessons. It's a required safety course. Do you want to keep the bruise as a badge of honor, or do you want me to take care of it?"

"Fix it, please," the freshman girl said. Her lip was swollen. She must have hit the wall of the tower at full tilt. "My mother is going to kill me."

"Your mother was two years ahead of me here at

Salem," Thyra said, taking her wand out of her blouse pocket. "And you never heard this from me, but she did the same thing."

Elaine giggled. "She did?"

Thyra smiled impishly at her and held the girl's chin still so she could work the healing spell on the abrasions. Elaine had done a solid number on her face. There was blood matting down her fine, blond hair. A whisk of the wand took care of that, too.

"Uh-huh. So did I. I guess it's something that young witches and warlocks just can't take anyone else's word for. We've got to go and try it for ourselves, even though everyone's warned us and we know better. Please, Elaine, try to remember that's *why* we tell you not to do things?"

"I'll try, Ms. Sanmussen." Elaine took a mirror out of her monogrammed school bag.

"No, don't use your dark mirror to look at yourself!" Thyra said, leaping to turn the glass down before it caught the girl's reflection. "You'll break the scrying spell. Mr. Hopkins has too much to do to reenchant everybody's glass every week."

"Sorry," Elaine said, fishing for a cosmetic mirror from her purse. "I forgot. Thanks." She looked at her face from several angles. "You'd never know I hit a wall."

"But you do know it," Thyra said, trying to inject significance into her tone. "Try to remember that."

"I will," Elaine promised. "I'll be back at three-thirty."

Thyra rose to let her out of the inner office and went to get the next student needing her attention.

The large outer room, which doubled as not only detention center but also group counseling chamber, lecture hall on private and often embarrassing subjects, and magical playroom when she turned her back, was full that Wednesday morning. Every one of the fifteen antique wooden chairs was occupied by guilty-looking students who needed her help. Thyra took a deep breath and scanned the faces.

Myra Salazar sat miserably near the window hugging a pillow to her belly. Thyra let her sit in the office during her Time of the Month. It was hard for any girl in a group to be the first to mature. It didn't help that the boys teased her that she had grown a full pelt of sable hair months before any of the other female werewolves her age. She raised a long nose as Thyra opened the door, then dropped it again to the velvet pillow. At least she didn't tear the cushions up anymore. The first couple of months had been rough.

"Your control is getting much better, Myra," she said, soothingly.

"Thanks, Ms. Sanmussen," the girl said, her voice muffled by the cloth.

"Thomas, you're next," Thyra said. A stocky boy with braces in his mouth, a wrinkled face, and wispy white hair clinging to a balding scalp stood up.

"Honest, Ms. Sanmussen, I only meant to go back in time *one day* to turn in a college aid application on time."

She beckoned to him. "Let's talk about it in here, and we'll see what we can do for you."

Thyra surveyed the curious and sympathetic looks the others sent after Thomas as he stumped after her into the office. She closed the door behind them.

Thyra Sanmussen was the last person to believe that she would ever have ended up as a school guidance counselor. Her years at Salem had been characterized by a series of disasters, both magical and physical, most of them self-inflicted, nearly all of them regrettably public. Her parents called her "curious." Her teachers said she was "undirected." The only person who saw her for the lonely girl desperate for attention that she really was had been Miss Sidley Proctor, the woman who had occupied that very office for thirty-five years.

"Getting in trouble is the wrong way to become popular, Thyra," Miss Proctor had told her over and over again. Miss Proctor was the epitome of what the novels called a dried-up spinster. She was small and thin, with delicate skin wrinkled like crumpled silk and fine white hair she wore in a bun on top of her head. Her hands were like little claws that had a web of blue veins on the backs. The one feature that kept her from being ordinary were sharp, dark eyes. Those eyes seemed to be able to see into book bags that concealed bottles of homemade truth serum, or into walls etched with magical graffiti that wouldn't appear until the school bell rang, or bore into the very skulls of students set on mischief and read their thoughts. Once she had made Thyra her particular subject, it had become almost impossible to get away with really good pranks.

In response, Thyra tried even harder to make a spectacle of herself.

There was the incident at the graduation of Rita Bargrim's class, when Thyra led a cadre of outlaw broomstick enthusiasts overhead just as the chancellor was giving the commencement speech. She felt she outdid herself at the sophomore class barbecue, summoning up her first fire elemental. She had been really proud of it, since elemental work was not scheduled until spring semester of her junior year. Too bad it had taken out most of the burgers and hot dogs that had been on the grill at the time. It had been worth the month she spent in detention to see the admiration on the other kids' faces.

Every time, she had ended up sitting across the desk from Miss Proctor.

"You are responsible for what you do," she always said. "I'm not asking you to account for yourself just to punish you. Admitting what you have done and accepting it is not only the correct way to grow into a fully mature person," at which Thyra always groaned, "but you cannot practice magic without being completely honest. You'll hurt yourself or other people, and I know you don't want to do that."

Thyra was ungrateful for her offer of help at the time, though in retrospect Miss Proctor gave her more credit than anyone else did. She never laid a truth spell on Thyra, as her parents often threatened to do. She just made her tell the truth.

"Because it is the right thing to do. You show so much promise. I hate to see you wasting it."

Thyra remembered how she used to roll her eyes at the ceiling, but Miss Proctor always took their sessions seriously. No matter how many stunts she pulled, no matter how many times she got sent to the office over one colorful infraction or another, Miss Proctor never gave up on her. She wouldn't have graduated at all, let alone with honors, if Miss Proctor hadn't been there for her. But she had not let memory be the only thing Thyra had of those days.

The stink-bombing of the school during finals at the end of her junior year had been her moment of crowning glory as the class clown and the straw that finally caused the administration to call for her suspension, or even expulsion. That rat Sigismun Doernan had turned her in, even though he had been part of the crowd egging her on as she lit the final candle that set off the spell. He had cheered the waves of green smoke that went rolling down the halls, then promptly disappeared. She had gotten one last look at his grinning mouthful of prominent teeth over the shoulders of the teachers who had surrounded her and herded her downstairs to the dean's office.

Thyra had had to wait there for hours until her parents arrived. There had been a lot of shouting between them and the administrators, to which Thyra had not really listened. She just sat miserably on the hard bench, dreaming up vengeance against Sigismun and taking one last moment of perverse teenage pride in her accomplishment.

I mean, she had thought, *the whole place REALLY reeks.*

She wasn't really worried about consequences until Miss Proctor showed up. The mob of warring adults fell silent and melted away like sheepish children, leaving no buffer between her and the counselor. The quiet tone of her voice cut through to Thyra in a way that no yelling or threats of punishment had.

"Thyra, I am really very disappointed in you."

Thyra hung her head. "I'm sorry, Miss Proctor."

The little woman tilted her head to one side. "No, you're not."

She could always cut right to the heart of the matter. She looked up at Thyra's parents, both much taller than she was. "We discussed this," she had said, holding out a silver goblet. "Do you give your consent freely?"

Both of her parents looked guiltily at Thyra, but they had nodded. Miss Proctor came to sit by Thyra.

"You are a teenager, so you have no real understanding of the karmic debt you owe to the universe, so it is the judgment of your adult support group that it be made obligatory. This," she had held out the goblet, "contains a potion that will lay a geas of responsibility on you. Specifically, when you finish your education, you will return here to Salem and take over my job as school counselor."

"What?" Thyra had yelped. "Not a chance! I won't do it."

"You will," Miss Proctor had continued, "and you will do it until you have paid back all of the care that other people have lavished on you and that you have wasted in such a cavalier fashion. You can use all of that boundless energy to help students who need a wise, guiding hand as badly as you do." Thyra had groaned. Miss Proctor wasn't having any of it. "This is not a punishment but a chance to redress the karmic balance. Be thankful I'm not requiring you to pay it back threefold. You'd be spending the rest of your life here instead of the couple of years I believe it will take you. I'm retiring then, and I believe you would make an excellent successor. Think of it as a learning experience."

"Not another learning experience!" Thyra had shouted. It was no use yelling or carrying on. The spell was going to be placed with the full knowledge and permission of her parents. It wouldn't do her any harm, physically or mentally, and it was better than being expelled.

Resentfully, she drank the melon-flavored potion and felt the warmth of the spell spread out through her body. Not too bad. Everyone watched her. She had been sorely tempted to grab her throat and roll around on the floor pretending it had poisoned her, but a new little voice in her head told her the act wouldn't be appreciated. In the back of her mind, she saw a little pointer like a gas gauge, with the indicator pinned all the way to the right, the representation of the karma she had to work off.

From that moment forward, Thyra realized she had to straighten out her life, or her sentence was going to be extended every time she created another "incident." No more making the gym teacher's uniform fall apart at the seams during calesthenics. No more spiking the vampire geology professor's liquid lunch with algae from the science lab. There was nothing left to do but apply herself to her education. To her own surprise she had earned A's.

Once she graduated, Thyra had had absolutely no intention of becoming something so dull as a guidance counselor, but the magic was there, prodding her forward like an invisible finger in her back. When she was asked at the university to declare her major, her mouth, her whole body, was ready to say "Drama," but what came out was "Psychology."

Eight years later, she had graduated with honors. She finished her master's degree simultaneously with her doctoral degree, and came away with high honors for both. That fall, Miss Proctor had retired, and Ms. Sanmussen had taken her place in the sunny office in Salem High, and if she expected the students to notice any difference, she had been disappointed. They didn't care who she was, or whom she had replaced. They just needed help.

It felt so strange to be back in that office again, on the wrong side of the desk. How Thyra resented those first few students who came in bemoaning their problems. A junior girl didn't know how to apply for a grant for potions research. A shy freshman boy didn't know how to cope with his new popularity on the football team when he manifested as a werebear. A young witch declared that she was Going to Die because she had fallen in love with her lab partner, who already had a boyfriend and couldn't see that she was alive.

"Figure it out for yourself!" Thyra wanted to shout at them. "You're so smart. You do it!"

But she had found the forms for grant proposals. She held back from calling the werebear a geek and advised him to hold on to his real friends from junior high and see if any of his new admirers still paid attention to him in his nonwere form. She sympathized with the lovesick girl and steered her toward the special-interest group on campus where her problems would be understood. The little gauge in the back of her mind crept down a minute notch. It felt good. In no time she would be out of Salem forever.

To her own surprise, she found herself getting interested in the problems she was hearing. By the end of the second month, she discovered that she had not snapped at anyone, not even once. She really threw herself into finding solutions, good ones that would keep the kids from losing faith in themselves. She realized it cost them something to come to her and ask, and she never made fun of them for doing it. She sounded so mature in her advice her friends would have been agog with amazement. She hoped no one would guess that she was faking it, repeating things she had read in her textbooks and stuff she heard on *Dr. Phil.*

Every so often she would feel the indicator move. She considered every notch down a reward, but it was incidental to how good she felt when one of the kids went away happy.

By the middle of her second year, she had stopped paying much attention to the gauge unless the needle dropped significantly. By the third she was surprised when she remembered it was there. Its presence played less and less importance in what she was doing. The students mattered to her. She cared what happened to them.

"Excuse me, I'm looking for the guidance counselor," a resonant male voice said from the door.

Thyra looked up. A broad-shouldered man in an expensive blue-gray suit was leaning into the room. He smiled at her. Thyra stiffened. He had grown taller and put on adult muscle, but she would have recognized that outsized dentition anywhere. Sigismun Doerner.

"Sigismun."

He blinked, as though adjusting his mental image forward as well. "Thyra? My God, what are you doing here?"

"I'm the guidance counselor you're looking for. What can I do for you?"

"I . . . uh, oh, yes. I'm the president of the event-planning company that holds fundraisers for magical-based charities. Salem students often act as ushers at our events. I, er, expected to see the old lady who used to be here. She's gone?"

"Retired," Thyra said. She recalled the last time she had really seen Sigismun, and resentment swelled up inside her large enough to choke her. She rose from her chair and started to reach for the wand in her blouse pocket. "*You're* the reason I'm here."

"Me?" he asked, puzzled. "I never told you to go into counseling . . ." His eyebrows sprang up on his forehead. "This didn't have anything to do with the stink bomb in junior year?"

"Yes!" Thyra had the wand in her hand and was trying to decide what would be the most fitting punishment for someone responsible for steering her life so far off course. How about making those big teeth the size of bathroom tiles? He wouldn't get too many jobs if he couldn't talk without sounding like a cartoon beaver, would he?

The little indicator in her mind appeared and started flashing red as the needle leaned alarmingly toward the "full" side of the gauge. Thyra batted at the air with her wand, trying to make the image go away. Then reality impinged, with a full load of guilt attached. If she lashed out at Sigismun, she would undo all the good she had done and would spend more of her precious years in that office. She forced herself to sit down again and played with the wand as though it were a pencil.

What had he really done to her? Ratting her out was reprehensible, but if he hadn't done it, someone else might have. As it turned out, the psychic hall monitor near the auditorium had already been on the intercom reporting the vision he had had of the culprit. She would have been caught no matter what. She realized the only person who was to blame for her present situation was herself.

What had she almost done? Had she really been about to use offensive magic on him? For a petty transgression years old? She wasn't a child anymore. What would Miss Proctor say?

"Yes," she repeated, forcing a smile to her face. "It seemed like the obvious profession for someone like me."

"I guess," Sigismun said. "I mean, there's nothing these kids would do that you didn't do years ago . . .

I'm sorry, that sounds offensive. I don't mean it like that."

"No offense taken," Thyra said. To her surprise, she meant it. She was relieved. The gauge twitched, but the needle receded again, but only to halfway empty. She had lost some ground, but that was only to be expected. What was another two years? "You just kind of . . . precipitated it, that's all. Thank you. It's been a learning experience for me."

Sigismun looked relieved. "Hey, then can I count on you to help round up some volunteers? I've got flyers . . ." He offered a stack of blue sheets from his briefcase.

"Certainly," Thyra said, taking them. "I'll have them distributed in homeroom."

"Hey, nice to see you, Thyra," Sigismun said, shaking her hand. "I bet you're really great at counseling."

"You wish," Thyra said, giving him a grin. The gauge went up a little.

Robbie Todhunter squeezed into the room under Sigismun's arm and ran to her.

" 'Scuse me, Ms. Sanmussen. You gotta help. Naffi's on the steeple, and this time he says he's gonna jump."

The gardens in front of the school's ancient tower were full of curious onlookers, both students and faculty. Thyra squeezed through the clipped yew bushes to the front of the building. The principal waved her over.

"That boy has caused trouble for the last time!" he declared. His face was purple with fury.

"What happened?" Thyra asked.

"He swapped two of the genie bottles in the history lab. The Ancient Studies teacher took it off the shelf and asked the occupant for an accurate historical tableau of the magi of the Golden Crescent from 2,600 years ago. He thought it was a new acquisition. It wasn't. This genie did as he was asked, but it was the third wish. When the lesson was over, he went free! Before he departed, he turned the entire department into a desert oasis, for fun. For spite, I say! There are fifteen camels on the fourth floor! Naffi did this on purpose."

"Naffi said it was an accident," a girl pleaded. "There are hundreds of bottles up there. He put the one he was looking at on the wrong shelf."

"I know him," Thyra said. And indeed she did. He was in her office at least once a week for playing jokes. He wasn't even close to her former standard, but the current staff had shorter patience than the teachers who were at Salem when she had been a student. "He's a good kid. If he says it was an accident, he means it."

"He's a prankster," the principal said, his brows lowered all the way to the bridge of his nose. "I've had enough of it. It will take the transformations teacher at least a week to change things back."

"Make it a school project," suggested one of the earth-sciences teachers. "It will be good practice for some of my advanced chemistry students to observe the heat exchange inherent in changing silicon particles back to wood floorboards."

"Well, perhaps . . ."

"What about Naffi?" Thyra asked, anxiously.

"Remember last week, when he rigged all the telephones to broadcast on the loudspeakers? No one could have a private conversation for an hour!" the school secretary said, shaking her head.

"He's out of here." the principal said, then realized to whom he was speaking. "I'm sorry, Thyra. Not everyone can make such a dramatic turnaround as . . . er, some people."

Thyra felt her heart turn over.

"Sure they can," she said. "Let me talk to him."

A crowd of girls must have come from broomstick practice to see the excitement. They were still in their gym suits and clutching school besoms. Thyra hurried to them.

"I need one of those, please. Which is the strongest?"

"This one, Ms. Sanmussen," said Elaine Bargrim, handing hers over. "It's not fast, but it's really steady."

"Thanks," Thyra said. She swung her leg over and urged the broomstick upward. She hoped the spell wouldn't give way. She had never perfected flying or even hovering without a broom. Slowly, she let the broom ascend, trying not to alarm the boy clinging to the narrow spire. When he saw her coming, he struggled to his feet, knocking a shingle off into the crowd below.

"Stay away from me!" howled Raffi. He was a thin-faced boy with long, straggly hair that had been made even more untidy by scrambling through the gable window. "No spells! I'll jump!"

"I'll keep back," Thyra said, evenly. He might not jump, but he was in real danger of falling. She glanced down. The emergency service was drawing a seal on the ground in chalk that ought to catch him if he did fall, but they might not get it done in time. She was his best hope. "Now, Raffi, you know we can talk. What happened?"

"I didn't do it on purpose," he said, looking sulky and terrified at the same time.

Thyra pressed her lips together. "You know, you always say that at first, and most of the time it turns out that you did."

"Not this time! It really was an accident, Ms. Sanmussen. I swear." A gust of wind blew Raffi's hair into his face. He spat it out. "How come everyone thinks I'm lying?"

"Because you do. We always have to pin you down to tell the truth, and that gets to be very old." In the back of her mind, Thyra could hear Miss Proctor's voice, and cringed a little. But Raffi didn't notice.

"I guess," he said, thoughtfully. "I mean, usually it's funny. This time it was a big mess, but that wasn't my idea. The genie didn't like the way Professor Kalmi talked to him. He only did what old Kalmi said because he had to, then *boom!* He turned the whole place inside out, with camels! I mean, for once it wasn't my fault, and no one believes me!"

"So that's worth throwing yourself off the roof?"

"How can I go back again?" Raffi asked, despairingly. "No one would believe me! Even when I was telling the truth! I felt like someone tore out my guts. I mean, I wasn't lying!"

Thyra looked him square in the eye. "Wouldn't it be nice to get back to the point where people automatically give you the benefit of the doubt?"

"Yeah. But they won't! You don't know what it's like!"

"Believe me, I do," Thyra said, edging nearer to him. He looked over the eaves at the ground far below and blanched. She was worried about him losing his grip. "Really. We should talk about it some time. I know you're telling the truth. You'll have to sit detention, and you will certainly have to work off some of the damages, but we can work together so you can start over."

"Can I really?" Raffi asked. His eyes were brimming with tears.

"I promise. If you promise to try, I will never let you down." She took her wand out of her blouse pocket and touched it to the tip of her nose. "Witch's vow."

Raffi's narrow face lit with hope. "I'll try, I swear, Ms. Sanmussen." He looked down at his own wand pocket and realized he didn't have a hand free. "Uh, I can't. I'll fall. Uh, do you suppose I can get a ride down on your broom? I can't get back in through that window."

Thyra edged her wooden steed around until her hip touched the roof line.

"Hop on," she said. "Let's get started on your new life."

Raffi scrambled onto the broomstick. The crowd below them cheered. Thyra felt a *pop,* and realized that her internal meter had dropped to zero.

Two months later, Thyra closed and sealed a letter she had written for one of her graduating seniors. The girl would be a real asset to advanced research at M.I.T. The Massachusetts Institute of Thaumaturgy wanted only glowing recommendations, and she was delighted to give credit where credit was due.

With no small amount of pleasure, she glanced up at the certificate on the wall. That May she had received that year's Florence Lamson award for excellence in student guidance. That had been completely unexpected and really gratifying. The principal had told her he was proud to recommend her for it.

"Congratulations." Thyra looked up. Miss Proctor stood in the doorway. "I felt the spell expire," she said. "You did very well. The principal told me what you did."

"That was hardly anything out of the ordinary," Thyra said, getting to her feet, "as you would know."

"Ah, but it was. How many of your fellow faculty members would risk being knocked off a broomstick by a panicking eleventh-grader they were trying to save?"

"I never thought of that," Thyra said, goggling. "I just saw myself getting up there and giving him a ride down."

"That's what set you apart, my dear. Your selflessness is most gratifying. You really have become an excellent counselor."

Thyra smiled at her.

"I owe it all to you," Thyra said, honestly able to mean what she said. "I really hated you when I started doing this, but I was surprised that I could actually do the job. It took a long time before I understood how much you did for me. I'm just passing it on. That's what you wanted me to do."

Miss Proctor nodded. "I knew you would be good at it. Because of your own experiences, you have an empathy for the children who come to you. They see you as one of them but with earned wisdom that gives you credibility. If they listen just a little, they become enriched by that piece of advice that will change the course of their lives."

Thyra blushed. "I never really thought about where I was coming from when I talk to them. I think maybe it's the desk. It gives me the perspective that the students don't have, because they're living it, and I'm looking at it from the outside."

"Well, your obligation to the universe has well and truly been discharged. You're free to use the rest of your life as you see fit. What do you think? Will you go back to drama school now?"

Thyra shook her head. "I'm staying," she said. "I'm surprised, but I love it. I wouldn't leave this place for the world. I don't need the karma-meter anymore. It's just what got me going. You knew that, right?"

Miss Proctor smiled back at her. "I felt exactly the same. That's why I spent my entire career right there in that very chair. Let me tell you a little secret: I got this job in precisely the same way you did, and I kept it for the same reason."

Thyra gawked at her. "You were a troublemaker? I wouldn't believe that in a million years."

Miss Proctor cocked her head. "You should. I was quite a hoyden. You can check the school records. I was nearly expelled twice. And my predecessor, Richard Winkelbotham, and his before him, going back nearly three hundred years. Keep that in mind. One day you may find someone just as promising."

"I've got my eye on a couple of kids now," Thyra said, with a twinkle. "But I think I'll wait until I find someone who needs that extra magical push like I did. I'd hate to let the standard drop after all these years."

A Family Thing

Sarah Zettel

Sarah Zettel is an award-winning writer of speculative fiction who loves to travel. Zettel's first novel won the Locus Award for Best First Novel in 1997 and her second book was a *New York Times* notable book of the year. Her short fiction has previously appeared in the DAW anthology *Pandora's Closet.* Her most recent novel, part of her Isavalta series, is *Sword of the Deceiver.*

WHEN Amber Bailey banged into Hannah Todd hard enough to send folders skittering every which way, I sat back and waited for Hannah to take her down.

"Sorry, Hannah," purred Amber. "Didn't see you."

On cue, her entourage giggled, and to my total shock, Hannah, my best friend and one of the badassiest kids in the whole school, just crouched down and started to pick up her folders.

That was when I saw her hands shaking.

Amber was just as suprised, but she didn't waste any time. "What's the matter with the punk witch-queen?" she sneered.

Anger burning, I put myself between Amber and my best friend. "Oh, look, Hannah. It's a skinny mass of no brains dressed like a ho."

It wasn't the best comeback, and Amber just looked

down her long nose at it. "So, Chase? Your mother turn you into a newt and forget to change you back?"

The toss of the blond hair was predictable. So was the giggling as the March of the Bitches trooped to their desks, making extra sure to step on some of Hannah's papers. I helped scoop them back into her folders and was shocked to see tears sparkling in her eyes.

Hannah? Hannah was *crying?*

"I know, Hannah," I said loudly. "But she can't help being *nouveau witche,* or how everybody knows she couldn't get in here until her Daddy gave the school all that money he made selling crystals to the summer pagans."

Okay, I'm a snob. My whole family's New England snobs, which are snobbier than any snobs on the planet. Comes in handy sometimes, though. Like when you want to see a newbie snot like Amber rear up out of her seat. At least now she was focused on me, instead of picking on Hannah.

"You . . . !" Amber shouted, but the bell rang, cutting her off.

"Sit down, Ms. Bailey, Ms. Good. We're on my time now," announced Mr. Schramm from the front of the room. Schramm was a little, bald wizard with a bristling gray beard who generally wore something blue with stars on it. Today, it was a Hawaiian shirt. "Ms. Todd, your seat also awaits you."

All of us slipped into our desks. Schramm was actually pretty cool, unless he decided you needed to be humiliated in front of the entire class. Hannah laid her folders down and stared at them. She rubbed her eyes, as though she might cry some more. My stomach knotted up. Something was really, really wrong.

"All right, heads up and minds focused!" Schramm clapped his hands together. "As I'm sure you remember, we are on Act III of *The Crucible*. Can anyone tell me . . . Miss Bailey?'

"Mr. Schramm, my father says we shouldn't be reading this play."

Mr. Schramm's eyebrows rose up to the place his hairline would have been. "Does he?"

"Yes," Amber replied primly. "He says it is mundane claptrap and utterly inappropriate for up-and-coming young witches."

This promised to be a good show, but I had other things I wanted to hear. I eased my cell out of my pocket. Hannah's gaze flicked between me and Schramm.

Schramm nodded, as if Amber'd just made a cogent point. "Of course you explained that our class is Mundane Perception of Witchcraft and that this play has a pivotal role in establishing the mundane disbelief in actual witchcraft. You held, I am certain, a long discussion on how belief, or nonbelief, affects the nature of magic itself, and so understanding how the beliefs of a particular time have been shaped is vital for efficient and effective magical practice.

"Or did you just complain you couldn't understand all the big words?"

The class snickered. My thumbs flew across my keypad, sending a message to Hannah.

U OK? U look bad.

Hannah had palmed her own cell. She typed one-thumb.

Up al nite w grandma.

Y?

Suddenly, Schramm raised his hand. My cell flew out of my fingers, smacking firmly into his palm.

"And yours, Ms. Todd." Hannah jumped as her cell flew into Schramm's other hand. "Since these are first offenses, in my class, you may have them back at the end of the school day." He tossed the cell phones into his desk drawer. "Any more protests or interesting messages? No? Good. Open your books . . ."

Hannah slouched down in her chair. Now I was flat-out scared. Usually, nothing gets to Hannah. She got into the country's best private school for witches totally on her own steam, and she's held her own for three years with all us snobs and bitches. It's one of the reasons I like her. Whatever was going on with her and her grandma, it was real and it was bad.

Thing is, I didn't even know Hannah *had* a grandmother. It's just her and her mom at home, and she never talks about her family, which is another reason I like hanging with her. In my house, we're all about family. We're Danvers Goods, direct descendants of Sarah and Dorcas Good of the Salem Witch Trials. Mom has this tendency to talk about them as if they might drop by for tea any minute. Hannah's always been in the *now,* you know? I'm related to half the magic-workers in Massachusetts, but she's the only one I can talk to about the possibility of cross-breeding mandrakes to get a more potent strain, or whether the wonks in the computer club are going to be able to invent a digital camera that can steal a soul.

Okay, so I'm a snob *and* a geek. But why's it all got to be about the past—brooms, black cats, and some dead woman's standards? Why can't we do something *new* with our powers? There's got to be something more to being a witch than family history.

Hannah agrees with me. Which is the main reason I like her.

Class was long. Hannah just sat there the whole hour, occasionally moving her pencil, pretending she might be taking notes. Finally the bell rang and we were all on our feet, scooping up purses and back-packs. Amber and The Brainless looked ready for a bitch pack attack. I grabbed Hannah by her shoulders and shoved her out of the room. The hall was crowded, as always. Salem High wasn't a big school, only about three hundred students, but that always felt like too many when we all tried to get into the halls at the same time.

"What is going on?" I demanded as I dragged Hannah toward our lockers. "Spill it!"

Hannah looked up at me, hopeless. "My grandmother wants to take me back to Germany."

I blinked. I'd heard every word she'd said, but I couldn't make them connect with reality. "She can't. Your mom won't let her."

"You don't say no to my grandma," Hannah whispered.

"Huh? Hannah! You're a witch! Tell her you'll turn her into a FedEx envelope and mail her back!"

She just shook her head. "She's not a normal grandma, or even a normal witch."

"So what is she?"

Hannah licked her lips. All around us swirled the riot of passing time. I could feel that internal crawling sensation that told me we were going to be late for fifth period, but I didn't care. I was so focused on Hannah that I didn't realize the hall had gone quiet, even though there were still lots of people standing around. I also didn't notice they were standing still.

Then what little color she had left drained out of Hannah's cheeks. She grabbed my arm. "Oh, crap, Chase. She's here."

I whipped around. A clear spot had somehow appeared in the crammed hallway, and in the middle of it stood a dried-up, ancient woman I could only assume was Hannah's grandmother.

She wore a black dress, high-necked and shapeless with a hem that came down to just above her ankles, which were covered in thick black stockings. A sturdy, black apron had been tied securely over the full skirt. Her hair had been bundled up under a beige scarf with blotchy roses all over it.

She should have been funny, or pathetic, but she wasn't. Her eyes were too cold and too alert, and they looked through me, as if I were a distraction, or an amusement.

Or a midnight snack. My throat had clamped shut. I wasn't the only one who felt it either. There's damn little that can make a whole high school of witches back up.

"Oma Tod," Hannah croaked. "What're you doing here?"

But Oma Tod wasn't looking at her. Her death's-head gaze swept the hallway, taking in everything: fluorescent lights, scuffed linoleum, all of us in our jeans and T-shirts and short skirts and cargo pants and our books on spell work, concentration, concealment, and Mundane Perceptions of Magic.

"This is it?" The withered woman smirked. "This is where she sends you to learn?" She all but spat the last word. "You come home now, Hannah."

"Excuse me!" Principal Carey shouldered her way through the crowd of stunned students. I felt a rush of relief, which was the last thing I expected to feel upon seeing our needle-thin, perfectly tailored principal. "I'm Diana Carey." She walked up to Oma Tod. "Can I help you?"

"I am come to take my granddaughter, Hannah Todd, home."

Mrs. Carey frowned. She felt it, too. This crabbed shadow out in broad daylight didn't mean anyone any good.

"I'm sorry." Mrs. Carey's answer was clipped and precise. "To release Hannah from school, I need permission from her mother."

Oma Tod snorted. "Her mother is of no consequence. Hannah comes with me now."

Principal Carey's smile was patient and sharp. "I will not release one of my students without authorization from his or her parent or guardian."

Behind me, I heard doors slam as the smarter kids beat it the hell out of there.

You know how you get to be principal of a witch's high school? Get to be in charge of three hundred angsty, horny, self-absorbed kids who think they can rule the world someday and who can, oh, yeah, levitate small automobiles and blow holes in cinderblock by concentrating hard enough? First you face down their parents. All of them. My mom's on the committee, so I've seen this. Principal Carey got her job because she's the most powerful witch in New England, maybe in the country—plus Canada.

With a flick of a perfectly made-up eyelid, the doors banged open behind Oma Tod. With another, we were all whisked back up the hall, including Hannah. The teachers were there, too, saying quietly and firmly. "All right, everyone, let's go, let's move."

Everybody was ready to be herded into the classrooms or down into the shelters. Everyone wanted out of there. I grabbed Hannah's arm, but she wasn't moving. It was as though she were glued to the floor, and for all I knew, she was.

Schramm had his hand on my shoulder. "*Now,* Ms. Good."

I obeyed, but slowly. Oma Tod straightened her shoulders. I swear the light dimmed, as if a thunderstorm had just moved in. A slow, sour wind blew through the open doors, swirling the hems of Oma Tod's skirt.

Principal Carey's knees buckled.

Painfully, one trembling inch at a time, the most powerful witch in the country knelt in front of Oma Tod.

"You understand nothing," Oma Tod announced. "I am older than you know, and the blood in my heart is drained from innocence itself. Go play your games with the other children and be glad I do not hunger today. I take what is mine and I leave you."

Oma Tod grabbed Hannah and marched through the doors, which slammed shut behind her. A boom like thunder rang through the hall. Schramm bolted over to Principal Carey.

"Get to the shelter!" he shouted at me over his shoulder.

I got, but not to the shelter. I got out the backdoor and out of the yard before everything went into lockdown. I had to get to Hannah.

I'm not a total moron. I messaged Mom and told her I was okay, and I'd be home by four. Mom's got a finely honed sense of worry and a magic mirror she found in an antique shop in Maine. If I wasn't home by four, she'd be all over it. School'd have a cow. I'd deal with that later.

So there I was, on Hannah's front porch, wondering what the hell I thought I was doing. Oma Tod had laid out the principal with one black look. And I was about to ring the doorbell.

Turned out I didn't have to, because while I was standing there trying to choose between being cowardly and being dead, the door creaked open.

"Come here, girl. I want a look at you."

The hair on my arms prickled as I walked inside. So, goddess help me, did my thumbs. I'd been around magic all my life, but I'd never felt like this. This wasn't Hannah's house anymore. Hannah's was a normal place; beige wall-to-wall carpet and off-white walls, furniture from Art Van and Ikea. This was a musty, ancient place of shadows and secrets, closed curtains and locked doors.

I head a chuckle and hard-soled shoes clacking on the foyer's linoleum. A shape emerged from the shadows, taking on the contours of an old woman as it approached.

There's going to be a low rumble of thunder any second. I felt a tide of pure attitude surge to the surface.

I put on a brilliant smile that would have done Amber credit and met the eyes that glittered like the ice you see right before your car goes off the road.

"Hi. I'm Chase Good. I'm a friend of Hannah's."

The old woman stared at me, her sunken mouth pursed in disapproval. "You're from that *school* she goes to." Her gaze took on the edge of sharpened steel. It took everything I had not to back up.

The thunder of Hannah's footsteps on the stairs broke the mood. *The spell.*

"Oh, Chri . . . Uh, it's okay, Grandma. Chase is a friend of mine."

Oma Tod wasn't mollified or impressed. "There is some power there. Some hint of old blood, but too weak and corrupted now."

Which was too much for me. Who *did* this old bat think she was anyway? "What is your problem? You don't think Hannah's a good witch? She's the best witch in the whole school!"

"Pah! It means nothing. She learns no way of power in that place."

"No way of power! She's got power you couldn't even touch if you tried. You couldn't even see half her mojo if . . ."

Hannah was beside me as if she'd teleported. "Sorry, Grandma. No one ever taught her manners. Come on, Chase. Let's go upstairs." In the next breath, she was halfway back up the stairs, dragging me behind her. I followed, not looking back, but I felt her grandmother's sharp gaze pricking my neck, even after Hannah had slammed her bedroom door.

She turned on me immediately. "Are you trying to get yourself killed?"

"What? She's all bluff, Hannah. A lot of scare spell." I wanted to believe it, really bad. Truth was, *I* didn't know what had gotten into me. I had just started up, and I couldn't stop. "What's she gonna do? Turn me into gingerbread and gobble me up?"

"She might."

I slumped down onto Hannah's bed. Nothing had changed here. Same yellow frilly canopy bed, same chipped white and gold furniture. Same mess. Thank goddess. It was easier to breathe and to think. "Hannah, who is she, really?"

Hannah collapsed into her desk chair. "She's not actually my grandmother. She's my great-great grandmother, or maybe great-great-great . . ." She let it trail off and then said softly. "She's from the old times. She's the Black Forest witch."

"The Black Forest? Like in Germany? Where all the Brothers Grimm stories come from?"

Hannah nodded. "Yeah."

I glanced toward the door, and my thumbs were prickling so bad I almost couldn't stand it. "So, when we're talking gingerbread, you mean she's the one . . ."

"Actually, that was her sister. Oma Tod's got eyes like a hawk, and she's very, very careful around ovens."

"Wow."

"Yeah."

"How'd you get over here?"

"During World War Two, my mother's mother found an American soldier lost in the woods. She ran off with him, came here, and had Mom."

"But I didn't think your mom was a witch."

"She isn't. In the old bloodlines, it skips a generation sometimes." I nodded. Our family got some non-witches in every generation. At least my folks didn't shun them, unlike some people. "Mom never told Dad about the witch thing, but then I showed up with the talent, and she had to tell him, and he got really mad and walked out on us, and . . ." Hannah shrugged. "I'm sure she never thought Oma Tod would care enough to come get me. Oh, by the way," she glowered at me, sounding like the Hannah I knew for the first time all day. "You weren't doing me any favors with the whole 'you can't touch this' thing. If I'm really, really lucky, she'll just know you're a stupid liar and *won't* make me prove it."

"But what does she *want?*"

Hannah's laugh was bitter. "You should get this, Chase. It's the family thing. She wants me back in the Black Forest. She says I won't learn to be a proper witch here."

"She can't do that, can she?"

"How's Mom going to stop her? Have her arrested? Oma Tod's got the evil eye, and I'm not being metaphorical."

"Wow."

"Yeah."

We sat there, Hannah stewing, me digesting. All this time, I thought I was being oh-so-nice, me with the Big Salem pedigree making a black-collar nobody my best friend, and it turned out her pedigree could eat mine for breakfast and still be hungry. It was an adjustment.

Look, I already *told* you I'm a snob.

"What if you could convince her you are a proper witch?"

Hannah ran both her hands through her hair. "How? Her idea of proper witching is poisoned apples and putting princesses into deathlike sleep for a hundred years.

I giggled, that little noise you make when you're either going to laugh or scream. "Maybe you could put Amber to sleep. I mean, who'd notice?"

Hannah shook her head again. "If I do anything with magic, she'll know what it is. She's like a magic gourmet. She can tell you just what you put in the spell and what it's going to do."

But I couldn't give up. We had to at least try, didn't we? "It wouldn't *really* have to be a hundred years. I mean, it could just be a few days, until she leaves . . ."

Hannah just eyed me sourly. "Have you heard a word I've said? She's *ancient*. She might be immortal. If I say I've put someone to sleep for a hundred years, she's going to come back in a hundred years and *check*."

Hannah hid her face in her hands. "What am I going to *do*, Chase? I can't even run away. She'll hold my mom hostage. She'll hold the whole flippin' town hostage . . ."

But while she was wailing, I felt the heavens open. Light poured down and birdies sang. I knew what to do. I *had* done Hannah a favor with my stupid bragging down there.

"Hannah, tell Oma Tod that you can't go back with her. Say you need to stay here to exact your revenge."

"What?" demanded Hannah, lifting her head. Her cheeks were red and tear streaked.

I grabbed her hands. "You've challenged Amber Bailey to a duel on Gallows Hill tomorrow at midnight for dissing you and your family. That's what I was trying to tell her down there, only you stopped me."

Hannah stared at me as though I'd lost my tiny little mind. "What are you talking about?"

"She wants you to be the Wicked Witch of Massachusetts? We'll give her a show that'll make her evil eye bug out!"

"Chase, she'll *know* we're faking it. She'll sense how weak the spells are!"

"Not if we don't use spells. You've got power she couldn't touch if she tried, right? I said so, right? Gimme the phone." I yanked her cell out of her purse and started dialing.

"What're you doing?"

"Calling my cousin at MIT. In the communications lab." I finished the number. "You would not believe the stuff they do up there. Third-generation holography, remote imaging, instant-read motion-sensor pixilated imagery. All kinds of shit."

The light began to dawn on Hannah, too. I saw it coming up in her eyes. "I can't, Chase," she whispered. "Oma Tod might get it into her head to help, and I can't put anybody in that kind of danger. Even Amber."

"Amber's not going to be anywhere near the place." The ringing started.

"But . . ."

"Would Oma Tod know Amber Bailey if she tripped over her? No? Right."

My hypernerdy MIT cousin—who couldn't have charmed a frog to jump, pedigree or no, but could make light do things it had only dreamed of—picked up. "Hey, Jimmy! It's cousin Chase. I need a favor. A big one, and you should do it because if you do I'll help you hex the Harvard-Yale game next fall." I winked at Hannah.

"This is what I need . . ."

Gallows Hill. In 1692 nineteen people were hanged there for being witches. Not one of them was, of course. The real witches in Salem, like Sarah Good, were not dumb enough to get caught by that bunch of losers. Still, it's a pretty spooky place. Every kid at Salem High has been dared to go up here at midnight sometime or other. Some of us actually have. I was just glad it wasn't Halloween. Then you can't swing a dead cat for all the tourists.

But it was March, a time when nobody in their right minds wants to be on an exposed hilltop in Massachusetts, so we had the whole cold, windy place to ourselves.

I was skipping school. I felt traumatized by the weird stuff that had gone on yesterday, and Mom was letting me stay home. Dad had to work (yes, he could have sent a doppleganger, except it was the day the auditors were coming). Mom was responding to the crisis of an unknown and possibly malevolent magic worker invading the school in her usual way. She had about six emergency committee meetings. So I was to rest and check in every two hours.

"I will," I promised as she kissed my forehead and hustled out the door.

I worried when Jimmy showed up with the Mixed Geek Assortment as well as the equipment, but he said he'd never get set up in time without help. He'd told them that it was all for a hack, which means practical joke in MIT speak. Our family is not the only Massachusetts institution with strange traditions.

Unfortunately it left me without much to do except check in with Mom and worry about Hannah. I messaged her a couple times and got no reply. By three o'clock, while Jimmy and the Geeks argued about the best way to set up the screen frames, I chewed my fingernails.

What if this didn't work? What if Oma Tod had already taken Hannah away? Or turned her into something? That's serious high-level magic, but I didn't doubt for a minute that Oma Tod could do it.

And if the plan worked, if Oma Tod came with Hannah to see our "duel," I'd be making myself a target for all that power.

I sat on a rock and wrapped my arms tight around myself. I was out of my tiny little mind.

At about four o'clock I called Mom and asked if I could sleep over at Josey's, who was also traumatized. Mom said yes. I called Josey and asked her to cover for me. She said yes.

About five o'clock, with the sun going down, Jimmy got me into the motion-capture suit, which is like a wetsuit with fuzzy ping-pong balls sewn on it. He helped me adjust the wireless microphone. It was already hard to see the screens. The whole show was based on teleprompters, Jimmy said, only better. This rig would pick up movement from the suit, pair it with some graphics, and project it to someplace I wasn't.

The last connection was made. Jimmy crouched down with his laptop and typed a few commands. There was a flash, and I faced myself, standing there in the motion capture suit.

I looked really stupid.

I waved my arm. Other Me waved back. I turned left. So did she.

Jimmy clicked a few more keys, and it wasn't me I faced. She was about my size, but she had a wealth of blond hair, was wearing low rider jeans and a tight halter top, which apparently had a pair of watermelons under it.

I glowered at Jimmy. He shrugged.

I raised my hands. Amber Plus raised hers.

"I'LL GET YOU MY PRETTY!"

A rage of colored lights exploded around Amber Plus.

"Cool!"

"And when Hannah retaliates, or if Oma Tod draws a bead on this, you'll be safe down over the slope." Jimmy showed me how to strap on the control gloves. "You just have to be in line of sight with the screens, and you can kill yourself however you want."

He showed me the command gestures. Over the next hour, I blew Amber up, turned her into a newt, and melted her into a puddle of green goo. Very satisfying. I was already thinking about how we could smuggle this into school.

I hugged Jimmy, thanked the Geeks, and hustled them all out of there. Jimmy swore to them over and over he'd be in charge of the remote monitoring, and, yes, he'd post the pictures as soon as he had them. As soon as they were gone, I hugged my cousin and made *him* beat it the hell out of there.

Then there was nothing to do but wait. It was cold, and the wind smelled like snow. The motion-capture suit did nothing to keep me warm. I had to pee, but I didn't dare take the thing off in case I messed up one of the billion connections. Suddenly, hanging my life and Hannah's on a bunch of high-tech stuff I didn't understand felt really dumb. Almost as dumb as saying the duel had to happen at midnight.

So I sat there, swinging from fear to anger to boredom, growing colder by the second. Finally, my watch beeped. Five to midnight.

I pushed the power button on the control glove. On top of the hill, Amber Plus appeared. I wanted her on display for Hannah and Oma Tod. I poured on the attitude, cocking my hips and thrusting out my chin, and my chest. I shook. I couldn't tell if Amber did.

Come on, Hannah, get up *here..*

Footsteps rustled in the grass. I couldn't breathe. They were coming. Hannah carried a camping lantern and wore her graduation outfit—flowing black robe and black cloak, a wand that was more like a Gandalf staff than those little things they wave around in the Harry Potter movies. Oma Tod stumped behind her.

I thought about giving out with my Margaret Hamilton imitation again, but I was Amber, right? That was not Amber's style.

I put both fists on my hips and said. "Oh, come *on!* Get up here already!"

"You want me up there, Amber Bailey?" called Hannah. "You got it!"

Levitation was one of Hannah's best subjects, and in the flowing black dress it looked really good, especially when the wind caught her cape and sent it billowing out like black wings as she landed on the crest of the hill three feet from Amber Plus.

Oma Tod did not look impressed.

I made Amber Plus yawn. "Ooo, the little witch can fly!" she/I said. "What else can she do?"

"You're gonna find out!" Hannah raised her staff, and the show was on.

I've got to give Jimmy and the Geeks full credit. Their light show would have done a heavy metal band credit. Amber Plus's aura glowed about eight different shades of green. Pops and booms sounded from all angles as she and Hannah went round each other, shouting nonsense spells and curses, staggering back, falling down, jumping up to toss out more lights and bangs.

Then, at last, Amber Plus fell to her knees. Hannah loomed over her. "Now, you upstart, you nothing, you will die!"

She raised the staff one more time, shouting like as though meant to bring down every ghost on Gallows Hill. I cowered back on my knees. "No! No!" and hit the controls to bring on the finale.

Amber melted into a gooey green mess at Hannah's feet and vanished in a cloud of steam.

Triumphant, Hannah turned back toward Oma Tod.

The crone had her arms folded and nodded, in what I prayed was an attitude of approval.

"Very good, granddaughter," Oma Tod said. "There is only one thing more to be done."

Hannah's face fell, but she rallied fast. "What's that, Grandma?"

Pain! Pain in my arms and in my shoulders, and that pain dragged me up the hill, shaking me around until my teeth rattled in my head and I sprawled beside Hannah.

"Did you think to deceive me?" Oma Tod climbed the hill one deliberate step at a time. "Do you think I have no eyes? That I am blind and cannot see who is beside me?"

"No, Grandmother, I just . . ."

"She just wanted to show you she is a real witch!" I shouted, picking myself up. "Hannah's one of the best at school! She's going to be valedictorian! You just need to give her a chance!"

"You will not talk to me that way!"

"You will not talk to *me* that way! I'm a New England Good, and this is *my* place!"

I called on my power. I dragged it up out of the ground, out of the blood in my veins. I called on the spirit and memory of Granny Good who tricked death in this place to lend me her aid. I felt myself crackle with power, down to my fingertips and the ends of my hair. How dare this outsider, this insolent foreigner, come here . . .

Oma Tod laughed.

She stretched out her hand, and it was all gone. Outrage and power drained out of me, and all of a sudden I couldn't stand up. I fell onto my belly again. In her hand, Oma Tod cupped a sphere that blazed sapphire blue.

I felt her fingers close around my heart.

"Very pretty." Her teeth gleamed in the light of my stolen power. "I'm hungry."

"Leave her alone!"

Hannah jumped. She didn't raise power, she just tackled her own grandmother, who stood there with my life in her hands.

Oma Tod fell backward. The sphere of my power shot into the air. Pain knocked the breath out of me. Oma Tod heaved Hannah off and scrambled away.

I stretched out my shaking hand toward the sapphire light.

"Please," I whispered to the goddess or Granny Good, or whoever might hear me. "Please . . ."

Slowly, the light reached toward me, as if it wanted to be home. I felt pins and needles on my skin, in my blood, and in my heart.

Oma Tod spun around, but Hannah threw her cape over her grandmother's head and grabbed her from behind. It would have been hilarious if I hadn't hurt so bad, if I weren't straining with every ounce of strength I had to try to drag my life back into my own body.

Oma Tod slammed her elbow right into Hannah's stomach. Hannah dropped the old woman, who landed on her feet easy as a cat and tore the cloak off. Hannah was on her knees, struggling for breath, and Oma Tod towered over her like a fury.

One spark at a time, my power filtered back into me. I could still barely breathe, let alone move. I caught Hannah's gaze, and fear shot through me.

We're gonna die. Oh, Goddess, oh, Mother, we're gonna die!

"You snake!" spat Oma Tod. "You and your little friend will beg for the oven before I am done!"

Slowly, Hannah pulled herself upright and met her grandmother's terrible, burning gaze.

"No."

"No? To me?"

"I've HAD it with you!" Hannah clenched her fists. "Go ahead! Make me suffer! Make me scream!" She seemed to grow taller with every word. Not with magic, but with a different kind of power, maybe the power of anger, maybe the sheer force of realizing you've become an adult. "You're the bad witch, the worst witch, the witch out of all the horrible nightmare fairy tales, but you know what?" Hannah's grin was wide and terrible. "That witch LOSES! Every. Single. Time. To the little girl, the clever brother, the pretty princess.

"You're just a thing from a story. You're a Disney cartoon! You're a flipping JOKE and YOU CANNOT WIN!"

Hannah's fury shone, brighter than any of Jimmy's light display, stronger than the power torn from my body. She was the night, the place, the power. She stood in front of Oma Tod and made her look small.

Oma Tod sagged. She trembled. There on Gallows Hill, the Black Forest Witch looked up at her shining granddaughter, and began to cry.

Hannah shrank and faded until she was nothing more than Hannah Todd again. She leaned over and slipped her arm around her grandmother's shoulders.

"It's okay, Grandma," she said softly. "Let's go home."

"So, she's gone."

We were back at school. In the girl's room, with the door wedged shut with a wad of paper towels so we'd have a warning before anybody tried to come in.

Hannah nodded. "This morning. On the plane. I didn't think Mom really needed to do that to her. She looked so . . . lost."

My eyes bugged out. "You can't feel sorry for her! She almost killed us!"

"I know. It's just . . ." Hannah shrugged. "She's my grandmother."

I nodded. Family. Can't live with them but somehow can't completely hate them. Not always. "How'd you do it?"

Hannah blinked. "Do what?"

I rolled my eyes. "Beat her like that! She was gonna eat me alive, and I couldn't move, and then you . . ."

"Oh." Hannah smiled as if she were being modest, but I didn't buy it for a second. "That was just Schramm."

"Huh?"

"Mundane Perceptions of Witchcraft. 'Belief or non-belief alters the nature of magic itself.' It's going to be on the final, remember?"

"So?"

"So, I know Grandma's the witch out of the fairy tales. That witch always loses. I just had to believe it. Really believe it, and she couldn't get through that."

"Wow."

"Yeah." Hannah picked up her purse and backpack off the edge of the sink and slung them over her shoulders. "Come on. Let's eat. I'm starving!"

I grabbed my stuff. "You oughta know, though. Amber says her dad's gonna get you kicked out of school, 'cause your grandmother endangered the class."

Hannah waved me off. "Don't worry. I'll take care it."

"Really?"

Hannah grinned. For a minute I saw her teeth were big and straight and sharp, just like her grandmother's. "Believe it."

Coyote Run

Debra Dixon

When she was young, Debra Dixon's parents wouldn't let her check anymore books out of the library until she got her nose out of them and learned to tie her shoes. As a teen she had to get an awful job—selling magazines on the phone—to support her reading habit. Now she writes to pay for her book addiction—a much better gig—and is the award-winning author of ten books and a frequent contributor to anthologies.

Izzy

I looked down at my hands, wiggling them a bit just to be absolutely certain I hadn't somehow become accidently invisible in the last twenty minutes. That's how long I'd been standing in the corner of the school office waiting for someone to tell me why I'd been summoned. I understood the first day back from the Yule break was always a train wreck. Really. I did. Every Tom, Dick, and Sabrina had a problem. I was more than willing to wait when Ms. Danderford, who'd been school principal since before dirt was discovered, held up a perfectly manicured finger and said, "Just give me a minute, Ms. O'Connell."

Her minute had turned into twenty. Enough time to mentally review every possible power screw-up from last semester. It had to be a screw-up. No one was summoned to the office for good news. The most likely screw-up was the "accidentally invisible" incident during the planetarium field trip. In my defense, every nonwitch normal in the planetarium had been looking up at the wonder of the universe and *not* looking at me go invisible. So I couldn't see how my occasional inability to properly control my magic was going to get me in trouble. I also couldn't see how I was going to get to my AP Government class on time unless I got pushy.

Unfortunately, I suck at pushy. I know this because I'm standing quietly in a corner beside a fake silk tree *and* because every single time Kale Yarbrough tossed a glance my way during a football game last semester I didn't take the opportunity to shove Katie Ford out of my way and cheer like mad for him.

Katie is not cursed with assertiveness issues. She shoved. She cheered. Petite blonde Katie is now dating Kale. Everyone calls them "KK." (As in: *"Is KK coming to the party?" "Have you seen KK?")* Couldn't you just throw up on KK?

Right on cue, one half of KK burst through the office door and rushed the counter in a flurry of blonde assertiveness. "You'll never guess. Her name is Tess, Ms. Danderford! She's the tiniest, scruffiest gray kitten. She wandered up yesterday, but I wasn't sure until this morning. A familiar finally chose me! I was so tired of being a freak! The waiting was awful. Thank the Goddess nothing's wrong with me!"

That's when Katie noticed *me*—the only other freak in school who didn't have a familiar. She tried to apologize. "Oh, geez, Izzy. I'm so sorry. I didn't mean . . . There's still time. It doesn't mean there's something wrong with—"

I cut her off with a forget-about-it wave of my hand. She didn't mean to call me a freak, but facts were facts. As the only member of the junior class who hadn't manifested a familiar, I now qualified for freakdom. Pretending I didn't qualify wouldn't make me petite, blonde, a girlfriend, or any less a freak. I mustered a smile and tried to be happy for her.

"Congratulations. A cat, huh? A classic." I nodded. "Good for you."

That sounded lame even to me, but what else was there to say? The truth was she wouldn't have cared if a lizard had shown up on her doorstep. We both knew people had been talking. Teachers were concerned. It wasn't natural to be almost seventeen and un-familiar.

"Oh, Izzy, you're the best!" Katie threw her arms around me and gave me a hug that confirmed her status as a clueless drama queen. "You'll get yours. You'll see."

While I tried not to snort—it's unladylike and rude—I couldn't stop the eye roll. I caught Ms. Danderford doing the same thing. We both bit down on smiles and looked away. Katie, who'd apparently forgotten we weren't remotely BFF, gave my arm one last squeeze for moral support.

"Call me if you need to talk to someone."

As if.

"I'm sure I'll be fine." *As soon as I figure out how to crawl into a hole somewhere or make you go away.* I tried the tiniest of magic nudges but missed her, misjudged the power needed, and slammed the door on some poor kid who'd been about to turn into the office. Air is not my strong suit. Katie jumped about three feet away from me, which was good. But I winced, which was bad. *(Notes to self: Never play poker. Add "bluffing" to the list of things you suck at.)*

Ms. Danderford looked at me and raised one eyebrow. Our moment of bonding over Katie's melodramatic nature was apparently done.

"Bad draft in the office?" I suggested as I stepped up to the counter.

"Sloppy," she corrected, then looked over my shoulder at Katie. "Congratulations, and go to class. Finn, wait. I'll just be a minute."

I froze.

Colin Finn? I'd slammed the door on Colin Finn? Geez, could the day get any worse?

Finn, a recent senior transfer from Ireland, was about the McYummiest boy who'd ever walked into Salem PHS #4. Black hair, blue eyes, melt-your-bones Irish accent. There was a little of the bad boy about him. A scruffiness that implied he lived life on his own terms. A paradoxical cool in the way he could be alone and never look lonely. In other words, he was just about perfect, and every ounce of his person implied that the girl who caught him would have to be more than a mere girl.

And I slammed a door on him. Great.

Not that it would have mattered to my chances with Finn even if I had been planning to stake a sovereign rights claim to him based on my vague Scots-Irish ancestry and unruly red hair. Far more aggressive girls than I had tried to get close to him. Finn was Teflon. Practically every vacuous boytrap in the senior class had flung herself at him. None stuck. In my opinion, that fact said a lot about Finn's intelligence and gave him the edge in the McYummy contest.

On the heels of my awarding Finn the McYummy, I felt a push of power riffle my hair. My gaze shifted to Ms. Danderford, wondering if she was making a point about how you push and control air in light of my fiasco with the door. She was a decent air witch, but she was busy looking for a file and paying no attention to me. Oh, so casually, I turned my head, looking over my shoulder at the only other person in the room. With perfect timing, as if he'd been waiting for me, he leaned more squarely into my line of vision by tilting his head. He studied me seriously for a moment, then one side of his mouth kicked up into something that might have been approval. Or an invitation.

OMG. The boy packed a wallop. His eyes should be illegal. They were a particular shade of blue that could slay any water witch for miles around. And I was way closer than any other water witch at the moment. I wanted to smile back, but it wouldn't be a subtle smile. No, if I'd didn't get a grip, I'd be smiling like a goon, a goon smacked by a two-by-four with little cartoon stars and birdies circling her head.

Get a grip, Izzie! Even thinking that Finn would bother to amuse himself air-fiddling with my hair—hair belonging to the junior freak girl who controlled magic so badly she slammed a door in his face—was ridiculous. He surely didn't even know my name.

"Whatever is the matter with my eyes?" Ms. Danderford sounded testy. "I can't read the label. It's all blurry. Does that say Isabella O'Connell?" She started to hold it out and then pulled it back. "Never mind. Must have been the light. This is your file after all."

I gaped with suspicion at Finn. Now he knew my name. How'd he do that? I didn't know, but I promised myself I wouldn't think at all anymore. Not around Finn. I turned back to the principal. "Ma'am?"

"I'm sure you already realized we had to change your schedule. No sense wasting time in Mr. Orlina's class on familiar magic until you have one."

Now I truly did feel like I'd been hit with a two-by-four. Because, *no,* I hadn't realized. I hadn't quite made that leap in logic. My chest felt as if someone had put me in a vise and was squeezing the air out of my lungs a twist at a time. She pushed the new class schedule halfway across the counter. After a tiny hesitation, I pulled the paper toward me. The Care and Feeding of Familiars was crossed off and beside it was written Individualized Grimoire Study—Library Work Program. I looked up, hoping there'd been a mistake. That my ears weren't working. Something. Anything.

Danderford closed the file. "That's a senior level class. Building your own personal Book of Shadows for your magic is serious business, but we feel you can handle it. Off with you now. We've both got work to do. And don't think I've forgotten your other problem." She glanced meaningfully at the door I'd slammed. "I'll expect you to spend some time doing pea drills as well." She had a thing for teaching air work using frozen peas because they were all different shapes and weights. It was harder than pushing uniform BBs around a table. "At your age you should certainly be able to control yourself better. You do those pea drills."

"Yes, ma'am." I avoided Finn's gaze as I left. I didn't want do that social nod where we both pretend I'm not a loser or that he hadn't heard my humiliation or that we'd catch up later.

I wanted away from there as quickly as possible. I was at my locker when I realized Finn must have thought I was much worse than a loser. A boy from Ireland and new to our school probably didn't know that Ms. Danderford meant "pea" drill and not "pee" drill. I'm not as dramatic as Katie, but it's not stretching the truth to say I just wanted to die. Chances were . . . McYummy thought I peed myself.

The first thing I planned to put in my personal grimoire was an earth spell designed to make the ground open up and swallow me. Yeah. I could use one of those.

Finn

Once Isabella left, the office felt empty, all the chaos that had poised on the knife tip of possibility fled with her. Finn liked a bit of chaos and uncertainty. It was part of who he was. Or at least who the High Circle wanted him to be. The principal pulled him into her private office, away from the secretary, and shut the door.

"You've left it a little late, young man." She didn't like him much because of what he was. Hadn't liked him from the moment the High Circle sent him into her school. She couldn't question the High Circle—no one did—which meant he got the sharp side of her tongue more often than not because she could question him.

She crossed behind her desk and drilled him with a look meant to chastise him. "There is no choice now. It'll have to be the water witch."

He looked at the principal. "Aye. It was always the water witch."

For a moment she looked stunned. Then slowly she sat down. "Isabella O'Connell isn't ready for this."

"I've not said she is."

"If she were strong enough in the power to have a familiar, she would have already acquired one. Why couldn't you have picked Katie?" Danderford drummed her fingers impatiently. "If I've ever seen a girl with a natural ability to manipulate and handle the dark magics it would be Katie."

"The other girl's mind wouldn't have survived. At least your Isabella has a chance." *If she can break away from the identity your doubts have created for her.*

As the silence grew, Finn imagined the look on the woman's face was close to the look that would have been on the faces of the adults who'd cared about him. If there had been any. He'd been as young as Isabella and alone when they called the coyote for him. The truth of it was . . . he wasn't much older than she was now. But witches treated you differently if you'd made the Coyote Run.

Only a handful of familiars scared the craft. Coyote was one. Coyote liked the night, liked magics worked in the dark. The witch with a coyote walked a fine line between the dark and the light. Power rippled in the coyote bond. Most parents believed coyote was nothing more than a scary story to make children happy to have gotten their timid mouse or songbird. The woman in front of him believed, and she didn't want coyote for Isabella. He could respect that.

"Would it help if I told you the coyote would have come with or without me?"

"Would that be a lie?"

"Some bit of it."

He had called coyote, but if not him, then someone else would have. No one got close to being sans familiar at seventeen without the Circle sending someone to call a coyote, just in case. An actual bond was too rare to leave to chance or to a young witch's ability to draw the coyote. The window of opportunity was small, just those few weeks before a witch turned seventeen. After seventeen there was almost no chance of a true familiar bond with any kind of animal. So the Circle would have sent someone, just in case Isabella was a witch to bond coyote.

Danderford picked up some files from her in box and centered them on her desk. She opened one to signal their talk was done. "You play by the rules. You tell her nothing. This is her choice. Do not make this seem an answer to her problems. Or power for the asking. Do not make it an easy choice for a girl who's struggling to find herself."

"Nothing is easy. Murphy's Law sees to that."

"Coyote sees to that," she snapped. "Mr. Olina would like a few words with you in private. He has some questions about exactly how the coyote bond works since it's so rare."

That sent his eyebrows up. "You told him?"

"Someone has to be ready to pick up the pieces if you break Izzy."

"Fair enough. An' will it be you who'll be pickin' up my pieces if I break Isabella? Or am just supposed to soldier on an' all?"

Finn didn't wait for an answer. Encouraging his anger was never smart. Everyone conveniently forgot he wasn't much older than Isabella and gave no thought to what they asked of him. He'd already had to watch one young witch crumble beneath her own doubts. He didn't think he could stand it again. Not that he had any choice. The Circle had been very clear about that.

Izzy

"Stop it! People are staring. Stop. It."

My pleading had no effect on Jordan, who was literally doubled over on the lunch table . . . chortling. She'd been my friend since third grade, and I'd never heard these noises before. I didn't know what else to call it except chortling. Or a seizure. You'd think she could have controlled herself long enough to offer a little support on my worst day ever. I leaned over to look at the little mahogany and white Cavalier King Charles spaniel at her feet. Somehow Andy always appeared for lunch. Or when there were french fries to be had.

I waggled a curly fry. "It's yours if you can make her stop."

Andy sprang into action, sitting up to put a paw on her knee, but he kept his gaze on the fry. Finally Jordan cleared her throat and wiped under her eyes. Not that she needed to. Her make-up was still perfect despite a few laugh-tears at the corners. Her special talents lay in glamour, as in "the casting of." I see a big career for her in photography, fashion design, or acting. If you sit close enough to her, a little of the glamor spills over onto you. She can't help it, which is why there is never an empty seat next to Jordan if she's in a group.

In self-defense I always sit across from her, especially at lunch when it's just the two of us. She doesn't mean to, but, lately, instead of the small spill-over glamour she usually radiates, she's been turning my hair an impossible shade of Goth black. And black is so not me; I can't pull it off. She swears she's not doing it on purpose.

The laughing? Now *that* she was doing on purpose, but at least she didn't look like she was having a seizure anymore. I tossed Andy the fry he'd earned.

"Are you ready to help me or do you need a little more . . . private time?"

"Don't be mad. It was funny! A water witch . . . peeing her pants. You gotta love the irony," she said and happily dug into her salad.

"What I gotta do is check in with Ms. Cortland in the library. I need books and I need 'em now. More than I can carry. So get up."

Jordan stopped in the middle of ferrying a tomato chunk to her mouth. "What lit a fire under you? Can't we finish our food?"

I waved my new class schedule and lowered my voice. "How long do you think it's going to take *them* to figure out that *I've* figured out I have the run of the Senior/Teacher section in the library? How long before they limit my access to only certain books? Right now I get to play with the good toys. The dangerous toys. They gave me a senior-level course. That means I've got a get-out-jail-free card and I'm going to use it. There's got to be a spell, a use of the power, new meditation ritual . . . *something* that's going to help me get a familiar. You know they don't tell us everything. Or those books wouldn't be off limits."

"You're serious?"

For a moment I considered banging my head on the table. "Yes, I'm serious. Listen. I'm not trying to outshine you with your Goddess-given talent or Elspeth Hightower with her hawk. I'm not trying to conjure up magic that will make me special and freak out my dad. My little sister's got that covered. Me? I'll be happy with a house sparrow or even a gerbil. I just don't want to disappoint my dad. He worries when things aren't . . . right with us."

"Uh . . . he wasn't so worried when he married the stepdragon and turned the house upside down." The way she leaned back and crossed her arms meant she thought she'd won the point. I'd been pretty vocal about being miserable with the stepdragon around 24/7.

I took a moment to straighten the black onyx ring on the middle finger of my right hand. Fiddling with the ring was a habit, as if it were my worry stone. My dad gave it to me not too long after Mom died. For his "grown up girl," he'd said. I was a lot older before I realized he'd been trying to buy some insurance. Onyx was a world champ at boosting protection, balancing a witch, reflecting those pesky dark energies that scared the crap out of him.

When your wife kills herself because she can't handle her power, you get weird. I understood. It was a little weird for me too. So, I defended him.

"Yeah, well, no matter what it looks like, he does worry, Jordan. If he'd just been trying to find a hottie, he didn't have to wait seven years. And maybe the 'rental unit was right. Molly called the stepdragon 'Mom' this morning."

Jordan gasped. "That little witch. She has finally gone over to the dark side."

That made me laugh. "Joan as the dark side is too funny. The woman is rainbows and s'mores. We're finally one perfect little magic family except for the fact the stepdragon is a normal and I'm a dud."

"You aren't a dud."

"Might as well be without a familiar to focus the bigger spells and add some power. Hey! If I can't figure out a way to make myself interesting to a familiar, maybe I can move to New Mexico and open up a crystal shop?"

"That's just whacked. There isn't enough moisturizer in the world! That's not happening." Finally she started moving, consolidating our trays to clear the table, talking to Andy out loud. "Go 'way. There's no food in the library. And you—" She stabbed a finger toward me. "Water witches don't reach potential until later. You know that. But if you think you need these books, then I've got your back. Or at least your backpack. Let's do this."

I smiled a little secret satisfied smile when she wasn't looking. I knew images of me as a sun-scorched, wrinkled, new-age crone would freak her out.

All around me were the spoils of war.

Earth, Air, Fire, and Water—A Balanced Approach

The Guiley Bates Treatise on the Ethics of Manifest Magick

The Forbidden Rituals of Slant

Consequences of Binding Spells

Familiar Fundmentals

Heathcott's Rites of Passage

Book of Shadows—A Complete Guide to Recording Your Magic in a Usable Grimoire

Grimoires—Creating a Compendium of Personal Spells, Herbal Potions, and Rituals

Fundamentals of Ritual Design

Designing Your Grimoire

My room looked as though the library had thrown up on it. In general my room looked as though *something* had thrown up on it. Just at the present, though, the mess was clearly librarian in nature.

I'd gotten almost every book I wanted except one. *A Study of Attraction for the Uncommon Familiar* was on a warded shelf. Arrgh. Understanding attraction was exactly the sort of research that might help. Well, at least I had something to work with, even if I was going to need toothpicks to keep my eyes open. Some of this stuff was dull, duller, and dullest. No help for it. Rubbing my hands together, I prepared to dig in.

"Need a break?" The hopeful voice was muffled by the door, but Joan respected my privacy. She wouldn't open it to be sure I heard. If I didn't answer, she'd walk away and try later. Best to get it over with now.

"Sure!" I pushed away a book on new meditation techniques and swirled my body around to swing my feet over the edge of the bed.

Joan wasn't anyone I expected my dad to marry. Well, to be truthful, it was the other way round. I never expected someone who looked like Joan to even date my dad, much less marry him. She was taller than him, drop-dead gorgeous in an I-look-like-this-when-I-get-out-of-bed-because-I-eat-right-and-exercise kind of way. She was homey. Always decorating. Put a new holiday wreath on the door every month. Even months without real holidays got a themed wreath.

Her cat wandered in first, wiggling his twenty-five pound butt through the door and launching himself toward my bed. Oliver seemed to take great pleasure in annoying me. Or he liked me. It's hard to be sure with Oliver. He'll throw up on your homework the moment you turn your back.

After Oliver, two pints of Ben and Jerry's ice cream appeared. "Your dad said you had a bad day. Care to drown your sorrows?"

I won't lie. I didn't wait for her to finish before I started reaching. "Yes, please. Peach cobbler. Yum."

"How are you?"

Well, this was new. Joan hadn't tried to do the bonding chat before. I guess my dad was more worried than I thought. He'd sent in a spy bearing gifts. However, my motto is never look a gift ice cream in the mouth. "I'm fine."

Nodding she parked a hip on an old leather trunk I had. There was a look on her face I hadn't seen before—a little less rainbow and more storm cloud. "Do I look like your father?"

"Excuse me?" There were definite storm clouds in her voice.

"He wants to believe it when you tell him you're fine. I, on the other hand, was a teenage girl once, and witch or not, it sucks swamp water when you're different. Do you think your dad is the only guy I was taller than? So, you'll have to come up with something better than, 'I'm fine.' Let's try this again. How are you?"

For a few seconds I dug at a chuck of peach. Then I said, "An eight on the freak-o-meter."

"Sucks. I had an eight once." When I opened my mouth, she waggled her spoon to stop me. "And no, I'm not telling. I'm taking it to my grave. Unless you'd like to share the details of your eight? Huh? Huh? Didn't think so."

We ate our ice cream in a companionable silence for a while. Then she planted her spoon in her pint and stood up. I watched as she dug into the pocket of her fleece pullover and fished out a small jewelry box. "I was saving these for your birthday, but I thought . . . what the heck. Wouldn't hurt to have a little something cheery on a day you hit eight on the freak-o-meter. Happy eight, Izzy."

Inside the box were black cameos to match my ring. When I looked my question at her, she said, "Yep. Black onyx. Protection and grounding. I looked it up in Molly's book of crystals and gems. Seemed an odd stone for you despite your ring. You always feel so solid to me, so grounded already. Not like Molly. So I thought maybe the cameos would be a better fit for you. Add a little something to balance that black. But what the heck do I know about magic?"

"Who cares? You know pretty," I said as I touched the small, carved white portraits on the black stone.

She smiled. "I do. Those are you. Carved special. Night."

"Me?" But the door was already drifting closed. I won't lie. I had a stupidly happy grin on my face, and against all logic I had a fleeting thought that maybe Joan deserved a better nickname than stepdragon.

I put the earrings where I could see them occasionally and got back to the book on new meditation techniques. My guess is my nose hit the crease in the book and I was snoring before midnight. That's where I'd probably have stayed if it hadn't been for Thunder Butt (a.k.a. Oliver).

The bedsprings rocked when he pounced on the

mattress, not coincidentally cracking my nose on the book as I bounced with the bed. Next the bed creaked beneath his weight as he picked his way carefully along the edge of the bed until he reached his objective—the small of my back. At that point, he executed the flop-with-elbow maneuver designed to move me to the edge of the bed so he could get comfy. Wretched cat. He'd gained weight since yesterday!

Experience had taught me that a swat made no impression on Thunder Butt. I pulled the textbook out from under my cheek and swung it behind me. "Get off, you cow. My bed."

The book swung through air. The weight at my back adjusted itself again. A shape much bigger than Oliver could ever hope to achieve.

You know that scream where you can't scream? Nothing comes out? I madc that scream, threw the book, and leaped out of bed fully prepared to catch my heart as it flew out of my body. I tripped on several books, bounced off the closet door frame, and sat down in the floor of my closet, having collected a fair amount of my clothes on the way down.

YOU ALWAYS THIS JUMPY?

Even if I'd wanted to answer, it's hard to talk with your heart in your throat. Slowly I dug out from the clothes burying me and peaked at the bed. Nope. Nothing there. "Hello?"

I REALLY DON'T THINK THE COAT HANGER IS GOING TO HELP.

I had a coat hanger in my hand, brandishing it like a weapon. I put it down. "Who are you?"

YOURS. MAYBE

"Ha!" I did a quiet little victory dance. "It worked! Wait. I didn't do anything that worked. You're invisible. What are you?"

No answer.

"You feel like a dog. Dogs are good," I offered as reassurance.

THEN I AM CERTAINLY NOT A DOG. WHAT WOULD A WITCH LIKE YOU DO WITH A DOG?

Suddenly the thoughts he thought into my head were darker, predatory even. I took a step back from the bed. A suspicion became a dread.

AH. SHE UNDERSTANDS FINALLY. LET'S HAVE A BIT OF FUN, SHALL WE, WHILE YOU'RE DECIDING?

"You're a coyote, aren't you? And you're about to mess up my life."

The only sound in the room was sound of the freak-o-meter hitting nine.

Finn

He'd worried when he kept missing her at school. So, today, he set himself against one of the interior columns with a line of sight to her locker to play watchdog. The principal said he couldn't push her to a decision, but no one said he couldn't watch her, conveniently be nearby if she needed someone who wasn't afraid of what she might be. Or who understood the cost of becoming that, what it did to the people around you.

Coyote made you pay for the power you got. He loved change. For sure he was one for givin' lessons. He'd turn you over in his mind until he found the key that let the shadows and passion loose to play. And then he'd chase you down until you faced yourself.

If Finn had ever seen someone with her shadow-self locked up tight, it was Isabella. He had more than a bit of air in his tool kit and a fair splash of water to go along with his fire and earth. The air and the water had given him a way into Isabella's thoughts that day in the office. The psychic feel of her surprised him. It was a rare girl who didn't get a bit nasty jealous when someone like Katie got everything. Rarer still was the girl who didn't throw a benny when her day had chased the devil down. No, this one kept her emotions on a very short leash.

What are you afraid of, girl? he wondered; then as the crowd thinned out, giving him a better view, he whispered, "And what *are* you doing?"

Right now she was having a bit of a tussle with her locker. The door kept jerking away from her hand and crashing shut each time she opened it. Interesting. Promising even, given the coyote nature when he first came to you on those ghost feet. Finn shaped air to better hear exactly what was happening over the noise of the last of the students shuffling off to class.

Finally Isabella looked to the empty space beside her backpack on the floor and hissed, "Stop it." Then she went back to the bizarre door-banging with no progress at all except in decibels. Without the other students to muffle the noise, the sound clanged through the hallway.

As soon as she had spoken to the nothingness beside her, as soon as he'd heard the exasperation in her voice, he knew an' for certain Isabella had a coyote problem. Now, what to do about that problem? On the one hand, he'd been told not to interfere. On the other hand, no one said he couldn't help a girl with a jacked locker. That being the case, he shoved off and headed for her.

By the time he reached her, she was arguing with that same empty spot . . . "I don't need to use power to open the door. Now, stop it!"

Bang.

"Isabella? Would you be havin' some trouble there?"

Bang. But this time she made the noise herself when she whirled around, backed up, and slammed her elbows into the row of lockers to stop herself. She look right gobsmacked. He'd never actually had quite that effect on a girl before. This one almost looked as if she'd be happier if he just turned around and walked the other way. And she looked tired, tired the way people looked when they'd been carrying around a secret too long.

Something had changed in her. He couldn't read her mind, not with anything like the clarity of earlier. She had grounded, shielded and centered as if her life depended on it.

Before he could say anything, the Gaelic-Celtic language arts teacher leaned into the hallway not three feet from them. She was tuned up to yell, but she stopped. He'd become a favorite of hers, so she just shushed them and waggled her finger for them to move on to their next class. He nodded his understanding and turned back to Isabella. Without realizing it, he'd put his hand on her arm and pulled her away from the lockers. Close enough that he could see only the top of her head without leaning back.

"I have sprites," she blurted to the top button of his shirt. "Not the lemon-lime kind. The locker kind. Don't worry. I'll deal with it."

"You have . . . locker sprites? That can rip the door out your hand, girl? Wouldn't that take a hundred sprites, give or take ten? It's a fair awful liar you are, Isabella. What's going on?"

TELL HIM.

"Aye, tell me."

Just that easily, he fell into coyote's trap.

Izzy

"Freaked" does not begin to describe the emotion that sent a chill through me. No one in my life knew about Wylie. But Finn . . . *Finn* just heard him. I hadn't even figured out how to tell anyone about him. My dad would flip. The dark familiars, even ghost familiars, aren't supposed to come for your daughters. It'd break his heart. Even worse, I hadn't been sure I *wasn't* crazy until five seconds ago. Until someone besides me heard Wylie.

All I could do was look at that empty space I knew was the coyote and then back at Finn. I'm not sure how many times my head moved back and forth before I asked the one question that might mean I was crazy after all. I needed to know if Finn actually heard Wylie or if he'd just heard me, as he had in the office.

"Were you reading my mind?"

He waited so long to answer, I thought he might not. "No."

Relief flooded through me. "Okay. I'm not crazy, but *how* can you hear him?"

Finn looked back at me. That's all. Just looked. That look bothered me because he looked . . . guilty. As if his current girlfriend had caught him with his ex-girlfriend and he was trying to figure out the best lie he could before he had to say something.

"You're about to lie to me aren't you?"

YES.

His eyes widened. Not much, but enough.

"Oh, you are so coming with me." For the first time in my life, I was pushy.

I was due for my individual study in the library and I didn't much care where Finn was due to be; we were going to the library. He didn't disagree. I retrieved my grimoire project from the locker, which Wylie no longer cared about. The door banging had just been one of his tricks from the last few days. Why had I thought having a familiar would be cool? I didn't understand this game. I didn't like this game.

CAREFUL WHAT YOU WISH FOR.

"I am." Finn answered. Then he looked at me as if it were *my* fault I had a whack job coyote. I really didn't want this to me my fault. Especially now that there might be someone else to blame.

We signed in and took the older of the two rooms in a back corner of the library. My stuff was piled in the middle of the table—both metaphysical and material stuff. All of it just sitting there "naked" on the table waiting for someone to sort through my life. I know there was a bigger issue at stake, but for a moment all I could focus on was that Finn looked better than me. Not a little better. A lot better. That made me mad. Go figure.

He wore this great blue shirt with tiny white stripes, white cuffs and collar. Perfect fit. I was wearing my favorite gray sweater except now one side was three inches longer than the other. This sweater was one of the things I grabbed and held on to for dear life to break my fall into the closet.

For the millionth time I wondered why I was always so off-kilter when it came to boys like Finn, who could sit there with all the answers and looking better than tidy. I was desperate and looked it. Grossly unfair. (I'm just saying.) The whole damsel-in-distress thing never works out in real life. The truth is, you usually look like crap and have to save yourself.

"What did you do?" I asked. A simple question. I'd learned it from my dad. Also the pacing back and forth was vintage dad material.

"You wanted a familiar."

"So you got me a *ghost coyote?* Like that was going to fix everything? Are you crazy?"

"Lower your voice and sit down." He snatched a chair out and waited for me to take it. I sat. He sat, leaning forward. "Do you know how rare the coyote bond is? Maybe twice every fifty years. It wasn't as if I had the idea all by myself. The High Circle is trying to improve those odds. So, I did what I was told."

His tone surprised her. "You didn't want to?"

Without answering her question, he said, "The bond is up to you. Only you. I can call one *to* you but only you can call it down. He won't be real until you do."

MAYBE THIS IS A GOOD TIME TO TELL YOU THAT HE DIDN'T CALL ME. YOU DID.

The thought fell like a hundred-year-old pine. At first there was the big crash and then silence while I absorbed what he said. Finn had nothing to do with this even though he'd meant to do the very same thing. Finally I forced my mouth to move.

"I–I didn't. I swear I didn't. I mean, occasionally I have a little trouble controlling the power, but I didn't call a coyote! I would have remembered that. Wylie?" He didn't answer. "Why isn't he answering?"

"Because the next move is yours." Finn's words were quiet, gentle as if he feared my reaction.

"Well, it's a mistake. I don't know what you people were thinking," I snapped. I heard my voice rising. The words coming too fast. "My father won't like this at all. The coyote? Do you know how much dark magic a coyote brings? That's just crazy. I need a bunny or something. That would work. Could you call a bunny?"

He stood up. He hadn't said a word but the disappointment was in his eyes. Oh, not the kind of disappointment you were supposed to notice, but it was there. And maybe a little doubt, as if he should have done something different. There was more he hadn't told me, and I didn't have a clue what it was. All I knew, somehow, was that it was important, and it had nothing to do with the High Circle. This was something deeply personal.

"Whoa, whoa! Where are you going? Aren't you supposed to convince me? Tell me how this is my last chance, especially if this is my true familiar? How there is no bunny in my future? We both know this is my last rodeo. Once I turn seventeen, stick a fork in me. I'm toast. Dude, is your Irish brain *getting* any of my clichés here?"

He smiled then, but he just picked up the grimoire notebook and a pen sticking out of the pocket of my backpack. "If you've got Rathsteiller as your adviser, be sure you use an affirmation on the title page. She loves a good affirmation." He flipped the book open, wrote something. "She'll like that one."

"The witch is the magic," I read. "What does that mean?"

"That I can't be helping you with. I don't know. She has it on the front of her grade book. I saw it once."

"Finn—" I knew I was going to regret this, but I'd

regret not asking it more. "What happens if I call coyote down?"

"Then you run. Either you beat him, or he beats you. Let's not be misunderstanding each other here. No one can help you. You'd not be getting a second chance at the Coyote Run. You lose, and you'll banjaxed—that's broken, no hope of repair."

He let himself out.

I think I knew what he meant about broken, because my mother was broken and she'd never had coyote in her life. I looked at the books in front of me and the library through the glass. I was in this room because I was already broken, too. Just broken in a different way, and I didn't know what way that was. I pulled the grimoire to me and opened it to a blank page. This book was supposed to be for my personal magic. I was about to make it very personal.

I wasn't sure what I expected, but something more original than a streak of lightning in the sky. It hadn't even hit inside the large circle I'd walked off. In fact, I suspected I'd screwed this up. Maybe taken too long to write the ritual and test the power blending. I needed all five elements, and I managed to scrape them up from inside me—even spirit—but for what? What piece of this had I gotten wrong?

I'd picked the old Clayton barn out on Chesney because these grounds had seen more unauthorized experimental teen magic than any other place. It was an open secret that the teachers cleared the place for residual power several times a year. Plus they reinforced the old barn so it could take a lickin' and keep on tickin'. It was really more of an extension classroom for the gifted.

Unfortunately, I didn't appear to be one of the gifted.

Maybe I should have picked up a copy of *Calling Coyotes for Dummies.* Oh, right. There *wasn't* one. I rubbed my eyes hard. I wasn't crying. I wasn't crying.

Slowly I picked up my grimoire and the candle I'd use for light. Stepping outside the circle I'd walked was going to feel like stepping across a big neon river of failure. How completely like the stupid craft to feed me a bunch of bull about calling down a coyote being something *only* I could do . . . if I couldn't *actually* do it? Why leave something so important in the hands of someone completely unsuited to the task?

I got so wrapped up in my rant that I think I missed the first low rumbling animal sounds from behind me and across the circle. It wasn't until a snarl was added to the base of that growl that I realized maybe I wasn't going to need that book for dummies. I had tennis shoes on, jogging pants with thermals, sweatshirt with thermals. I was ready for everything but Wylie. He was gorgeous, more Eastern mountain coyote than desert from what I could see. Gray. Big. And I couldn't feel any lightness in that animal soul.

Snarling and snapping, he eased another step into the clearing. I backed away a step. I'd never win this foot race. There'd have to be another way. *Find safety and outwait him, maybe?* I kept one eye on him and tried to check for the barn with my peripheral vision. Uh-oh. The barn was gone, and in its place was a small cottage, looked like two stories. Easier to hole up in. If I could get there . . .

Each step he advanced, I retreated, knowing that eventually he'd make a run at me in earnest. If I didn't make that porch before he caught me, well, I didn't want to think about that. This had to work. For me. For Dad. For Molly.

Watch his haunches. Won't they bunch before he pushes off to run?

When he exploded, there was no warning. He went from standing still to at my throat, or he would have if I hadn't pushed air at him to slow him down. Thank Danderford for those freakin' pea drills. I made the porch, then door, and finally I was inside with the bolt thrown. I'd won. Then Wylie landed on the door so hard I bounced off it. That door wasn't holding. Not long. I poured everything I knew about metal and wood into that door and watched it buckle again anyway.

I didn't wait to see how long before it failed. I took the steps two at a time. I found a bedroom with a solid door and closed it. I piled as much furniture in front of it as I could. I wove some binding spells and to heck with the consequences. I paced and had a hysterical moment when I realized I knew just how the three little pigs felt.

Nervously, I reached for my ring. It wasn't there. I'd taken off my jewelry when I showered. This whole Coyote Run thing was not going well. The one decent protection I had against what was coming up those stairs was lying on the bathroom sink. I wasn't confused about what was coming up those stairs anymore. That coyote was pure dark magic. Power like nothing I'd ever seen. The kind of power that would sweep over you and eat you up. I didn't want that anywhere near me. I was having trouble imagining how anyone could have thought I could win this fight.

I heard snuffling at the door. Then a thump. The furniture was helping, but the next thump rattled it. Okay, that wasn't going to hold. Not forever. I needed that onyx for protection. I tried to recall every scrap of my notes from Relocation Magics last year. They worked best with items that were personal, with specific detail you could recreate.

Wham. The funiture shuddered. I paced and tried to conjure up my ring. Nothing.

How hard could this be? It was just a round stone in . . . a setting. I wore it almost every freakin' day and I couldn't remember the setting? I should know it as well as my own face!

"Wait. Yes, oh, thank you, Joan." I concentrated and the two most beautiful cameos in the world plopped into my hand. I began one of the standard shielding spells.

When I did the thing in the hallway freaked.

Crash. This time the door splintered and the furniture moved several inches away from the door. I was running out of time. I refocused on the cameos, connecting with the onyx, grounding, shielding, centering, and sending everything I had against the darkness coming through that door. But it was like feeding oxygen to a dying flame. That coyote roared back to life, tearing a hole in the door and almost clearing a path through the furniture.

I was out of time. I saw the grimoire where I'd tossed it on the floor in my hurry to stack up the furniture. Snatching it up, I tried to find something that might work. The coyote out there—I'd stopped calling him Wylie—was quiet for now. I didn't know why. And I wasn't complaining. Maybe it had gotten hurt on that last rush at the door.

I considered jumping out the window and running, but I was right back to the first moment I saw that animal. I couldn't outrun it. Not on my best day with six months of training. This couldn't be about foot speed. It couldn't. The Coyote Run came down to a witch and that beast. That nagged at my mind.

A witch and that beast. A witch and that beast. A struggle.

Suddenly I looked at the grimoire, at the door and then the cameos in my hand. The beast had gone crazy when I'd used the onyx to keep him out. He backed off when I stopped, as if we had a truce. And I realized my mother had never found that truce. That darkness had eaten her up in the struggle.

I touched one of the pages in the grimoire. *The witch is the magic.*

Finn had known. He just couldn't tell me.

It doesn't matter how dark the magic. The magic

serves the witch. Not the other way round. You can't deny part of who you are. To do that is to be broken.

I began to rub the cameos, chanting. Just as the beast broke through the wall of furniture, I flung the cameos away and welcomed the magic home.

When I came to in the middle of the circle, a big fur ball was laying on my chest staring intently at me. The teeth were still just as big, but the noises were smaller. Just a gentle chuffing at me to see if I was really awake.

GET UP. I'M HUNGRY.

I started to laugh but I couldn't because I had no air.

"Lad, get off the nice witch."

HE'S BACK AGAIN. I CAN BITE HIM.

"You can try, boyo, you can try. But you'll have to get through her first."

I struggled out from underneath Wylie and found a slightly bigger version of him at Finn's side. I smiled, stupidly happy. "Your coyote is bigger than my coyote."

"Aye, and that's one of the finer points I've been trying to explain to your Wylie there. Her name is Reese. She's how we found you."

"Oh, no. I can see her." Looking around and up at the soft daylight stealing into the area, I gave a fake scream. "I'm going to be grounded for a year. I'm dead. It's daylight. I've been gone all night. Please tell me you brought a phone that gets a signal." When he handed it to me, I said, "Good lad." He laughed.

The phone call with my father wasn't pleasant. I'm grounded for year or something close. When I asked to speak to Joan, he grumped (he wasn't through yelling), but he put her on. I apologized for losing the cameos. She wasn't mad at all. That astounded me because she'd gone to so much trouble. When I told Finn, he said, " 'Tis only a stepmother that would blame you for that."

"But she is m—" Then I laughed. "Never mind.

You're absolutely right. Only a stepmother would would blame me." I realized the light inside me that kept threatening to lift my feet off the ground was happiness. I liked it. I looked at Finn and said, "What now?"

Those Irish are fast bunch of boys. He kissed me. Now I'll have to explain to my father why training with the boy I want to date doesn't really violate the rules of grounding.

You Got Served

Esther M. Friesner

Multiple Nebula Award winner Esther M. Friesner is the author of over 30 novels and over 150 short stories as well as being the editor of 8 anthologies including the popular *Chicks In Chainmail* series. Her latest titles include *Temping Fate* (Puffin) and *Nobody's Princess* (Random House), whose sequel, *Nobody's Prize,* will appear in 2008. Educated at Vassar College, she went on to receive her Master's and Ph.D. from Yale University, where she taught Spanish for a number of years. She lives in Connecticut with her husband and two all-grown-up children.

"AT least you don't have to wear a hairnet." Cathy gave her cousin Josie a sprightly smile. The two young women were having breakfast in the townhouse apartment they shared thanks to the machinations of Josie's mother. As annoying as Josie found this morning's conversation, it wasn't a patch on the one she'd had three months ago with Mom—the "This won't take a minute, dear" telephone chat that had gotten Cathy wedged into Josie's life and living space. *That* one began with Josie's forceful rejection of the whole idea, countered by Mom's insistence that Cathy's only alternative was living out of garbage cans *and* in them. It ended with Josie's "*I give up!*" and Mom's self-satisfied, "Only if that's what *you* want, dear."

So Cathy moved in, bag and baggage and conversations like this one, which Josie had inadvertently begun by saying, "Here's your breakfast. At least you'll appreciate it. Oh, God, I hate my job so much, I wish I was dead and unemployed!"

That was when the chirping started. Cathy was a chirper, one of those provoking, peppy people, happily stuck in a universe where dreams came true if you knew how to stay spunky, find the wishing star, and bake a mean chocolate chip cookie. Belief in fairies was strongly suggested but not mandatory.

Josie had only wanted to vent a bit, then go to the job she'd come to loathe. (Quitting was not an option: It paid too well.) But apparently Cathy couldn't tell a vent from a vehement cry for help. In between bites of the lavish breakfast Josie had placed before her—a *haute cuisine* riff on bacon and eggs—she harangued her morose cousin about finding the upside to employment as cafeteria supervisor at Salem Township Public High School #4.

Now she dragged a scrap of English muffin through the dregs of her breakfast eggs and concluded: "I can understand how working at the same high school you used to go to can be kind of weird, but you *did* always want a career in cooking, you're getting paid oodles of money, and you *so* don't have to wear a hairnet. That's *something* good, isn't it?"

"No hairnet, right." Josie spoke dryly enough to reduce the Pacific to a handful of salt and fish bones. She drank her breakfast, a cup of bitter green tea. "How silly of me to feel so miserable when I get to work without a net. Whee."

Cathy's pale brow wrinkled for a nanosecond. Then she did a bungee jump back to the status quo of her scarily sunny disposition. "Oh, Josie, you've got *such* a wonderful sense of humor! I wish I could be as funny as you." She continued enjoying the last of her breakfast.

Josie studied her cousin's face carefully, with the

objective interest of a trained naturalist. Strive as she might, she could not find any trace of irony in that young woman's upbeat worldview. *Why did I even* try *telling Cathy about how much my job sucks?* she thought. *It's like trying to make a kitten understand that— Well, it's like trying to make a kitten understand* anything, *really.* She got up from the table and emptied her tea into the sink.

"Is that all you're going to have?" Cathy asked. "A cup of tea?"

"Half a cup," Josie said.

"It's the same thing every morning: You always make me such yummy breakfasts, but you never eat a bite."

"If I wanted to poison you, I'd stick arsenic in your strawberry lip gloss. I just don't have an appetite on work days."

"But breakfast is the most important meal of the—!"

"*Don't* say it. Or say it, but lock up your lip gloss. I am a self-supporting adult and you are not my mother. I don't have to eat just to make you feel better."

"You don't need to bite my head off." Cathy folded her arms and actually looked annoyed. Then she ruined the effect by adding: "Of course if you did bite my head off, that'd count as breakfast, which as you know is the most important meal of the—"

Josie slammed the apartment door loudly enough to draw complaints from neighbors across the street.

All during the bus ride to work, she did her best to think about anything but her destination. A catalog of shattered dreams and blasted hopes failed to distract her. Thundering herds of grim coulda-shoulda-wouldas out of her past were no match for the dire power of a hideous here-and-now. No matter where she directed her thoughts, they invariably came swooping back to a single, chilling fact: It was *Nutrition Is Magic, Too! Day* at Witch High.

Josie got off the bus and made her way to the school kitchen. Her two assistants were already there, impeccably turned out in crisp pink uniforms. You couldn't beat witchcraft when it came to whipping up designer knockoffs. If not for the white bib aprons that were part of regulation cafeteria wear, her underlings could have passed for a couple of Ladies Who Lunch rather than Lunch Ladies.

Josie muttered an obligatory "G'morning" and went into the break room, right off the kitchen. A plasma screen television dominated a space furnished with lounge chairs featuring built-in heating and massage options. She stalked across the thickly carpeted floor and entered the door to the locker room and spa area. Here showers, a hot tub, and a sauna beckoned the weary food service worker. The air was thick with lush aromatherapy exhalations. She paused to read the bulletin board notice saying that Yuri, the on-call pedicurist, was taking Friday off for a *Hunks of Spadom* calendar shoot, but Antonio, the resident masseur and former romance novel cover model, would be standing in for him.

Note to self: Never *let Cathy find out about these on-the-job bennies,* Josie thought. *She'd strangle me with my own hairnet. That I don't wear.* She changed into her uniform, tied her apron strings, and went into her alcove office to deal with e-mail and paperwork.

"Josie?" Marie, the taller and older of the two assistants peeked around the open office door. "It's nine, and you still haven't given us today's recipes."

Josie rested her cheek on her fist. "What difference is it going to make?"

"Not much," Marie admitted. She reached behind the bib of her apron and pulled out her wand. "Not to the kids, anyway. But if you don't give us the recipes, we won't know which ingredients to use. It'll cause pantry inventory discrepancies. You know what happened last time."

"Uh-huh." Josie took her own wand out of the top

center drawer of her desk. The sealing spells that kept it safe from anyone's touch but her own crackled when her fingers closed around the slim length of koa wood. "The Faculty Appreciation dinner. I was dealing with one of Mom's long-distance meltdowns, so I left you and Barb to your own devices. You improvised the students' lunch and used up most of the supplies we needed for the dinner. I didn't have the budget or time to order more, so I replaced them with *conjured* ingredients."

"It almost worked. If only you'd—" Marie abruptly clapped a hand to her mouth.

"It's okay, Marie, I can't fault you for speaking the truth." Josie gave her assistant a reassuring pat on the arm. "If only I'd graduated from this school instead of washing out in my senior year, right? If only I'd managed to master fixative spells. Anyone can conjure a bag of flour or a dozen eggs out of thin air. Preventing them from dissolving *back* into thin air isn't so easy. Will you ever forget the look on the principal's face when that forkful of Chantilly potatoes melted like snowflakes halfway to her lips? Or when the roast beef gravy just . . . evaporated?" Josie couldn't help giggling.

"Or when that entire death-by-chocolate cake suddenly turned into fudge-flavored lace?" Marie put in.

"Well, the *real* ingredients in the cake didn't vanish. I just didn't have enough for the whole recipe. It looked absolutely scrumptious before it *eroded* like that." Josie giggled again. "I've never seen so many grown women cry!"

"Good times," Marie said. "Most of those old cows were the reason you and I and Barb flunked out of this place. I *like* seeing them cry."

"You're going to see *me* cry if we don't get lunch on deck. Here you go." Josie handed Marie the day's recipes, then stood up and decreed, "Ladies, man your cauldrons!"

While Barb and Marie fulfilled her instructions with

their usual combination of hands-on efficiency and wands-on spell craft, Josie's thoughts slid back into the abyss. *Look at them go, and with smiles, yet! Don't they care that their hard work goes to waste, day after day? What's wrong with them?* A darker cloud settled over her mind. *Maybe the only thing wrong here is me.*

Lunch hour crept closer, but there was no last minute panic in the school kitchen. Under Josie's able direction, Barb and Marie had the food cooked and out on the line with time to spare. They took care of the basics, but her hand alone fine-tuned the seasoning and added those little creative touches that made the difference between mac-'n'-extruded-cheese-food-product and *penne au gratin.*

Not that it matters, she thought. *I should let this stuff go out onto the serving line as-is and spare myself the heartache, and yet—* She sighed as she dusted a snowflake pattern of freshly chopped parsley over the top of a brown rice casserole. *—and yet, I can't help myself. Cooking's what I do. It's what I* love *doing! It's not my fault that it all goes down the slop-chute day after brat-packed day.*

Barb murmured the spell that would keep the big metal pans full of veggies, Tofu Surprise, skinless broiled chicken, and assorted healthy side dishes at the perfect temperature. Marie gave the rows of wholesome desserts a final alignment. Josie deployed the serving utensils—spoons, spatulas, ladles, and tongs—then went out front to survey the lunchroom. She stood by the cafeteria doors and checked the brightly colored posters on the walls, the big banner above the food line, and the decorative signs labeling each menu offering. *Nutrition Is Magic, Too! Day* was the principal's idea, and what could Josie do but implement it?

What does that woman imagine this will accomplish? Turn a cage full of hellspawn into well-nourished *hellspawn? Does she think they'll change their junk food guzzling ways just because she's plastered the room with food pyramid propaganda?* Josie shook her head wearily. She'd seen to it that though the day's offerings lacked salt, sugar, and fat, they were attractive to the eye and brimming over with tastiness. But would anyone ever know, let alone appreciate her art? She knew the answer.

She trudged back behind the counter, picked up her spatula, and awaited the onslaught. The lunch bell rang, the cafeteria doors opened, and the students streamed in. Their animated chatter filled the air as they swarmed the lunch line. Show-offs made their trays levitate and glide along, no-hands. The Popular Girls took a moment to cast a spell over their chosen table, which was promptly enveloped in a hedge of poisonous thorns. The sports-mad clique staked out their turf in much the same way, except their method for discouraging squatters was to give their lacrosse sticks unnatural life and set them on guard duty. Outsiders who tried to slip into one of their chairs got whacked upside the head.

Josie took deep, steadying breaths, waiting for the first student to reach her station. She'd assigned herself the main courses, the worst position on the line. *I'm either a nice boss or a masochist,* she thought. She didn't even try to smile when she asked the girl, "What would you like?"

The girl peered through the steamy glass at her choices, tossed back her long brown hair, and wrinkled her nose. "What's *that* stuff?" she demanded, pointing her wand at the meatless main dish.

"Tofu Surprise," Josie said, and immediately regretted not having left her response at just *tofu.*

A wicked grin spread across the student's face. Her wand barely twitched. A great bubbling surged up from the heart of the serving pan as a dark fissure split the beautifully garnished surface of the Tofu Surprise. Hissing and spitting, a bile-green demon leaped out of the crack and flew up to perch on one of the overhead lights. It was carrying a banana cream pie, but not for long. A flash of scaly paw, and the pie smacked Josie right in the face. Even though she'd known what to expect the moment the pie appeared, she lacked the talent to get her own shielding spell up fast enough to block it. She'd barely begun to scrape whipped cream out of her eyes when the gooey evidence vanished.

"Surprise!" The student gave her a cherubic smile and flounced down the line to the cheers of her friends.

"Awwwww, I wanted to do that one," said the next girl. She contented herself with making the herbed new potatoes assemble themselves into tiny snowmen, which drew cries of "Lame!" from the onlookers.

After this there came a succession of students who seemed to be too sophisticated for sophomoric humor, even though Josie recognized them as members of the sophomore class. They all requested the broiled chicken. A younger, less cynical Josie would have felt relief at this respite from questionable, food-based humor. The hardened, experienced Josie knew that the demure display was simply a prelude to the dropping of the second shoe, and it was going to be Goliath's hobnailed boot.

While she waited for whatever nastiness the sophomores had in store, she watched how the other students approached the day's nutritious offerings. Josie's ears rang with "Ew!" after "Ew!" from the students, with "Yuck!" and "Ugh!" thrown in for variety. The best behaved waited until they reached their tables before using their magic to turn Tofu Surprise into cheeseburgers and fries. The rude ones didn't bother putting off the inevitable. They changed their servings of brown rice pilaf into chocolate fudge cake the instant it hit the plate. Some spotlight hogs didn't even wait that long, transforming veggies into slabs of double-cheese pepperoni pizza while the broccoli and carrots were still on Barb's serving spoon. Two or three of the students left well enough alone, though

Josie knew it was not out of any concern for the cook's feelings; they simply lacked the witchcraft for the job and begged their more magically adept friends for help the instant they sat down.

No one bothered to *taste* Josie's original creations. No one.

A shriek of glee arose from the sophomores' section of the cafeteria. The broiled chicken pieces were rising from their plates and coming together in midair, assembling themselves into a giant rooster with a beet salad comb and wattle, tomato eyes, and legs made out of massed pineapple spears. He crowed lustily and attacked the juniors' tables. The juniors countered by forming a spell circle and summoning forth the remaining Tofu Surprise right from under Josie's nose. The shuddering mass flew across the room and coalesced into a colossal anthropomorphic figure even as the last of the brown rice pilaf arose and solidified into a hefty club. The Abominable Soy Man seized his glutinous weapon and swung savagely at the broiled zombie fowl while the students laughed, hooted, and made side bets on the outcome of the battle.

"I quit," said Josie, just before the demon on the light fixture conjured up a fresh banana cream pie and got her one more time.

"It was only a food fight," the principal said. "Mind you, I am somewhat concerned that one of the students actually conjured up a demon. That's forbidden, according to school policy. Disciplinary action must be taken. Such a shame, too. Gemma is a senior and one of our best students."

"You sound like you're thinking of expelling her," Josie said. "I wish you wouldn't. Sure, she sicced a demon on me, but all it did was hit me with a pie."

The principal smiled in her most placating manner. "Now you see why you can't leave us, Josie? Where could we ever find someone else with such forbearance?"

"I don't know, but you'll find out. I'm still quitting. Gemma and her banana cream demon are just one small part of the problem."

"Ah! So it *did* bother you. Never mind, I'll take care of it. Please say that you'll give me a *chance* to regain your goodwill." The principal went on to promise that the students involved in the lunchtime melee would apologize as soon as they cleaned up the cafeteria. She also offered Josie a make-nice bonus so obscenely huge that only a fool or an independently wealthy heiress would turn it down.

Josie was neither. She'd uttered the Q-word in the heat of the moment, knowing full well that she'd never have the nerve to follow through. She rescinded her resignation, though she felt her stomach clench as she spoke the words the principal wanted to hear.

All the way home, she couldn't get over the sensation that she was still covered head to toe with banana cream pie. It was a persistent, soiled, sticky feeling. *Even after you pull out all the arrows, a target's still a target, and that's all I'll ever be to those kids. Oh, well, I can probably buy myself a nice, new bull's-eye with that bonus money.*

Cathy was already home by the time Josie got there. The moment she came face to face with her perky cousin, Josie knew that the only thing worse than the day she'd had would be rehashing it for Cathy's benefit. And she would *have* to rehash it, for Cathy was one of those obtrusive people whose "Do you want to talk about it?" was actually a thinly disguised "You had *better* talk about it, because I'm not going to give you a moment's rest until you do!" Josie feigned the smile of a beauty pageant finalist, in hopes of throwing Cathy off the somber scent.

Too little, too late. Cathy could detect unhappiness the way a shark could scent blood in the water. The chirping began.

"Poor sweetie, you look soooooo *grumpy!* Bad day at work? Do you want to talk about it?"

Josie took the coward's way out and 'fessed up straightaway. The only thing she kept out of her recitation was the rather *special* nature of Salem Township Public High School #4. Those who had no magic had no need to know about it, and the nonmagical parents of all students—and former students—had their perceptions and memories gently altered as the administration deemed necessary. Thus the day's spectacular debacle devolved to: "The kids didn't like what I served them, so they staged a big food fight. I wanted to quit, but the principal talked me out of it." *Or was it all talk?* Josie wondered. *She bought me off, but did she use a few gentle persuasion spells as backup? How would I ever know? You have to be a* successful *witchcraft wielder to tell when something that subtle's being used on you.*

Cathy clicked her tongue in sympathy. "That's just awful. I know! Let's bake cookies and eat them for supper and rent Mike Meyers movies and forget all about your nasty ol' day."

Cookies? Josie's jaw dropped. "You did *not* just say that. You did not just suggest that we slap a cookies-and-comedy adhesive bandage onto the sucking chest wound that is my life. Do you *know* why I can't stand my job? It's not because of the brats I have to feed, or the way they despise everything I try to do for them. It's not the humiliation of working at my old school while the rest of my classmates travel the world, doing exciting things I can't even dream of.

"No. It's because I had a dream too, one I had since I was a teenager. I was going to be a chef! Not a cook, a *chef.* A mistress of *haute cuisine,* creating dishes to make the angels drool! If I'd paid as much attention to my classwork as I did to recipe books and cooking contests, I wouldn't have flunked out of high school. But I didn't care. It set me free to attend one of the best culinary schools in the country, and once I graduated I knew I'd be another Morimoto, a Batalli, an Emeril! I had *everything* planned."

She paused and took a deep breath. "Everything except genius. Funny, you can't plan for that. I'm a good chef, Cathy, maybe a *great* chef, but I'm no genius. So I dropped my dream and got the best job I could find, and when I say 'best,' I mean the one that pays the most. If I can't die happy, I'll die rich, and have enough money for restaurants where *real* chefs are living my dream."

Cathy's normally blithe expression was gone. "Josie, I am *so* sorry. I didn't know. Is there anything I can do to make it better?"

"Oh, God, you *mean* that. You actually believe there's something you can do to help me." Josie laughed. Now that she'd told Cathy everything that was troubling her, she *did* feel better. Who knew?

"Yes, I do." Cathy looked miffed. "Thanks for making fun of me."

"Trust me, I'm not. I wish I could be more like you, truly *believing* we've got the power to turn our lives around." She gave Cathy a quick hug. "It's no use, but thank you." With that, she went into her bedroom and shut the door.

"Thank the god and/or goddess of your choice, it's Friday." Barb dumped flour into a big stainless steel bowl.

"Thank him, her, them, and/or it after lunch." Josie rummaged through the drawer that held the serving utensils. "Where are our spatulas?"

"They're missing?" Barb called back over one shoulder. She used her wand to crack a dozen eggs at a time and add them to the batter under construction.

"Missing or invisible," Josie replied. "It'll be kind of hard to cook pancakes without a spatula."

"Pancakes for lunch," Marie mused aloud. "Plus syrup and a bunch of gooey toppings. Then you've got us serving desserts with enough fat and sugar to clog an elephant's arteries. Are you trying to bribe the kids fast or kill them slow?"

"Curses, my master plan has been discovered." Josie twirled an imaginary mustache. "If they're going to detour all our lunches into Empty Calorie City, we might as well beat them to the punch. It's efficient *and* it takes away all their fun. Mwahaha, and so forth."

"Why don't we use our wands?" Barb asked.

"Possible, but exhausting. Why strain our spell craft trying to pinpoint the *one* pancake we need to flip on the griddle or drop onto the kid's plate when all it takes to get the job done is—"

"—a spatula?" Marie held up a large, red example of the utensil in question.

"Where did you find that?"

"In here." She pointed at an open drawer under one of the kitchen worktables.

"I thought I checked there already. I guess I didn't look carefully enough."

"Maybe it's a gift from the students," Marie suggested, passing the utensil to her boss. "To say they're sorry for yesterday."

"Or a new prank," Barb put in. "To say they're not."

"It's too soon for another 'joke.' The principal would skin them alive." Josie studied the red spatula closely, then glanced back into the drawer. "Huh! What's this?"

"Please don't let it be a snake, please don't let it be a snake, I know those kids are capable of anything but *please* don't let it be a snake," Marie muttered, eyes squeezed shut.

Josie pulled out a small white envelope. "It's the rare albino flat-bodied viper in its rectangular phase, with my name on it." She tore open the envelope and read the note inside. "Huh! The spatula's a gift from my cousin Cathy. The note says she's leaving it with the school secretary, she hopes I get it before lunch, and that she knows it's a silly gift but she hopes it flips my frown upside down."

"Flips your frown upside down? Permission to gag, ma'am," said Marie.

"Permission denied."

"So why didn't the secretary leave your cousin's gift out in plain sight?" Barb asked.

Josie shrugged. "I bet she got a student to bring it. 'Ooh, let me hide this in a drawer and take away all the other spatulas so the Lunch Lady will go crazy looking for them, and when she finally finds it, it'll be a *surprise!*'"

"I am never having kids," Marie announced.

"You should; they're delicious." Josie tossed the red spatula in the air and caught it easily. "Okay, ladies, it's pancake time. Let's get those jacks a-flapping."

The pancake recipe was Josie's original creation, and serving them on the line was her job alone, both because she was the handiest with a spatula and, today, the only one. Soon three massive trays were filled with flapjacks. Josie used her wand to cast a fast heat-and-texture-retaining spell over them and waited for the lunch bell to ring.

The atmosphere in the cafeteria that day was subdued, even somber. Josie frowned. That stale old war movie line—*It's quiet.* Too *quiet.*—filled her mind and set her nerves on edge. *How silly,* she told herself. *You should be* enjoying *the respite. Smile, fool! They can sense weakness.* She slapped on a brittle grin and greeted her first customer: "Hi! What would you like? We've got—"

"I don't want pancakes." The girl was sullen. Josie recognized her as one of the clique that hung out with Gemma, summoner of the dread Tofu Surprise demon.

"So do what you always do: Take the pancakes and change them in something you *will* eat."

"Why? So you'll have an excuse to get *me* expelled, too?" the girl snapped. She sounded mad, but Josie saw more than anger in her eyes. There it was, peeking out from behind the glare of defiance and resentment: fear.

And I know why it's there.

Josie's mind echoed with the principal's voice: "Gemma . . . one of our best students." She thought back to her own days at Witch High and the cliques who ran the place even then. In normal schools, popularity bred power. Here, power bred popularity. At a school where life was bounded by "Abracadabra," "Oops," *"Aaaiiieee!"* and "Sorry about what I did to your head," the best students *were* the best because they had the most magic. They were also the most feared because they had few qualms about testing that magic on others.

If you weren't one of the sorcerous elite and you wanted to survive until graduation, you took a lesson from the remora, the clever fish that swam alongside sharks. Lesser predators didn't dare get close enough to attack it, and when the shark feasted, the remora benefited from any scraps that drifted its way. Human remoras—Witch High students who attached themselves to the most powerful magic-wielders as cronies, sycophants, and minions—told themselves there was nothing shameful about toadying to the shark; the shark was their *friend*. It was a comfortable existence until you took their shark away.

You didn't like *Gemma,* Josie thought, regarding the girl before her. *But she was all you had to protect you from the rest of the so-called Popular Girls here.* Still clutching the red spatula, she said, "I didn't ask the principal to expel Gemma. I asked her *not* to, but she might've misunderstood."

The girl opened her eyes wide in false innocence. "You're saying it was an *accident?*"

"Yes, that's exactly what I'm—"

"Like *this?*" She whipped out her wand and flicked it at the serving pans filled with flapjacks. A host of wingless giant bats appeared in midair, midnight black and shrieking. The student giggled and waved her wand again, causing pair after pair of pancakes to attach themselves to the bats' backs. The creatures took flight on round, sugary wings, swirling about Josie's head. She couldn't help screaming.

"Stop that!" Barb pulled her wand from her apron pocket and slashed at the bats. They swelled up like black, hairy balloons until they popped. The results were quite unappetizing.

"Pancakes and bat guts," said the student, deadpan. "Yum-o. At least now you're serving us something *creative*."

"Hey, I serve you hellions *lots* of creative meals!" Josie protested. "Except you always—"

"Always what?" said a cold voice from the cafeteria doorway.

"Gemma!" The name went up from the lips of every student, except for the ones already trying to flee or hide. Even the few who pronounced it with joy sounded nervous, and with good cause: The former Witch High senior strode across the room, her magic a cloud of sizzling, blue-white energy dancing around her. She was all in black, she came attended by a slavering wolf, and she did *not* look happy.

As if they'd rehearsed the move for years, Barb, Marie, and Josie drew their wands in unison, the tips aimed for the silver alarm box high on the cafeteria wall. Before they could utter the first syllable of the Summon Principal spell, Gemma murmured the word "Fetch." The wolf's skull split into three identical heads at the ends of three serpentine necks. They shot out like fanged streamers and snapped the wands out of the women's hands. Three quick chomps of their jaws and the wands were splinters.

Gemma patted each wolf head in turn. "Who's a good boy? *You* are. Yes, you are," she cooed. Then she turned a far less indulgent look on Josie. "Well? What are you waiting for, Lunch Lady? I'm hungry. Do your job." She pointed her wand at the serving pans. A few pancakes remained untouched by the recent batty brouhaha, though the magical flurry had leeched away the effects of the heat-and-texture-retaining spell.

Heart pounding madly, Josie forced herself to look unafraid. *They can sense weakness.* "You don't want pancakes; you want payback."

"And plenty of it," Gemma said. "You ruined my life, getting me expelled just because you couldn't take a joke."

"I didn't ask for—"

"Don't try stalling me with lies." The rogue student waved her wand, and the entire cafeteria was laminated in translucent green. "I got an A-plus in Advanced Shielding. Even the principal will need an hour and serious backup to break through that. More than enough time for what I've got in mind." Resting her free hand on the three-headed wolf's back, she sashayed over to the nearest table and sat down. "It's real simple, Lunch Lady: Feed me. If I like what I taste, you're home free. If I don't . . ."

Josie's spine stiffened with the courage born of knowing she had nothing left to lose. "Forget it. We both know you're going to despise anything I serve you. You never gave my work a fair try before. Why should I believe you'll do it today?"

"But it'll be *fun!* A precious memory to comfort me when I'm a Witch High flunkout failure like *you.*" Gemma snapped her fingers. Something sparkled in midair for a moment before she popped it into her mouth and swallowed. "Even you should recognize a truth crystal," she said, licking her lips. "It guarantees that I'll give nothing but honest responses for one hour. *Now* will you play?"

Josie gave the girl a mistrustful look and said nothing. Gemma sighed dramatically. "Do you have to make this so hard?" She glanced at her lupine servant. *"Fetch."* Two of the wolf's heads snaked out, seized Marie and Barb, and reeled them in, each held captive by her right wrist. Josie watched in horror as the fiend tightened its hellish jaws just enough to draw a trickle of blood. The women whimpered.

"All right, you win!" Josie cried, raising her hands. She was still holding onto the red spatula, which made her gesture of surrender look like she was about to conduct an edible orchestra. "What do you want me to cook?"

"Don't go to any trouble. Just serve me the same thing you were going to give my friends." Smirking, Gemma indicated the sorry remains of the lunch pancakes.

"That's not fair! They've gone cold, and some of them have bat bits on them, and—"

"But you *did* make them, and that satisfies the terms of our agreement." Gemma sat down at the nearest cafeteria table. Her grin was worse than the wolf's.

"At least let me heat—"

"*Now.*"

"Fine." Josie turned toward the kitchen. "I'll get the pancakes."

"No, *they* will." Wordlessly, Gemma directed a group of the apprehensive student spectators to bring out the serving tray, the assorted pots of toppings, and a place setting. "I wouldn't want you to try any last minute magic. Not that I think you've got the skill, but why take chances? You know what they say about a broken clock."

Josie flipped a pile of flapjacks onto Gemma's plate. *Well, I finally got my wish,* she thought. *One of these miserable whelps is actually going to give my cooking a fair taste test. Then she's going to kill me, because no matter how good these pancakes once were, now they're cold and sodden.* She topped the stack with sliced bananas, chocolate chips, and a trickle of caramel sauce, shoved the plate at Gemma, and dully muttered, *"Bon appetit."*

Gemma was grinning as she snapped up her first forkful. Abruptly, her gloating look vanished. Her eyes went wide. "No," she said. "This is—is—*delicious!*" She began to sob with frustration. "These pancakes are *hot* and *light* and *yummy*. The toppings are *delectable*. It's like eating sliced angel wings!"

Josie was taken aback by the onslaught of praise. "Uh . . . thanks? I guess this means you're going to leave now and—"

"Not on your loathsome, hash-slinging life!" Furious, Gemma sprang up from the table, wand in hand. "Cookie, you're still going down!"

One of the other Popular Girls dared to speak up: "Gemma, you said that if you liked what the Lunch Lady served you, you wouldn't—"

"I *lied,* stupid! I wasn't dumb enough to pop a truth crystal when I set the terms of the challenge."

"But that's not fair. It's, like, the first thing we're taught here, being true to your word. It's in the Student Honor Code and junk."

"Whose side are you on? You're *my* friend! Friends are all I've got, now that I've been kicked out of school. You want fair? Fair *this*, you traitor!" Gemma raised a wand sheathed in writhing flames of black, crimson, and bilious green. The students shrieked and rushed for the cafeteria doors, forgetting that the exits were sealed. Their fingers scrabbled futilely against the glassy surface of the shielding spell just as Gemma aimed all her dreadful power at the one girl who'd spoken up for Josie.

"No you *don't!*" Without thinking, Josie jumped between Gemma and her intended victim. She brandished her spatula as if it were the mightiest of wands, sweeping it up to meet the titanic blast of dark sorcery.

The spell hit the spatula.

It was rather a let down. There were no fireworks, no explosion, no sizzle of vaporizing flesh. There was only a delicate *boing!* as Gemma's magical attack struck the small, flat piece of plastic and rebounded, bowling the girl over with her own power. She went tumbling backward until she bumped up against one of the tables, where she sat dazed and slack-jawed, but otherwise unharmed. Her three-headed wolf dropped its hold on Barb and Marie, howled dolorously, and vanished in a puff of kibble-scented smoke.

Josie drew closer to the stunned girl. "Are you all right?" she asked. "Do you want a glass of water?"

Gemma blinked, then focused her eyes on Josie. "I don't want any water, dear Lunch Lady." Her smile was radiant, sweet, and a little creepy. "I *do* want you to accept my apology, and to forgive me for having been so nasty to you, and to know how I sorry I am that I never even tried any of your fabulous cooking until today. Oh! And I *really* want more of those super num-nummy pancakes." She batted her eyelashes. "*Pleeeeeease*?"

"Ew," said Josie.

Cathy looked up from her copy of *Cosmopolitan* when Josie came home from work that day. "Did you get my present?" she asked brightly.

Josie nodded. She was still holding the spatula as tightly as a drowning man might grasp a life preserver.

"I hope it cheered you up. There's nothing like a surprise giftie to turn a frown upside-down."

"Not just a frown." Josie stared at the spatula. "This thing turned a batch of ruined pancakes into a gourmet treat. It turned a destructive spell back against the one who cast it. It changed the spell itself into something that turned my worst enemy into the sweetest, most appreciative student I ever met. It turned the principal's decision to expel Gemma into a second chance for the poor—"

"Well, of course it did, silly. That's what spatulas do. They flip stuff. And the right spatula can turn all *sorts* of things heads over heels."

"Uhhhh . . . Cathy? Where did you get this spatula?"

"I made it. It's what I do, creating custom tools for . . . our kind of people." She smiled.

"Uh-huh. And *where* did you say you went to high school? I know you didn't go to Witch—I mean, to Salem—"

"Honestly, sweetie, do you think there's only *one* high school like yours? It's a big country. It's a bigger world."

"Yes, but—"

"Look, Josie, the enchantment on the spatula doesn't last forever, and it's a beast to perform. It was a miracle I was able to cast that spell in the first place. Are you going to waste time asking questions, or are you going to use my gift to flip something *important?*"

Josie frowned. "Like what?"

"Like your life." Cathy took the spatula from her cousin's hand and placed it on the floor. "Hop on. One flip and you're on a one-way trip to becoming the culinary superstar you've always dreamed you'd be."

"Fine." Josie kicked off her shoes, set the tip of one foot on the spatula blade. "But I'm not going to wear a hairnet."

Remedial Magic

Bill McCay

Bill McCay says his pen seems to have two settings—grim and goofy. He can play it very straight—the *Star Trek* novel he wrote with Eloise Flood, *Chains of Command*, put the characters through some hard times (while also becoming a *New York Times* bestseller). His five *Stargate* adventures blended action with humor, while the *Riftworld* novels he did with Stan Lee reversed that mixture. Among the dark tales of revenge in the anthology *Vengeance Fantastic*, his submission came across more like "Fantasy meets Looney Tunes." As for the tone of this story, well, Bill did mention that he wrote part of it while waiting in an emergency room to get treatment for his own mother . . .

SINCE Mom had gotten sick, Saranne had joined the 2:30 Club—the rush of kids who left after the final period of the day without staying for after-school activities. There were a lot of them, even for Salem Public High School #4, otherwise known as Witch High.

Saranne had a spark of regret at ditching the Art Club—it was the one part of school where she felt as if she fit in. Witch High was no picnic when you reach junior year and you're still in Remedial Magic. Freshman year, the class had been full of kids who needed help in controlling a talent. Beyond that, the program was aimed at helping kids with a flicker of talent, nurturing them into a useful place in magical society—or flunking them out.

That approach didn't seem to help Saranne. She tested with very high potential for earth magic, but her power tended to manifest itself in very strange ways. When a wannabe bully had cast a spell on Saranne, she had not only grounded the attack itself, but had also drained away all the energy from a very expensive prespelled wand, turning it into a highly carved but worthless willow twig. After that incident, nobody had messed with Saranne. In fact, her manifestation as a magic sink had gotten her excused from spell casting classes. She'd been banned from the flightorium to keep the crash count down.

However, Saranne had done well with the regular curriculum and scored high on magical theory—all without learning conscious control or a practical application for her talent. And in Witch High, practical application—use of power—was the name of the game.

Not only her magic but also her blood made her an outsider in school life. Saranne's family tree linked her with the Brownes, one of the founding families of Salem witchdom. But her branch had been shunned for two generations. Both Saranne's grandmother and mother had married nonmagical types—"mundanes," "nulls," "mortals," or the term witchfolk especially used to disparage them, "cowen."

Saranne sometimes wondered if it was Mom's rebellious streak showing, some sort of swipe at her supercilious Browne relations that she'd married a man named Dan Cowan. It was a perfectly normal name—maybe too normal. In the original Scots, it meant a person who didn't comprehend an art or who was self-taught.

In Witch High, of course, it was like waving a red rag in front of a bull. Certainly, it seemed to complete the job of isolating Saranne at school—"Saranne wrapped too tight," as classmates referred to her.

Actually, she was Sarah Anne, but she had elided the two names into "Saranne" as a toddler when her mother had called out, "Sarah Anne Cowan!" after some infraction or other.

As often as not, I'd keep on doing whatever I was doing back then, Saranne thought as she made her way through the crooked downtown streets. *Why should I be any different now?*

Her family lived within walking distance of the school, in a not very desirable part of town. But they had the ground floor of a house that some successful merchant had built about a hundred and fifty years ago, and Mom's artistic sense had made it comfortable and beautiful . . . and home.

Saranne picked up her pace. The late autumn sky was already getting gray. She wouldn't have much time.

These days, Mom's energy and attention tended to fade with the daylight—"sundowning," the doctors called it. After five years of battling the malignancy inside her—surgery, chemo, other therapies—Mom had a right to be tired.

But to Saranne, the hour or hour and a half they had after school was precious, a reminder of what life had been before Mom got ill. Mom knew it, too. She carefully rationed her strength, saving herself for a lunch-hour phone call with Dad and her late afternoon time with Saranne.

With two houses still to go, Saranne already had the key out of her pocket. She opened the door to the house, went down the hall, and stuck her head into the parlor. A woman in a light-blue nurse's aide uniform met her.

"Hi, Mrs. A," Saranne said. "How are things going?"

"It's been a quiet day," Mrs. Addabo replied.

"Your mother asked me to make some tea." She withdrew, tactfully giving them some alone time.

At first, Saranne had resented having the short, dark, gray-haired woman around the house all day. She locked her door to keep the intruder out. Finally, Dad had taken her aside. "Saranne, your mother needs the help. She'll get more rest and wear herself out less if she doesn't have to keep smoothing things over between you and Mrs. A."

So Saranne had tried hard to make nice with the aide, even helping out in the kitchen when Mrs. A prepared supper. And Mrs. A had tactfully found things to do somewhere else in the house while Saranne sat with Mom.

"Good day at school?" Mom asked.

"Pretty average. The Lords of the Dark Dimensions tried to invade, but we fought them back," Saranne replied with a grin. "Luckily, I only had to blow up the cafeteria to save the world."

Mom smiled and ran a hand through Saranne's brown hair. "The savior of the world needs a haircut."

"Not to mention losing about fifteen pounds," Saranne said gloomily.

"Dig out the albums," Mom demanded in a mock-stern voice. "You'll see that I looked exactly like you when I went to Witch High."

And look how you grew up, Saranne thought. Even with the bones showing under her skin and a scarf covering up where her hair used to be, Mom was still beautiful. The best Saranne could hope for would be to grow up as a blurred copy of her mom—a shaggy, porky blurred copy.

Mom instinctively changed the subject. "Tell me something evil that happened today."

Saranne smiled again. "We were talking about the Salem Witchcraft Trials in history," she said. "I mentioned how several of the executions settled some bitter real estate disagreements—including a tract of land that went to our Browne ancestors. That really put Rina Browne's perfect little nose out of joint."

"Oh, yeah," Mom laughed. "Nothing better than annoying a Browne cousin."

"Is that why you took the name Cowan?" Saranne had to ask.

"I married your father because I loved him—and still do. As for the Brownes . . ." Mom shrugged. "Well, I knew I wasn't going to see any family heirlooms turning up at the bridal shower. They had cut my mother off years before I was born."

"That went pretty deep with Grandma, didn't it?" Saranne said.

"She never talked about it," Mom admitted, "not even in the hospital when she got sick." She paused for a second. "To answer your question, though, I figured it might raise the blood pressure for some of our snootier Browne relatives. They keep tabs on us, you know, even if we are below the salt."

Mom looked at Saranne. "Mostly though, your father and I were just interested in creating a life together. And I think we did pretty well with that."

"With your pictures," Saranne said. Mom illustrated children's books, invoking her talent in subtle ways that literally created visual enchantment. Her work had won awards, even if the kind of pay she got from publishing didn't make them rich.

"Your father certainly contributes too," Mom said. Dad worked as an editor, fixing up books instead of doing the woodworking he loved. His nimble hands not only fixed the old house, they also helped make the place much more livable. "Where would be we without his medical benefits?"

The old, basic resentment rose up to choke off any words from Saranne. Yes, Dad's benefits paid for mundane medicine for Mom, but no medical miracles. The witchcraft practitioners they had approached—the ones they could afford—hadn't offered any miracles, either. Even though witchcraft had its basis in healing, these healers told them that the cancer was too far along, that they couldn't stop nature from taking its course.

Saranne said nothing, but she held onto Mom's hand fiercely. *If you need a miracle, I'll find one,* she promised. *I will.*

The days got shorter, and so did Saranne's after-school time with Mom. Worse, Mom grew steadily weaker. She faded more quickly, and their conversations tended to become more monologs as Saranne strove to find the funny side of life at Witch High. Sometimes she'd bring out some clay and make caricatures of teachers and classmates. Imbuing some part of herself into these improvisational sculptures was the closest she'd come to using her earth powers—and it made Mom laugh.

The bad news came in the middle of an Alchemical Theory exam. Saranne had studied, but she found herself distracted. This was one of the classes she shared with Rina Browne. For some reason, Saranne kept looking over at Cousin Snooty. Had Rina decided to dress down for the exam? That blouse she was wearing screamed "Unfashionable!" even though Rina had covered most of it with a sweater.

As much as she tried to concentrate on the exam formulas, the discrepancy nagged at Saranne's attention. Then she realized there was something else, a tickle of magic. Not splashy spell casting, but the sort of magic Saranne struggled to understand, the sort imbued into a material.

Then she understood. That blouse wasn't just unfashionable, it was old—the sort of thing Rina's mother might have worn to school. Magister Arminius, their instructor, constantly harped on what good grades Rina's mom had gotten. With his bent-over physique and heavily wrinkled face, the teacher looked old enough to comment on class standings of his students' great-grandparents.

So Rina had turned to the past to help her out. She'd dug out that ancient blouse and was using it for passive magic, channeling her mother—or rather, her mother's knowledge of alchemy.

Rina was cheating.

Saranne's internal debate over whether to bust her cousin was interrupted by a knock at the door. Old Arminius stumped over, muttering a few Words that would make things uncomfortable for whoever was interrupting.

But the person on the other side of the door was Assistant Principal Parris. "I've come for Saranne Cowan," she announced. Then, to Saranne, "Please take your books."

All of Saranane's insides seemed to congeal into one icy lump as she followed Ms. Parris into the hallway like some sort of golem.

"Your mother had taken a turn for the worse," Ms. Parris told her when they were out of the classroom. "The nurse's aide called for an ambulance, and they're at the hospital."

Good old Mrs. A, Saranne thought.

"So Mom is still . . . alive." Her jaw muscles were so tight, the words seemed to creak their way between her lips.

"Yes, but you'd better get your coat and head over there quickly," Ms. Parris said. "I've already called a cab. The school will pay for it."

Saranne felt strangely numb, cut off from her usual grounding hold on the earth as she rode in the cab. She never could recall whatever she'd seen out the windows. It was as if she'd been a feather batted around by vagrant winds.

They had put Mom in a private room—never a good sign. "Your mother became unresponsive," the nurse at the duty station explained. "She seems to be slipping in and out of consciousness."

When Saranne entered the room, Mom was awake, but she looked strangely shrunken, even though the hospital bed was much smaller than the four-poster she shared with Dad. Mom raised a hand from the white cotton blanket, and Saranne seized it. She couldn't help noticing that the flesh looked like translucent wax as she gently rubbed it, as if she could somehow force health into it.

"I was afraid I wouldn't see you again." Mom smiled, but her voice had dropped to a breathy whisper.

"Mom, *no!*" Saranne couldn't help the way her voice went up.

"We've talked about this before," Mom told her. "Remember, no regrets."

"No regrets?" Saranne said bitterly. "You're a Browne—if you were really living like one, would you be here, or would we have every medical thaumaturge in the country crawling out our ears?"

"I came to terms with being a Browne years ago," Mom said. "And as for pursuing more magical treatment—well, I came to terms with that, too. It didn't matter how much money we spent, Sarah Anne. Nothing was going to work. So I tried to make the best of the time we had—"

"It's not enough!"

"It's all we have, love."

Mom sank back, and they waited in silence—mutinous silence on Saranne's part—until Dad arrived. She left her parents to have a few minutes together. Soon enough, though, Dad appeared in the doorway.

Saranne took her place on the other side of the bed from Dad. They each held one of Mom's hands—Saranne had the one with the intravenous needle in the back. "I love you," Dad said.

"Me, too," Saranne added.

"And I love you both," Mom replied.

There didn't seem to be much to say after that. What little talking they did wasn't about anything much. Dad remembered silly stuff from the days when they'd first gotten married and Saranne was just little.

More often than not, Mom's responses were just squeezes of their hands. Her eyelids kept closing, but then she'd open them again with an almost apologetic smile.

But Mom's strength visibly faded, until finally she shut her eyes and couldn't be roused. When they talked to the doctor, he merely nodded as if this were to be expected.

"Is Mom in a coma?" Saranne asked.

"You could say that," the doctor replied.

"People come out of comas," she plowed on, in spite of the look Dad gave her.

The doctor paused for a moment, weighing his words. Saranne noticed that oncologists—cancer doctors—did a lot of that. They didn't want to give patients and their families false hope, but they didn't want to crush all hope, either.

"I don't think we've ever seen that in cases like this," the doctor said gently.

Saranne wasn't sure whether that was the royal "we" or just a corporate "we"—referring to the experience of the entire hospital. Either way, she didn't care.

Well, then, I guess "we" are all going to be surprised when Mom comes out of it, Saranne thought grimly.

They must have eaten something in the hospital cafeteria—what, Saranne had no idea. Whatever it was, she choked it down, eager to get home to the family computer.

Dad called a few friends and family members with the news, then dragged himself off for some exhausted sleep. Meanwhile, Saranne set herself up in front of the keyboard, got online, and began researching comas. Whenever she hit the words "terminal" or "final," she'd switch to another Web site. There was still a lot of stuff for her to learn. She discovered that a coma could be the body's way of conserving energy when it was really needed—like, for instance, to cure itself. However, coming out of a coma could be a time of great danger. Sometimes, Saranne read, the effort of returning to consciousness seemed to exhaust a patient's resources—with fatal results.

That wasn't going to happen to Mom, Saranne silently vowed. She was going to return to the world strong—cured, even. Saranne already saw a way to do that . . .

After her all-nighter on the computer, Saranne had to keep stifling yawns as she headed off to school the next morning. Even walking around in a bit of a daze, Saranne still noticed the glances and whispers all around her. *Looks like my interrupted exam made the Witch High gossip grapevine,* she thought. *I haven't gotten this much attention since I drained that witch-bitch's wand.*

Even the girl at the next locker actually looked at her and gave a brief nod. But the real surprise was when Rina Browne suddenly appeared. "I heard about your mom," she said. "I'm sorry."

Saranne was surprised to get any expression of sympathy from her cousin. Then she noticed that Rina had taken care that none of her fellow Queen wanna-Bees were around to notice her acting like a human being.

Thrusting her head forward, Saranne spoke in a cold but quiet voice. "You'll be even sorrier if Magister Arminius hears about what you were doing on that exam. And he will unless you do what I ask." Her lips twitched in an expression something like a smile. "You may suck at alchemy, but I know you're a whiz at spell casting."

It took Rina a day to research and set up the spell. She appeared at Saranne's house the next afternoon with a knapsack of supplies. Coming into the parlor, she looked around, especially at the patchwork of oriental carpets that covered the floor in glowing colors. "Beautiful." She almost said the word under her breath.

"What?" Saranne asked, "You figured we outcasts would have to live in a hovel somewhere with mud floors?"

She didn't mention that despite Mom's careful magic, the carpets had been carefully laid in that pattern to hide worn spots. The furniture in the room probably spanned two centuries, but nothing was a fancy-schmantzy antique. It was just good, solid, comfortable furniture built to last—and also to survive an active child. Saranne rested her hand on the seventy-year-old couch piled high with colorful cushions where her toddler self had played at mountain climbing.

"Sorry." Rina made a production of searching through her bag so she wouldn't have to glance anywhere else—or meet Saranne's eyes. "It was just—unexpected."

"Yeah, I guess your folks wouldn't want you to learn how the other half lives. Or rather, the other ninety percent."

Rina fumbled a little at that, and Saranne couldn't resist twisting the knife a little. "I guess they'd be so disappointed with your own transgressions."

Now Rina actually winced. *Don't push it,* Saranne warned herself.

Rina brought out an old grimoire, looking odd with a fringe of Post-its jotted over with cabalistic symbols sticking out. She also had several candles and some vials of various colored powders. "Where do you want to do it?" Rina asked.

"I thought the kitchen table would be good." Saranne looked doubtfully at the spell makings. "Unless you're going to be scorching a pentagram or something." Because of her disability, she'd never been allowed into the spell casting labs.

"Nothing like that," Rina assured her. "And you have the other stuff?"

Saranne dug in her pocket and came out with an earring—half of Mom's favorite pair. She wore them almost all the time, which made them perfect for what the girls were about to do. Then Saranne unclipped the chain she wore, removing the prism pendant that Mom had given her when she was little. Again, this was something that had rested against Saranne's skin almost all her life.

"Okay, this will involve the principles of contagion and similarity." Rina must really have felt nervous to be rehashing the theoretical part of the spell, something that Saranne had already outlined. "I tried to find an existing spell with the same sort of structure, so we could get the effect you want with only a little tweaking. Oddly enough, the closest turned out to be a spell for creating a love token."

"You think I don't love my mother?" Saranne could feel her face getting hard.

"No, no," Rina said hastily. "I meant I was looking for a spell with the same kind of . . . connection."

"Oh." Saranne relaxed a little, realizing that this whole thing was making her a little nervous, too. "Now, you'll need these things to be wrapped together in something, don't you?"

Rina nodded. "The spell doesn't actually specify. It would be a twist of canvas, or a felt jewelry bag could do the trick—"

"How about this?" Saranne reached into her pocket again. This time she came out with a small knit figure, a smiley-faced monkey with a long pipestem tail. The head and lower body were already stuffed, but the chest remained empty—and open.

"You made this?" Rina asked as Saranne deposited the little figure in her hand.

"Yeah." Saranne hadn't just inherited something of Mom's artistic talent. A bit of Dad's nimble fingers had gone into her makeup, too.

"It'll be fine," Rina said. "I brought a scrap of silk to wrap up the jewelry bits and a couple of essences. Then we can put the whole thing inside this."

"You can," Saranne told her.

Rina shook her head. "You have to be here, too.

This isn't just any—" she fumbled for a moment—"normal—connection we're making."

"But what if I screw it up?" Saranne asked. "What if this condition of mine sucks all the *manna* out of everything in the middle of the spell?"

"We don't have a choice." Rina's voice sounded desperate. "I tried every compendium I could think of—this one has been in the family since the 1700s. It's not like we're trying to catch the fancy of some passing stranger. What you want is a bond that I've never seen attempted before. It's not going to work unless you're physically present."

Saranne spend a moment in hard thought. "But I won't actually be participating, will I? You don't need me to chant or anything?"

Rina shook her head.

"Then this is the way it will have to be," Saranne told her.

In the kitchen, Saranne looked up at one of the blackened beams Dad had uncovered and restored. Behind her, Rina worked on the table. Saranne closed her eyes and did her best to shut her ears as her cousin started chanting behind her. Luckily, this spell needed no dramatic invocations or Words of Power. It was designed to be a personal, private bit of magic.

Even so, the spell made its presence know through Saranne's other senses—the smell of the candles, beeswax impregnated with various essences, some sharp, some almost unbearably sweet. Magic showed in the subtle play of forces within the room, invisible but not impalpable, as the gooseflesh on Saranne's arms testified.

The unexpected flash of light penetrated even Saranne's closed eyelids, but that was nothing to the sudden vibration deep within her, as if a disembodied finger had penetrated her soul to pluck at her heartstrings—a resonance demonstrating that the spell had taken.

Rina handed over the completed charm, and Saranne sewed up the opening in the yarn body with trembling fingers, still afraid of destroying the magic within.

"Now all you have to do is touch it to your mother and keep it close to her," Rina said.

Saranne gestured toward the pipestem tail. "I'll use that to hook it over the headboard of her bed. If anybody asks, it's a get-well mascot."

None of the mundane medical types would realize that this good luck charm was the real thing.

"You want a soda or something?" Saranne had stocked up on snacks, figuring that Rina might need a little refreshment after her unauthorized spell casting.

Rina declined the offer, obviously eager to get out of there even as she struggled to be polite.

She paused in the doorway, though, to ask the question that was uppermost in her mind. "So now we're square, right?" In spite of her best efforts, a note of pleading crept into Rina's voice. "You won't need to talk to Old Arminius or anyone else?"

"As long as the charm works," Saranne told her coolly.

She paced around the parlor, impatiently waiting for Rina to get out of the area before Saranne showed her own eagerness, rushing off to the hospital.

Mom's room was dim when Saranne arrived. It made a kind of heartless sense. Why bother with even a reading light when the patient wasn't aware enough to appreciate it?

Still, Saranne found herself glad for the shadows as she took out the charm. Dangling it by the tip of its flexible tail, she let the magical monkey touch Mom's forehead. Saranne staggered as if she'd been pulled off her feet, fighting a sudden feeling of weakness and vertigo. Almost instinctively, she pulled the yarn figure back and found her footing become steadier. The voracious pull diminished to a barely perceptible draw. Saranne permitted herself a quick smile, hooking the monkey charm's tail so it would hang directly over Mom.

The spell worked! It would channel energy—vitality—from Saranne to Mom, helping her to recover.

When Dad arrived that evening, Saranne sat reading aloud beside the bed. She looked up from her book. "They say that reading is good for people in comas." Her lips quirked in a grin. "I just hope Mom doesn't mind that it's an assignment for school."

Dad's eyes flicked to the brightly colored yarn animal hanging from the headboard. "I made it for good luck," Saranne said. "You told me that Mom used to call me Monkey when I was really little."

That got a dubious look from Dad, but he didn't say anything. Instead, he went to the other side of the bed and held Mom's hand as Saranne kept reading. That was fine, except for the fact that she kept yawning at least once per page.

Finally, Dad said, "Let's get you fed and put to bed. I know you haven't gotten much rest over these past few days. Do you have any more homework to do?"

Saranne yawned again. "Nothing that can't be put off."

She went home and slept like the proverbial log. The only problem was that when she got up the next morning, she still felt tired.

Saranne went to the kitchen, where Dad had left a bowl of cornflakes and some fruit for her on his way out the door earlier. Grabbing a bottle of milk and a spoon, she began wolfing down the cereal, suddenly ravenous.

"Guess I'm eating for two these days," she told herself with a laugh. That didn't make the hunger go away, though. Saranne found herself scrounging through the refrigerator for something extra, finally constructing two peanut butter and jelly sandwiches, which she polished off in short order.

That day at lunch, she astounded the cafeteria staff by asking for extra helpings of everything. Even then, her stomach began making embarrassing noises in the middle of her last period.

Saranne went home, fixed herself another snack, and headed off for the hospital.

By the end of the next week, Saranne and Dad fell into a pattern. She would go to the hospital and do homework, reading aloud to Mom. Dad would get over there after work, visit Mom for a while, and then he and Saranne would either grab a bite to eat or get some takeout.

It wasn't so very different from the times when Mom would be working against a big deadline. Though Mom was usually the chef of the family, at times like those, Dad and Saranne had to fend for themselves. They'd have to bring food into Mom's studio and force her to eat.

Dad's eyebrows rose a lot over how much Saranne was packing away, but he didn't want to say anything. She figured he was probably afraid to shatter whatever facade of normality they had going.

The staffers at the hospital were a bit nonplussed, too. Mom's vital signs had been steadily declining since she'd been admitted. Now, however, they held steady. Some days, they even showed improvement.

The days kept getting shorter as autumn waned toward winter. Mom's vitals continued slowly but steadily edging upward. Saranne, on the other hand, showed signs of slowing down. Dad began hinting that she might start up with the Art Club again, at least a couple of days a week.

Saranne knew that wasn't going to happen. She didn't have enough energy these days to handle her regular homework, much less extracurricular activities. Except for the reading she did with Mom, Saranne was falling further and further behind on assignments.

Often, after a day in school, she felt so tired that even the stuff she read aloud didn't stick in her memory.

So what if my grades end up in the toilet? That won't show until the end of the quarter, Saranne thought. *At the rate Mom is going, she should be back by then.*

So Saranne kept on with the program until she got a jolt one day when she arrived at the hospital. "I'm afraid your mother had a bit of a downtick today," the young woman on duty at the nurse's station told her. Was it her imagination, or did Saranne really detect a sense of satisfaction, even relief, under the concern the nurse was projecting? That nature was finally taking its course?

Saranne didn't have time to consider any of that. Instead, she ran into Mom's room without a word. It took her only a second to see that the charm was no longer in place on the headboard. "Where's Mom's lucky monkey?" she demanded.

The nurse looked a little taken aback. "I guess we moved it when we were tidying up today—"

Saranne's eyes roved the room, finally spotting the knitted figure on the bedside table—farther away from Mom. Carefully picking up the charm by its tail, she restored the monkey to its position on the headboard.

"Maybe it's silly," she said over her shoulder to the nurse, hoping she wasn't laying it on too thick. "But it's been good luck for Mom since we put it up. At least it gives Dad and me some hope."

The monkey remained undisturbed after that.

In the next week, the weather took a real turn for the worse. Saranne never had a problem with the chills before, but now it seemed she felt the cold right in her bones. Winter was coming early this year, and winter in Massachusetts was definitely not for sissies. Salem's location on the coast meant that the air was damp. Add a chill in the wind, and the air developed a rawness that cut through coats, sweaters, and Saranne's flesh itself.

Too bad stuffing myself hasn't worked, she thought. *Looks as if I could do with a nice, thick layer of blubber.*

Even when she was really chowing down, Saranne hadn't gained weight. Then her appetite began to flag. It quickly got to the point where she couldn't even look at all the food she used to inhale. Just managing to eat the amount she usually did was beyond her.

Saranne paid no attention to the effects of the Secret Spell Diet until one evening when she looked up from pushing food around her dinner plate to find her father staring at her.

"Are you okay, Dad?" she asked.

He just shook his head. "It's just—I never realized before how much you look like your mother."

After dinner, Saranne took a long look at herself in the bathroom mirror. She knew she couldn't wear what she called her "fat pants" anymore, and even her skinny pants were getting kind of loose. But the image reflected in the mirror came to her as a shock. It *was* Mom's face looking back at her—Mom before she got sick (or at least too sick), Mom with hair, although she'd never have let it get so long and tangled.

"Whoa," Saranne said in a quiet voice. She even had the famous Browne cheekbones, just as Mom had predicted she would. Is this why guys had suddenly started talking to her in the halls between classes?

It didn't matter. Nothing did until Mom was safely back among the living.

Soon enough, Saranne had a hard time believing she'd ever gone through a phase of gorging herself. Just looking at food sent a sick feeling through the pit of her stomach. Instead, she found herself using what seemed like gallons of mouthwash to get rid of the strange metallic taste in the back of her throat. It reminded her of the time when she was three and had climbed the bookcase in the parlor to lick the brass statuette on the top shelf. Mom had nearly blown a gasket over that.

Now, though, that brassy taste kept growing until it finally overwhelmed every other flavor in Saranne's mouth. She wound up popping the very strong lemon balls Mom had just about lived on before going to the hospital.

Funny little blisterlike sores began popping up, first on Saranne's hands and wrists, then on other parts of her body. She just put ointment on them, thankful that the cold weather kept her covered up in long-sleeved sweaters.

Saranne had a harder time hiding the narcoleptic fits that began hitting during the school day. One moment she'd be fine and alert, at least as alert was she could expect to be these days. The next, she'd be out—not zoned out, but dead asleep.

Most teachers didn't even say anything—maybe they thought it was a commentary on their lecturing style. They would just take the opportunity to make a loud noise—coughing or dropping a big, heavy book on their desks.

At least, that was pretty much what happened until Saranne fell out in the middle of alchemy class. Magister Arminius took it personally, hollering at her in a mixture of English, Latin, and German. Usually he'd have backed up his invective with a couple of nasty sendings, but even in his anger he remembered that would be a waste of energy—Saranne's inexplicable ability would just ground his spells.

"I–I'm sorry, Magister," Saranne stumbled through an apology if only to stop the yelling. "I don't feel—"

A sudden lurch in her stomach gave her an instant's warning to run for the wastebasket in the front of the class. She didn't have all that much to heave up—just a piece of toast, some tea, a lot of bile, and some liquefied lemon sour balls. She blinked as the smell wafted up at her, afraid it would start her off again.

"You are excused, Miss Cowan." Old Arminius pointed to the door.

Beneath his outstretched arm, Saranne saw Rina Browne's horrified face staring at her.

Saranne stood in the girl's bathroom. She'd already washed out her mouth several times. A paper towel soaked in cold water covered her face, helping her to revive.

That's when she heard the door open. "You've got to stop this." Saranne recognized the voice—it was Rina Browne.

Peeling away the towel, Saranne looked at her cousin.

"I didn't realize how far things had gone till this afternoon," Rina said. "You've got to break the spell. When you came to me with this idea, we specifically excluded the Black Arts, because of what your mother could become. But don't you see, Saranne? This spell is turning your mom into a vampire before she's even dead—she's sucking the life out of you!"

"Mom's almost back now," Saranne talked over her cousin's words. "Maybe if I went to the hospital and pushed it—"

"Maybe it will kill you!" Rina cried. "If you won't stop this, I–I'll tell."

Saranne glared at Rina. "Yeah? If you do that, you'll have to tell everything." She stalked out of the girls' room, hoping Rina didn't notice her unsteady steps.

She headed for her locker, got her coat, and walked out of Witch High. The sky was giving the full winter preview—it was snowing, although the precipitation that landed was more like sleet. Saranne was glad the route to the crosstown bus was downhill.

Alighting from the bus, Saranne took a deep breath. She had always thought that the three blocks from the bus stop to the hospital ran on level ground, but she'd discovered lately that it was a small but ever more perceptible uphill journey.

Today it was more like scaling the slopes of Kilimanjaro. The wind had veered round till it was in

Saranne's face, scything through her even as it peppered her face with stinging ice pellets.

It's for Mom, Saranne thought as she plodded on. Her heel skidded in the icy accumulation on the sidewalk. Bad, that. If she fell, she might not have the strength to get up.

Pushing one foot in front of the other, Saranne finally made it to the hospital. She went straight to Mom's room. This wasn't the time to deal with comments or questions from any of the nurses.

She had to lean against the headboard of the bed as she took up the charm. Hand trembling, she touched it to Mom's forehead again. The world went gray edged with black. Saranne felt as if she were dropping feet first in a vertiginous descent that would make her earlier near tumble to the pavement about as serious as a sneeze.

But beyond this sickening fall into—whatever—she heard a weak "Saranne?"

Mom's voice.

Saranne struggled to steady herself, but her response came out almost as weakly. "Mom?"

Suddenly she felt two pairs of hands on her upper arms, pulling her back. The room swam into focus. Rina was there—so was Ms. Sanmussen, the Witch High guidance counselor.

And Mom's eyes were open.

"Rina told me everything," Ms. Sanmussen said. "She showed me the spell she attempted."

"Attempted?" the word came out as if Saranne's speaking machinery needed oiling. "But it worked!"

"It worked because you imbued it with something far more than Rina was attempting," the counselor said. "Don't you see, Saranne? You found a way to use your potential. You have it in you to become a great healer—the kind that doesn't come along for generations."

"I guess I should be proud," Mom said softly. "You wanted me around so badly, you finally tapped your abilities." Her whisper grew stern. "But you nearly squandered your talent and your life to bring me back. That won't work, dear. You have to let go."

"So I'm a great healer, but I can't save you?" Bitterness worse than bile filled Saranne's mouth.

"No one has the power to keep two souls burning at once," Mom said. "Not for very long."

"It's the fate of healers—even mundane ones," Ms. Sanmussen said. "They lose those close to them through freak medical conditions."

"You gave me a gift, to see you come into your own life," Mom said. "But you have to let me leave mine. Otherwise—I refuse to live if it means burying my daughter."

Those last words came out in the strongest voice Mom had used yet. She reached to her breast, took hold of the little monkey charm, and clenched it in her hand. "*Recuso,*" Mom said.

The room swung giddily around Saranne. She took a deep breath, feeling stronger than she had in weeks. But Mom—

Mom lay in the bed, her hand to her stilled chest, but a gentle smile remained on her face.

"It's the end," Saranne said as Rina flung her arms around her to hold her tight.

But she also knew it was a beginning.

Homecoming Crone

Pauline J. Alama

Pauline J. Alama's first fantasy novel, *The Eye of Night*, was a finalist for the Compton Crook Award. Her work has appeared in the anthologies *Rotten Relations, Mystery Date*, and *Sword & Sorceress XVIII*. She lives in New Jersey with a supportive husband, an imaginative child, and two cats who are not on speaking terms. A lapsed medieval scholar, she once presented a conference paper on "The Witch Trial of Jesus." This story goes out with thanks to the Writers of the Weird Workshop of the Science Fiction Association of Bergen County and two indispensable witches.

FOUR weeks into her first term at Witch High, Maria Caspari was starting to wonder if the Spanish Inquisition would have been better for her health.

It was a lot like the junior high she'd escaped from, but here, the Wicked clique didn't just have cool clothes and cutting remarks. They had designer wands and the latest curses.

They ran in a pack like jackals, and when they fused their powers, they could do some ugly stuff. It had taken her an hour in the nurse's office to unravel the spell they'd cast on her that morning: painful boils, some in unmentionable places. She'd missed Spell Composition, her best class. Now it was time for lunch, and she wasn't sure she wanted to brave the cafeteria. The Wickeds would be there, and they'd probably curse her with nausea.

She slunk downstairs to the crypt level to get her lunch from her locker. If only she'd mastered that Summon Remote Object spell in the back of the text! Crypt level was full of blind alleys, perfect for ambush. Why hadn't the school administration closed them? Were they Wicked too, or just dense?

Round a corner, she encountered an unexpected sight: the Wickeds closing in on someone else, for a change.

The victim was a girl in a peasant blouse decked with bright Indian embroidery and little round mirrors. Her face was as bland as the blouse was flashy: milky pale, WASPish, framed with light brown hair. Probably a Witches of the American Revolution kid; those Old Salem snobs gave Maria almost as much grief as the Wickeds. Still, she had to feel for the girl, with all those Wicked wands pointed at her.

Bella Rizzo towered over the bohemian from the height of stiletto heels, pointing a lipstick at her and snarling, "You're gonna tell Featherby you cheated."

"I didn't," the girl said calmly.

"*I didn't,*" Bella mimicked. "Listen, grade-grubber. You're going to tell Featherby you *did*, or else—"

"Or else what?" The girl narrowed her eyes at the lipstick. "You'll give me a tacky makeover?"

Maria flinched. Bella's lipstick was a wand, and a powerful one. The hippie WASP was in for a nasty surprise.

"Hey! Leave her alone!" Maria charged at the Wickeds without any idea what she meant to do to them. Her wand wasn't even out—not that it mattered, since she hadn't gotten the hang of wand work yet.

Bella's sidekick Taylor smirked at her. "Hey, look—the freak and the geek."

"Coming to save your lover?" sneered Lindzee, and all the Wickeds cackled.

"Think they'll go to Homecoming together?" snorted Taylor. "Which one will be Homecoming Queen?"

"You mean Homecoming Crone!" Bella pointed her lipstick at Maria and fired off a curse. Maria felt her knees stiffen, her back bend. She looked down at her aching hands and saw her grandmother's gnarled old claws.

She glared at Bella with eyes full of fire. Behind the Wickeds, a wastebasket burst into flame.

"Shit," said Taylor, "which one did that?"

"Shit," thought Maria, "I'm gonna get expelled already." With that, Bella's designer handbag exploded in flames.

"Fuckin' A!" Bella flung the bag away and, jumping straight to the wrong conclusion, pointed her lipstick at the milk-faced girl. All the Wickeds followed suit. Bella snarled, "That was a Fendi. Bitch, you're gonna fuckin' die for that."

White-hot jets of power shot out of every Wicked wand.

"No!" yelled Maria, unable to stop the slaughter.

But the bland-faced bohemian just flung up her arms, catching their force lines on the mirrors sewn to her blouse. Every jet of light reflected back to its origin. In an instant, Bella was writhing in pain, her skin blistered and burned. Taylor was bent double vomiting, and Lindzee, Madisyn, and Tory were just screaming like particularly foul-mouthed banshees.

"You are *so* dead," Bella said, but she uttered that threat in retreat as her beaten band turned and fled.

The girl in the mirror blouse turned to Maria. "Thanks for coming to the rescue."

"You didn't need rescuing," Maria muttered, shamefaced.

"No," the girl admitted, "But it was kind of novel, having someone on my side. You on your way to lunch? Can I buy you a slice?"

"Um, cool," Maria said. It was the first time all month someone had wanted to eat with her, let alone replace the stale sandwich in her locker with something more appetizing. "But what about—?" She gestured mutely at the wastebasket and Bella's abandoned bag, still burning. "I don't wanna burn the school down. I mean, not exactly. Yet."

"So earth the power," the girl said.

"Oh." Maria had read about the technique, but so far, they hadn't raised enough power in her classes to need much earthing. "Um—"

"Freshman, aren't you? I'll help. Grab my hand. We'll gather the fire back into you, and from there into the ground."

It sounded impossible—even dangerous, bringing all that fire back inside her—but when the stranger grasped her hand, Maria felt a coolness like sea air, relieving the heat inside. After that it was easy. She left two scorched footprints on the floor, and the Fendi bag was ash, but at least the ashes were cold.

"Thanks!"

The girl shrugged. "It's nothing. Shall we go?"

"Um, I hate to trouble you, but can you unravel their aging spell?"

"It's gone already," the girl said. "As soon as you took the fire back, the spell burned up. Fire likes you."

"Great," said Maria. "The school hates me, and fire likes me. I am having *such* a great year."

"Yeah, me too," the other girl said. "Let's go."

They went out the fire door that was always propped open and headed for the nearest pizzeria. "So," the bohemian said, "you've had trouble with the Wickeds, too?"

"Since day one," said Maria heavily. "*What* is their problem?"

"Their *problem,*" said the girl, "is that they think it's all about power. And that power always means power *over* someone. And they wouldn't know power from *within* if it bit them on the ass." She brightened. "It will, one of these days."

"Wow. How do you know all this stuff? Who are you, anyway?"

"Holly Mays," the girl said. "You?"

"Maria Caspari."

"What do you like?"

"Huh?"

"On your pizza," Holly said, as she led the way into the hot and crowded pizzeria.

They ordered and waited. The noise in Nona's was deafening, but Maria was too full of questions to wait. She hissed in Holly's ear, "What was Bella foaming at the mouth about?"

Holly grinned. "I got 100 percent on Ms. Featherby's Magical Theory test."

It took Maria a moment to grasp the ramifications. "Featherby grades on a curve!"

Holly nodded. "They all failed. They were trying to intimidate me into lying, telling Featherby I cheated, so I'd fail, the curve would change, and they'd pass. Hey, is it my fault they suck at theory? If Daddy buys you a wand preloaded with spells, you don't learn, do you?"

They took their pizza onto the school lawn. At first Maria glanced around nervously for their enemies, but Holly murmured something inaudible and a sphere of mist formed around them. "Stealth bubble. That should give us a few minutes' private conversation."

"Wow," Maria said. "That's senior-level magic. Are you—?"

"Sophomore," said Holly. "I do a lot of independent study."

Maria eyed her appreciatively. "You can do so much stuff already, and you're only a year ahead of me. I'm dying to know what you did to the Wickeds with the mirrors."

Holly smiled. "Nothing, in a sense. Everything they

do is bound to come back to them, sooner or later. I just sped it up."

"How?"

"I sort of make like the moon, the way it reflects everything that comes to it."

"I wish I could do that! I—I don't know anything," Maria said, feeling dangerously close to tears, or worse, combustion.

"But you've got a lot of raw power," Holly said. "Those fires!"

"Power, sure. But I can't control it." Maria sighed. "There used to be a lot of magi in my family, but now it's rare. The last one was my great-aunt, and she died before she could teach me anything. These are her clothes." Maria furiously clutched her shapeless off-white skirt. "They're charmed against self-immolation. I haven't learned to do it myself, so I'm stuck wearing hers for safety. She wasn't much for color."

"At least your complexion has some color to it," Holly said appeasingly. "Think how much worse it'd look on *me*."

"Everyone in the family says it's great that I'm a mage, but they treat me like a ticking bomb. Come to think of it, I *am* a ticking bomb. Aunt Clara spontaneously combusted in the *shower*. I could do that, too, any minute."

"Hell of a thing to have hanging over you," Holly sympathized. She didn't back away. Maria's respect for her rose another notch.

"What about you?" Maria said. "I bet you come from a total witch family, learned spell casting at your mother's knee and all that."

Holly laughed. "Yes and no. I was raised in the Craft, but you'd be amazed how closed-mouthed Mom can be about anything with power to it. 'Coven secrets, dear.' But at least she didn't lock up her books."

"Maybe . . . could you teach me?" Maria said. "I hate feeling stupid. In my old school, I was, you know . . ."

"Normal?" Holly guessed.

Maria shook her head. "Like you. The one that wrecked the curve. It wasn't always fun, but at least it was a familiar sort of isolation. Then puberty hits and congratulations, I'm a fire mage. Wherever I go, things burn. I get into Witch High, and suddenly I'm in Remedial Magical Practice with everyone else who can't control their magic: a few werewolves who go wolf at the full moon, a were cocker spaniel who goes dog at the half-moon, and this girl who drools snakes and cockroaches when she speaks. They all gang up on me when the teacher's not looking. Well, all except the cocker spaniel, when he's a dog. They're a friendly breed."

"If you're having so much trouble," Holly said, "why stick your neck out to defend a stranger?"

"Well, they make me mad!" Maria said. "The Wickeds think they own the school. And the other kids let them. Even the teachers seem scared of them. It's–it's–it's just wrong."

"Yeah," Holly said. "You want to do something about that?"

"Boy, would I love to. But what could *I* do?"

"Wrong question," Holly said. "It's more like, what could *we* do? Fire's my weak element. I'm really strong with water and air. But you, you're like fire with a face. We could make a great team."

Maria's black eyes grew wide. "You think we could work together?"

"I think we just about have to," Holly said. "I've been, well, scrying on the Wickeds. I think they're planning something really vicious."

"Aren't they always?"

"Something big. Whatever it is, I want to derail it. You want to help me?"

She almost protested that she couldn't do anything. But just being asked made Maria feel twice the mage she'd been that morning. "I'm in!"

* * *

Holly invited her over to study the next afternoon. Maria approached the Mays house warily. It was, as she had suspected, very Old Salem: a landmark gabled house full of impeccably well kept antiques. On either side of the fireplace were tasteful alcoves with gleaming classical statues of Artemis and Apollo.

Holly swept past this grandeur into a small bedroom that seemed entirely carpeted with books. "Welcome to my lair. Pull up an encyclopedia and sit down. We can work here, if you don't mind the mess."

"I love it," Maria said. "It's like a library without the obsessive-compulsive cataloging system. Is this where you work with your, um, coven?"

Holly looked sheepish. "I've been, uh, working solo, which is an entirely valid path for a witch, with, you know, many historical precedents."

Maria suppressed the impulse to respond, "So, you don't have any friends either?" Instead she said, "Anyway, I doubt you want me experimenting in *here*. Pity to set all this on fire."

"Oh!"

"I usually work—well, in the bathroom, you know. Less flammable, even if Aunt Clara did manage to combust in one."

"All right," Holly said, "we've got bathrooms, too." She grabbed two plastic action figures off her nightstand and led the way to an imposing marble bathroom with gleaming brass fixtures. She set her two action figures on the rim of the tub and sat next to them.

"Um, are those—what are they for?"

"Well, they're not necessary—we do entirely secular magic in school, of course, since it's public school—but at home I like to have my goddess and god figures with me," Holly said.

Maria stared at them. They looked an awful lot like comic-book superheroes.

"Hey, they've got more personal meaning to me than those museum replicas Mom and Dad use," Holly said defensively.

"Yeah," said Maria. "I have a couple of images, too, that I don't show in school." She pulled from her pocket two laminated holy cards: a Sacred Heart image of Jesus and a Madonna of the Revelation crowned with stars.

Holly raised her eyebrows for a moment. Then she shrugged. "Dion Fortune said all gods are one."

"Cool," Maria said. "Now, how should we start?"

"What have you been working on?"

Maria winced. "Mainly methods of containing the inner fire. None of them work. It seems like the harder I try, the more it breaks out. Today I set the fire extinguisher on fire."

Holly considered. "Have you tried making the fire your friend?"

"Huh?"

"Look, it's part of you. Like, maybe it's your gift? Get to know it." She squinted at the Sacred Heart picture. "How come your Jesus has flames on his heart?"

"I don't know," Maria admitted. She'd always been drawn to this picture: Jesus with his heart bursting out of his chest as if he couldn't contain it. She'd never asked questions about it.

"He's perfect for you," Holly said. "Why don't you, like, meditate on that while I get some candles?"

She returned with brand-new beeswax candles, probably from certified organic beekeepers, in a gleaming candelabrum. Holly struck a match, lit one, and set the candelabrum on the toilet tank for lack of a better level space.

"What should I do with that?" Maria said.

"Just look at it, for now," Holly said. "You see fire as something that burns houses down. But think how important your kind must have been back when you couldn't just turn on the stove. There must have been times when the fire mage was the life of the tribe."

Maria gazed into the flame, trying not to glance uneasily at the snow-white lace curtain in the window behind it.

The curtain caught fire.

"Okay, so we have a little excess," Holly said. "We can handle it. You're going to take that fire back into yourself and earth it, just as you did in school. You were okay then, and you'll be okay now. And if things get too hot for you, I'll help."

When Holly put it that way, it didn't sound impossible. Maria opened her eyes wide and took the fire back in.

Holly inspected the curtain. "Hey, you're getting better at this. It's barely scorched."

Maria cringed, wondering what the parents who'd paid for the elegant curtain would say when they found it "barely scorched."

But Holly's spirits didn't flag. "Now, I wonder if you could try something. Can you take the candle flame into yourself, even though it didn't come from you?"

Maria bit her lip. Was Holly trying to trick her into self-immolating? "Can *you* do it?" she challenged.

Holly stared at the candle a few moments, then shook her head. "Fire's not my element. But maybe we could do it together." She set the candelabrum on the floor between them and took both Maria's hands, making a circle of their arms. Again, Maria felt a welcome coolness in her touch. Together they enveloped the tiny flame, and in an instant, it was not on the candle wick at all. In the air between the girls hovered a bright spark of heat. For a few moments they let the spark float between them, before it came to Maria like a dog to its mistress, and she let it in.

"Awesome!" Holly breathed. "Now can you put it back on the candle?"

Full of fresh confidence, Maria fixed her eyes on the candle and tried to breathe the flame back onto it.

The result was a bit unexpected.

"Oh! Sorry! I guess I misaimed. I'll take that back—"

"No, don't just yet," said Holly, turning to the mirror to admire her hair, which had turned red. "In fact, leave it this way. I like it."

After that, magic sessions with Holly became the highlight of Maria's life. They practiced water magic by the docks, where Maria set some floating garbage on fire, stirring up a furor about the local marine environment. But such mistakes became rarer, and Maria's confidence grew.

She felt ready for anything by the time Holly announced that she had found out the Wickeds' plans: "They're scheming to take over Homecoming."

"Is that all? The fiendish plot is to win a *popularity contest?*"

"It's not a popularity contest. At least, not this year," Holly said. "Haven't you heard? They're bringing back the traditional Homecoming Rites that were banned in 1950. It's controversial, of course, because of the 1949 disaster—"

"What happened?"

Holly frowned. "I couldn't find out exactly. I think the administration must have used magic Bindings to hush it up. But the yearbook has a black-rimmed picture of a girl who died that year, and the Homecoming Mysteries have been banned ever since."

"Homecoming *Mysteries?*"

Holly nodded. "The traditional crowning of the Homecoming Queen goes back to ancient rites of sovereignty and fertility. The school is built on ground consecrated to the powers of earth by the first Salem witches. They tapped those powers to protect the colony from hostile forces, human or natural. Some say their rites never lost power over the prosperity and security of the land—and today it's not just Massachusetts but the whole United States."

"National security in the hands of some teenage queen bee?" Maria gulped. "No wonder they banned it."

"You see the problem?" Holly said. "There's one more thing about 1949. Ever hear about McCarthyism?"

"You bet," Maria said. "My dad says his father lost his job in that witch-hunt—um, I mean Red Scare."

"Exactly," Holly said. "Total paranoia about national security. It happened just a few months after Homecoming went wrong."

"You think it came from here?"

Holly shrugged. "There's no way to prove it. But if someone screws around with rites designed for the protection of the land, that's just the sort of madness I'd expect."

"And if the Wickeds take control of the rites, that's just the sort of thing they'd make of it: persecuting people who are different."

"Right," Holly said. "Not that they're interested in politics. They'd just see it as one more way of getting power in the narrow things they care about."

"*They* may not be interested in politics," Maria mused, "but maybe their demons are."

"Their *what?*" Holly choked.

"Demons," Maria said. "Didn't you know? That's why they're not afraid of karma. The demons tell them they won't suffer the consequences of their actions. Of course, they lie."

"Hold on," Holly said. "I know you're not from a witch family, but let's get this straight: We do *not* use demons to do magic."

"Oh, I know *you* don't use demons," Maria said. "But the Wickeds do. I see them."

"See what? Guys with horns?"

"No, no! That's the cartoon version," Maria said. "They're spirits gone bad. I see them as a–a sort of nasty aura. I thought you could see them, too. I started seeing them around the same time I started working with you. Wait, no," she said, as the thought struck her for the first time, "It really started with Bella's aging spell. Like I aged into the Sight, or something.

But even before I could see them, I knew about demons from Aunt Clara's diaries. They seduce people with promises of power over others, but they only want to enslave us all. My kind have fought them for generations."

Holly wrinkled her forehead. "So, like, you think you're supposed to kill these demons?"

"Not kill," Maria said. "That would make us no better than them."

"Good. Because, in case I forgot to tell you, everything you do—"

"—comes back to me. I know. But anyway, no one can kill a demon. They're immortal. But magi can, like, recycle them."

"WHAT?"

"They need a link to some earthly being to act in this world. Magi try to detach them, send them back to their sphere. They always reappear in another form, but it takes time. Besides, every time they come back, they get another choice between good and evil. Every now and then, one of them decides to change. Usually that takes much more than detaching: sacrifice, love unto death, perfect forgiveness, that sort of thing. Way out of my league. I don't think I'm up to forgiving Bella, much less her demon."

"Whoa." Holly put a hand to her head. "I'm having trouble fitting this into my worldview."

Maria shrugged. "That's how I've felt about most things I've learned at Witch High. And some things I learned with you." She looked at the ground. "Are we still partners?"

"Of course," Holly said. "I've just got to get my brain around this. So, if you're right, it's really the demons that want to take over Homecoming."

"Yeah. The Wickeds probably just *think* it's their idea."

"Whether it's the Wickeds or something behind them," Holly said, "they'll want one of their clique to be Homecoming Queen."

Maria nodded. "Probably Bella. Her demon's the boss."

"So's she. All the others are just me-toos. Imagine Queen B robed in powers of Sovereignty. She'd start World War Three."

"So, is our job to keep the ritual pure, so they can't take it over?"

"I don't know," Holly said. "The rite goes back before democracy as we know it. Some witches gloss over that, like we've always been one happy democratic family, indivisible under Goddess, with liberty and justice for all—but I don't buy it. Back then, people believed in kings and queens, and this is about crowning a queen. Maybe they were right to ban it."

"Then are we trying to stop it?"

Holly shook her head. "It's too late to stop it. Mom's in the PTA, and she says the principal's already summoned the Mysterious Stranger who chooses the Homecoming Queen. You don't just disinvite a powerful spiritual entity."

"Should we tell them about it?"

"I tried," Holly said. "Even Mom doesn't believe me."

"Then what can we do?"

"I don't exactly know," Holly confessed. "But look, there are different kinds of power. We know the Wickeds believe in power *over* people, and they'll reinforce those strains of Sovereignty. But you and I, we believe in power that doesn't make someone else powerless. If we're there—and if we can raise enough power together—maybe we can draw the rite toward our kind of power."

They skipped the football game and the parade—modern innovations of no importance to the rite, Holly said—and met in the evening, ready for the dance.

"Hey, you look fabulous!" Holly gushed when Maria came to the door.

"Thanks," Maria said. She was still stuck with Aunt Clara's wardrobe, but it was colorless no longer. She'd tie-dyed her dress in fire colors, vermilion and gold. It didn't look like something to wear to Homecoming, but it didn't look like Aunt Clara, either. "So do you."

Holly's hair was still red, reflected over and over in the mirrors on her blouse. "Thanks," she said. "Come out to the back yard. We need to touch the earth today."

Shivering under the bare trees, they cast a circle amid brown oak leaves, then held hands and breathed slowly, listening to each other until they breathed in unison.

"Now?" Maria said at last.

Holly nodded.

They'd agreed in advance that neither should take precedence; each would invoke her deity simultaneously. Their two voices wove into each other, fragments of each invocation ringing out in the other's pauses:

"You do not want your children to be slaves . . ."

". . . raise up the lowly, cast down the mighty . . ."

". . . that gives life to the cosmos . . ."

". . . sets captives free . . ."

". . . mother of all . . ."

". . . prince of peace . . ."

". . . touch us, change us!"

". . . renew the face of the earth!"

By the time they'd done chanting, their arms seemed to encircle a mountain of power, its roots deep in earth, its summit in the clouds, its heart in both their hearts. But they did not know how they could carry it to school.

They need not have worried. The power carried them where they were needed. Without taking a step, they found themselves in the Old Gymnasium on the crypt level, where the Homecoming Dance was beginning.

Loud pop music pulsed from enormous speakers. Maria raised her eyebrows. "*This* is Traditional Homecoming?"

"*Don't drop the energy,*" Holly hissed. "Chill out. There's a reason for everything. The flickering strobe lights. The throbbing bass."

"Inducing trance?" Maria guessed.

"Yeah."

"Should we go along with it?"

"I think so," Holly said. "The gods that brought us here won't stand us up. Trust them. Dance."

They joined the undulating crowd, dancing with everyone and with no one, according to the ancient tradition of girls at high school dances. They did not watch each other; each one scanned the room to see what would happen. Nonetheless, they always sensed the link between them, the power they bore together like a team of yoked horses.

For a time, Maria almost passed into dream, hypnotized by the rhythms and the strobe lights and the forces swirling around her: the deep-earth energies of the Homecoming Mysteries and the bright dance of fire and water between herself and Holly. Then another rhythm broke into her dream, sharp and jarring: the demon power of the Wickeds.

She turned toward them with her eyes half lidded, keeping their fire in check.

Beside her, Holly murmured, "Sorry I doubted you."

"Hmm?"

"It must be the shared power. I see the demons now, too."

"We can handle them," Maria said, hoping it was true.

"Look, Taylor," Lindzee trilled, "you were right: here's the freak and the geek dancing together."

"Oh, my gawd," Taylor drawled, "Caspari, it's dark in here, but not dark enough to hide your ugly face."

For once, Maria had the perfect response. "Is it too

dark for you to see what you're carrying? Now *that's* what I call ugly."

"Who asked you, dyke?"

Part of Maria wanted to lash back, but something buoyed her up, raising her above the taunt. She went on as if Taylor hadn't spoken. "You think you're driving the demon, but it drives you. You think it feeds you, but in the end, it'll eat you."

"Shut up, asshole!"

The Queen B herself bestowed a glance on them. "You two are so dead. Don't you know they've restored the old Homecoming Mysteries? This year's queen will have real power over things on the earth and under the earth. And my first act as queen will be to bury you."

Holly cut in. "*You'll* bury us? What makes you so sure *you'll* be queen?"

Bella rolled her eyes. "Whattya think, the Mysterious Stranger's gonna pick a lame ass like you?"

"Who said I was thinking of myself?" said Holly mildly. "But we'll find out soon enough. Here he comes!"

They all followed her gaze to the Stranger, a shadow among the strobe lights, cloaked, hooded, and gloved in black. His black mask was fringed with feathers in the colors of autumn, apple-red and grain-gold, the only touch of color about him. Not an inch of skin could be seen.

"Tall," murmured Bella. "Must be one of the basketball team."

Holly snorted—and then was silent, intent only on the Stranger.

He sailed through the dance with the grace of a professional among amateurs. He moved through the room like the wind, passing from point to point without seeming to touch down between them. He flowed from girl to girl like a heartbreaker, now dividing a couple, now partnering a solitary girl for a few measures before leaving her as lonely as before. He lifted his masked face as if scenting the wind, made a slow, searching turn, then moved on, all without ceasing to dance.

Bella strutted toward him with a sultry swing of the hips. The black-robed stranger bowed to her, then twirled and slipped away before she could follow.

"Tease!" Bella hissed, and stalked after him, her catlike grace a match for his own, her silk sheath dress as black as his cloak, her glittering nails as red as the feathers around his mask. Every nail-tip was charged with demon energy. A glittering net of power extended from her fingers.

For a moment Maria despaired. The stranger was as predatory as Bella and as drunk on power. Surely he was only toying with them all. Surely any moment he would turn again and choose Bella as his queen.

But instead, he offered his arm to Holly.

Bella leveled her wand. Her demon gathered its forces to spring upon her rival.

Maria rushed at her, screaming the only distraction she could think of: "You're wrong, Bella. I'm the one who torched your Fendi bag!"

Bella dropped her wand in surprise. It rolled away and crunched under another dancer's foot. Her spell misfiring, she spat out a curse that resolved into snakes on the floor.

Sitting next to the snake-drooler in Remedial Magic, Maria had become a connoisseur of snakes. Only one was really dangerous: as luck would have it, a desert creature. "Hot and dry, hot and dry: creature of fire, no less than I. Come be friends!"

Really, it was not so different from taking a flame into herself; as she opened herself, the snake shimmered like a mirage and melted into her inner fire. It wasn't bad, but her skin felt odd. Scaly.

Taking advantage of her distraction, the demon sprang at her—and Maria surprised herself as much as anyone by breathing fire from her mouth, enveloping the demon in flame. With a sharp cry, it lost its grip on the material world and disappeared.

One down, four to go, Maria thought. It was only when she looked down to tick them off on her fingers, and found claws instead, that she noticed she'd become a dragon. Everyone was staring at her in disbelief—everyone except Holly, who grinned at her over the Stranger's shoulder. "I knew you had it in you!" But she never stopped dancing with the Stranger. And he never stopped gazing at his chosen partner, the one person in the room who showed no fear of the dragon.

Suddenly, Maria thought, it was clear: Holly must be Queen. She'd bring their shared power to the queenship and make it benign. The land would prosper, safe and at peace.

But she wasn't the only one who noticed the Stranger's choice. The Wickeds were regrouping. Bella still sat wandless on the floor, tangled in her own snakes, spouting curses that misfired without the demon. But Taylor, Lindzee, Madisyn, and Tory were all training their wands on Holly. Their demons tensed, ready to pounce, as attentive to Holly's every move as the Stranger was.

They must *not* be allowed to interfere. Finding the link between herself and Holly still strong, Maria gave all the shared energy to Holly, shrinking back into human form as Holly shimmered and grew into a creature of winds and dancing tides.

Drained, Maria waited for Holly to defend herself with her doubled power. But the dance went on as if Holly and the Stranger were too entranced to notice the forces gathered against them.

It's up to me, Maria thought. This time it may take a sacrifice. "Hey, you demons! You always like to prey on the weak. Well, here I am, emptied, no power left. Are you still scared of me?"

The Wickeds turned their wands from Holly to Maria, uncertain what to make of her. "You smoking something?" Tory said. The demons simply pounced.

Maria braced herself for the onslaught, but it never came. Holly spun away from her dance partner and caught the demons' power on the million mirror-facets of a sleeve of sea-waves, sending it back to them.

The shock of their reflected power sent the demons shrieking back to their origins. The Wickeds reeled from the blast. Taylor fell stunned. Lindzee's wand shattered. Madisyn broke a spike heel. She fell against her girlfriends, and they all tumbled like bowling pins. Maria found she could almost feel sorry for them: kiss up to Bella, kiss up to demons, and where does it get you? Ass-up on the dance floor with your magenta panties showing.

"Splendidly done," said the Mysterious Stranger. "I am not accustomed to claiming two queens in one year. But I am loath to part so glorious an alliance. Let us see if your courage lasts when you see my face."

Behind the mask grinned a bare, bleached skull. The Stranger unfurled his right hand, and a grave opened in the earth at the center of the dance floor.

"Of course," Holly murmured. "It's what we all come home to."

With his left hand, the Stranger drew from under his cloak something that looked at first like a bloody heart, but proved to be a cut pomegranate. "Daughters of Air and Water, Daughter of Fire, will you be Crones of the Earth?"

Maria's stomach lurched. But Holly was already tasting a seed of the pomegranate.

"You're stepping into that grave?"

Holly shrugged. "It's all right—I think. But you don't have to join me."

"What, upset the balance? Lose my best friend?" Maria reached for a pomegranate seed. "I'm in."

The Stranger smiled. "Only four seeds apiece, my dears. You don't want winter to last too long." He touched a withering-cold hand to each girl's cheek. This time it did not terrify Maria to feel herself aging.

She saw Holly, too, going gray and bent, her blue eyes brighter in a nest of worry lines and laugh lines.

They followed the death's-head into his cavern. "Come, my brave queens. I have much to teach you before the kiss of spring restores your youth."

After that, Maria thought brightly, I'll never need Remedial Magical Practice again.

Late Bloomer

Karen Fox

Karen Fox has always enjoyed adventure and the paranormal, and it shows. Her first two books were futuristic romances for Leisure—the second, *Somewhere My Love,* was a RITA finalist for Best Paranormal. She followed these up with a contemporary fantasy set of four books for Berkley and a time-travel romance and historical romance with a hint of paranormal for Zebra. Following her Air Force husband, she's lived in Tacoma, Charleston, Biloxi, and Belgium while raising three children and working full-time. She works on the annual Pikes Peak Writers Conference and is a member of Pikes Peak Romance Writers and Pikes Peak Writers. A member of The Romance Writer's Association, Karen spent the last four years serving on the National Board of Directors.

"BUT I don't want to go." Fourteen-year-old Abbi Symes turned sideways in the front seat of the car to face her mother. If she had to do this, she'd die. She'd just die.

"No more arguing." Her mother waved her hand toward the passenger door and it swung open. "Now go."

Heaving a dramatic sigh, Abbi snatched her backpack from the floor and climbed from the vehicle.

The weathered redbrick building before her appeared small and decrepit, at odds with the lively chatter rising from the steady stream of students filing inside.

Though the sign on the gate read SALEM TOWNSHIP PUBLIC HIGH SCHOOL, NO. 4, the symbol of the crescent moon and sun below it told her all she needed to know.

Witch High.

She'd heard enough stories about the place from her older brother, Gilbert, to know she didn't belong here. She pivoted to plead once more with her mother, but the car had already turned onto the main street.

She was doomed.

Steps dragging, she joined the flow into the building, then froze as she passed the threshold. *Mab's Marbles!* The interior in no way resembled the exterior. The hallways were wide, the ceilings cavernous, painted to resemble the sky. Illumination from above lit the place as brightly as the sun, yet she saw no discernible lights.

Yeah, this was Witch High, all right.

Jostled from behind, she stumbled forward, then concentrated on finding her first classroom. All first year students were required to take Essential Witchcraft courses in order to pinpoint their inherent magic.

Like that was going to help her.

Here it is. The Art of Healing. She slid into a wooden desk toward the back of room. Maybe no one would notice her there.

Many of the other students knew each other and chatted enthusiastically, sharing which teachers and classes they had. Abbi hadn't gone to any of the below-grades magical tutoring, where the others had probably met each other. Even her parents had agreed it would have been a waste of money.

She managed to remain unnoticed until Mr. Turner called the roll. "Abigail Symes?"

"Here."

Most of the entire class swiveled to look at her, no

doubt recognizing the last name. Symeses were well-known in the witch community. Warmth crept into Abbi's cheeks, and she dropped her gaze to her desk. The teacher continued calling names, and the students' attention moved elsewhere.

"Psst."

Abbi looked up to see the girl in front of her hissing. "Me?"

The girl—Belinda Rochester if Abbi remembered right—smiled. "You're Gil Symes' sister?"

Abbi's answering smile faded. "Yeah."

"He's such a hunk."

She shrugged. Other girls obviously thought so. To her, he was an annoying older brother. They looked nothing alike, Gil being tall, blond, kind of good-looking, and brainy while Abbi was average with carrot-red hair and a peppering of ugly freckles over her face and arms. The only thing they shared were blue eyes.

Gil was a powerful witch. He'd passed Advanced Sorcery in his junior year and now as a senior was taking the Masters of Magic classes. Of course, both their parents were esteemed witches in their own right so it made sense.

Except that Abbi possessed absolutely no magic at all.

Belinda swung back toward the front as Mr. Turner began speaking. "Welcome to the Art of Healing. As you probably know, nearly sixty percent of all witches are born with a natural healing talent. We're going to teach you how to focus that talent and learn some herbal potions and remedies as well. Open your books to page ten. We'll start there."

Abbi had inherited the Symes intelligence, her one good trait, which made book learning easy. However, actual implementation of anything magic caused problems.

Since it was the first day of school, she made it all

the way to her last class before her secret was exposed. Spellcasting. She *hated* spell casting.

The teacher, Ms. Cherry, started with creating fire. Abbi groaned. Every witch there had mastered that skill by age ten. But not her. She couldn't even generate a hint of smoke.

As Ms. Cherry passed, each student curled then opened his or her palm to reveal a ball of flame. Belinda, who'd made it a point to sit next to Abbi in every class they shared, even produced a large cube of fire.

Ms. Cherry paused. "Ah, Ms. Rochester. Excellent. I can see that fire is one of your strengths."

Belinda beamed. Not many witches possessed a mastery of shaping fire. For a majority, the simple creation of fire was enough. Those with the ability to control and use it usually went on to high positions in the Witches' Council.

The teacher stopped by Abbi. "Ms. Symes?"

Closing her eyes, Abbi concentrated with her entire being on igniting a tiny wisp of flame. Nothing.

She opened her eyes to find Ms. Cherry frowning. "You may recite the spell if necessary, Ms. Symes."

Abbi's chest hurt as if her lungs were suddenly too small. She tried again, focusing on her palm. *"Accendo."*

Nothing.

"Can't you make fire?"

Abbi dropped her gaze, her stomach twisting now. "No."

The class exploded with laughter. "Even six-year-olds can make fire," Belinda said, derision coating her words.

Abbi winced. So much for that friendship. Of course, she suspected it had been built more on who her brother was than her own winning personality. "Well, I can't," she snapped.

"Perhaps your talent lies in a different area."

Though Ms. Cherry's words were intended to reassure, Abbi caught the quick rolling of the teacher's eyes as she turned away.

The whispers pelted her at once. "Sure you're Gil Symes' sister—?"

"Probably adopted."

"Shouldn't be here."

Tears welling, Abbi bolted. Not that it helped. Moments later, she was lost, disoriented by the twisting hallways that grew and shrank as she passed through them.

Unable to focus through the blur of her tears, she sank to the floor, her back against the wall. She'd told Mom and Dad she didn't belong here, but they'd insisted she just had to discover her magic. They refused to accept that a child of theirs could be magicless.

Wrapping her arms around her knees, she buried her face on top of them. She wasn't coming back. No one could make her. *No one.*

"Ab? What are you doing here?"

Swallowing hard, she didn't look up. "Go away."

"Come on, Abbi. What is it?" Her brother, Gil, squatted beside her and lifted her chin so he could meet her damp gaze. "Bad first day?"

"I shouldn't be here. I'm not a witch." A sob punctuated her words. "You got all the magic."

"That's not true. You're just a late bloomer."

Anger flared. "Like Mom and Dad haven't been saying that for years. I think if I was going to bloom I'd have done so by now."

"Not necessarily." A new voice intruded, and Abbi focused beyond Gil to see a too-good-looking-to-be-true guy. Dark-haired with equally dark eyes, he smiled at her to reveal twin dimples. Her pulse jumped in response. "Trust me."

"Who . . . ?"

Gil tugged Abbi to her feet. "Ab, this is Rupert Damani. He's taking Advanced Sorcery this year, so

I'm tutoring him." He shot Rupert a rueful grin. "This is my sister, Abbi."

Rupert extended his hand. "Pleased to meet you."

"You . . . too." Half afraid, Abbi placed her palm in his, her gaze focused on the floor. His warm fingers surrounded her hand as he gave it a quick squeeze. She glanced up to see his warm smile still in place.

"Why don't you come with us?" he asked.

"With *you?*" He still held her hand and she found it difficult to speak.

He released his grip so he could use his hands to gesture toward the interior of the school. "I found myself drafted to head up the float brigade this year. I talked Gil into helping me conjure up the float chassis."

"Gil?" She glanced at her brother. Could she?

Gil didn't appear as enthusiastic as Rupert, but he nodded. "Sure. Come with us."

They led her through a winding maze of hallways and staircases until they reached the flightorium. It put the largest state stadium to shame, stretching wider and longer than any football field in existence and boasting a ceiling that disappeared into the heavens. Abbi squinted up. How far did it go?

Obviously any type of interschool sports had to be conducted elsewhere. Witch High's true nature was a tightly guarded secret.

On one end of the room, several students practiced their antigravity control, soaring through the air on brooms, skateboards, and even one rowboat. As Abbi gaped at them, Gil led her toward a smaller group gathered in one corner.

Rupert greeted the three girls and two boys. "Hey, everyone. Thanks for coming. This is Gil's sister, Abbi. She's going to help us, too."

Help? Dread soared through her veins. Not if it involved magic.

Abbi moved to one side as the group conferred, discussing the size and theme for the homecoming float. With the parade on Saturday, they didn't have much time to put it together. Of course, magic helped.

Though they could only use it for the chassis, since the other schools in the area had to rely on more mundane means to build their floats. The headmaster insisted on fairness.

After much discussion, Gil and Rupert drew a rectangle on the wooden floor, then stood on opposite ends. Gil nodded at Rupert, and they recited the spell together.

"Build us a structure strong and fleet,
To last a period of just one week.
Include the grid to hold the flowers
And propel it by antigravity powers.
Make sure we have an artistic form
And include our mascot, the unicorn."

Before they finished the last word, tiny darts of light appeared within the rectangle, zipping from one end to the other, more of them appearing as each grew in size. Slowly, the lights melded together, creating a shape, then a solid form. Within minutes, a large structure stood inside the lines. The school's mascot, a majestic unicorn, stood proudly at the front, while a tall maypole took up the center. Three benches circled the maypole, creating secure spots for the court to stand and wave.

"Great job, guys." One girl, Lydia, a senior as were most of the others, stepped forward. "Now it's my turn. I'll teleport the flowers here."

She murmured several words beneath her breath, then clapped her hands. Buckets of cut flowers appeared on the floor around the float—daisies, roses, carnations, lilies, and Abbi's favorite, small but brilliant violets.

"Excellent." Rupert sent Lydia the brilliant smile that Abbi had experienced earlier. Even now, seeing it created a hitch in Abbi's breathing. "Let's get to work."

The grid surrounding the lower portion of the float glowed in a variety of colors, indicating which flowers went where. Abbi could make out the school's sun and moon logo on the side facing her as well as letters forming the words, Salem High #4.

Fasten the flowers in the slots—she could do that. It required nothing more than a steady hand and willingness to help. Joining the others, Abbi found she enjoyed working with the flowers. Their scents and textures appealed to her. She caressed a delicate rose petal, inhaled its perfume.

Since her family lived on the penthouse level of a city apartment complex, she rarely had much contact with nature. Her sole achievement was nurturing an African violet for several years in her bedroom.

Time flew as she tucked the blossoms into the grid. To her relief, this small group accepted her and chatted with her easily. No doubt knowing Gil was her brother helped, but he'd left for his class after creating the chassis. Would they still like her if they knew she was a talentless witch?

Rupert paused by Abbi. "You're doing a great job," he said. "Thanks for helping out."

"I'm glad I could."

"This will take most of the week. You gonna help us tomorrow?"

Abbi hesitated. If she had her way, she'd cut school forever. "I . . . don't know."

His warm gaze met hers, as intimate as a caress. "I'd consider it a personal favor if you would."

At a loss for words, Abbi nodded and blushed. *Goddess!* Nothing looked worse than a blush on a freckled face. But Rupert only grinned and moved on, leaving her tingling. She'd never experienced this before. Was this some kind of enchantment he'd learned in his upper-level classes?

If so, why didn't the other girls seem to be affected?

The hooting of an owl signaled the change of classes and—in this case—the end of the school day. *At last!*

They worked a few more minutes before Rupert called a halt, and Sandi, a sophomore, cast a moisture spell over the flowers to keep them fresh. As they broke apart to go their separate ways, Rupert paused by Abbi.

"I'll see you tomorrow. I have an after-school sorcery class now. Guess they don't want me to blow up the school with kids in it." He grinned at her, then walked off.

Abbi followed the flow of students in the hope of actually getting out of this place, but she found herself turning at one hallway, her feet leading the way without any direction from her mind. When she found herself before Ms. Cherry's classroom, she gulped.

A summoning spell. *Mab's Marbles*! She was in trouble now.

"Come in, Ms. Symes." Ms. Cherry's voice came clearly from the classroom.

Her hands cold, Abbi ventured inside. The teacher sat at her desk and glanced up as Abbi approached. "You bolted from my classroom."

"I'm sorry." Abbi swallowed the lump in her throat. "But I . . . I couldn't stay. I don't have any magic. I shouldn't be here at all."

Ms. Cherry looked as though she agreed. "That's not for you to decide. Your mother insists you have talent."

She'd talked to Mom? Abbi was *really* in trouble.

"May I ask where you went?" Ms. Cherry asked.

"I joined my brother and Rupert Damani in decorating the float."

"Ah, the homecoming parade is this Saturday, isn't it?" The teacher pursed her lips. "I'll admit we got off to a shaky start. Why don't you take the rest of this week to work on the float, and we'll see how things stand next week?"

Relief flooded Abbi. She beamed. "That would be great."

"But I do expect to see you here ready to learn next Monday."

"Yes, ma'am."

When Abbi finally made her way out of the school, she paused and glanced back. Maybe she'd survive.

Maybe.

The taunts began the next morning as soon as she walked inside. Belinda stood beside a group of lockers, surrounded by several other girls. "Gil Symes' sister has no magic," she shouted as Abbi passed by.

The girls with her stared and pointed as if Abbi had sprouted horns and turned green. So, of course, the students nearby had to gape at her as well. Abbi blinked back tears and kept her head high. Gil had promised her the crowd would move on to something different in a day or two. She wanted it to be *now*.

In her Circle Casting class, she managed to learn the basics easily—the drawing of the circle, lining it with sea salt, casting out negative energy. Only when she went to set the circle did she fail.

But here she wasn't alone. Several others couldn't set the circle either. This time a small girl with unruly dark hair bore the brunt of the teasing. Pandora Barstow was half-witch, half-mundane, with only a tentative control of her erratic but powerful magic.

Instead of setting a circle, Pandora made hers explode, tossing salt into everyone's eyes. While the others, especially Belinda, derided the girl, Abbi made it a point to offer Pandora a hug.

"It'll be all right," she told the shorter girl. "You'll get it in no time."

Pandora shook her head, her eyes downcast. "I . . . I can't make it behave the way I want."

Abbi forced a smile. At least, Pandora *had* magick. "That's why they make us come to school."

A hint of a smile touched Pandora's lips. "That's true."

Belinda elbowed Abbi, knocking her into Pandora. "The two of you deserve each other." Belinda had the haughty look down to perfection. "One who can't handle her magick and the other without any."

Pandora flinched. Seeing it, Abbi whirled on Belinda. "Leave her alone."

Something in her expression must have told Belinda that she meant it, for Belinda shrugged and strolled away. But not before she tossed one last comment over her shoulder. "Why would I want to waste my time on you anyhow?"

"Thank you," Pandora whispered.

"Ignore her." Abbi repeated what Gil had told her. "Her kind needs to pick on someone to feel important."

"But she cast a circle the very first time she tried." Awe lingered in Pandora's voice.

"That still doesn't make her better than anyone else." Abbi said the words, but couldn't quite convince herself to believe them. She had no talents. In this place, she *didn't* belong.

Only the warmth of Rupert's smile when she joined the float group kept the day from being a total disaster. He crossed the flightorium floor to pause before her. "Bad day?"

"Not great," she admitted.

He caught one of her hands in his and led her toward the float. "It'll get better."

She wasn't so sure of that. "Promise?"

His smile twinkled in his dark eyes. "Promise." He tugged her into place beside him by a pile of flowers around the unicorn head. "Work with me here."

Releasing her hand, he lifted two bright daisies and placed them in the unicorn's face. "*Glowsati.*" Immediately, the dark gold centers became the creature's glowing eyes.

"Wow." Abbi couldn't stop her exclamation. "That's awesome."

Rupert winked at her as he dropped a pile of lilies in her hands. "Can you put those on the mane?"

"Sure." She moved closer in order to reach the mane and found herself just a hand's breadth from where Rupert worked on the opposite side of the unicorn's face. Concentrating on tucking the lilies into the wire-framed mane, she found her chest tight. Why was he being so nice to her? Because Gil was his friend?

"Rupert . . . ?" She started to ask, then stopped. He'd think she was an idiot.

"Yeah?" He glanced up, his gaze meeting hers over the unicorn's head.

She shook her head with a tight smile. "Nothing." She wanted to look away, but his dark gaze held hers, his usual mischievous light becoming solemn.

He started to speak, paused, then started again as if unsure. Rupert? Unsure?

"Rupert?" she asked, her voice quiet.

The corner of his lips lifted in a wry smile. "I need to tell you something."

At the seriousness of his tone, Abbi flinched. Was this where he told her he didn't want her working with them anymore?

"There was a time when I thought I'd never have any magic," he said in one quick burst.

She stared at him. Rupert? Without magic? He was in Advanced Sorcery. Only witches with a lot of power and skill took that.

"I know what you're thinking." He flashed her a quick grin. "But it's true. I was thirteen before I had any glimpses of my abilities. I couldn't make fire, cast a spell, anything."

"You're just saying that because you want me to feel better," she retorted. And it was working. If a witch as talented as Rupert came late into his magic, she still had hope.

"No." Rupert placed his hand over hers atop the wire head. "I had to find my trigger, which in turn awakened my powers. In my case, I was nearly hit by lightning chasing my dog after he'd gotten out."

"A trigger?" Abbi had never heard of that. Gil's magick had always been there.

"Some of us need one. I understand what you're going through. It's tough, but you'll make it."

His reassurance gave Abbi the courage to confess her deepest fear. "What if I don't have any magic?" She hated the waver in her voice. What if she remained a null for all of her life? She'd disappoint her parents, her brother . . . herself.

"You do. I'm sure of it." He gave her hand one more squeeze, then returned to work. "Trust me."

She wanted to trust him. Could he be right? Could her magic be out there waiting?

Why not?

By the time they finished for the afternoon, she found herself joining in the group's lighthearted teasing. They treated her as if she belonged, whether she had magic or not.

Maybe Witch High wouldn't be so bad after all.

If the other students would leave her alone.

The remainder of the week went quickly. Her natural aptitude helped with the book learning, and she scored high points there. It was on application where she failed—which Belinda never let her forget.

Joining Rupert and his friends to work on the float every last period made the ridicule bearable. By Friday, it was finally beginning to look like a true entry for the parade. The unicorn appeared alive, magick making its eyes glow and nostrils snort.

As a group, they stood back to admire it. Rupert stood by Abbi's side. "Great job, everyone. No way can Werewolf High do better than this." He nudged Abbi's shoulder as he referred to their archrival—the only other school in Salem with otherworldly students.

"Especially you, Abbi. I can tell the areas where you worked. The flowers look more vibrant."

"Thanks." Abbi couldn't stop a large smile from escaping.

"Yeah, thanks a lot." Sandi produced a mock pout.

Rupert spread his hands. "Hey, only calling them as I see them."

Sandi took a step back to examine the float, then placed her hands on her hips. "I hate to say it, but he's right." She grinned at Abbi. "You have the touch."

"We'll have to remember that in the future," Doug added. He rested his arm around Sandi's shoulders and gave her a hug. "Give it one last watering before we leave."

As Sandi muttered a quick spell to cast a light mist over the float, Rupert spoke. "Remember, everyone. Be here at eight tomorrow morning so we can get it hooked up and over to the parade route."

"Will do."

"Sure, boss."

"Whatever you say."

The group broke apart, and Rupert fell into step with Abbi. "Excited about the parade?" he asked.

"I think I am." She smiled up at him. He'd worked a miracle. In just one week, she'd become a part of Witch High. Or at least a small part of it. "Our float is going to be the best."

"Of course. We'll be able to take the best float trophy to the dance." He hesitated for a moment. "Abbi, would—?"

They rounded a corner and nearly collided with Belinda. The other girl cast Abbi a dark glance, then beamed at Rupert. "Rupert! There you are." She sidled closer to him, placing her hand on his arm. "I heard you don't have a date for the Homecoming Dance tomorrow night. Poor thing. I will go with you after all."

Abbi's heart dropped into her stomach. Rupert had asked Belinda to the dance? *Belinda?* Was he nuts?

Sure, Belinda was a knockout, but Abbi would rather eat nails than spend time in the girl's company. Abbi hadn't expected to go to the dance herself, but the thought of Rupert taking Belinda made her ill. She'd expected better of him.

"I'm sorry, Belinda." Rupert smiled at the girl but freed his arm from her hold. "I don't recall asking you."

His words didn't faze her at all. "You must have forgotten. All that sorcery stuff."

"I don't think so. Besides . . ." He wrapped his arm around Abbi's shoulders. "I'm already taking Abbi to the dance."

Abbi stiffened slightly in surprise. He was taking her? No, he was using her as an excuse not to go with Belinda. She didn't blame him.

Belinda looked from Rupert to Abbi, her scowl darkening. "You must be joking. She's a null."

The smile vanished from Rupert's face. "I'm taking Abbi." His tone left no room for doubt.

With a disgusted huff, Belinda pushed past them, jostling Abbi as she went. "You'll pay for this," she muttered.

Abbi tried to dismiss the threat. What could Belinda do to her? Any spells used against a member of the school resulted in immediate expulsion. She doubted the other girl would risk it.

Besides, she was more concerned with Rupert. She glanced up to find him watching her, his gaze intent.

"You will come with me, won't you?" he asked.

Abbi forced a smile. "You don't have to do this. It's enough that you told off Belinda."

He muttered something under his breath, then gently turned her to face him and raised her chin with one hand. "I know I don't *have* to do this. I *want* to do this."

"You *want* me to go to the dance with you?" He

could ask any girl in the school from freshman to senior and they'd say yes.

"Yes. You." His devastating smile appeared. "I was just going to ask before we ran into her."

Abbi stared, unable to believe his words. Rupert wanted to take her to the dance. Her! Her mouth moved but no words emerged from her dry throat.

A teasing light appeared in his eyes. "So, will you?"

"I . . . yes." She found herself grinning foolishly. "I'd like that."

"Good." He drew her closer and placed a quick kiss on the tip of her nose. "I'd like it, too."

Walking again, he placed his arm about her shoulders. "I'll pick you up at six," he added.

"Okay." She was going to the dance. With Rupert. Abbi barely felt the floor beneath her feet. Glancing down, she ensured she wasn't levitating.

It only felt that way.

Abbi arrived the next morning to help hook up the float and found the group staring at it in horror. Glancing at the floral design, she gasped. "Oh, no."

Icicles hung from the frame, the flowers wilted beneath the icy cold, the vitality gone. It resembled a sodden kitten more than an award-winning entry.

Rupert broke an icicle off and wrapped his fingers around it. "This was done by magic." Anger deepened his voice.

"Who would do such a thing?" Sandi asked.

Abbi closed her eyes in despair. Belinda. This was her revenge. All because Abbi agreed to go to the dance with Rupert. Didn't the girl realize she'd hurt more than Abbi?

She opened her eyes to meet his gaze. He grimaced, silently agreeing with her assessment.

"It . . . it was me."

They all turned toward the timid voice behind them. Abbi blinked. Pandora?

"I . . . I didn't mean to. I . . . I'm sorry." Tears trickled down the smaller girl's face.

Rupert approached her, his anger gone, gentleness in its place. "What happened?"

"I . . . I came early with my friend, Tabby. She wanted to practice her flying." As Pandora spoke, another girl stepped to her side, her expression equally distraught.

"It's my fault," she said. "I couldn't control my broom, and Dora tried to stop me."

"I . . . I used a freeze spell." Pandora added.

Abbi already saw where this was leading. Poor Pandora had powerful but uncontrolled magic.

"It worked." Tabby indicated her drenched clothing with a grimace. "But it also went everywhere." She darted a glance at the destroyed float.

"I'm so sorry." Pandora literally wrung her hands.

Rupert touched her shoulder in a reassuring gesture. "You didn't mean it. Accidents happen." He turned to face the float. "We should be able to fix this. We're witches, aren't we?"

The others nodded with little enthusiasm, and Doug sent out a slow warming spell that removed all traces of ice. But the flowers remained limp.

Rupert cast a more powerful spell that revitalized the ribbons and trimmings but again failed to restore the flowers. "Flowers are alive." He lowered his hands. "It'll take someone with more magic than I to bring them back."

Lydia started down the hallway. "I'll get the headmaster."

If anyone had the power to fix this, it would be Headmaster Abernathy.

"Poor things." Abbi approached the float and cupped a drooping rose in her palm, aching to see such beauty destroyed. She focused on the bloom, wishing it back to life. "You'll be okay," she whispered.

A bolt of liquid fire abruptly ran from her head to her toes, tearing a gasp from her throat. It poured from the tips of her fingers in the form of glittering sparkles. Suddenly exhausted, Abbi fell to her butt on the flightorium floor and stared in amazement as the sparkles danced, grew, expanded to surround the float in a shimmering net.

Equally amazing, the blossoms revived, regained their color, and radiated a healthiness beyond what they'd had before.

"Wow." She'd never seen anything like this.

"Wow indeed." Rupert slid his hands under her arms and helped her to her feet, allowing her to rest against him for support. He bent to whisper into her ear. "Told you the magick was there."

The float almost glowed as the others cheered and clapped. "Why didn't you tell us you were a nature witch, Abbi?" Lydia demanded.

"I . . . I didn't know." Abbi had never had much contact with nature.

Though her African violet had thrived.

"A nature witch is very rare," Rupert added. "I foresee different classes in your future, Abbi Symes."

He waved a hand at the other students. "Let's get this float hooked up. We have a parade to attend."

Even Pandora was smiling as everyone snapped into action. When Abbi finally felt as if her knees would support her, she drew away from Rupert, missing his warmth at once.

He caught her chin and turned her to face him. "Will a very powerful witch still condescend to attend the dance with me?" Though his words held a teasing note, his eyes were serious.

"Nothing would keep me from it." Aside from her exhaustion, Abbi didn't feel any different. She was still herself but apparently not a null after all.

"Good."

Abbi walked beside Rupert as they entered the homecoming dance in the main hall and enjoyed the way Belinda's eyes widened at spotting her. Now that

Abbi had found a way to access her own magic, she doubted the other girl would be much trouble.

Abbi wore a dress she'd conjured herself from her African violet—velvety, dark purple, form-fitting with a scent of violets. Rupert's eyes had gleamed when he saw it.

Now, he hoisted the large silver trophy over his head. "Witch High is the best," he shouted and was answered with cheers.

They'd won the Best Float Award in the parade.

But Abbi felt as though she'd won it all.

The Price of Gold

Sarah A. Hoyt

Sarah A. Hoyt has sold over sixty short stories to such markets as *Weird Tales*, *Analog*, *Asimov's*, and *Amazing*. These days her short story writing takes a backseat to her novels—the magical British Empire series from Bantam (starting with *Heart of Light*); the Shifters series from Baen Books (starting with *Draw One in the Dark*); the space opera, also from Baen (starting with *DarkShip Thieves*); and, under the pen name Sarah D'Almeida, the Musketeers' Mysteries from Prime Crime (starting with *Death of a Musketeer*). Sarah lives in Colorado and, when not typing furiously, can be found plotting (never mind what) with her husband, minigolfing with her teen sons, or rolling around with her pride of cats.

WHEN Michael Laurel disappeared, everyone had an opinion.

Everyone but Maria, who could barely remember Michael and who really didn't want to hear about someone disappearing—because she often felt like disappearing herself.

Yet there was no escaping speculation. Early morning, walking into school, past the office door that had been left ajar, she heard the first one.

"I don't know if he's dead or just beyond the reach of our magic," the principal of Witch High said. "We should never have admitted him. Family or no family. I know that the Laurels are an old magic family and all, but the boy had not a drop of talent, not one. Poor kid."

Maria shook her head. That was too bad. She knew what it was like to be a misfit. Maybe Michael should have stuck to mundane schools. His parents had money and pull—they could have afforded the best for him. Or maybe he would not have done any better anywhere else. Perhaps it was not his lack of talent, but how little he cared, that governed his lack of magical ability. She found this was true for most of her classmates.

At fourteen Maria was too tall for a frame that hadn't quite filled in yet, and she had a cloud of unruly red hair. But worst of all—or perhaps best, only that was not how she experienced it—she was the best witch at Witch High. By far. At her command, with the careless wave of a hand, she could turn Witch High itself inside out. Without even trying, she could change her ratty school clothes into a sparkling ball gown. At her whim, and with very little effort, she could change her desk to solid gold. Barely thinking about it, she could take a tattered, half-bald broom, found on the street, and cause it to fly with the best brooms produced by the best aviation broom houses.

Her parents had sent her to Witch High because, though they were both sorcerers, they were not at her level. They couldn't teach her to control her power as she needed to. Her father worked as a day trader, putting his premonition ability to good use in the mundane world, and her mother used her transforming ability to run her distinctive designer clothing shop in the small, expensive Massachusetts suburb where they lived.

They functioned like mundanes, and in the mundane world.

They neither craved nor wished for the kind of power that more magic could give them. And, if truth be told, Maria scared them a little, with her untrammeled and unimaginably powerful magic. Which was probably why, she thought, they left her alone with her books most of the time.

They didn't want to get caught in the crossfire if she messed up with it.

They were afraid to let her play with the other little girls in their very mundane neighborhood, too. After all, most ordinary people no longer believed in magic, and it was better that way. It wasn't so long ago that those with special powers had been hanged or burned at the stake.

By sending her to Witch High, a school designed for witches, they'd thought she'd have enough friends.

By the end of her first semester there, Maria had learned this wasn't true. And she didn't even care. Not that much. She went to school, and she did her work, and she slouched through the hall in clothes that she could make far more glamorous if she cared, which she didn't. Why bother? Everybody was too afraid to approach her no matter what she wore.

On the day after Michael disappeared, the hallways were decked in posters for the coming witch ball. Magical letters glowed out of the walls proclaiming *Music by the Magical Jive; Broom Waltz; Foretelling and Magical Matching.*

The posters were ornamented with pictures of girls and boys in their magical best—which considering the exchange students who came to Witch High from secret portals all over the world meant everything from tuxedos to wizard robes—twirling madly in sparks of stars.

Maria didn't even notice the posters. She didn't pay any attention to them on purpose. To go to dances, you needed to have a date, or at the very least a friend. And Maria had no friends in the school. She made the best grades effortlessly. And then she went home to watch TV and dream she was a normal teenager with no power at all. One of those many ordinary girls she saw in her neighborhood every day. One of the many who didn't dream that every school fed into Witch High—as really happened in mundane schools over the world. Most had a secret entrance to Witch High and the magical world where young witches and wizards got trained. And Maria dreamed that no matter where she ran away to, once she went to school, she ended up back at Witch High.

Alone again. Too powerful to have friends.

"We really should never have accepted him," the flying teacher said. She was a tall, gangly woman with angular features.

Maria was helping her put away the brooms after flying lesson, because there were always two of three of the students who couldn't quite control the brooms and left them scattered all over the landscape, from the nearby fields to the play areas for the young kids in Witch Elementary next door.

The teacher didn't have that much magic. She was just good at flying. But she could not farsee where, in the thickets of bushes, in the rolling grass leading down to the river, the missing brooms might hide. And she had no idea how to bring them back unless she was physically riding them.

So Maria stayed after school and farsaw where the brooms were, and she waved a hand, and pulled the brooms to her by the force of her magic.

The first lost brooms were, together, in a thicket at the end of the school grounds. Maria didn't need to foresee that they'd been abandoned by a young couple who'd used their ineptitude at flying as an excuse to ditch their mounts and walk back, hand in hand, through the spring-flowering woods. Stacey and Paul had used up the entire period that way and got remarkably little flying done. But when push came to shove, they'd pass the class, and what else did they need? No employer in the mundane world out there would hire people just because they flew brooms better. Only witches even knew people could ride brooms.

Maria guided the two brooms, side by side, to the pile of the other brooms, against the gym wall. "I heard the principal say that," she told the flying teacher. "That he was only accepted because of his family. I always wondered why he was here, how he always managed to be promoted every year."

The flying mistress gave her a worried look, then sighed. "The Laurels are very well off, very influential in the wizarding community. They refused to admit their son had no talent. And, you know . . . what if they were wrong? Sometimes I wonder if people know what's best for their children when they push them into programs like this, that they are totally unsuited for."

Maria nodded. "Sometimes I wonder if I . . ."

The flying mistress gave her a startled, worried look, as though she could read what Maria didn't say. That sometimes she wondered if Witch High was the best for her, too.

"Oh, my dear, but you are who the program was designed for," she said. "Not, that," she added piously, in the tone of someone reciting a spell—and it must be one, because every teacher said this at least once a day. "You're any better than kids with no magical talent. Of course not. It's just that everyone is gifted in a different way, and your gifts are perfect for this school."

And Maria nodded and blushed and didn't say anything else. Instead, she pulled the next missing broom from where it had been ditched—in the middle of the river, where Will had doubtlessly taken an opportunity to have a swim on this sweltering day.

But she wondered if it was true that the program was designed for people like her. Looking at the flying teacher, so lonely, so quiet, so gawky-awkward, she wondered if it was true for anyone.

The program tried to control these highly talented

magical kids by telling them—a hundred times a day—that they were no better than those without magic. Maria understood that. They were clearly afraid that witches would decide they were better than normals, or a different species, and turn on them.

Only, the thing was, in the long history of witchcraft it had never been the witches who decided to eliminate those with no power. Always it had been the other way around. There was strength in numbers, and most people had no magical power. Which made them . . . what was expected.

Many of the kids in Maria's class spent their lives disguising how powerful they really were once they were out in the real world. And disdaining learning new spells. And forgetting their abilities.

Maria didn't seem to have the knack of it. She liked magic. She liked performing magic.

Of course being the top kid in the class didn't make her very popular. She expected she would end up like the flying teacher someday—tall and talented, but gawky and awkward. And alone, very alone.

"If I hear there was any bullying that caused him to disappear," the vice principal said, magically broadcasting his voice over the lunchroom. "There will be severe punishment. You must remember that your magic does not exempt you from common, decent behavior. You're not better than the kids with no magic. You're just different. Each person is gifted in their very own way."

Maria, sitting alone at the table in the corner bent her head over the peanut butter sandwich into which she had transformed the tuna sandwich her mother had packed her and thought what a load of nonsense it all was. Yes, everyone might be gifted in a different way—but if you had a gift for shaping flint tools, it wouldn't do you much good in the twentieth century. And if you had a gift for witchcraft, a gift so large you could not deny it, then even your witch classmates could ostracize you. And if you had no gifts and were sent to a witch school . . . well . . . They'd probably ostracize you, too. Only more so.

She didn't know if Michael had been bullied, but he didn't need to be to feel awful. But she felt awful anyway. All isolated and alone.

She looked around the dark wood tables—she'd once peeked into the lunchroom at a mundane school, and she'd been shocked at the Formica tops, the plastic chairs, the linoleum floors with handy drains. She supposed, though, if custodians couldn't magically clean the place up, no matter what happened inside it, those dreadful indestructible fittings would be better.

Here, the oak tables, the broad wood chairs looked better, but she knew that mundane schools couldn't be worse than Witch High for cliques and groups. The pretty witches hung together, as did the powerful wizards. Students specialized and made groups of that specialty. And they used their magic to make themselves popular. Vast giggling groups of glamour-intensive people whose magic made them popular ate together everyday.

And ignored people like Maria, who were too serious, too intense, too whatever . . . and people like Michael, who had no power at all.

Bullying would be merciful by comparison to being treated as invisible. Sometimes Maria thought she could vanish into thin air and no one would know.

"Michael didn't go home last night," the vice principal said. "And our foretellers can't find him anywhere. He's not in the magical dimension, nor in any of the schools Witch High connects to. We can't find him at all. There are two reasons for this—either he's been kidnapped by a more powerful magical entity who is hiding him, or . . ."

The VP never said or what, but Maria knew what was meant. They couldn't find him because Michael was dead.

While the vice principal thundered on about bullying, she wondered if he had been bullied, and if that was the reason he'd gone missing. Or if he'd simply been as ignored, as lonely, as disconnected as she was. So left out that he eventually just disappeared. It could have happened that way, she thought. Some days she thought she could burst like a soap bubble, just a little "pop" and she'd stop existing.

Posters of Michael appeared on the walls of the school by sixth period. Alternating with the posters of couples twirling and the glamorous enticement to witches ball, there were the pictures of Michael, serious-solemn, staring from the walls. The top of the poster said MISSING and the bottom MICHAEL LAUREL. And that was all.

No explanations. No indication where to look for him.

The picture itself showed a dark haired boy, with overgrown, lank hair and intense dark eyes staring out at those who walked by. And walk by they did. Groups and couples, and the occasional loner like Maria. They walked by laughing or talking, or thinking of their multidimensional geometry quiz.

It was as if the posters were as invisible as Michael was.

Maria wondered what good the posters could possibly do. They were even easier to ignore than Michael had been.

Perhaps that was why, toward the end of the evening, she used her magic, on an empty hallway, when no one was looking, to pull one of the posters off the wall.

She spread it out on the white carpet of her room after school and stared at it a while.

The family's large house in the mundane suburbs was empty and echoing. Her parents were out at a dinner given by dad's company or his clients or something. Maria didn't know which and cared even less.

After doing her homework, including studying what had gone wrong at Salem back when for her history class and memorizing the new weather-changing formula for physics, she sat down in front of the poster, staring at it.

Michael didn't look special at all. He never had. They'd been in the same schools since elementary and though Maria had had her share of crushes on boys at school, she'd never even thought of Michael as a possible crush object. He just was. A boy like any other. With no magic.

Like she was just a girl like any other. With too much magic.

They didn't have the same classes, of course. Michael was in remedial everything, from transformational physics to arcane architecture. He would pass every year, but as far as she knew, he never shined at anything, despite his high-talent family. Maybe it was just one of those things.

And every year he was a little quieter at recess. Every year he sat alone in the lunch room. Every year.

Even she wasn't that isolated.

She stretched out her hand to the face that showed in tridimensional projection in the poster. And at that moment she heard it.

Help.

The quiet cry was in Michael's voice, and it sounded both urgent and despairing.

For a moment she thought it was built into the poster, and then she realized that was not it, not at all. It was just she'd been thinking of him. And she'd established such a connection in that moment that she could hear him.

Half fearful, even afraid she might be communicating with the dead—which was a course she wouldn't even take till eleventh grade—she extended her mind in the direction of that cry for help, and she asked, "Is this Michael? Where are you?"

It took a long time before she heard a reply, and

when his voice came to her, it was as if from a long way off. "Yes, I'm Michael," he said. "And I'm trapped." And then, faintly, echoing only in the deepest reaches of her mind: *Help me!*

The sane thing to do, Maria knew, would be to call an adult for help. But as she reviewed, in her mind, the adults she could reach—her parents or the teachers at the school—she realized that wouldn't do. For one, her parents were at a business dinner. And they wouldn't believe her anyway.

As for the school . . . well, given that their farseers hadn't located Michael after a serious interval of massive effort, why would they believe Maria had found something? Maria knew that adults in general and teachers in particular hated to be shown up by kids. Even at Witch High.

So this was up to her.

She got out her materials for Meditation and Concentration class. It was obvious she could not find Michael as she found the broomsticks, by thinking about it. Something more was needed. Meditation and concentration were how Witch High students were taught to improve their skills.

And though Maria didn't need it, her skills were so strong, she had dutifully done her lessons and knew what to do. From her backpack, she extracted the requisite candles and incense and set about creating a circle around Michael's poster. Then she closed the blinds on her windows tightly and sat down on the floor, looking at the poster of Michael and thinking of where he might be.

Suddenly, without transition, she found herself before him in a landscape that appeared to be completely composed of gray spiderwebs. Buildings, land forms, humanlike figures . . . all was shrouded in gray evanescence.

Only Michael had color and looked fully alive, as he stared out at her.

"Where?" she asked him, but even as she asked, she got the mental coordinates of his location, the feeling of where it was.

In the mundane school in Maria's neighborhood there was a stall in the bathroom—the third from the left, on the second floor bathroom—where, should a student with magical ability who was intended for Witch High enter, the back wall opened and allowed access to the front hall of Witch High. The arrangement was the same at other "magnet schools" that fed Witch High with exchange students. The passage conveyed the kids from their world into another world, in which humans had never existed, and from there to Witch High. There, in those in-between-our-space-and-time pathways, the students circumvented the laws of physics and commuted to Witch High instantly. Once at Witch High they could indulge in broom flights and do all the magic they wished. And they could get to school without fearing a repeat of what was called in the school's textbooks The Salem Incident.

Most people, Maria knew, were never able to open the gateways between worlds on their own, or at least most students weren't. They took the gateways they used on faith, just as, in their mundane regular world, they took computers and automobiles on faith, without the slightest idea how they worked.

They never realized that the gateways transitioned to Witch High through other dimensions and strange new worlds.

But Maria had long since figured out how to open those gateways. She'd traveled every path she could find along them. It had been more than an idle quest for challenges to her abilities. She'd been looking for a society she would fit in. She hadn't found one, but she'd seen a great variety of worlds, from places where technology had never existed and Earth was ruled by magic priest-kings to worlds where her kind was sniffed out and hunted down on first appearing.

Because of that last kind of world, she'd stopped traveling the secret pathways connecting Witch High to the universe—or universes. But now, she could sense that Michael was trapped in one of these secret worlds. And clearly he was being held there, not visiting of his own free will.

How should she proceed from here?

She stepped over the circle of candles to the door of her room, which she locked. All she needed right now was for her parents to find the bedroom empty while she looked for Michael. They'd mess with her set-up and give the alarm and set in motion massive interference by the school's teachers. Those teachers hadn't been able to find Michael. What good would they be at finding her? And couldn't they disturb her plans and leave her trapped in that other dimension, too?

She was better off handling this one herself.

Getting her school backpack, she picked out of her magics case—for the Elementary Magic class—such elements that amplified her natural powers. She could tell from the faintness of the sensations he was sending that Michael was a long way off—as such things went.

Einstein was right, even in the magical world, about all things being relative.

She sprinkled dragon's blood powder on the candles and lit an incense stick scented with jasmine from the suspended gardens of Babylon—harvested from a world in which they still flourished. Then she sat down and concentrated on the *signal* coming from Michael, and on homing in on it.

For a long time nothing happened. Then there was a *whoosh*, as though a doorway had opened and she was being sucked into a long, long dark tunnel.

This had never happened before. This shouldn't happen at all. When she opened a gateway somewhere, she knew that there should be no space or time in between. You stepped in, and there you were. But she'd neither moved nor stepped anywhere, and yet . . .

Dark, cold wind blew, pulling at her clothes, whipping her hair into a red tangle. She tried to scream, but the wind blew hard against her mouth and seemed to rob her of breath.

I'm going to die, she thought.

And then she was dropped, head first, into a gray, indefinite landscape.

She fell sprawling onto something that felt like centuries of accumulated cobwebs. And rolled to face upwards, to see Michael staring down at her.

He was much paler than in his missing posters, and he looked cold and scared. Very scared. "What are you doing here?" he asked. "Are you a prisoner, too?"

From somewhere, more felt than heard, came the sensation of a door clicking shut with a definitive, irrevocable sound.

Oops.

"Why would you want to come to join me in this prison?" Michael asked. He waved his hand around at the surroundings, which were not a proper world at all. Just the same cobwebby stuff everywhere. "I asked you to get me out, not send company for visiting hours." His lips were thin and tight, very tight, and he looked way upset, as if she'd disappointed him on purpose.

"Well, pardon me," Maria said, getting up and dusting the gray stuff from her clothes and hair. "I didn't know where you were, and I didn't know what else to do. Besides, I'm pretty sure I can get us right out of here and back home."

"You can?" he asked. "You're sure?"

"Well, no," she said.

With a small frown and a look of fear, he said, "But . . . they won't let us."

"They?" Maria asked.

He waved his hand again and bit his lip. "The guardians."

"What guardians?"

"The people keeping me here."

She frowned at him. Was there really anyone there? Any type of guardians? Why would they care? Why would they watch? "I didn't see anyone coming in," she said, stubbornly.

And before the compounds she'd burned to get here could lose their effect, she applied her power to the effort of getting them back home. Closing her eyes, she concentrated on the picture of her bedroom in her mind.

For a brief moment, cold and dark enveloped them, the wind tore at her face, her hair. She heard Michael say "Oh!" in a tone of great despair. And then there was nothing but the two of them, sitting alone in the gray cobweb world.

"Great work," he said.

"It's only a first try. I can do better with a little information. Who is holding you prisoner?" she asked. "And why?"

"It started because I couldn't do magic," Michael said. He'd sat down, in a corner, half leaning on the gray cobweb stuff and looking entirely too much like he'd become comfortable with it and it didn't disturb him anymore. He was wearing jeans and a black T-shirt that looked as if he'd slept in them, which she supposed he had. There was a hole in the knee of his jeans.

"What, not at all?" she asked, startled. She'd thought it was impossible to be at Witch High if you couldn't do any magic. After all, what would the point be? Even if your parents were magicians, what could they think was achieved by sending their nonmagical offspring to a school where people learned to control magic?

He shook his head. "Not at all. My parents said

they never detected any, you know, not even when I was very little." He picked at a frayed portion of his jeans, on the knee. "They did the regular checks, to make sure I wasn't getting in trouble." He shrugged. "If it weren't for the fact that dad is one of the great sorcerers in the country, I'd never have thought magic really existed before I entered the school."

"But then why send you to Witch High?" Maria asked, baffled. "What did they expect you to learn?"

Michael squirmed a little against the gray cobwebby stuff. "Well . . . you see . . . My father runs Astounding Effects, the—"

"Special effects company for movies?" Maria said.

"Exactly. And he uses magic for most of it, and he expects me to inherit the business. He hoped my little problem was just that I didn't believe in magic, and that seeing it at work would eventually . . . free my latent energies. They said, Mom and Dad, that no son of theirs could be completely devoid of magical power. Nothing I said or did could change my mind. They thought it was some kind of childhood rebellion. I wish that was all it was . . ."

Maria snorted. What his parents had done seemed like a crazy thing to her. While magic mostly bred true, scientists long ago had decided inheritance of the gift couldn't be a straight genetic thing. Some people were magicians whose parents had never had any power at all, and other people who couldn't light a mage-light had parents who were both sorcerers.

Magical talent played by its own rules, and every witch knew it.

Her snort, surprisingly, brought a hint of a smile to Michael's face. The first she'd seen since arriving. "Yeah," he said. "You'd think they'd know better." And he shrugged. "So they sent me to the Witch Middle School first. And then when time came for me to be accepted for Witch High . . ." He shrugged. "You know how there are people who sell things . . . to help kids boost their powers?"

Maria nodded. "The shops." She said. Salem, even mundane Salem, was a witchy tourist trap these days, full of little shops that sold charms and spells to the mundane along with the talented. There was a whole village full of the stores, some selling scams, some vending the real thing, down a narrow path from the school.

Michael shook his head. "Not the shops. People who approach you, when you're out walking, outside the grounds, or on your way to the shops . . . and sell you things."

"Like drugs?" Maria asked blinking. No one had ever approached her, but then she didn't often go out of the school grounds or down the beaten path to the village—and even when she did, she was usually accompanied by one of the teachers.

He shook his head, then shrugged. "Well, not really, though they do sell dreaming powder, that makes you . . . never mind . . ." He shrugged again, as if in answer to a question she hadn't asked. "I was desperate, okay. I knew it wouldn't be a good idea. Most of these people aren't exactly on the up and up . . . They make you think of all the bad legends, of the poisoned apple and Snow White. But I was desperate. My father was so sure I could do it, I could do magic, if I just tried . . . He was so disappointed and kept insisting I was lazy or didn't try . . .

"So I bought . . ."

He looked up, and for a moment their eyes met. His were unfathomably dark. A black so deep it was hard to tell his pupil from his iris. And yet, if you looked really close, there seemed to be dark blue specs caught in all that black, shimmering in the light. They made his eyes look like a deep, dark summer night with stars.

"I bought paint."

Whatever Maria might have thought of, paint had never crossed her mind. Nor would it ever. She blinked. "Paint?"

"One of the people . . . She said she could sell me

paint that would make my paintings magical. That would make them alive—make them entrances to other universes. Capture life in them. And you, know, I thought . . ." He shrugged. "I liked to paint. I figured, what harm could it do.

"So I bought it. And I started using it. And the school decided I had magic for giving life to inanimate creations. Just the sort of thing my father wanted me to have. So I kept buying the paint . . ."

"But . . ." she said. "That must have been very expensive."

"It was," he said. He picked at the hole in his jeans some more. "You see, every time I bought another bit of paint—and mostly I bought gold to mix in the other paints and give them magic—they took a bit of my soul in return. Until they had all of it. And then my body followed, and now they've captured me here."

There were many things Maria wanted to say, starting with "How could you be so stupid?" and possibly ending with "Your soul?"

But she didn't say anything. It seemed to her like a bad bargain and a crazy one at that. Why would he want to pay with his soul to be allowed to go to a school he was thoroughly unsuited for in the first place?

Instead, she stared at Michael. He looked up. "I'm sorry to have got you into this. You should see if you can port out alone. You see . . . they're never going to let me go."

But Maria was thinking. If Michael was truly who he thought he was—just a kid and devoid of magic—why would anyone want to steal his soul? And why would anyone want to keep him here, prisoner?

"Why would they want you?" she asked. "I mean . . ."

"I don't know." He frowned. "Perhaps they eat you? Or your soul?"

"It can't be right," she said. "If they planned to have you for dinner, they'd be fattening you up. You don't look exactly healthy—I bet you haven't eaten in days. And if they ate your soul, they would have done so when they took it away a bit at a time. You'd be an empty husk to them now. They wouldn't just let you sit here and not do anything to you."

He shrugged. "What does it matter why? I'm a prisoner. You're not. You can go back alone." And then, earnestly, he added, "Come on, we barely know each other. I mean . . . I've seen you in the hallways . . .You don't owe me a thing."

She started to shake her head, but why be so noble? He was right. She barely knew him. And besides—and besides—if she left here, she would have a much better chance of freeing him from back where her base of power was. Especially now that she knew where he was.

All of her heart wanted to take off for home and tell him she'd be back. But her mind told her she didn't know who might be listening. It wasn't the sort of thing she should blurt out into the open at a time like this.

She turned her back on him—he was looking forlorn and curiously small sitting against the wall of the space that had to be some form of cell between the worlds—and she thought of her room. Now that she wasn't trying to take him with her, there wasn't even the cold wind, or the sensation of fighting against the current. Instead, there was a soft plop, as of a lid opening. And suddenly she was in her room. Alone. And she had a lot to do.

"Laurel residence," the male voice said, with a certain strain of tension in it.

"This is Maria Malcom," she said, using her talking-to-stuck-up-adults voice. "I'm one of Michael's classmates."

"Classmates?" the man asked. The Laurels' phone number was in one of the most expensive neighborhoods in one of the most expensive areas of town. Maria's area code wasn't in the same rarified air.

"Witch High," Maria said.

"Oh," the man said.

"Has anyone called you, demanding a ransom?"

"No."

Well, that eliminated the small possibility that the forces that held Michael had simply kidnapped him for a ransom. That would mean that the keepers believed that Michael must have some sort of power. And if he did . . . it would be in his paintings. Had to be. After all, that was the only place that anyone looking for it had detected magic. But what could Michael's power be? And what could it mean? Why would it be so singular that anyone would kidnap him for it?

She hung up the phone without noticing, without caring what Michael's father thought. If Michael took art as a course at school, and he must if it was what the school thought his talent was based on, some of his paintings had to be at the school. And she needed to see them.

Breaking into Witch High should have been impossible. But it was an old tradition with students. As long as none of the kids tried to break into the teacher's lounge or the school records, it was reasonably easy to get in. Maria knew how to juice the system. She simply concentrated on making the door to her closet a gateway into the front hall of the high school.

And arrived there as the bell rang and a throng of students milled around her.

She had a moment of panic, that she somehow had spent so much time in Michael's prison that it was now the school day again. Then she remembered the school took students from all over the world. Even with some magical time-jumping, that meant it might have shifts that operated around the clock.

Maybe she wasn't jumping out of her temporal reality.

Her backpack on shoulder, she slouched toward the art room.

"Maria!" the art teacher said. He was a dark haired man of Mediterranean origin and with the sort of expression that looks like he expects you to turn into a raging bear at any minute. "What are you doing here? It's not school time for you."

She nodded. "I know. It's just . . ." and then all the lovely excuses she had thought up crumbled to ash, making way for the truth. "I'd like to see Michael Laurel's paintings, if I may."

"Michael's?" the man said, surprised and then, his eyes widening, as he no doubt told himself they were teenagers after all. "I see . . . he was . . . a friend of yours?"

"Yeah. He's my friend. We've been going to the same schools forever. And I've never seen his paintings," Maria said, trying to strike the right chord of sadness and longing.

The teacher sighed. "He's talented enough in art. Nothing spectacular, mind. I mean, the art itself is very good, but as for magic-imbued images, he's no Leonardo da Vinci. He'll never be able to change history with his paintings, or to convince people of things just by their looking at them." He sighed. "But he's good enough. There's a chance that as he grows, his paintings will acquire life, on their own, and then he'll be able to work in movies or such."

"As he grew, I should say," the man amended himself. "I am very much afraid poor Michael is no longer with us."

"Don't say that!"

Maria's look of genuine horror must have swayed him. He must have decided their relationship was more than Maria was letting on. He led her through the class, where various students worked diligently at their notebooks and paper. Against the wall were a row of very short and wide drawers, each one marked with the student's name.

He opened the one that read "Michael Laurel." "Help yourself," he said. "Just put them back neatly when you're done."

And with that he turned his back on her and went back to his class, walking between the rows, encouraging some students and correcting others. Maria wondered if he was abandoning her because he didn't want to turn his back on his class or because he thought that Maria might get emotional or because he couldn't bear to look at Michael's work himself right now. It didn't matter.

She turned, instead, to do what she'd come to do. Pulling the pictures out of the drawer, she sensed them for magic.

First she felt the obvious glamoury of the paints, but then . . . but then . . . beneath them she sensed something else. Some vital energy, some strong power. Something she'd never felt before. And one thing she was sure of. That power couldn't be related to the gold.

The pictures that had gold in them—mostly pictures of fairylike castles and one amazing landscape of autumnal trees—felt . . . like tawdry magic. The type of magic that, were it a flavor, would taste of bubble gum. But there were others with no gold at all that felt like the wild, swirling, unexplained magic.

And then at the bottom, at the back of them all, there was one picture she recognized from her own experiences. It was the cobweb world—all gray, indistinct mush, forming things you had to guess at. Walls, and floor and something that might be people. And suddenly she understood.

Reverently, carefully, she put the pictures back in the drawer. And then she used magic to open the lock on the supply cabinet and to slip a case of markers and a notebook into her backpack. The class, absorbed in their work, did not see her.

Gatewaying back to Michael was harder this time. The wind bit at her clothes and seemed to form icicles upon her open eyes. But when she got there . . . when she got there, Michael got up startled. "You just left," he said. "How could you?"

"Never mind," she said. And handed him the notebook. "Draw," she said. "Draw a nice room, with a doorway in it. And remember, the doorway leads somewhere you know. Your house. The school."

He stared. "What?"

"Just. Do. It."

He gave her a *you must be crazy,* look, but then he sat down and drew.

She could sense the feelings rolling from him. It started with annoyance that she was forcing him to do this. But as he drew, he became more and more involved in what he was doing. And when he was done, and flung it at her with a "Now what?" the room he'd drawn was perfect and enticing.

It was a white-walled room, with wicker furniture, a quilt draped over the arm of a cushion-smothered chair. The door on the wall was oak, slightly rounded.

"Where does that lead?" she asked, pointing.

"To my room," he said, and crossed his arms, as though daring her to do her worst.

"Right," she said. And put him into the drawing. It was a moment of intense concentration. A moment of wishing him in the drawing.

He said a surprised "Oh," and there was a feeling of a breeze as he disappeared and air rushed in to replace where he had been.

Slowly, Maria looked down at the paper. For a moment she thought it hadn't worked. And then she noticed that in the drawing the door that had been closed was open.

When she ported back to her own room, the candles had burned almost down to the carpet. She started blowing them out and putting them away hastily.

She was doing a spell to clean the wax off the

carpet—Mother would have a fit if she saw it—when the phone rang.

"Maria?" Michael's voice, shaking slightly.

"Yes." She looked in the number ID window on the phone. It said Laurel. She felt a great relief. "Yes. Oh. You made it home."

"Yes," he said.

For a while neither of them talked. And then he said, "How did you do that? And what does it mean?"

"Do what? Oh, you mean . . . the painting? I think you create miniuniverses, Michael. That's why they wanted you. A lot of the creatures—fairy or demon—that trade in the sort of gold paint you bought are not very good at creating things. You can create little worlds. Each of your paintings is a world."

"What? But all those people looking for magic . . . They never . . . They couldn't detect . . ."

"No, of course not. They were looking for one of the identifiable talents. But, Michael, the world they kept you prisoner in was something you drew."

"Oh, that," he sounded comfused. "I realized that, but I thought they were mocking me. You see, I drew that because it was what the school made me feel like. Like a place with no outlet."

"So you drew the perfect prison for yourself," Maria said. "That's why I told you to draw something with a door somewhere safe."

"And you put me in it. How did you do that?"

"That . . . " she shrugged. She saw herself in the mirror—her hair a mess, her clothes all torn and worn. And she realized she would have to go back to school tomorrow. And her life would still be a prison. Why did she care what she looked like? No one would hang with her anyway. "I have more magic than is good for me. That's why . . . well . . . no one talks to me."

"They say you could turn the whole school inside out, if you wanted to," Michael said. "Or make it disappear. They're afraid of you. I've heard them talk."

"Yeah, well. I don't want to turn the school inside out." She paused. "Most of the time."

He coughed, and she could swear it had started as a laugh, and he'd disguised it.

"So I have talent," he said in a wondering tone.

"Just not a type that the school can measure." She grabbed her brush and started attempting to comb her hair.

"What else is new," he said from the other side, and she had the distinct impression of a grin behind the words.

She thought he would look very attractive with a grin instead of his usual scowl.

He was silent a long while, and at last she said, "I guess I see you at the school? Tomorrow?"

But he just said, in a tiny, tiny voice, as if he'd suddenly regressed ten years in age. "So . . . so . . . Do you want to go to the Witch Dance? Or . . . do you have a date . . . or . . ."

"I don't have a date," she said. "And yeah, I could go with you. I think I'd like it."

"Right, then," he said. And again she had the impression of a grin behind the words. "I'll see you at school tomorrow."

"Okay," Maria said.

She hung up and put the phone down carefully. And then she stared at herself in the mirror, in her scruffy jeans and ratty shirt that looked as if they'd been scoured with steel wool. She concentrated and glared at her image. She felt the softness of silk against her skin.

The mirror showed her a slim redheaded teenager wearing a dress that appeared to have been sewn together from the shimmering wings of a butterfly.

Let the other girls at the dance eat their hearts out. Like Michael, she'd been holding herself back. It was long past time for her to bust out of the prison of her own making. One step at a time. She ran her hands down the silk. It was a very nice first step.

The House

Diane Duane

Diane Duane has been writing science fiction and fantasy professionally for more than twenty-five years, working on such projects as her continuing *Young Wizards* novel series (now approaching its ninth volume) and licensed properties such as *Star Trek* (on which she's worked in more forms than anyone else alive). With more than forty novels in print and various television and film works screening worldwide, she somehow also finds time for train travel in urban Europe and dining in the Alps.

SHE lay facedown on her bed, clutching her pillow over the back of her head, and moaned, "It's useless. *Useless!*"

In the hallway outside her bedroom, Brianna's mom had the linen closet open and was stacking sheets in it: Bri could smell the lavender water from here as her mom sprayed it onto layer after layer. And for the moment, the light clean scent infuriated her. Her mother's compulsive housewifeliness didn't usually bother Brianna so much except at moments like this, when the world was ending and how nice the sheets smelled wasn't even slightly germane.

"Sweetie," her mom said, "maybe you should just wait a few days and ask him again."

"It wouldn't help," Brianna muttered. "He'd just

get the idea I really wanted to do this project with him."

"Yes, but you *do* really want to do this project with him."

"That's not the point!"

From out in the hall came the perhaps understandable long silence as her mother tried to parse this statement. Brianna had noticed that her logic and her mom's sometimes just didn't intersect, and occasionally serious annotation became necessary. "If I ask him again," Bri said, pulling the pillow up a little so she wouldn't have to shout, "he'll tell everybody that I was desperate. It'll be all over school. My rep will never recover."

"Which rep are we talking about, honey?" her mother asked, pausing to spray some more lavender water, and then to sneeze. Her mom was allergic to lavender, which always added a slightly surreal quality to this operation in Brianna's eyes.

"My reputation as an independent kid who doesn't need anybody's help to get the job done!"

"Well, you don't, if you ask me. So do it without him. If he's not smart enough to want to pair up with you on this science fair thing—"

"*Para*science, please, Mom! This is not just people fussing around with anemometers and toy erupting volcanoes. It's going to be the main event of Heritage Week!" Though she *had* seen Carol Anne Naylor's plan for a *real* miniature exploding volcano, genuine magma and all, and had been consumed by envy at not having thought of it first. If it worked, it would be terrific, and even if it malfunctioned, that could still potentially be desperately cool. After all, there was never any guarantee when you were working with a fire elemental, even a baby one, that it wouldn't get out of hand—

Another few sneezes came from outside, and then the sound of her mother shutting the linen cupboard. A few seconds later her mom came in and sat down on the bed beside Brianna, smelling strongly of lavender. "All right," she said to Brianna, "I'm missing something here. What exactly is it that makes Arthur Etchison so necessary to what you've got in mind?"

His eyes. His shoulder muscles. His haircut. His— But there was no point in getting into this line of reasoning with her mother. Brianna pulled the pillow up over her head again, this time with reason, as she was blushing again. It was the curse of her life: she had always been an easy blusher, and this year, when Arthur arrived at school from England, an exchange student, *yes, and I'd exchange any ten of our guys for one of him, he is just* so—Brianna moaned again, feeling as if her face should just about be able to scorch the sheets under it at this point. "Mom, it's just such a *good idea!* He's the King of Shop. He's got a way with metal, it *listens* to him. You should see him under the hood—" *Wouldn't I like to get under* his *hood!* said one completely unrepentant part of her mind; in response, the blush scaled right up to blowtorch level. She started talking faster, hoping to distract herself. "And nobody, *nobody* else has even thought about doing anything with the paraphysics of magic swords. Everybody's all hung up on organics this year, the specific gravity of potions and catalytic thaumachemistry. Or else this vague paperwork stuff, diagramming hexes, the structural analysis of spells." She waved a hand from under the pillow. "Airy-fairy stuff where nothing's likely to blow up or make a mess. Nothing concrete. Nothing *practical.*"

Her mother sat quiet for a moment. "Okay," her mom said. "So if you can't ask him again to help you, what *are* you going to do?"

Brianna was tempted to cover her head with the pillow again . . . except that wouldn't help her solve the problem. "Think of some other project?" she said after a moment.

"Sounds like a possibility," her mother said. "Let me know if you need any help with that." She got up.

"By the way, I'm going down to the mall later. Let me know if you want to come."

"What're you getting?"

"Just some clothes, honey." She got up and stretched, heading for the door.

Brianna winced, as for her, there was no such thing as *just* clothes; they were a statement of who you were and how you felt from day to day, self-revelatory, vital. But not so for her mother. Brianna took the pillow off her head and sat up, sighing. Her mom was a little on the plump side for her height, the gray in her hair needed touching up, and no matter how Brianna tried to work on her to style herself up a little, her mom never saw the point. Her jeans were all the wrong cut, her tops made her look like a sack of potatoes, her skirts—no, the less Brianna thought about those, the better.

Her mother paused in the doorway, looking oddly at her. "Sweetie, you're looking awfully flushed, are you all right?"

The Arthur-blush hadn't worn off yet, and the realization started making it come back. *"Mommmmmm!* I'm *fine!"* Brianna said, desperate not to be looked at. She launched herself off the bed, past her mom, and out into the hall, through a long zone of lavender-smelling air, down the hall past her brother's bedroom and down the stairs. There at the bottom of the stairs she paused, not sure where to go or what to do.

Books. Books are always good. If nothing else, they make you look busy. She went to find where she'd dumped them when she came in from school, on the breakfast nook table in the kitchen.

Her brother Mick was there, cooking—never a safe time to venture, in as her brother's tastes in food sometimes veered into the wildly experimental. Walking very softly, Brianna tried to sidle in past the refrigerator and failed: the door flipped open right in front of her face. *I don't even have the protection of hearing him working now,* Brianna thought, annoyed. At the start of this last semester, Mick had been fast-tracked into sixth-grade nonverbals and had been seriously sucked in by what he (and everybody else, at first) perceived as the luxury of not having to say a spell out loud any more. Eventually, like everyone else, he'd get over it. Brianna merely hoped that would be soon, as living in a house with a twelve-year-old "silent" magic user closely resembled playing in traffic.

For the moment, the smartest thing to do was stand still. Vague thumping and rattling noises came from inside the fridge. "What are you making?" Brianna said, more or less to the refrigerator door.

"Spaghetti," her brother said and slammed the door shut without touching it. The half-open jar of pasta sauce he'd been looking for was floating across the kitchen to him; the skinny, redheaded, floppy-T-shirted shape working at the stove put one hand out and caught the jar without looking at it, while staring down into the steam from a large saucepan and fishing around in the pan with a fork. "You want some?"

"No thanks," Brianna said, carefully making her way past Mick on the storage-cupboard side of the kitchen.

Mick looked over his shoulder at her. "So what about Arthur?" he asked, and then turned his head away again to watch as a single strand of spaghetti shot up out of the pot and hit the ceiling over the stove. There it clung, while Mick stood bizarrely counting. "A thousand two, a thousand three—"

"What *about* Arthur? And what in Hecate's name are you doing? That's going to fall down and burn somebody!"

"No it's not," Mick said. Sure enough, the strand fell down into the pot again. "Another thirty seconds, I think . . .You sure? I'm using the sauce with extra garlic."

"No thanks," Brianna said, "our antivampirism unit isn't for another three weeks, why rush it?" *Besides, it takes the garlic smell a little while to wear off, and if I* do *ask Arthur again tomorrow—* Her book bag was where she'd left it. Grabbing it, Brianna retreated to the far side of the breakfast nook, over by the conservatory windows, plopped down in the lounge chair there, and started going through it.

The textbooks were all the normal parascience books for her year, and she'd sweet-talked Mona, the school librarian, into letting her have a couple of the more advanced reference works that didn't normally leave the building. *She knows I'm good for them.* And Brianna sighed. *Maybe that's the problem with Arthur. Maybe he thinks I'm too much of a library babe. Too much of a geek.*

Then Brianna let out a breath at her own insecurity. *I'm not gonna waste anymore time on it,* she thought. *I'm going to assume it's a lost idea. If he asks me about it in the next few days, fine. Otherwise, I'm going to have something else ready, because if* I *mention it to him again, he may just think,* Hey, what a great idea!*— and hand it off to one of his little clique.* Brianna was not quite willing to admit that she had been a willing enough member of that clique until recently. There were still plenty of girls willing to follow Arthur around Salem, both the town and the school. *Done with that now,* Brianna thought, reaching for the thickest and brainiest of the books. *No more being one of the sheep.*

Brianna sighed and opened the book in her lap, the *Materia Magica,* intending to spend a while scanning it for more parascience fair ideas. But it was dry as a broomstick's bristles—ingredients for spells, mostly, both organics and synthetics: how they were isolated, how they were combined, what went with what and what emphatically didn't. Botanicals, *mineralissimae,* animal extracts and contributions . . . She scanned through the index, trying to spot something that might be useful.

Mick glanced over at her, recognized the book, and returned his attention to the pot. "You're wasting your time going all techie on him," he said, fishing out another strand of spaghetti and looking at it thoughtfully. "The way to a man's heart is through his stomach."

Brianna looked up scornfully at her brother. "You know any *men* we could ask about that?" Brianna said.

Mick just fished out another strand of spaghetti. "Seriously," Mick said. "Why don't you do something about food?"

"Food!" Brianna rolled her eyes. "Please. *So* home ec."

"What's the matter? Afraid you're gonna put back some of that puppy fat?" Mick looked over his shoulder at her again and gave her a wicked look as another strand of spaghetti shot toward the ceiling.

Brianna stared after it as it hit the ceiling and clung. *One thousand . . . two thousand . . . three thousand . . .* It fell back into the pot. "Only puppies have puppy fat," she said. "As you'll discover if you keep annoying me. And will you *stop* that? Dad's gonna have a fit when he sees. You know how he is about not making more cleaning work for everybody."

"He won't see," Mick said, getting the spaghetti drainer down from the pot rack and dropping it into the sink. "I'll have it cleaned up by the time he gets home from work."

Brianna sighed, turned her attention back to the *Materia Magica's* index. Boredom, boredom from A to Z, nothing nearly as cool as a magic sword . . . She wrinkled her nose at the A's, and turned to the Z's and started reading the materials-and-ingredients index backward in weary desperation. *Zyzzal, zugreb, zingiber, zameron, zacinth—*

Something stopped her. She glanced back.

Zingiber? What the heck is zingiber? Brianna peered at the index listing. *Page 966—*

She paged back through to the entry in question and found herself looking at a double-page spread of strange roots like clutching hands, as well as a fair amount of leafage in odd shapes. *Zingiber. The genus containing the true or "common" gingers used in normal spicery, as well as the uncommon gingers* (Z. castrava, Z. amnemosyne, et al.) *used in magic. All varieties originally native to mainland Europe but now widely imported into the New World and Asia for use in sorceries involving mindchange, persistent illusion, edulent work, and fast-growth imaginary constructs. Also used for routine herbal medicine (as a carminative and sialogogue, and for stomach disorders) and culinary purposes (e.g. Asian food, confectionery gingerbread, etc.)* . . .

Brianna sat staring at the page. *Gingerbread?!*

Her mind went instantly back to the shelf of fairy tale books that still sat above the headboard of her bed. In her mind's eye Brianna could see the image of two kids standing hand in hand in front of a little cottage with dark golden-brown walls, the windows made of rock-candy glass, the shutters piped around with ornate icing designs, the roof hung with sugary icicles. And outside the gingerbread Dutch door, a little old bent-over lady in a shawl, beckoning them in. Down the years, from the memory of the faintly scandalized eight-year-old witchlet staring at the illustration, the verse floated: "Nibble, nibble, little mouse. Who's that nibbling at my house?"

When she was eight, she had mostly been indignant about how the witch looked. "It's just a stereotype, honey," her daddy had said while she sat on his knee and he read her the story. "They didn't know any better. *We* know witches aren't like that." And she did know it, since her dad was a witch of great experience and skill, living successfully in both worlds and never needing to catch and fatten up any little kids for the table. Nonetheless, that little house had stayed on her mind for a long time. *Something about the candy-cane drainspouts, I think.*

Now, though, that house suddenly meant about a

hundred different things. Stereotypes. Legend. Heritage. *The image you can't escape,* Brianna thought, *and can't understand. The one you try to ignore . . . unsuccessfully, because it's just too popular and keeps popping up no matter how many times you try to whack it down.*

There it was, hanging in front of her mind's eye along with that ancient illustration, but far more glorious in prospect. A short exhibit on the history of the archetype, some illustrations and other-cultural referents—and then standing there by itself, in the middle of the school gym probably, The House. Gingerbread, candy-cane drainspouts, and all.

Then Brianna slumped back in the chair. *But this is so* old . . .

She was about to chuck the book to one side when, resolute, that confident voice in her head said, *So old that it's* new!

Brianna stared at the book. *But think of all the work, and all the time sorting out the details will take. You couldn't build a house out of gingerbread. Not really.*

Could *you?*

Brianna sat there, no longer really seeing anything around her as she thought. All her mind was taken up with the image of The House. *You know,* she thought, *nobody could have made that up. Someone, some witch,* did *that. Someone saw it, once. And then the story got passed along orally . . . until the Brothers Grimm heard it. And wrote it down, just as they heard it: yet another crazy thing that witches did.* Leaving out the cannibalism, of course, which (as Brianna knew from her history of witchcraft classes) came from a different set of mythologies, farther east, and had gotten itself embedded into the German motif-set somehow.

But it doesn't matter. What old witchcraft did, new witchcraft can do. After all, we've got all these new techniques and technologies, so much better analysis of how and why spells work . . . And it's Heritage Week. If the project pulls in witchy heritage issues along with the science aspect—

Brianna sat and thought about that. *Synergies.* Miss Levenson, her arcane- and parasciences teacher, was all about synergies. *Her favorite word. She would absolutely okay this.*

Brianna pushed the book aside and jumped up out of the chair to go upstairs to the storybook shelf in her bedroom. As she passed Mick by, she said, "You know what?"

"What?" He picked up his pot and turned away from her to dump the spaghetti into the colander.

"You *may* just have been right," she said. "I may just let you live."

"Aww, and after I was all set to look into the puppy fat thing for you," Mick said, making what he apparently thought would pass for big puppy eyes at her.

"I emphasize the 'may,' " Brianna said. But she still punched him lovingly in the head on the way out of the kitchen.

Being Brianna, all that evening she changed her mind back and forth at least six times about the virtues of this project versus the magic sword. Absolute certainty was not something she had a rep for. But by morning, the gingerbread was beginning to grow on her. *Eww,* Brianna thought as she got dressed—and she was taking unusual care over it, wearing all new clothes that no one had seen—*gingerbread growing on you, weird image, didn't need* that *one!* The gingerbread project did have this virtue: it *sounded* good. It had some depth to it.

Assuming, Brianna thought as she walked up through the school's front gates, *I can get some of these concrete details worked out first. The size was an issue, and there was always—*

—Arthur, standing there by the front doors, with the usual gaggle of adoring ones around him. Brianna's heart sank. *Not what I wanted to be dealing with just yet. I haven't even had homeroom!* She swallowed and then just went by, letting them see the new skirt and the stylish new shirt-top, perfect for one of those cool Salem mornings: headed on through, acting as though she had places to go, people to see.

"Brianna!" Arthur said as she went by, the tone of voice being half *Looking good, girl!* and half *Did that for* me, *did you?* And there was just enough emphasis on the second half of the tone to push her right by him with a smile that was maybe a little more cursory, a little cooler, than she'd originally intended. She could hear the murmur from the other girls gathered around him and then a couple of giggles.

She blushed again, got annoyed over it as she made her way in and down the hall to where her locker was. *Never mind,* Brianna thought, shoving some books in, taking out some others, *now the ball's in his court. I'm not going to chase him. He has a chance to catch up with me after homeroom. I've got an optional free period then, he knows that.*

Homeroom came and went, with the usual subdued gossip and people muttering about unfinished homework or some long-prepared research spell that had gone wrong at the last minute. Brianna sat through it, eager to get out the door and find Arthur waiting for her there in the hallway. When the bell rang for people to go to their first-period classes, Brianna lingered, in no rush to be first out. But when she finally meandered into the hall, there was no sign of Arthur.

Ooookay, she thought, *we're playing it cool. Never mind, two can play at that game.* And Brianna headed down the hall and back toward the parascience wing.

The library was on her way. Brianna paused in the doorway of the glass-walled space and leaned in, looking down between the shelves. "Ms. Mona?" she said.

The librarian put her dark-haired head out from behind a shelf further down the room. "Who—oh, hi, Brianna."

"Ms. M, can I hang onto this for a little longer?" Brianna held up the *Materia Magica.* "I think I'm onto something hot."

"Sure, you go ahead. If anyone needs it, I'll message you."

"Thanks—"

Brianna slipped out again and headed down the hall. She had a couple of stops to make with her other science teachers to clear what she had in mind; that took only a few minutes each. Then Brianna headed toward the labs. They were split between the newer science annex and the older rooms, some of the ancient lead-surfaced lab tables with their arched faucets and little sinks bearing many scars of spells that had gone wrong. Near the glass window looking into Lab 3 was the table that had been turned entirely to stone the time the basilisk got out of its hood. Down past there were the newer lab and technical parasciences rooms, and the first of these, seen through its windows to the hall, looked more like a kitchen than anything else. Brianna pushed the door open and swung in, glancing around.

She couldn't think when the subject, or the room, had last actually been called Home Economics. These days the class was called Family and Consumer Science and was an elective, taught only for a quarter semester every year because its uptake was just so *small.* There were usually a few guys who got involved with it, seeing it as a gateway to some kind of career in food service management, and a few girls who were usually already excellent cooks and felt like taking a class that would be no effort for easy credit.

"Ms. B?" Brianna said, standing there and glancing around. The place was empty—there were normally no classes this early in the day. "Ms. Baldwin? . . ."

No answer. Brianna was just turning to go when, in the middle of the room, between two of the stainless steel cooking demo stations, a cloud of black smoke burst up from the floor. Out of it, a moment later, walked Ms. Baldwin, fanning the air in front of her a little.

She peered at Brianna through the smoke. "Wilkes, isn't it?" she said. "Brianna Wilkes."

"That's right." It had been a couple of years since Bri had taken home ec, but Ms. Baldwin was as famous for her memory as for her other oddities, which stuck out somewhat even at Salem. Ms. Baldwin seemed sometimes to be genuinely rooted in some other century, only visiting or working in this one because the pay and benefits were better. And if there was a teacher in the place who genuinely looked like a witch, it would have been Ms. Baldwin—though of course no one would have dared say as much to her, since she also taught the Power Potions class *without ever referring to a text,* and no sane person was going to get even *slightly* rude to a person who could keep that kind of dangerous stuff contained in her head. She did, however, wear shawls and strange-looking old gingham dresses; and she had the somewhat wayward white hair, the classic longish nose, the classic "crone's" narrow chin, those little wrinkled eyes . . . as well as a complete disdain for the magical "plastic surgery" that could have left any thoughtful witch looking her waist size instead of her age. No one was clear why Ms. Baldwin was so insistent on letting her body look so traditional, especially in Salem. But anyone who thought about asking her probably also immediately thought about the Power Potions class and shut up.

"So what brings you in today?" Ms. Baldwin asked, moving over to one of the demo stations to turn on one of the cooking hoods and clear the smoke away a little.

"I need some advice," Brianna said. "I want to build a classical witch's gingerbread house. Full size."

"Why, goodness, Brianna dear," she said—and Brianna blushed because it was so bizarre to be called "dear" by a teacher—"doesn't a gingerbread house seem a little . . . *retro?*"

The word "retro" itself surprised Brianna, coming from Ms. Baldwin's mouth. "Well," Brianna said, "right out of the box, I guess so. But say 'witch' to half the population, at least in the same sentence as 'fairy tale,' and they'll say 'gingerbread house.' Seems like a cultural slamdunk as a Heritage Week project."

This line had worked as well a few minutes ago with Mr. Johannson, the General Arcana teacher who was coordinating the Parascience Fair entries, as it had with Brianna's own parascience teacher Ms, Levenson. Now Ms. Baldwin blinked at her thoughtfully. "Unless," Brianna said hurriedly, "you think it was just a myth . . ."

"Oh, not at all," Ms. Baldwin said. "That kind of thing wouldn't just occur to some seventeenth-century peasant out of the air, as a rule. It's the construction that's likely to be a problem." She pulled out a lab stool and sat herself down on it.

"I did some research last night," Brianna said, "and some of the sources aren't even sure it was actually made of gingerbread. Some versions of the story just say 'bread.' "

"I know," Ms. Baldwin said, "but it probably *was* gingerbread. Bread was considered holy in those days: staff of life and all that. But specifically, you have to put salt in bread, not just to make it palatable but to stop the yeast from working before you bake."

"And salt's one of the antimagic elements," Brianna said, "like plain cold iron and running water."

"So there you are," said Ms. Baldwin. "You try building a magic house out of bread, you're going to run into trouble. Early gingerbreads, though, wouldn't have had salt in them, not just so that the flavor of the ginger wouldn't be interfered with but because there was no yeast or other leavening to worry about—they were more like cookies than cakes. The cakey gingerbreads decorated with gold leaf and all that fancy whatnot didn't start turning up until the eighteen hundreds."

"Oh," Brianna said, and pulled open her notebook again to start making notes. "Great! So . . . how *do* you build a gingerbread house with magic?"

Ms. Baldwin blinked at her. "One big enough to house an old woman and a couple of kids," she said, "and an oven big enough to shove one of the kids into when he gets fat? Brianna dear, I'm a cook, not an architect. I've done a lot of regular gingerbread houses at Christmas time, with magic and without . . . and believe me, even a little one with walls no taller or wider than a cookie sheet can be a nuisance to keep standing. All mine needed cardboard reinforcement layers. I don't even want to *think* about how much marshmallow fluff I used as mortar last year. Or how long it took me to get it out of my hair." Ms. Baldwin actually shuddered. "And as for what they used in the old days, well, I doubt they had marshmallow fluff . . . so your guess is as good as mine as to what spells or mortar they used. Do tell me what you figure out."

"Uh," Brianna said, "okay . . ."

She went out sadly. *And it was all looking so promising until now,* Brianna thought. *I don't have time to work all this out from scratch. If I just did a miniature one . . . But that would be lame.* Especially after what she'd had in mind for the magic sword: the real thing, full size. This would just be too much of a comedown, and once again her rep would suffer.

Outside the home ec lab door she paused, looking up and down the hall and wondering where to go with this next. More research, she thought. *It'll have to wait until the afternoon; I've got Spell Construction next. Or else just dump the whole idea and go see if the magic sword thing is still alive . . .*

She sighed, and strolled, and thought; and then off to the left, as she passed the organic parachem lab, something caught Brianna's eye.

She paused. *What the heck is that?* Brianna thought. On the lab table nearest the door to the hall stood a perfectly clear construction, like glass, spiraling up three feet or so from some kind of pedestal. At first Brianna thought it was some kind of strange lab glassware she'd never seen before—something left over from one of those rainy-day situations where Mr. Donswitz the parachem instructor started hauling out his alembic collection. But no, there was just this twisted column of glassy stuff, sparkling slightly around the edges with the greenish-white sizzle of the remnants of spell artifact; and standing there, watching it, was a guy in jeans and a T-shirt and a jean jacket, his arms folded, looking vague.

Brianna stood still and tried to remember who he was, but she couldn't find a name to pin to the face. It was a nice enough face, under shaggy, not-quite-stylish hair. A Salem student, yes, but not one Brianna had ever spoken to. "He's in a different circle," was the way Brianna's crowd at Salem would usually put it—meaning a different social circle as well as a different magical one. On the surface, the saying might just indicate a preference for a particular kind of witchcraft. But normally, truly, it meant somebody was too dumb, too plain, too angry, too weird, too . . . different.

He looked up at her now, and Brianna was startled by the intensity of the gaze: blue, like almost everything else about him, but not the worn blue of the denims. A paler blue, like early sky or cold water: uncertain. Or, if there was certainty, it was the kind that was thinking, *This is going to go wrong, too, isn't it.*

Brianna blinked and then pushed the lab door open. "Uh," she said, "hi."

"Hi," the guy said, looking slightly shocked.

"You looking for Mr. Donswitz?" Brianna said, going over to the table and looking at the strange twisted thing. "I think he's out this week."

"Oh. Yeah. Uh," the guy said. "No. I just wanted to get this done before class started."

"What is that?" Brianna said. And then she laughed. "Sorry. I'm Brianna."

"Dirk," he said. "Dirk Willis. Yeah, I know." He looked up at the glass thing. "It's called a barley-sugar twist."

"A what?'

"Barley sugar. It's a kind of candy they used to make in Europe. Sometimes they would make sticks of it that were twisted like this. But it's also an architectural form—they named this style of pillar after the candy."

"Barley sugar," Brianna said, staring at it. "Is this actually *sugar?*"

Dirk laughed, looking embarrassed. "Uh, yeah. It's a pun. I did it to win a bet. Someone in my physics class bet me that nobody could actually make a weight-bearing one out of sugar. Dumb bet." He said this with satisfaction, but no malice. "See the way this twists, three times in twice the twist's width—" He pointed at one section of the pillar. "It's incredibly strong. DNA has the almost same twist. The main difference is that the interior bracing in DNA is more obvious. It's another echo of the helical shape that keeps turning up in nature . . ."

Brianna stood there nodding and looking at the column. Inside, though, she was seeing once again that image from the storybook on the shelf over her bed. Not just the gingerbread house, itself, but the detail. The candy slates on the roof, the sugar-glass panes in the windows, the porch. *With pillars that looked like this—*

Brianna looked at Dirk, who had his head a little on one side and was eyeing his creation while he talked like someone already wondering whether there wasn't something wrong with it and whether it could be improved. ". . . not really about sugar, though, but they were always giving it weird names. They also called it the Salomonic column, but it didn't actually have anything to do with King Solomon. It was just that in the Vatican there are these two big columns, and they were supposed to be the original front columns from the great Temple in Jerusalem, their names were Boaz and Jachin, and they—"

"Dirk?"

He stopped and looked at her. "What?—Oh, no, it's nothing to do with Solomon and the genii, that was just—"

"Dirk!"

He stopped again.

What Brianna really wanted to say was, *You are a king geek among geeks!,* but that would be seriously counterproductive at the moment. So instead she said, "I need to do—something kind of weird."

Dirk turned that sideways-cock-of-the-head look on her and looked, for the moment, completely like a bird. To Brianna's utter astonishment, he also went pale. "Weird *how?"* Dirk said.

"For my parascience fair project."

He suddenly looked very much relieved but also puzzled. "You mean you're not doing the sword thing with Arthur Etchison?" Dirk said.

She stared at him. *"What?"*

"This morning before everybody went in, he said he'd had this great idea, and you were just the one to handle the execution and do the heavy lifting."

Brianna went ice-cold, then flushed hot a second later. *"He'd* had—!" *Why, that big-mouthed, stuck-up—!* "Well, no, I am not," she said, not caring for the moment that she sounded furious. "And he is just very wrong. Arthur can just go forge his own sword and stick it right—" Brianna stopped herself. "—Where magic swords are usually stuck," she said. "As a rule, stones are involved, I believe."

Dirk gave her a crooked smile—an odd look, but one Brianna still liked much better at the moment than Arthur's. "Okay," he said. "So what about the project? What were you going to do?"

"A gingerbread house," she said. "Full size. At least, I want to. But I don't know how. And Ms. Baldwin wasn't much help." Then she laughed. "Well, yeah, she was, but only to give me a sense that you can't just whip up a whole lot of gingerbread by magic and then stick it together and expect it to stay up."

Dirk sat back in his chair and tilted his head sideways again, but this time the effect was more considered and less freaked-out. "Well, no," he said. "The stresses would be all wrong for the material. It would weigh too much. Then there's interior and exterior bracing to think about, and—" He paused. "You know, the smartest way would be to grow it."

Brianna stared at him. *"Grow* it? Gingerbread?"

Dirk shrugged. "Sure," he said, "why not? That's probably how the witch who built the original managed it. You take some of the ingredients of gingerbread—" He paused, thinking. "Well, ginger, obviously. Flour. Water. But you know—" He suddenly got a very canny look on that face: the eyes positively came alive, like those of someone who was getting ready to play a trick on the world. "You could make this really strong if you used live ginger rather than the dry ground-up stuff. That might have been what the original witch did, too. Get the live organic material to grow up *through* the stuff that was alive at one point—the flour—after you'd complexed the water in with it. You'd get an internally braced solid structure. Like reinforced concrete, but organic."

"Prestressed gingerbread?" Brianna said, and laughed. "Are you serious?"

"Sure. It'd come out almost like wood if you got the water mixed correctly with the flour, kept it even enough. You could even just suck the water molecules into the spell right out of the air." He turned suddenly from her to the computer. "Let me check the school weather station, I need to see what the relative humidity is—"

Brianna was astounded. "I hadn't thought about doing this today, wouldn't it take more time, I mean—"

"Why would it? Once you've designed the basic structure, and laid whatever shape you're imagining over the construction spell, you can collapse the spell and then reenable it anywhere you want it."

And suddenly he turned his back on his barley-sugar pillar and headed for one of the computers by the window, pointed at its mouse, wiggled it. The screen came up out of black, displaying a kind of wire-frame diagram of the pillar. "That's so wild," Brianna said.

"What?" The structure?"

"No," Brianna said, and laughed. "That your two columns have names."

"Oh, yeah," Dirk said. "They're even in Tarot cards, in some decks. I think they symbolize the union of opposites or something." He snapped his fingers, and the wireframe diagram vanished. "Meanwhile, there has to be a blueprint first," he said. "And then the spell to prestress the structure." He sat down in the typing chair in front of the monitor and began drumming his fingers on either side of the keyboard, a thinking gesture. "We have better flour than they used to have in the old days; the protein structures are different. The old stuff, it'd have been what we would think of as a really *crude* whole grain prestressed. Even with the crudest flour we can get, you're going to be working with something that's a lot better milled. And then there's the question of the windows. First you'd have to—"

"Whoa, whoa, wait!" Brianna said. "Too much, not all at once, give me a minute!" She pulled her notebook out and started making witch-writing on the outer cover; it would sink in and slide itself onto the lined paper inside.

"It's okay," Dirk said. "Don't get stressed, this will

all transfer to my laptop, and it can share it with your notebook." He started typing, and the beginnings of a blueprint began assembling itself on the screen. "Basic stuff first?" he said. "Just the physical design. You tell me how you see it."

"Yeah. Then, if it's going to be a grown thing, we'll need a couple of contagion and sympathetic magic routines to hold the growth in . . ."

Dirk nodded, typed, occasionally stopped to use the mouse. A basic floor plan started to appear on the screen, with space for the spell fragments to be inserted and locked into the design. Dirk was really good with the CAD; if his thought processes made him seem scary-smart, maybe that was a good thing here. *And who knows what he thinks of my thought processes,* Brianna thought. *Probably finds them a bit lame.* But that wouldn't matter if she pulled this off.

"If *we* pull this off," Dirk said.

The blood ran right out of Brianna's face: she could feel it leaving her white and cold. *"What did you say?"*

"Sorry," Dirk said, sounding completely unconcerned. "I have the underhearing gift sometimes, when work's involved." He said it as if he was discussing the weather, and boring weather at that. "I don't pay any attention to it, mostly. It's usually things that people'll say out loud, sooner or later. Sometimes they even think they *did* say it. No big deal."

Brianna gulped. His voice was the voice of someone who was completely used to no one paying any serious attention to him. But the pain the concept caused her was apparently either invisible or unimportant to him: He went right on with what he was doing at the computer. "There," Dirk said, "just the basic walls-windows-and-roof stuff. Interior design can wait—"

And outside the lab, a bell rang—the bell for the end of first period. "Oh no!" Brianna said.

"What's the matter?" Dirk said. "Plenty of time later. If you're not too busy—"

"Me?" Brianna said. "Oh, no. No! We can meet after school—"

"If you don't mind," Dirk said.

"Mind? You're only saving my life," Brianna said. "Not to mention helping me stick it to Arthur."

Dirk's look was amused. "What time?" he said.

"One forty-five?" Brianna asked. "Is that too early? I don't officially have a last period today."

"Sounds fine," Dirk said.

Behind them, the barley-sugar column was levitating up off the lab table as Dirk stood up. "Here, let me get that for you," Brianna said, and pointed at the door, whispering the basic portal spell; the door swung inward for them. "Dirk—"

"Don't thank me," he said. And just for a moment he gave her a look that was less than strictly blue-on-blue. "If it works, then yeah. And isn't that Arthur down at the end of the hall? Looks like he's looking for somebody."

"So it is," Brianna said. "Later!" And she swept on down that way to instruct Arthur as to the potential placement of potential magic swords.

When Brianna walked in her front door with Dirk after school, she was praying that her brother wasn't there to start teasing her. But there was no sign of him. Relaxing a little, Brianna headed for the living room to see if there was anyone around. If there was, she wanted to get the necessary introductions over with; then she and Dirk could get out in back of the house and get to work. "Mom?" she said as she turned the corner from the front hall.

Instead of her mom, she found her dad there, sitting cross-legged in the middle of the living room floor, surrounded by a number of piles of perfectly hovering levitating paperwork, and sorting through one pile that he was holding in his lap. As they came in, he glanced up and gave Brianna and Dirk a somewhat surprised look. "Hi, sweetie. Are you running early? Or am I running late?"

"I'm early, Daddy. I had a last period study hall I didn't need. Got more important things to do. Daddy, this is Dirk."

"Dirk Willis," he said. "Hi, Mr. Wilkes."

"Hi, Dirk." Brianna's dad took the pile of papers in his lap, boosted them into the air and left them hanging there; then he plucked a neighboring pile down into his lap and started riffling through them. Brianna's dad ran an accountancy firm in Salem. If all his clients on both sides of the metaphysical divide described his skill with figures as magical, he just smiled and said that all his clients deserved the very best he could do. "You kids don't need to be working in here, do you?" he said. "This place is going to turn into a paperwork blizzard if these piles get bumped into."

"No, Daddy," Brianna said. "We're going to be out in the back; we'll be working on our parascience fair project."

Brianna's dad nodded and looked away, unconcerned. Knowing her dad, she could just hear him thinking: *Oh, the Magic Sword thing fell through* but refusing to say anything about it out loud. She hoped desperately that Dirk couldn't hear him thinking it. Brianna started blushing, then pushed that, and the embarrassment about it, aside; there was just no time for it now. She and Dirk headed out toward the back door and into the backyard.

On the other side of the screen door, Dirk stood on the steps and looked around him with a strangely satisfied expression. "Good," he said.

Brianna regarded him with astonishment, as this was a word that had never occurred to her in connection with her back yard. "Good?" she said, incredulous. "What we've got back here is crabgrass city. This is *good?*"

Dirk grinned at her a little. "Well," he said, "this process could get a little bit . . . destructive." He glanced around at the expense of scraggly, dried out, weed-ridden "lawn" that constituted the Wilkes' backyard. "If there was anything like landscaping back here, I could feel guilty about what might happen to it. And it might take time to put it back."

Brianna shook her head, laughed, and walked out into the middle of the crabgrass, looking around at it. "Dad keeps saying he thinks the ground is cursed. Mom keeps saying he put too much bonemeal on it a few years ago, and it's never recovered. Dad has no green thumb whatsoever. Any plant he touches usually just withers right up."

"That might come in useful later," Dirk said. "But never mind it now. You have the bag?"

Brianna nodded, and from the schoolbag over her shoulder pulled out the plastic grocery bag that had taken them the better part of the after-school afternoon to fill with the right ingredients. They had spent lunch going over the *Materia Magica* together, working out the exact characteristics and species of the ginger they were going to need. Then they wound up teleporting out on the sly to three separate supermarkets, one after the other, looking for the right kind of ginger. The difficulty was that all the ginger rhizomes looked approximately the same, whether they were magic or not: There were few signs to guide you with certainty to the kind you needed. But finally, in the fourth supermarket they'd gone to them—an Asian supermarket that specialized in supplying the local Chinese restaurants—they had stumbled across the right stuff. Now, as she handed Dirk the bag, he rooted around in there and pulled the knobby golden root out, regarding it with satisfaction.

"This has to be what they used," he said. "Must have gotten to Europe by coming all the way down the Silk Road. It doesn't look like much, does it?"

Brianna shook her head. From the carrier bag she

pulled out a sack of whole wheat flour that they'd picked up at the first supermarket they'd gone to. "Is this going to be enough for the whole thing, do you think?"

"Should be fine," Dirk said. "Under the Law of Contagion, part stands for all. If you can hold the right imagery in your head, it's not the amount of material that will matter; it's the quality of the imagery and the amount of power you apply to it. Like you saw before, with the barley-sugar column. That whole thing came out of one sugar packet from the cafeteria and a lot of intent." Dirk walked around the weedy expanse of the backyard for a few moments, pacing. "Okay," he said. "You got it all into your notebook out of my laptop, I think—"

"I think so," Brianna said. "Let's give it a shot." She pulled the notebook out of her shoulder bag, paging through it past the notes she'd been making all day for the posters and other visual aids that would be mounted in and around the gingerbread house. Brianna sighed at the sight of the scribbles, all of which were going to need extensive work in the computer to smooth out the wording. But it was going to look good when it was done, especially all the data about the cultural background of the house and the worn-down "magical" rhymes that still persisted in some versions of the Hansel and Gretel story. Probably there'd also be room for some heartfelt commentary about how witches should not allow their cultural heritage to be peeled away from them, even if it sometimes seemed of dubious value or correctness in this modern time. "We are all part of *all* of our heritage," it would go; "we can't afford to try to cherry-pick the parts we want to keep or the parts we'd prefer to throw away. The context can only be understood in terms of the entire picture. And this is part of the picture, no matter how stereotypical it looks and how many calories it seems to contain . . ."

But right now the fancy verbiage could wait. Brianna put her notebook down on the ground. Then she stood over it for a moment, held her arms out in the proper invocatory gesture, and called up in her mind the words that she would need to kick it out into expansion mode.

Dirk suddenly looked a little concerned. "You *do* have a visual-blocking 'glamourie' field around the edges of this place, don't you?"

Brianna paused, grinned. "With my brother?" she said. "Oh, yes. And it's robust. When Mick built his first rocket ship to go to Mars, the neighbors never even noticed the ignition."

"That would pass for robust," Dirk said. "Okay, let's go for it!"

Brianna said the words. Immediately the notebook began spreading itself across the backyard, like an oversized picnic tablecloth covered with designs—the very specific spell diagram necessary to let the ginger do its job, and the outlining of the "blueprint" for the house itself. She and Dirk had gone back and forth about the basic design, but at the end of a long discussion it had seemed simpler to go for something that would duplicate a German peasant's cottage of the 1600s rather than a prettied-up version that might have more room for people to stand around inside, but also possibly be accused of being less realistic. The final result—two rooms, one with a small bed for the witch and a tinier one for Gretel, the other containing a sort of condensed kitchen/dining area, complete with nasty small cage—had satisfied them both and would, Brianna thought, impress everybody who saw it. "We'll get as close as we can to archetype," Brianna said, as she now looked over the fully expanded blueprint where it lay glowing on the ground, "without getting fetishistic about it."

Dirk gave her an amused look. "Is there anybody else at our school," he said, "who would use the words 'archetype' and 'fetishistic' in the same sentence?"

Brianna actually paused, wondering if that was

something she ought to be blushing about—then laughed out loud, because the look Dirk was giving her was nothing whatsoever like the looks she either got from Arthur or dreamed about getting from him. "Probably not," she said, "so if you won't tell on me, I won't do it again. Is the magic ginger ready?"

"It was born ready, as far as I can tell," Dirk said, and walked out into the middle of the cottage plan. "I think you'd better put the flour down first, though."

"Right," Brianna said. She walked out onto the plan after him, and carefully tore just a corner off the bag of flour. "Is it going to need a whole lot of this, or will just a little be enough?"

"Keep it light," Dirk said. "You're going to want to have enough to resurrect the design when you put it up in the school gym, or the parking lot or wherever."

Brianna started to head for the outer edges of the diagram—then changed her mind. *No, better do the inside first—you'll be less likely to mess it up.* Cautiously she sprinkled the flour over the glowing spell-tracery of the "blueprint," covering up the lines that marked where the interior walls would rise. "I feel like the kids in the story," she said. "Except without the breadcrumbs."

Dirk watched how she was walking, not looking up. "What breadcrumbs?" he said. "I thought when the wicked stepmother tried to lose them, they used rocks or something to mark their trail."

"Pebbles," Brianna said, finishing with the outlining of the interior walls and moving to the outer ones. "And that time Hansel and Gretel got home okay. The stepmother wouldn't let them bring rocks the next time, though. That's where the breadcrumbs come in. Hansel improvised with the bread the stepmother gave him. But the birds ate it."

Dirk shook his head, still watching carefully to make sure the lines were being covered evenly. "What kind of parents take their kids out into the woods to lose them on purpose?" he said.

Brianna shook her head as she finished the second exterior wall and headed for the third one. "The story says the parents were starving," she said. "Or afraid they were going to. But it still sounds kind of fishy to me. If everybody around there was starving, how come the witch had food? And enough of it to fatten Hansel up, too."

Dirk shook his head again as he fished around in his pocket for something, came up with it: a couple more packets of sugar from the school cafeteria. "You missed a spot there." he said.

"Yeah." Brianna went back to do it again, then headed for the fourth wall. "I mean, it's all very strange. What's the moral?"

"Being an honest woodcutter doesn't pay well?" Dirk said as he ripped the sugar packets open. "Don't get married twice? Stay out of the woods no matter who takes you in there? Become a witch and always have plenty to eat?"

Brianna snickered as she finished the last wall. "Maybe," she said, "there *isn't* a moral?" She stepped away from that last corner and took a turn around the blueprint, checking to make sure that all the outlines were properly covered.

Dirk was shaking his head. "Always a moral," he said, and broadcast the contents of one of the packets over the design, then sprinkled the contents of the second one in front of where the door would be. "Sometimes they just hide it better than usual." He glanced up as Brianna finished her round. "You ready?"

"All set," Brianna said.

Carefully Dirk placed the ginger root in the middle of the blueprint, in the place prepared for it, and stepped back. Then—

It was a twofer spell, so there was no way around it: they had to hold hands. This was the prospect that had given Brianna delicious shivers when considering what it would be like with Arthur, but now she only felt excited to see what was going to happen. When she took Dirk's hand, which he held out to her without really looking at her, the only shiver Brianna got was because his hand was cold. *Can he really be nervous that this might not work?* Brianna thought.

He had his laptop open now, and Brianna had her notebook. The electronic resource and the magically written one had coordinated with each other so that each was now carrying the complete version of the spell. Together they began to read the invocation to the Universe and the listening Aion-spirit of Magic, the force within everything that made witchery work, and with that solemnity done, they went on to the concrete stuff, the instructions for the spell that were more like the ingredients of a recipe than anything else. Normally this part of a spell bored Brianna, but this afternoon, for some reason, she started to feel like laughing out loud when they got past the mystical stuff and started invoking the chemical fractions of the ginger root which produced the prestress/reinforcement part of the spell. "Sesquiphellandrene, bisabolene, farnesene," she and Dirk chanted together, and Brianna had to choke back a snicker as she wondered who, or where, Farnes was. "Cineol, citral, gingerol, shoagole, *zingerone!*"

"Sounds like Italian food," Dirk said under his breath, and then they both cracked up together.

And in midlaugh, the spell took, and took off. The ground humped and bucked, the lines of the diagram writhed and slid and then reared up proud of the ground, getting taller and thinner, shifting their shape and color. *Oh, no,* Brianna thought at first, *did we get something really wrong?*—because the color was green. But then she realized that she was seeing the ginger root starting to do its business, its virtual leaves growing outward into the spell-pattern, sheeting up along the uprearing lines of the floor plan, then flattening out and spreading sideways and upward like some odd veiny green wallpaper. And up after them went the flour, going weirdly liquid and spreading itself across the green leafery like confused wallpaper paste as the walls grew and stretched upward. It had only been a few breaths now since the Italian food joke, but the walls had already reached the height of Brianna's and Dirk's heads and were growing higher still. Brianna craned her neck to see the roof forming, its peak pointing itself, the chimney sprouting upward in the midst of the whole business like an afterthought.

"Almost there," Dirk said under his breath.

"Are you sure?" Brianna said. "Did we forget something? Look at it, it's still green, what if it—"

—and all at once, the green faded, darkened. "That's the dessication routine cutting in," Dirk said. Brianna breathed out, relieved, for there was no mistaking it: The flour stopped looking pasty, started looking brown. A heavy scent of ginger filled the air. The color of the walls darkened further: golden brown, dark brown—

"Here we go," Dirk whispered. All in a rush, with a strange crackling noise that at first sounded like paper burning, the ornamental sugar routine went off. Once more the fizz and sparkle of spell artifact seemed to be everywhere; for a few moments, as the crackling noise got louder, Brianna wondered if they'd plugged too much energy into that part of the spell. It was running enthusiastically all over everything, like yellowy-white sheet lightning. But the crackle faded away, and Brianna saw the skin of mint-wafer rooftile start growing down over the roof, watched the licorice chimneypot form at the top of the chimney, grinned as ribbons of red spiraled down the white tubes of the candy-cane drainspouts. Rock-candy icicles formed at the roof corners, icing-sugar snow piled itself tastefully over the nougat windowsills: the windows sheeted over with perfect sugar glass an inch thick. A very creditable fake wood-graining ran down the textured gingerbread-and-halvah front door. And on either side, as the last of the spell effect grounded itself out and fizzled away, there they were, on either side of the door: two twisted pillars, one slightly golden and one slightly green, both clear as glass.

Brianna shook her head, let go of Dirk's hand, and went up to one of them. She licked her finger, touched the column with it, and then licked her finger again. No question: It was sweet.

"Barley sugar," she said. "You joker you."

"Boaz and Jachin," Dirk said. He went over to scratch at the surface of the nearest wall, got back a few satisfactory crumbs of perfectly baked gingerbread, and then leaned against the wall, grinning, dusting a little confectioners' sugar off his jeans.

Brianna shook her head, so impressed. After a moment she looked over at him. "How do you know all this stuff?" she said. "How do know so much, and nobody knows that you know so much? And you're so— "She shook her head, waved her arms, hunting for the word, not finding the right one. *"Useful!"*

Then Brianna was shocked at herself, and horrified, thinking maybe she'd said the wrong thing. Mostly what guys wanted to hear, in her experience, was that they were cute, or strong, or something like that. But Dirk just smiled. "Useful's good," he said. "You could be a lot of worse things than useful." And just for once, he looked her in the eye.

She blushed, looked away.

"Useful's good," Dirk said again, and this time he looked away too. "Look, though, we should take this down before the humidity changes too much. The Law of Contagion won't be flouted: The effect's going to keep trying to spread if you don't put a stasis around it. And you don't want to do that until you've got it where you want it, finally."

"Yeah," Brianna said. She reached between the pillars of the doorway, pulled the top half of the Dutch door shut by its wrought-licorice handle, and checked to see, in the keyhole underneath it, what they had both expected to see there: a gold-leafed, hard sugar key. Brianna turned it, pulled it out.

The whole house simply faded away into the air, leaving nothing behind but some dusty confectioners'-sugar lines on the crabgrass, like the limit lines of a peculiar-looking tennis court. In the midst of the lines lay the ginger root and a scatter of whole wheat flour. Brianna went to these, picked them up, and dumped them into the flour bag, making sure she got plenty of the flour to guarantee the contagion effect would duplicate the house correctly. "I guess we just keep this somewhere dry until Friday." She counted days in her head. "Wow, it's only three days!"

"During which we don't have to do much," Dirk said, looking satisfied as they headed back toward the house. "Except watch everybody else going insane doing last-minute stuff on their projects."

"Excuse me," Brianna said. "There's still the posters and the visual aids."

"Oh, you won't need any help with that," Dirk said, sounding most insincere. "You're perfect for handling *that* kind of heavy lifting—"

Brianna snickered. "Just get your butt on inside," she said, "and check my spelling."

Between homework and other after-class business, Friday afternoon came around all too soon as it was; and Brianna was starting to feel the strain as early as Thursday night. By Friday morning, when Dirk stopped by the house to help her carry everything over to school, her nerves were in tatters. "Don't you think we should put it up and take it down just once more," she said to Dirk, as they rolled up the last of the display materials, "to make sure it, you know, goes up and down all right—"

"You just want to fiddle with it for anxiety's sake," Dirk said. "You'll start draining energy out of the spell, and it won't work right tomorrow. Let it be."

"But if we—"

"Do what Arthur's probably doing with his right now," Dirk said, "and start obsessing with it? I don't even want to think about it."

They were standing over the dining room table, looking at the main poster, STEREOTYPES AND SORCEROUS REALITY: AN INTERCULTURAL CONTEXT, before they rolled it up into the last of the mailing tubes that Brianna's dad had brought home from work. He had already left for the day. Now her mom came wandering in from the kitchen wearing a set of faded sweats that had been respectable once, perhaps during the Jurassic, and Brianna could barely spare the energy to be mortified by them, she was so keyed up. "Does that sound too pompous?" she muttered. "Should I have put it all in caps like that, does it look like we're shouting? Shouldn't we—"

"No," Dirk said. "Yes. And no. Come on, Bri, this isn't going to get any easier."

"It looks lovely, dear," Brianna's mom said. Brianna let out an exasperated breath, because her mother said that about everything.

"No," her mom said. "Seriously. You're going to be a big hit, and what's his name, Arthur, is going to wish he hadn't been so dismissive. Just you wait."

Her mom kissed her good-bye, patted Dirk on the shoulder as he finished with the mailing tube, and more or less pushed them both to the front door. "We'll be down around starting time," she said. "About four, is it?"

"Four-thirty," Brianna said. She was astonished to find that she was actually shaking. *I am such a wimp! I can't believe it! Oh, what if this doesn't work—*

And that was the state her brain was in until nearly three-thirty, when the Parascience Fair setup began. Mr. Johannson and the other parascience teachers were all in their glory, running in and out between the school gym and the parking lot next to it, ordering people around. Ms. Levenson, Brianna's parascience teacher, looked as unnerved as Brianna felt, though she couldn't understand why; it wasn't as if Ms. L. has any pressure on her or anything. "Brianna," Ms. L. said, pushing her curly hair back and trying to look in several directions at once. "No, Richie, not there, we can't have a sprite so close to that fire elemental; you're going to have to move down to table fourteen! That's right. Brianna, what is it?"

"We were supposed to set up in the middle of the gym," Dirk said, "but that whole area's full already. Looks like the original setup plan got thrown out. Where are we supposed to put our project?"

"This is your little house, isn't it?" Ms. Levenson said, running her hands through her hair again and looking harried. She always looked a bit like an ostrich at the best of times; now she looked like she might suddenly turn into one—an alarming prospect, since shapechange was a specialty of hers.

"Uh, not so little, Ms. L," Brianna said, glancing around her nervously. "We're going to need a fair amount of room—"

Mr. Johannson, on his way into the gym, stopped next to them. "Dirk," he said, "Brianna. The house?"

"That's right."

"It'll have to be out here," he said. "Put it over there." He pointed toward the end of the parking lot. "Nothing flammable?"

"Oh, no," Brianna said.

"Fine, then he won't be a problem."

"He?" Brianna said, or rather squeaked. "Uh, Mr. Johannson—"

Too late. He was heading back into the gym. And "down there," holding his arms out over the blacktop and reciting a preliminary spell, was Arthur Etchison.

"No choice, I guess," Dirk said under his breath. "Bri, don't freak."

Together they made their way down the parking lot to where Arthur was standing. Near him were Donna

Mbele and a few of Donna's friends—Michele and Laurene and Belle—looking on with that expression of interested hangers-on everywhere. As Brianna and Dirk headed for them, those heads turned, and the expression on the girls' faces got strange—amused, and in one or two cases a little nasty.

Arthur, for the moment, wasn't looking. He had his eyes closed, and under his outstretched arms, an anvil was taking form. Brianna looked at this with some skepticism. "Shouldn't there be a stone under it?" she said.

Arthur opened one eye. "Brianna," he said. "Dork."

Brianna's eyes narrowed. She glanced over at Dirk, who was standing there with his hands in his pockets, looking completely unconcerned. "Prince Arthur," Dirk said.

"Shouldn't that be 'king'?" said Laurene, sounding hostile. It looked bad on someone so small and blonde and delicate.

"Takes more than just a sword," Dirk said. "Bri, let's get these put up, shall we?"

The two of them had a parking place to themselves. They uncased and unrolled the posters and other visual aids they'd brought, and put them up on their stands at the top of the parking place. "Bri?" Dirk said.

She was watching Arthur and his anvil. It was completely manifested now, soulsteel that he had called up out of the earth just as she'd suggested someone might. And now he produced more steel, a small ingot of it this time, sourced from one of the local steel mills—the only thing about this process that didn't have to be magical. Finally, Arthur reached into a case down by his feet and produced the flint hammer. It had been sung over to talk it into being harder than the steel or the anvil. Brianna knew exactly what the words would have been: She'd told him half of them. But now it was Donna who was holding Arthur's spare hand and helping him say the words, with just about the same half-swooning look that Brianna probably would have been wearing.

"Brianna," Dirk said.

She turned. He was holding out the shopping bag to her, the one with the flour and the ginger root in it. "Let's get this laid out," Dirk said.

Brianna felt her face going tight with anger. "I'll do it," she said. "The way I've been obsessing over it, I've got it by heart." And she started pacing out the outline of the house, sprinkling the flour there, not looking up any oftener than she had to because Arthur was hammering the steel on the anvil now, and the sound was getting into her head and giving her the beginnings of a headache—as were the amused grins of the girls around Arthur. *Talk about a comedown. Starts out with something really hot, a magic sword, winds up with cookie dough . . .*

Brianna turned her back, finished the third wall of the house, turned the corner of the design and started laying down the fourth one. In the midst of this, out in the secondary parking lot, she heard a sound she'd have known anywhere: her mom's car door shutting. Here they come. *And they'll see me and Dirk with a cookie house and Arthur doing something really cool.* She started to get angry.

Bri, Dirk said inside her head. *You want to get a grip on that—*

No I don't, Brianna thought. *Because no one here knows what I can do. No one thinks I'm all that smart or that serious. I'm usually kind of the fluffy one. They're gonna think* you *did most of this.*

Dirk was quiet for a moment. Brianna let out an angry breath. She knew that kind of silence. It usually meant embarrassed agreement.

You don't strike me as all that fluffy, Dirk said. A *fluffy person wouldn't have pulled together all the cultural-context stuff that makes this actually mean something instead of just being something that goes boom like a fake toy volcano. And a fluffy person would* definitely *not use the words 'archetype' and 'fetishistic' in the same sentence.*

He was trying to make her laugh, but she wouldn't do it because inside her head, blocking the laughter, was the sound of the hammer. White fire was going up from the enchanted flint. Inside the anvil and the metal Arthur was forging, the spell he was reciting as he hammered was having the desired effect. The steel writhed, shuddered, and abruptly lengthened itself, bursting into blade like a flowing bursting into bloom. The fire was completely magical, so it didn't burn: Crosspieces burst out of the hilt end of the blade, and Arthur dropped the hammer and seized the sword by its new hilt. Then he held it up high, and it glittered, and green fire ran up the blade, making Arthur looked like a superhero. The light of the sword's fire caught in the eyes of all the girls around him.

He ignored them, though. He looked at Brianna, and his smile was unusually mean. "See what you could have had," it said. And aloud he said: "No matter what else you do—you blew *this*." And he looked at Dirk. "For him."

And Arthur laughed.

Brianna stood there in the middle of the diagram with her fists clenched as Arthur's laugh got right into her head.

"Oh, yeah?" she said. "Did I really."

"Brianna," Dirk said. "Maybe you shouldn't—"

"Yeah, Bri," Arthur said, "maybe you shouldn't. You might strain something. This was never going to be the kind of thing you could manage yourself. You're a follower, not a leader. You couldn't—"

Brianna stepped into the middle of the diagram they'd traced out and raised her arms.

"Let's just see," she said.

She hardly even heard herself speak the Invocation to the Aion of Magic, but she saw heads turn toward her from all around the parking lot, as people looked at her from tables with placards and experiments and grimoires set out on them. She couldn't hear anything that anyone was saying. *We'll see what I can't do by myself!* she thought, as around her everything started getting dark and ginger-smelling. I *saw this witch's vision over all these years.* I *found my way to the technology I needed to make it happen. I even made the friend I needed.*

Or maybe he *did,* said another voice inside her head. *But never mind that right now. Let's just do this.* And when the hand took hers, it felt natural. There was no thrill, no fear, just a sense that this was the way it was supposed to go.

They said the spell. Down on the ground between them, the ginger root started putting out its broad leaves. All around them, the sugar-and-flour blueprint went afire with spell artifact. Brianna got just a glimpse of Arthur's face going dim, dark, vanishing outside growing walls that were briefly pale, then very suddenly dark brown. The walls, then the roof, shut the afternoon light away. Everything smelled strongly of ginger. The sound of their voices got close and muffled. And finally there were no words left to say, and Brianna and Dirk were standing in cookie-walled dimness, with just a few squares of sugar-filtered light to suggest what was going on in the outside world.

"It looks okay." Brianna said, glancing around.

"Only one problem," Dirk said, looking around him with some alarm. "There's something we didn't fix before we did this spell. This was supposed to be put up *inside,* remember? There was going to be some limitation on the amount of water in the air, to keep it the same size." *And,* Dirk added silently, looking over his shoulder, *you weren't supposed to be really, really pissed off when we did this.*

Brianna sneezed. The ginger scent was very strong. Inside, everything was as they'd designed it: the little beds, the uncomfortable cage, the wall-built bake-oven big enough to take a child or a very small witch. "Come on," she said, "let's see how it looks."

She made her way to the little Dutch door, opened it, stepped out. Dirk came out after. Brianna paused only long enough to make sure that Boaz and Jachin, the barley-sugar columns, were there. They were. But then, glancing around, she noticed that all their display stands around the house, with the carefully made posters hung on them, were . . . different. They were, in fact, all made of gingerbread. Incredibly thin gingerbread, the laser printing on them now looking like incredibly thin icing.

Brianna's mouth dropped open. So had the mouths of various other people. Her mom and dad, for example, who were making their way over the grass from the farther parking lot. And Arthur, for another. He was standing over a gingerbread anvil . . . and as Brianna watched, Arthur was staring at the thing in his hands: a hand-and-a-half cookie sword, with piped icing twining around its quillons.

Arthur's clique, too, were all staring around them in astonishment. All the tables that had been placed out in the parking lot were now gingerbread. Brianna turned around and looked at the gingerbread house.

Her eyes widened. It seemed about three times as tall as it had been. It had little castle-towers of gingerbread, with ice-cream-cone pointed roofs, dusted with icing. It had stained-glass candy windows, and ribbon-candy pennants flirting from the tops of the towers. The low afternoon sun struck it, looking unusually golden. In fact, the gym building behind it looked almost as golden, almost as if—

The scent of ginger on the afternoon air was overwhelming. Brianna looked up and gasped as she realized that the gym, and the science wing, and indeed, the body of Salem Township Public High School #4 behind it, was . . .

. . . gingerbread. It looked wonderful in the afternoon sun. In fact, the way it looked was going to create a problem for Brianna, because the main body of the building stuck well up past the concealment field that would have been protecting the parking lot . . .

"This is now officially beyond serious," she whispered, going cold with fear. But Dirk was looking at her with something like an odd pride.

"You don't do anything by halves, do you?" he said. "You did a transformation on the whole place. You are *hot stuff!*"

Brianna smiled at him, still terrified, but happy terrified. Then the happy fell off abruptly at the sound of the deep voice from behind her.

"So, will someone tell me exactly what we're going to do about this?" said Mr. McAllister, the principal of Salem.

Brianna gulped as she turned to face him. He was standing there with his hands clasped behind his back, looking up and over her at the main building. Mr. McAllister was never a very impressive looking man, balding on top, with kind of a beer belly under the inevitable three-piece suit. But he was (as he had to be, in this job) one of the most powerful witches in Salem, if not the state . . . or on the continent. He eyed the long brick facade, now faultlessly restated in brick-textured gingerbread, cinnamon-candy quarry tile, and sugar glass, and said, "It's magnificent. If a bit . . . overdone?"

"I'm so sorry," Brianna said, "I didn't mean to—"

Mr. McAllister gave her a look. "You shouldn't say that," he said, "since plainly, you did mean to."

"Am I in trouble?" she whispered, unable to believe that she wasn't, as turning the whole school into an advanced confectionery structure was almost certainly going to be trouble for somebody.

The vice principal came up behind Mr. McAllister, leaned over him—Mr. McAllister was a bit short. "The outer glamourie field is built for catastrophic overrun," Miss Winchester said in his ear. "It caught the visible effect; the normals outside won't have seen anything. We're all right."

"Very good," Mr. McAllister said. "Brianna—"

Her insides went cold.

"You'll be needing to see the counselor tomorrow," the principal said. "A power surge like this typically needs a management course to help you keep it in order for the next year or so. In the meantime, please decommission this witchery, all right? Which has unquestionably won the Parascience Fair's award for most impressive use of mantic energies." He looked over at Ms. Levenson, who was shaking her head at the cookie sword and cake-gingerbread anvil, while Arthur Etchinson cursed under his breath and his clique, suppressing their snickers, slipped quietly backward to avoid being caught outright in desertion. "Maybe the first prize, if we can finish everybody else's judging. So please get on with taking this down, will you?"

Brianna nodded, raised her arms. Dirk reached up, and once again took one of her free hands.

Told you there'd be a moral, he said, and he smiled at her.

Brianna blushed.

Patrick Rothfuss

THE NAME OF THE WIND

The Kingkiller Chronicle: Day One

"It is a rare and great pleasure to come on somebody writing not only with the kind of accuracy of language that seems to me absolutely essential to fantasy-making, but with real music in the words as well.... Oh, joy!" —Ursula K. Le Guin

"Amazon.com's Best of the Year...So Far Pick for 2007: Full of music, magic, love, and loss, Patrick Rothfuss's vivid and engaging debut fantasy knocked our socks off." —Amazon.com

"One of the best stories told in any medium in a decade. Shelve it beside *The Lord of the Rings* ...and look forward to the day when it's mentioned in the same breath, perhaps as first among equals." —*The Onion*

"[Rothfuss is] the great new fantasy writer we've been waiting for, and this is an astonishing book." —Orson Scott Card

0-7564-0474-1

DAW 111

Tanya Huff's

Blood Books

Private eye, vampire, and cop: supernatural crime solvers—and the most unusual love triangle in town.
Now a Lifetime original series.

"Smashing entertainment for a wide audience"
—Romantic Times

BLOOD PRICE
978-0-7564-0501-4
BLOOD TRAIL
978-0-7564-0502-1
BLOOD LINES
978-0-7564-0503-8
BLOOD PACT
978-0-7564-0504-5
BLOOD DEBT
978-0-7564-0505-2
BLOOD BANK
978-0-7564-0507-6

To Order Call: 1-800-788-6262

DAW 75

Tanya Huff

Tony Foster—familiar to Tanya Huff fans from her *Blood* series—has relocated to Vancouver with Henry Fitzroy, vampire son of Henry VIII. Tony landed a job as a production assistant at CB Productions, ironically working on a syndicated TV series, "Darkest Night," about a vampire detective. Tony was pretty content with his new life—until wizards, demons, and haunted houses became more than just episodes on his TV series...

"An exciting, creepy adventure"—*Booklist*

SMOKE AND SHADOWS

0-7564-0263-8 $6.99

SMOKE AND MIRRORS

0-7564-0348-0 $7.99

SMOKE AND ASHES

0-7564-0415-4 $7.99

To Order Call: 1-800-788-6262
www.dawbooks.com

DAW 46

MERCEDES LACKEY

Reserved for the Cat

The *Elemental Masters* Series

In 1910, in an alternate Paris, Ninette Dupond, a penniless young dancer, recently dismissed from the Paris Opera, thinks she has gone mad when she finds herself in a conversation with a skinny tomcat. However, Ninette is desperate—and hungry—enough to try anything. She follows the cat's advice and travels to Blackpool, England, where she is to impersonate a famous Russian ballerina and dance, not in the opera, but in the finest of Blackpool's music halls. With her natural talent for dancing, and her magic for enthralling an audience, it looks as if Ninette will gain the fame and fortune the cat has promised. But the real Nina Tchereslavsky is not as far away as St. Petersburg...and she's not as human as she appears...

978-0-7564-0488-8

And don't miss the first four books of
The Elemental Masters:

The Serpent's Shadow	0-7564-0061-9
The Gates of Sleep	0-7564-0101-1
Phoenix and Ashes	0-7564-0272-7
The Wizard of London	0-7564-0363-4

To Order Call: 1-800-788-6262
www.dawbooks.com

DAW 23

Raves for the previous anthologies of Denise Little:

"A winning treat . . . this low-key pub crawl is surprisingly consistent, delivering a punchy blend of shocks, laughs and otherworldly action."

—*Publishers Weekly,* for *Cosmic Cocktails*

"Denise Little has put together some really nice collections in the past few years, and it's gotten to the point where, if I see her name as editor, I know I'm in for a worthwhile read."

—*Chronicle*, for *The Magic Shop*

"Given the career of an English boy named Harry, the creation of an American school for magic-workers was inevitable. Not inevitable was that the place be a fount of intelligent entertainment. Editor Little's judgment helps make it such, and the comprehensive folkloric expertise she displays."

—*Booklist*, for *The Sorcerer's Academy*

"Exceedingly well done."

—*Booklist*, for *The Valedemar Companion*

"*Familiars* is a load of fun to read for the fantasy fan or anyone who wants a good escape. Little has gathered fifteen highly original short stories that deal with magical companions." —Kliatt, for *Familiars*

"After finishing this anthology, readers will never look at magic shops and new age/metaphysical bookstores the same way again. Little aptly describes the anthology as a 'collection of stories of the changed fates and challenged minds of the amazed consumers—both mundane and magical—who dared to shop at a Magic Shop.' Buyer beware!"

—*The Barnes and Noble Review* for *The Magic Shop*

Also Available from Denise Little and DAW Books

Enchantment Place
A new mall is always worth a visit, especially if it's filled with one-of-a-kind specialty stores. And the shops in Enchantment Place couldn't be more special. For Enchantment Place lives up to its name, catering to a rather unique clientele, ranging from vampires and were-creatures, to wizards and witches, elves and unicorns. In short, anyone with shopping needs not likely to be met in the chain stores. With stories by Mary Jo Putney, Peter Morwood, Diane Duane, Laura Resnick, Esther Friesner, Sarah A. Hoyt, and others.

Mystery Date
First dates—the worst possible times in your life or the opening steps on the path to a wonderful new future? What happens when someone you have never met before turns out not to be who or what he or she claims to be? Here are seventeen encounters, from authors such as Kristine Kathryn Rusch, Nancy Springer, Laura Resnick, and Jody Lynn Nye that answer these questions. From a childhood board game called "Blind Date" that seems to come shockingly true . . . to a mythological answer to Internet predators . . . to a woman cursed to see the truth about her dates when she imbibes a little wine . . . to a young man hearing a very special voice from an unplugged stereo system . . . these are just some of the tales that may lead to happily ever after—or no ever after at all. . . .

Front Lines
It is only since the advent of battlefront reporting, of turning on your television and seeing actual wars in progress, putting names to faces, "meeting" both soldiers and civilians who are caught in the day-to-day struggle for survival, that war has become more personal and the true price of combat has become real. Diane A.S. Stuckart, Laura Resnick, Josepha Sherman, Jody Lynn Nye, Dean Wesley Smith, and others here visit the front lines of battle in stories that range from a chemical experiment gone horribly wrong . . . to a young recruit who may hold the key to "understanding" the enemy . . . to a U.S.-Canadian conflict where the team attempting to broker peace is a joint Palestinian-Israeli unit . . . to a half-mortal knight trying to avert a war with the Elfin Host . . . to a Battle of Trenton fought against seven-foot-tall Saurians. . . .

Hags, Harpies, and Other Bad Girls of Fantasy
From hags and harpies to sorceresses and sirens, this volume features twenty all-new tales that prove women are far from the weaker sex—in all their alluring, magical, and monstrous roles. With stories by C. S. Friedman, Rosemary Edghill, Lisa Silverthorne, Jean Rabe, and Laura Resnick.

The Magic Toybox
Thirteen all-new tales about the magic of childhood by Jean Rabe, Esther Friesner, David Bischoff, Mel Odom, Peter Morwood, and others. Here toys come to life through the love and belief of the children who play with them. A tiny Mr. Magoo yearns to escape the Old Things Roadshow and get home to the woman he'd been stolen from. A child slave in Rome dreams of owning a wooden gladiator—could an act of magic fulfill his dream? Can a ghost who's found refuge in a what-not doll solve a case of unrequited love?